Dead Tide

"[A] fleet, unnerving thriller. . . . Kadow, taking a leaf from Patricia Cornwell's forensics . . . keeps spinning out mysteries so brilliantly . . . nobody will stop reading halfway through." —*Kirkus Reviews*

"Show[s] killer instincts. . . . Jeannine Kadow has mastered the art of dangling possibilities in *Dead Tide,* an intriguing thriller about a serial killer." —**Minneapolis Star Tribune*

"*Dead Tide* is a fast-paced, exciting story with dual plot lines." —*Romantic Times*

"Intriguing. . . . You won't see where [this] mystery's headed. Secrets, secrets, and more secrets." —*The Clarion-Leader* (Jackson, MS)

"Chilling. . . . Kadow ushers you into the depraved mind of a serial killer as it's never been expressed before. From the suspenseful prologue, she never lets you up for air for more than a brief moment, before thrusting you back into the cruel world of a madman. Very highly recommended." —I Love a Mystery

continued . . .

Burnout

"Kadow piles on the suspense . . . a heart-stopping journey." —*The Washington Post Book World*

"Genuinely disturbing. . . . If you're faint of heart, don't go near this one." —*Chicago Tribune*

"Compelling . . . dramatic . . . ingenious twists." —*Publishers Weekly*

"[A] knockout . . . staggeringly well-done." —*Kirkus Reviews*

"Shattering . . . a riveting suspense thriller with a plot that moves like wildfire." —*Lake Worth Herald* (FL)

"Compelling characters . . . [a] fast-moving tale." —*Roanoke Times & World-News* (VA)

"Kadow offers the reader uncanny insights into both the mind of a killer and that of an FBI profiler. A harrowing and ultimately gratifying read."
—Gregg McCrary, former FBI profiler

Blue Justice

"There are horrific images in this novel that no reader will soon forget. The pages turn."
—Robert Daley, bestselling author of *Prince of the City*

"On par with the top works of Cornwell, Rosenberg, and Palmer . . . action-packed . . . mesmerizing. . . . Ms. Kadow will climb to the top faster than a speeding bullet."
—Painted Rock Reviews

"A lightning-fast tale of police intrigue . . . swift, action-packed, and suspenseful."
—*Romantic Times*

Also by Jeannine Kadow

Blue Justice

Burnout

DEAD TIDE

a novel of suspense

Jeannine Kadow

A SIGNET BOOK

SIGNET
Published by New American Library, a division of
Penguin Group (USA) Inc., 375 Hudson Street,
New York, New York 10014, U.S.A.
Penguin Books Ltd, 80 Strand,
London WC2R 0RL, England
Penguin Books Australia Ltd, 250 Camberwell Road,
Camberwell, Victoria 3124, Australia
Penguin Books Canada Ltd, 10 Alcorn Avenue,
Toronto, Ontario, Canada M4V 3B2
Penguin Books (N.Z.) Ltd, Cnr Rosedale and Airborne Roads,
Albany, Auckland 1310, New Zealand

Penguin Books Ltd, Registered Offices:
80 Strand, London WC2R 0RL, England

Published by Signet, an imprint of New American Library, a division of Penguin
Group (USA) Inc. Previously published in a New American Library hardcover
edition.

First Signet Printing, November 2003
10 9 8 7 6 5 4 3 2 1

For Captain Mitch Kadow
My Brother, My Hero, My Friend

ACKNOWLEDGMENTS

A very special thank-you to my editor, Genny Ostertag. Her inspired and extraordinary editing was invaluable to me as I navigated the challenging waters of writing *Dead Tide*. I would also like to thank the local residents of Nantucket who opened their lives and hearts to me, and in doing so revealed the magic and mystery of their island.

PROLOGUE

She was a strange water warrior stranded on land, six feet tall, muscled and young, dressed in a neoprene wet suit with a forty-pound weight belt loaded at her waist, twin dive tanks harnessed to her back, and a five-inch knife sheathed along her shin. Flippers were strapped down tight to the tank pack, regulator and dive gauge console securely tucked under the straps. A buoyancy vest harnessed her torso, and a silicone dive mask wound around her left bicep.

In the water she would feel weightless, but here on the rocky coastal cliffs of Massachusetts, on this cold October night, her load was painfully heavy. Still, she forced herself to run. The elements were on her side. Night was a cloak, and the wind was her friend, speeding her along, and the dense swirling fog was a divine misty curtain separating her from the all too mortal hunter in hot pursuit.

Behind her, dogs barked, and for the first time she heard his heavy boots beating the cliff scrub, gaining ground.

She reached down and touched the knife for reassurance, but five metal inches were no match for him—armed as he was with nightscopes, firepower, and a pack of eight trained Dobermans. She willed herself to keep moving, scrambling up a steep incline on all fours.

The sound of surf crashing against rocks was deafening and close now. She broke into a run, oblivious of the searing pain of dive tanks banging against her spine and the agony of shale slicing the soles of her feet. If she could just make it to the ocean, she might have a chance.

She had gear. He had none.

And she was navy SEATEC, trained for escapes like this. She knew how to plunge into rough surf and kick through breakwater, swim out to open sea.

Freedom, freedom, freedom, she chanted silently, running toward the Atlantic.

The hunter's voice carried on the wind, the terrible shapeless tenor pitch she had come to fear. Suddenly, ominously, sounds took the form of words: "End of the road, girl! Watch yourself now! It's a long hard fall!"

She stopped, inched forward one step at a time, feeling the earth with her toes. Five small steps and she hit the edge. She backed off.

The Dobermans were close, growling their hunger.

"End of the line," the hunter called out from behind.

She turned and saw only the dense swirling fog.

"Game's over, girl! You fought well, and I'll tell you what: You won! It was just a game, to see what kind of soldier you really are! Come on back with me now."

She was not fooled by his sweet assurances promising her life. He was a liar, a thief, evil incarnate.

And he had her trapped. Panic rose; sour bile burned in her throat.

He would never let her die quickly. He would never grant her that. He would revel in her slow death and celebrate as she first lost her pride, her heart, and her soul.

Her only option was to jump, but the fog concealed her view of what lay below. To jump risked death on the rocks. A water landing could be deadly, too, like hitting cement if the cliff was too high. If the drop was fifty feet, she might make it. Seventy? She still had a chance. Cliff divers in Acapulco jumped seventy-footers for sport. Her heavy gear would add speed to the fall. She might survive seventy, but more than that—ninety or a hundred—and she would surely die.

"Ashley!"

He was close.

She moved to the edge and folded down in a deep crouch—thighs tense, steely, trained quad muscles bunched and twitching, ready.

Jump or die by his hand.

She had jumped in training from hundred-foot cliffs in Puerto Rico on fine August days. Those summer leaps were tactical maneuvers, nothing more than games played by soldiers who felt indestructible.

Then, not one of them dared to imagine the hell of capture, of being held prisoner. Not one of them knew the agony of a slow, torturous death. Back then jumping was a gymnastic maneuver, a circus trick in the sunlight, a performance, a fun-filled free fall into a warm tropical sea.

She had never jumped into frigid water when she was injured and weary and burdened with so much gear.

"Ashley . . . Ashley . . . Ashley!"

She looked back and saw the dogs, closing in, straining at their leashes, rising up and clawing air, howling and panting, wild over her fresh warm scent. She heard his boots slam down, saw the shape of his body hurtling through the mist.

Ashley took a deep breath and jumped, springing out, away from the deadly cliff face. SEATEC skills kicked in. Her body made dozens of precise adjustments: head tucked down, eyes squeezed shut, elbows locked at her sides, arms crossed over her chest, legs knifed straight and tight together in the perfect aerodynamic form.

She dropped forty, fifty, sixty, seventy feet and hit hard, slicing straight down through the thirty feet of turbulent water. Thirty-five, forty-five, fifty-five, and she was still falling. She tugged a cord and gave the buoyancy vest a blast of air. The vest inflated slightly. Her falling slowed. She gave the vest another blast, and drifted up ten feet, where she hung suspended at the point of perfect aquatic equilibrium.

Two hoses stemmed from the top of the dive tank pack. One was the line to the regulator, the second to the LED instrument panel, which was a rectangular box with compass, air supply, CO_2, and depth gauges. Lungs burning, ready to burst, she found the regulator and shoved it in her mouth, sucking hard, exhaling, and sucking again until the burning was spent and her breathing was slow and rhythmic, relaxed.

Eyes still squeezed shut, she pulled the dive mask off her arm and fit it over her face, blew through her nose to clear the water out, then opened her eyes and peered into the gloom. Her instrument panel floated in the current, a glowing green snake, the only light in her dark world.

The Atlantic seeped in between neoprene and her skin, so cold it burned. In October, in the Northeast, the surface temperature averages fifty-four degrees. Now at forty-five feet under, it was cold enough to kill. Shivering, she pulled her flippers on and began to kick.

A strange night fish, she thought, *finning through a sea.*

She reached around and touched the two tanks on her back. Two tanks. Two hours of life. She pulled in the green glowing snake out of habit and checked the gauge. Incredulous, she shook it and checked again. Her tanks were nearly empty. He had promised her they were full. He had lied. The gauge said she had twenty minutes of air—twenty minutes. The tide was sweeping her east, away from land, into open water, and there was not enough air in the tanks to swim anywhere at all except back to the cliff shore, where he and the dogs would surely be waiting.

Go back into the waiting arms of the hunter or give herself up now to the water.

She chose the sea, and the numbing Atlantic cold was a blessing after the earthly panic, the hot, endless captive's fear. She let the swift cold current sweep her along until she had sucked the tanks dry. Then, exhaling, she ascended, kicking slowly, one hand held high overhead in traditional form.

At forty feet the ocean was still dark, but at thirty blackness brightened to green gray, and at twenty feet a strange light pierced the water in spears.

Her heart fluttered. Adrenaline rushed.

Night fishermen! she thought, spiraling up through the glowing water. *Deep-sea fishermen with a boat!*

The rays of light were as bright as her new warm hope.

She broke surface, spit out the regulator, and gave the buoyancy vest a blast of air. It mushroomed up, holding her head high out of the rolling swells. She waved and shouted. Her voice was feeble against wind and waves and rain. The light slid away. She splashed and yelled and kicked. The light swung around and caught her, blinded her. She heard a motor kick over, a boat edging in.

Fishermen! Dry blankets and hot coffee. A safe ride home.

A winch hummed, and the net came down from the sky, falling around her, gathering her, saving her. It slowly lifted her out of the cold swells into the rain. The outline of the fishing boat was visible, the sharp prow and small square cabin.

Machinery groaned and metal shrieked as the net was reeled in, suspended, over the open deck.

Hanging high up, swinging in the wind, she saw the outline of the fisherman below. He carried a flashlight and aimed it at her face. The winch groaned. Slowly the net lowered some and she was blinded again, looking straight into the hot light.

"I ran out of air," she shouted, squinting. "The tide was strong. I don't know how far I drifted. I don't know where I am."

"Right where you belong, Ashley. You're with me."

He turned the light on his own face.

Her fear of him exploded into a final futile fury. She fumbled for the knife sheathed at her shin, grabbed it and sliced through the net, aiming for his throat at the same time he wrenched her wrist back. The knife fell, clattered on the deck. She kicked and clawed and twisted, but the hunter had her netted and hanging in midair, swinging lightly in the wind.

"Ashley," he whispered, lowering his catch into his arms and holding her like she was his bride.

Dark in her wet suit, curled in a protective shell, the warrior was gone and a cold terrified young woman lay in her place, helpless and hopeless and scared beyond belief. She tasted rain, tears, salt, blood, and jute—the cold, heavy, wet net of her capture.

The hunter stroked her head, and when he spoke his voice was a caress, too.

"You fought well, Ashley. You fought hard. But you never had a chance. You're mine. Game, set, match. Let's go on home now. It's a fine night for a swim."

CHAPTER ONE

The storm hit at midnight, waking me from my nightmare to the furious sound of water: rain slamming against windows, hammering the roof, pouring off eaves, twenty-foot breakers crashing on shore. My heart was slapping hard, my body shaking with fright. It wasn't the water that scared me, but the unfinished dream and the malevolent face in it that haunted my sleep—thin copper hair plastered flat to his skull, parchment skin, limpid eyes, and pale thick lips moving as he whispered those unforgettable words, "Touch the fire, Lacie. Reach out and touch the fire."

I kicked aside sweat-soaked sheets and sat straight up in bed.

Thunder drowned out the roar of the Atlantic as lightning cast my hands in its harsh white light. Ravaged with scars, curled and useless, they were flesh-and-blood proof that the nightmare was a savage memory and the face in it belonged to a killer named Edward Beane.

My hands were destroyed when I was ten, in a car fire Beane set that trapped my father and burned him alive in the seat next to me. In a crazy attempt to save him, I plunged my hands into the fire. When I pulled them out, they were two torches burning bright in the Massachusetts night. The flames were a foundry, melting my skin, devouring muscle and tendon, eating all the way through to the bone.

I survived, but sometimes in the years that followed, when I looked at my stumped, ruined fingers and remembered the horrific agony of father's infernal death, I would wish I had not.

I wear black gloves in public. Always. Even in summer. I hide my hands from the world and mostly from myself. They are bitter reminders of the accident and the terrible weeks twenty-three years later when Beane returned, cutting through my life in a vengeful finale, killing the father of my daughter, and very nearly my daughter and me, too. His reign of terror culminated high up on a mountaintop in the winter-frozen Tetons, where he held my thirteen-year-old girl hostage behind a wall of fire, a funeral pyre he had built for me.

I fought hard, using my feet like powerful hands I did not have, savagely kicking with the razor-sharp crampons that were buckled to my boots, forcing him back into the flames. I heard his screams and smelled the stink of his blazing body as I crawled closer still to watch him burn.

I saw the agony on his face, witnessed flesh wither and hard bone cave in.

Melting snow ran black with his ashes, a cold river rushing around me, the wet, dark water of his death.

My nemesis was dead.

Now, ten months later, it was October in Nantucket, and despite the fury of the storm, I fell into a good deep sleep, feeling safe, believing nothing could burn this night, not even the flames of hell—not on this night, in this storm, not with the cold pure water of heaven pouring down.

CHAPTER TWO

He was standing by the pool naked when the midnight storm hit and the Heavens came down. Lightning flashed. He looked up at the natatorium skylights, at water sluicing off glass, and listened to the sound of hard rain beating against the double steel doors.

Water, knock, knock, knocking. Water trying to find a way in.

He flexed his lats and exhaled, satisfied; then he went back to powdering the inside of his wet suit. He held a square container of talcum upside down and tapped it gently. Powder sifted out, a fine light dusting that would make the black rubber slide over his skin in a sensual way.

The preparation was a ritual. He worked slowly, with precision and care. When the dusting was finished, he put the powder down and caressed the suit.

The dressing was a ritual, too. He worked slowly, relishing each move.

Left leg first, followed by right, he rolled the neoprene up, tugging lightly and stretching, getting maximum extension for the ultimate fit. The suit slid over his knees, up his thighs, across his hips and torso. He shrugged it over his back and shoulders and up along his muscled arms. The zipper ran from crotch to chin. He pulled it closed and smiled at the cool, slick feel of his second skin. Sheathed head to foot in the black neoprene, he looked like a diver but felt like Poseidon, an invincible deity, so much more than a man.

Somewhere out at sea, the storm was blowing full force, churning the currents, changing the tides, sucking the ocean floor up in gales of golden sand.

Somewhere out there the elements clashed. Water beat earth, waves swelled high, the great Atlantic scraped the sky.

But that was outside, and he was in—next to the pristine water of his own private sea.

There was another reason for satisfaction this night. The net had come down, the catch safely brought in.

He took a deep breath and jumped, hit water, and began to swim.

CHAPTER THREE

When I woke again, the rain had stopped and the bedside clock glowed 9:00 A.M. It was late by my usual working standards, but I took my time getting up, lingering in bed and then again in the shower, and when I finished drying my hair, it was half past ten. There was no reason to hurry on this Monday morning, no one waiting and nowhere special to go. I was on the tail end of a medical leave of absence from WRC-TV, the NBC affiliate in Washington, D.C., where I anchored the six o'clock news.

It had taken five surgeries spread over nine months to painstakingly rebuild the flesh of my face that had been burned away in that final fiery confrontation with Beane. Now the scars were almost healed. Angry red surgical welts had dulled to dusky shadows. With careful lighting and the right makeup, they would not be visible at all. Bald patches on my head where my hair had been burned down to the scalp had filled in. My long hair was healthy again, a riotous red gold, ironically the color of flame.

I was still painfully slim, a hundred and five pounds stretched across a five-nine frame, but the lost weight accentuated the high plane of my cheekbones and made my blue eyes appear huge. The camera would like that, I thought, tapping the mirror once for luck. I was due back on the set on November 1, in two weeks' time.

My long convalescence had made me restless. I missed the studio, the station, the newsroom buzz, and my news director, Harry Worth. I was one of those rare anchors who wanted to do more than just read copy. The entire process from start to finish was what thrilled me, going out after the news, hunting it down, digging it up, and then in pictures and words telling my audience *the story*.

Looking at my reflection, I was happy with what I saw and felt the outside of me was finally ready again for on-air work. As I dressed and made breakfast, I wondered if the inside of me was, too, if I would be able to concentrate and anchor with my old ease.

As much as I wanted to go back, a big part of me wanted to stay right where I was, hidden away in my beachfront house on an island where money had bought security and privacy in a crime-free town. Healing is an intimate process, and despite my very public life, I am an intensely private woman—that is why I chose the island.

Nantucket's heritage is profoundly Quaker, a solemnity expressed by the courtesy of locals. They recognized me and knew my story, but there were no prying questions or long, speculative sideways glances. Only quiet kindness and the right to live out of the public eye; they granted me that. It is the Nantucket way.

Then there is the physical island itself, five hundred square miles unique to the planet, formed by prehistoric ice floes—a sacred place some say, a mystical remnant from when the world was born. Forty percent of the land is nature preserve. In summer, fuchsia roses tumble over white lattice fences and lush grassy fields turn the color of lime. In fall, cranberry bogs splash across the moors, flushed crimson with rich ripe fruit. In winter, the color cast changes to a hundred shades of gray—the sun to slate, the ocean platinum, skies to steel, and the fog to heathered silver.

And always, there is the sound of the sea.

I loved Nantucket mostly because it was surrounded by the ocean. Seeing water all around, hearing the rhythmic roll of the surf breaking endlessly on shore, gave me an elemental comfort. With so much water I imagined nothing could burn. Thirty miles out at sea, cradled by the mighty Atlantic, I believed I was out of harm's way, that nothing could hurt me.

"What the hell do you do with yourself all day?" Harry had asked at first.

"This and that," I said, keeping the truth to myself.

What did I do? I counted gulls and rolling waves. I counted minutes and hours as time swept me away from the violent past, hoping that when enough days went by the nightmares would leave me, that I would wake up miraculously cured, inside and out. When that didn't happen by midsummer, I counted some more. Ten days. Thirty. A hundred, then two. Two hundred and forty-nine days since I kicked a killer into the fire.

A hundred and five days since Jack walked out of my life.

That one sneaked in, a stubborn refrain, my renegade heart beating out the time.

Jack was the reason I found my daughter on the mountain that January night. I loved him fiercely, but Federal Agent Jack Stein hunted child killers. His work put him cheek to cheek with the worst of mankind, and I couldn't live with that—waiting for the phone to ring, for someone to tell me that Jack had finally met his match, that this time he had lost. So I asked the impossible. I asked him to quit.

He would not give up his work, and I could not give up my fear.

Locked in a hopeless stalemate, Jack left.

I remember the sound of his hiking boots solid and heavy on my Cape Cod deck, how he stopped halfway down the steps as if he were going to turn back, but changed his mind and kept right on walking across the drive and into a waiting taxi. That morning the fog was heavy and wet, interminably gray.

Today the fog was a translucent veil, misting black storm clouds and an angry sea. In my study, big bay windows faced the ocean, framing the view like a work of art. A small aquarium sat on the sill, filled with living treasures from my daughter's summerlong visit: a starfish, two angels, a glowing green gobi, a funnel-nosed clam. She knew all the Latin names. *Angelus imperator* was her favorite, an angel named after a king.

I dropped a pinch of food into the tank, took my coffee to the desk, and flipped through the morning mail, all of it junk: five pool-supply catalogues, two of them pitching dive gear and one, inflatable pool toys. I had been inundated with all kinds of aquatic-related catalogues over the summer, even though there was no pool on my property, even though I did not swim. I tossed the whole lot in the trash and spent the morning researching concepts for feature stories I planned to produce back in the newsroom.

My home office was a precision-built professional indulgence. On one wall were five twenty-four-inch color TV monitors mounted in a row, allowing me to watch news on the three Boston affiliates, the small local station on the Cape, and CNN at the same time. On the adjacent wall was a six-by-four-foot home theater that had an infrared connection to my laptop. Any visual from the Net could be viewed directly on the big screen in real time or downloaded and burned straight to DVD.

My ultraslim IBM notebook was the Ferrari of multimedia convergence technology, a journalist's dream, with an integrated cell phone capable of visual transmission, video player, television, and word processor all in one. I accessed the Internet via satellite linkup, a miraculous wireless technology that enabled me to work virtually anywhere in the world at optimal speed, uploading and downloading large video files. The Cybernews Archive was my principal research resource, a one-stop digital library of archive news content from all the major networks, and I was downloading relevant footage straight to DVD when Harry called in.

"Morning," he boomed. "Hell of a pounding the East Coast took last night. Hell of a storm."

"You didn't call to talk weather," I said, smiling. "What's on your mind?"

"You. Have you seen the D.C. papers, the tabloids, the major city dailies?"

"Yes."

Newspapers and magazines were piled high on my desk. The reporter bylines were all different, but I was the page-one lead story in each. All the old details of my life were documented, the tragic story retold, complete with pictures of my burned-out Washington, D.C., town house and my daughter's frightened face. Looking at the photos of Skyla, I was grimly satisfied that she was tucked away at an elite Maryland boarding school under an assumed name. I lived in fear of copycat criminals, that some psychopath might grab my girl and put her through the nightmare all over again.

"Fifty billboards around town are plastered with your picture," Harry went on. "We're running thirty-second radio spots at five-minute rotations in drive time, full-page print ads in the *Post,* and heavy round-the-clock promotion right here on WRC. Our slogan is simple and strong: 'November 1: Lacie Wagner Comes Home to WRC.' Just in time for the fall ratings sweeps. Action News has slipped to third place in the market. When you were anchoring we were number one. Ad sales is selling off your old ratings, selling what they're calling the Lacie Wagner effect. Their collective ass is on the line."

"Not to mention mine," I quipped.

"Are you ready?" Harry asked. "Do you feel up to it now?"

I grinned. "I've got a dozen ideas for features. My brain is working at high speed."

"It's not that."

"Then what?"

He hesitated.

"We're friends, Harry. Say what you mean."

"You've been away a long time. You need to walk into the newsroom strong and confident. Nothing less. I'm wondering if your psyche's healing as well as your skin. You've been through hell and back again, Lacie. Don't underestimate the psychological fallout. I only want what's best for you. Don't worry about the promos or the ratings or the station or me. If you need more time, just say the word."

"*Work*, that's the word. You know the way I'm wired. Work will be the best thing in the world for me. November first, I'll be back on the set."

"Okay, then!" he said, obviously relieved. "Excellent. You're the big story here. Be prepared for that."

We said good-bye, neither of us knowing Harry was wrong. The big story was coming right at me as unexpected and powerful as a fast-breaking wave—a story unlike anything I had ever covered, imagined, investigated, or dreamed.

At quarter past three, I stopped and changed into black sweats, loaded a waist pack with water and my cell phone, and headed down a battered wood walkway to the beach for my afternoon run.

I lived on the east side of the island, in Siasconset, a wide, wild stretch of sparsely populated shoreline fully exposed to the Atlantic. Moorland rolled on for long empty miles off the back of my property, the Atlantic swelled endlessly in front, and sand dunes spilled north and south as far as the eye could see.

My house was one of three perched on the bluff: a 150-year-old two-story Cape Cod with white shutters, French-paned windows, a widow's walk, and an old-fashioned wraparound porch too charming to be called a deck. Like all the old island houses, cedar shingles had been weathered by the elements to a soft driftwood gray.

To the left was another vintage island classic, closed up for the winter, shuttered and locked. To the right was a split-level home built of the same island cedar—but where my house was old, this one was new. Shingles were light caramel, the color of fresh cedar before sun and ocean spray beats them down.

On Nantucket, development is tightly controlled. Building plans must be approved and for that reason alone the architecture of the new house puzzled me. The lines and materials were traditional but details were out of balance and scale: The widow's walk was too big, there were too many triangular eaves with half-circle attic windows that looked like eyes, and too many modern skylights that stuck up from the roof like smokestacks.

The windows were huge twelve-foot-high rectangular sheets of plate glass facing the beach. I imagined how they must have groaned and shuddered in the full frontal attack of the previous night's storm. Even from where I was, standing on shore, I could see right inside. The house reminded me of an aquarium.

Bulldozed land ringed the house like a raw scar, as if the workers had hurried off before the job was done. A pool had been dug, tiled sapphire blue and filled, but there was no decking. It was left surrounded by dirt and now even though it was October, the pool had not yet been covered and closed.

On sunny days, it shimmered iridescent blue, like a glittering square-cut stone nestled in the earth. At night, lit, it was a slick, wet mirror, an azure gem glowing in the dark.

When rain came down hard and fast as it had overnight, the pool bled; water overflowed, spilled out, poured in rivers down the bluffs, turning sand and soil to heavy mud.

The house was named Angel's Reef, and a man lived there alone. He was not on holiday or one of the weekends-only crowd. He stayed on through September and October, long after the island's summer population had gone. I saw him almost every day on my afternoon run, surf fishing, casting gracefully in late-day sun. I was never close enough to guess his age, only to see that he was dark-haired and tall with a good lean build. He always lifted a hand in greeting from afar. Polite acknowledgment. We never spoke.

On this afternoon, I had the beach all to myself. The wind was sharp, the clouds dark and heavy with the promise of more rain. I started out slowly, cutting right to the north. As my body warmed, I picked up speed and ran with a fierce fast pace, needing the burn of athletic exertion. The pain of pushing my body to the limit cleared my mind and, even as my feet flew across sand, lifted me high to a place where there was only the moment—a place where past and future, like memory and nightmares, simply did not exist—and it was then that I felt happy and light and free.

CHAPTER FOUR

.

A collector's item.

A splendid nautical instrument with pedigree.

Three extendable cherry wood legs raised the telescope five and a half feet high. The shaft was four feet long, hand-hewn, hammered brass, circa 1800 with state-of-the-art opticals, two twin objectives, powerful enough to spot a whale a hundred miles offshore, clear enough to pick out craters on the moon. But the subject that interested him today was neither planet nor fish. It was female, a half mile down the sand, running the shoreline fronting his house.

Beautiful, Vale thought, tracking her, *a two-legged gazelle in full flight.*

He had been watching her since May when she had first moved in. She ran every day at three-thirty sharp, in the wind, heat, fog and rain. Nothing stopped her. She was precise and exact. He could set his clock by her afternoon run. Just for fun one day he did.

In the summer she wore a black bikini brief, tiny tight black tee, black baseball cap, and the gloves, always the gloves. On those warm days, she ran barefoot on the hard pack, darting into and out of the surf. There was a childlike innocence to her game, the impulsive joy of a woman who thinks she is unobserved, totally alone.

Now she was bundled in black sweats. He missed her summer-bare legs, the mile-high thighs on display, the curve of her backside, the bounce of her breasts. But even covered up, she had beauty and grace. He zoomed in tight on her face until it filled the optical round. She turned suddenly and glanced up at his house. His pulse quickened. She was too far away to see him, of course, but right then, looking into his lens, it seemed as if she could.

She had eyes the color of cobalt, high-flying cheekbones, and full, sensual lips. On television, she was striking in a controlled elegant way. But here now free on the shore, her face unpainted and hair tossed by the wind, the natural woman was a hundred times more beautiful.

Lacie Wagner, he said out loud to himself. On November 1 she would be back in D.C. anchoring the news. She was leaving Nantucket. He had no time to waste.

Vale stepped back from the scope and watched her with his naked eyes, running right up tight to the surf, teasing the tide line, kicking seashells and driftwood, flotsam tossed up in the storm—running, running, running like the wind, into the wind, north, toward the Old Whale Rock.

CHAPTER FIVE

One mile turned into two, and the Old Whale Rock came into view. It was a geographical anomaly, a cluster of gray-black boulders jutting out of the shallows like the head of a whale. Locals said it just appeared one day as if the tidal shelf had shifted suddenly in an undersea quake. There were plenty of other explanations that had nothing to do with science and everything to do with island superstition, stories of how the rock was an oceanic rebuke for the hundred-year slaughter of whales, or a divine reprimand for throwing Indians off their native land.

To me it was a destination, a marker in the long stretch of beach, something to head for, a place to turn around. In high tide only a small tip of the rock was visible. I sprinted the last half mile on the wet hard pack, letting waves come tantalizingly close and chase me in a made-up game. Just as I hit the rock a big one caught me by surprise, breaking hard and rushing up fast, soaking me to the knees. Happiness snapped to horror when I saw what the water had washed in.

I wanted to push her away, leave her to the tides and the fish.

I had had enough of death.

I should have turned around and left her.

But there she was, facedown, loose-limbed, and lifeless, curving around my ankles, weighing down my feet, and as the wave receded, sweeping her back out, I couldn't help myself. I tossed my waist pack high up on dry sand and waded in after her.

She wore a black wet suit and a fully inflated buoyancy vest, twin dive tanks harnessed to her back, a weight belt loaded around her small waist. She had booties but no flippers or mask, and her hands were bare. Her face turned slightly in the water, and I saw enough of the horrible damage to know without question the diver was dead.

A thick strand of seaweed threaded around her tanks like the rope to an anchor. Standing waist deep in the shallows, I pulled at the slippery kelp, cursing through tears, hating the weight of her against me, the way the surf tossed her body between mine and the rock. Her head hit granite hard in bone-cracking thumps, and her hair floated in a fan, sticking to my knees. I tugged and pulled and cursed the tight seaweed knot, but could not break the kelp. The wind was rising, and the surf turning rough. I waded out. The beach was more than a quarter mile wide and deserted. The closest house was my own, two and a half miles back. I didn't dare leave, so I took the cell phone from my pack and called 911.

CHAPTER SIX

Assistant District Attorney Hinks was standing at the dock in Hyannis with a state trooper when the call came in.

"Floater in Nantucket," the young trooper said. "That's your county and mine. Want to come along for the ride?"

"Let's go," she said, dropping neatly into the cigarette boat.

It was a metallic red three-engine monster named *Ruby,* a 1,500-horsepower triple-header confiscated in a sting—now the ace perk for Cape Cod state troopers and local assistant DAs. On a flat sea they could make the crossing to the island in the same time as a plane. With the moderate chop Hinks was looking at, it would take an extra fifteen minutes.

"You driving?" the trooper asked.

"Of course," she said, taking the keys. Hinks always drove. It was a control thing.

She turned the ignition. *Ruby* was feeling good. The engines kicked right on over.

Hinks grinned. Anticipation stirred in her chest. Massachusetts law gave state troopers and the DA's office investigative jurisdiction over drownings and any other unattended deaths on the island. For a long time Nantucket had been basically crime-free, but things were changing fast, and the real world was sneaking in. The last Nantucket drowning had led Hinks straight to a heroin-ring bust and a high-profile prosecutorial victory that turbocharged her young career.

Slipping out of the port and into open water, Hinks opened the throttle and let *Ruby* fly. She steered standing up, and that made for a striking sight: long legs firm on the deck, white-blond hair rippling in the wind, full female curves of her body on powerful display.

Hinks was blessed with beauty and brains—a formidable combination that guaranteed a great future. Mixed in was a healthy dose of three of the seven deadly sins: pride, envy, and greed—a fierce triple-headed hydra all her own.

As the speedboat roared out of the harbor, her pulse ticked up from a fourth potential sin: Lust.

Tom Wheeler would be at the scene in Nantucket. He was the island's ME, and Hinks would do just about anything—hell, Hinks would walk on water for a chance to get next to him.

CHAPTER SEVEN

The temperature dropped; ocean spray fell like rain as I waited on the hard pack, watching the empty horizon, the dark sky, and the lifeless body beating rock. The humming of engines carried on the wind. A battered old pumpkin-colored Jeep came streaking down the beach and pulled in next to me. The driver got out.

He was six four and wore a black wet suit that showed off bulging biceps the size of most men's thighs. He carried a black medical bag in one hand, a fat dive knife sheathed at his waist, and a Nikonis waterproof camera slung over one massive shoulder. Although he must have only been in his early forties, his head was totally bald, smooth and well-shaped, golden from the sun.

"Ms. Wagner? I've seen you on television," he said. "Tom Wheeler."

"Nantucket PD?"

"I'm a surgeon—the only surgeon on the island, in fact. I step in as medical examiner whenever we get an unattended death."

"Unattended?"

"When someone dies who isn't under the care of a doctor. Doesn't happen much around here, but it looks like we've got one today."

He dropped the medical bag and sprinted into the water with surprising grace for such a big man. Surf crashed against his chest, splashed up in his face as he barreled ahead, snapping pictures of the body in situ. Knife steel flashed silver. Wheeler cut the kelp, grabbed the tank pack, and used the force of incoming waves to haul the diver in. When he had her up on the dry sand, he took close-ups of the body and gear.

"How did you find her?" he asked.

"I was running tight to the surf line here when a big wave carried her in."

"Frankly, I'm surprised she washed up at all."

"Why's that?"

"Nantucket's a tiny dot of land thirty miles out in the middle of the Atlantic. The way the tides and currents work, this isn't an easy target to hit. That and the fact the tide's going out. There've been times when fishermen have fallen overboard in full sight of the island, but their bodies never washed in—even in high tide. The ocean doesn't give up the dead easily—not here."

"How many drownings do you get on average each year?"

"One or two," Wheeler said. "Swimmer or diver goes out and never comes back. The currents are mean, and the water's cold. Folks forget that. They go in thinking the Atlantic's a goddamn bathtub.

"State police will have to talk to you, take your statement. A trooper's on his way now from Hyannis Port. Nantucket PD will escort him on out here."

"Why would state police get involved in a local situation?"

"That's standard procedure anytime there's an unattended death or drowning on the island."

"Her buoyancy vest is fully inflated," I said. "How can you be sure she drowned?"

"I'm not sure yet. Could've been a heart attack or embolism." He checked her air pressure gauge. "Empty. Same old story. Too far out, not enough air."

He snapped a close-up for the record.

"Strange time of year to be sport diving," I said, "given the cold water and lousy visibility. What about commercial divers?"

"There's nothing commercial out there. No rigs. No salvage—private or military."

"I couldn't help but notice that her body's pliant. Rigor hasn't set in."

"Right," Wheeler said, examining her hands. "Whatever happened, it was recent. A day or two at sea, she'd be blown up twice her size and smell like death itself. Other than the salt water, there's no odor at all."

"Wouldn't the cold water temperature slow down decomposition?"

"Sure, but it wouldn't slow down the hungry scavengers. She's got lacerations on her palms that sure as hell aren't from fish."

He turned one up for me to see the deep cuts.

"More than a couple of hours out there, and the sea life would've taken their share. Her hands would be chewed up, not cut up like this, and just like you noticed, rigor hasn't yet set in. That alone tells me she died in the past twelve hours."

Beyond the breaking surf the sea was relatively calm with gently rolling swells. The buoyancy vest troubled me. I was thinking about how it should have held her head high up out of the water even if the swells were twice as big as they were earlier in the day. Even if she had been knocked unconscious, that vest should have saved her life.

Wheeler rolled her over on her back. Her head flopped to one side. He put a hand under her chin and brushed the hair away to see if it was a local girl, someone he knew.

"Christ," he said.

Facial flesh had been pummeled featureless, ripped and ragged, brows obliterated, nose smashed, and lips gone. Shards of bone jutted forth, fine white splinters, and three front teeth were missing. Out of the ruined mass, one eye was open and staring, vivid blue.

"Beaten?" I asked.

"No. There's no subcutaneous hematoma, no bruising at all. I'd say the surf and the rock did this postmortem, when she was stuck in the kelp. She took quite a pounding out there."

He took close-ups, then let the air out of the vest, and tugged on the wet suit zipper, working it down. She was nude under the neoprene, high breasts, ribs and stomach covered with festering circular craters seared deep into her flesh.

"These sure as hell aren't thermal burns," Wheeler said.

"If fire didn't do that, what did?"

"Radiation. That's my guess."

I had seen wounds just like them when I interviewed Yoko Shimada, the daughter of a woman who died in Nagasaki during the war. She had laid out pictures of her mother's corpse reverently while telling me how she watched radiation sickness kill her mother slowly, as it ate holes in the flesh that looked like burns.

"Five weeks," Yoko had said. "Five weeks of fever and frightful pain. Eight hundred and forty hours of suffering. The people who say the bomb kills fast lie, Ms. Wagner. They lie."

"Do radiation burns appear simultaneously with exposure?" I asked.

"Not unless the victim's exposed to atomic fallout from a nuclear plant disaster or some major incident like that—in which case her wet suit would've melted. There's no way it would be intact."

"What about a low-dosage exposure or contact with nuclear waste?"

"She'd get radiation sickness. Burns would come up over time as a result, couple of weeks, three at least. In my mind that's most likely what happened."

"Three weeks into radiation sickness?" I asked. "How would she feel?"

"Sick as a dog."

"Not to mention the mind-blowing pain of salt water in those open wounds."

"Right."

"If she was as sick as that, why on earth would she have been out scuba diving?"

Wheeler just looked at me, as if I had the answers.

I didn't.

But I planned on getting them.

CHAPTER EIGHT

Sunset on Siasconset, the tide running out, the sky bleeding color and light, night falling.

Wheeler and I waited in his Jeep with the heater on high. He switched his headlamps on bright, lighting up the dead girl in an eerie way. The featureless face in profile, pale exposed breasts, sternum and belly all glowing white while everything else was black—the wet suit, the tanks, the burns, the wet matted hair.

"I've never seen anything like this," Wheeler said. "Never seen anything even close."

I wanted to run out and cover her with a blanket, shelter her from the elements and our own fascinated eyes. She did not look like a tired swimmer in repose. Tanks still loaded on her back, she lay high and unnaturally arched in the sand. Supine, arms at her sides, palms up, open to the skies, she looked sacrificial, like a classic figurehead come unlashed from the prow.

Beyond the spill of headlamps, the beach was pitch black. The state flag on Wheeler's radio antenna flapped furiously, pointing out to sea. The wind was offshore and strong, blowing up veils of sand, whipping white streaks across the water, beating against our windows and whistling in through a hundred tiny cracks, chilling me to the bone. My hands were hypersensitive to the cold. Damp leather gloves were sheaths of ice, but much as I wanted to, I would not take them off, not with Wheeler right there next to me and state police on the way.

The radio played something classical while a police

scanner crackled on the dash. Wheeler sat with me in silence, watching the night, the waves, the wind, eyes always moving back to the dead girl heaped high on the sand.

At six, the first lights appeared way off in the distance coming from the high north end of Siasconset Beach. They were just tiny pinholes winking in the black; then they grew into distinct halos of blazing headlights and powerful running lights as a blue Land Rover pulled up, Nantucket PD.

The driver swung out, a big man built like a fighter, with steely gray hair buzzed flat in a military cut. He wore faded jeans and a blue parka.

"John Colter," Wheeler said. "Nantucket's chief of police."

A young man dropped down from the passenger side.

"Trooper Quinn," Wheeler said. "State police."

Quinn held the door while a woman got out.

"That's Hinks," Wheeler said. "Assistant DA for Cape Cod and the islands."

Hinks was long-legged and tall, five ten, with broad square shoulders, a lush heavy chest and white-blond hair razored down tight to her head. The severity and maleness of the cut made her all the more striking, revealing the formidably flawless complexion and perfect bone structure of a classical Swedish face. Her features were strong—the jaw, the nose, the wide full mouth, high sweeping forehead, and prominent cheekbones. She was dressed in black jeans and a turtleneck.

As we got out of the Jeep, a second, younger woman in blue jeans emerged from the back of the Rover.

"Kiri Hannover," Wheeler said. "She's an oceanographer from Woods Hole Institution across the sound. Kiri knows more about the tides and currents on the Cape and here on the island than anyone else. State police use her whenever they want forensic tidal work done."

Kiri was barely five feet tall and had startling white-blond hair like Hinks, but she wore hers long and straight. Her skin was pale and her delicate features finely drawn. A white diamond pierced her nose. On her the effect was sweet rather than rebellious. Standing next to Hinks, she looked small, and when Wheeler walked up she looked positively tiny—a fragile, ethereal doll.

Of the six of us, I was the stranger.

Wheeler made brief introductions and moved on, summarizing his findings.

Hinks stood close next to him, listening carefully, asking questions, and touching his arm from time to time in a way that said their relationship was more than professional. When Wheeler finished, she knelt next to the body, going over the detail of the ruined face and burns.

"Kiri," she said, "I want you to work up a computer simulation of the tides and currents here at the rock going back twenty-four hours."

"You're looking for a probable entry point?" John Colter asked.

"Right," Hinks said, rising. "I want to know if she washed in from somewhere local here or if she came in from across the sound."

"I'll need to log in compass readings at the shoreline," Kiri said, "triangulate the body's position, and see if there are any geographical anomalies to take into consideration on account of last night's storm. A mile in either direction should cover me."

"John and Dave will take you in the Rover," Hinks said, brushing sand off her thighs. "Tom, there's nothing more to learn here tonight. You can go ahead and bag the body. Ms. Wagner and I are going to walk a bit, enjoy this good island air."

She wanted me alone, one on one, and moments later we were.

"Lacie Wagner," she said. "You're an *investigative* reporter, *anchorwoman* from Washington, D.C., the one we all read about a while back." Her tone was patronizing, full lips pressed in a hard tight line.

"Lot of disturbing things about the body," I said, "things that don't add up, don't you agree?"

"Seems to me I'm the one who should be asking the questions. I am the assistant district attorney, and this is my case."

"Good. I like to get my facts from the top. What are you thinking? Where does the investigation go now?"

"You're a witness, Ms. Wagner. And that means you answer questions, not pose them. Now tell me exactly what happened this afternoon and why you were on the beach in the first place." She was intimating that my finding the body was somehow suspect and reason enough for her obvious contempt.

"I live here," I said.

"Beachfront."

"Yes."

"City news must pay real good."

"We were talking about the case. What do you think about the radiation burns?"

"Burns?"

"The wounds on her body."

"Who said radiation did that?"

"The ME here on the scene."

"He might be wrong. It's too early to do more than guess now, ahead of an autopsy. Shoot, they looked like fish bites to me. We've got these big-mouthed suckerfish in the bay. Why, if you're not careful they'll suck your skin right off."

"Through a wet suit?"

"Looks to me like fish did the work," she said, sarcasm so thick I couldn't miss it.

"Looks way bigger than that," I replied.

"Run-of-the-mill drowning, that's all."

"I don't think Dr. Wheeler would agree with you."

"Fish, Ms. Wagner, taking lots of good-sized bites out of our floater here."

"Wheeler said she wasn't dead long enough for sea life to start feeding."

"Christ, so now he's suddenly a fish expert, too? One thing I know is fish, and the fish in these waters are voracious. Nantucket fish. Old as time and twice as hungry. They chew up bodies faster than most."

"Are you stonewalling me?"

"I am advising a *witness* to not let her imagination get the best of her. Stick to the facts, and the only fact we don't know is what kind of fish made those bite marks."

"You treat all press this way?"

"Just putting a lid on wild-eyed speculation, the kind of tabloid hoo-ha that gets people all riled up."

"I'm not a tabloid reporter."

"You're a witness, like I said." She handed me her card. "That's my mobile. If you decide to leave the island, give me a call first."

"Does that mean I can't?"

"No. It means just what I said: Keep me apprised of your whereabouts. Now tell me the sequence of events—what happened here today."

I went over my story. When I finished, Hinks flipped on her flashlight and pointed it at my face.

"Humpty Dumpty," she said softly. "Humpty Dumpty with big-city pay and high-priced plastic surgeons. They did a good job putting you back together again. Too bad they can't do the same for our Jane Doe. Go on home now, Ms. Wagner, watch TV—leave the investigating to me and my team."

Hinks was gone before I could reply, moving fast in long-legged strides across the sand, back at attention, white-blond hair bright in the night.

"The body goes to Boston," she called out to Wheeler. "I want Miles to do this one himself. Check in with me when you get there, Tom, I don't care how late."

The Rover pulled up. Hinks climbed in and slammed the door. The Rover turned a neat 180-degree circle heading back the way it had come, taillights red glowing embers in the dark.

I went to Wheeler. He was on his knees in the sand, working a black bag over the body.

"Why are you leaving the gear on?" I asked. "Wouldn't she be easier to handle without tanks?"

"The gear's evidence. This is a suspect death." He loaded the body into the back of the Jeep. "Come on. I'll give you a lift home."

I got in. He slipped in beside me and we rolled slowly south, bumping along down the beach, shadowy bluffs sliding by on the right side, the ocean on the left.

The Jeep was small, and even though I kept my eyes trained straight ahead, the mound of body behind me was visible and close enough to touch. It bumped the back of my seat from time to time, bag crackling like popcorn, tanks clanking inside.

"Sorry you've got to ride with her like this," Wheeler said. "Couldn't run an ambulance out here on the sand, and truth is my old Jeep is the unofficial transport wagon for most of the island's dead."

"What about the funeral home?"

"Oh, we've got one in town. Jimmy Hanson's place. But Jimmy's old hearse is so shot it's up on blocks half the time. The other half when it's running, Jimmy's off drinking someplace, and good luck trying to find him at just the same moment that you've got a body to bring in. We don't even have a proper morgue here on the island, so we use Jimmy's fridge when we need to."

"Doesn't that compromise security, and break the chain of clear evidentiary protection when you do that?"

"Yes, indeed. Just drives home the point of how different small-town life is, Ms. Wagner."

A light rain started to fall. Wheeler flicked the wipers on and turned off the beach, rumbling up a man-made ramp in the sand to a snaking dirt road up on the bluff. The island had hundreds of them, unmarked narrow trails winding for countless miles. They were the sole access to the Siasconset shore and beachfront houses like mine. Asphalt was not used much because winter storms washed the roads out and in winter they were hard to repair. Dirt roads were cheap, practical, and quickly fixed.

Wheeler's suspension was shot. The Jeep pitched and rocked, and the dive tanks in back clanked, reminding us the dead girl was right there with us. Wheeler swerved to avoid a pothole. Branches of scrub oak whipped my window and clawed the door.

"Why are you taking the body to Boston?" I asked.

"We're not set up or authorized for autopsies here. Nantucket's got its own protocol for the dead."

"Which is?"

"We've got a local DA in town, Frank Marshall. When someone dies unattended, I call Frank and describe the circumstances surrounding the death. He talks to Hinks and then decides if an autopsy is needed or not. In certain kinds of deaths it's a waste."

"Such as?"

"Last week for example, Harry Darnell went to sleep and never woke up. He was eighty-nine years old and under a local doc's care for heart trouble. There was no foul play or any reason to suspect it. An autopsy would've just caused grief to his widow. A tox screen was good enough, and I did that myself.

"Drownings here typically don't require an autopsy. Usually it's obvious that's what took place—a witness or two who saw the unlucky swimmer yanked out to sea by a riptide—or a whole boat full of people who saw a drunk fall overboard."

"But tonight is different."

"Oh, yes. You can say that again."

"What time's the autopsy slated for?"

"Who, what, where, why, how, and when." He stopped the Jeep and looked at me hard. "Are you interviewing me, Ms. Wagner?"

There was some of Hinks's contempt in his voice.

"I'm a journalist," I said, "and this is a story."

"Okay," he said reluctantly. "I'm a practical man, and the way I see it, you'd stay up all night getting the information some other way. Might as well get it right from the source. Keep you from bugging folks, driving them nuts on the phone, or worse yet showing up at the DA's with a camera and crew. If you have more questions, then go right on and shoot."

"How are you getting the body to Boston?"

"By air."

"Medevac chopper?"

"A chartered Cessna. And I'm going along for the ride."

"Why?"

"You tell me."

"Hinks wants an inviolate unquestionable chain of evidence, and the body and the gear that's on it is all the evidence she has. You're the legal escort."

"Right. Miles McKenzie is the chief ME up there. He and I will do the autopsy first thing in the morning."

"You're assisting?"

"Wouldn't miss this one for the world. For a part-time medical examiner out in the boondocks like me, this body's forensically fascinating. I've never seen anything like it and probably never will again."

"McKenzie has his own staff. Why would he let you assist?"

"We're old friends. Go back a long time, all the way to med school."

I saw an opening and took it: "Take me with you."

He stepped on the gas. "Not a chance."

"I want to observe."

"A reporter in the autopsy suite?" Wheeler laughed. "No way."

"I'm going to be there."

A whisper of a smile skated across his lips. "Reporters."

"You say that like they're snakes."

"They are."

"The wrong kind, maybe."

"And you're the right kind?"

"I'm a journalist. I respect the law; I respect privacy. I don't hound people. I may push the envelope from time to time in the interest of breaking a story, but I never forget who the victim is, and I never forget my obligation to honor the rights of the bereaved."

That was not entirely true. I had always been the first one at the front of the news pack in my black suit and camera-ready makeup, ringing the doorbell, shoving the mike in someone's face, asking the hard questions because I believed my disability made me more empathetic, that somehow my wrecked hands gave me the right to stand in the living rooms and on the front lawns of the victimized and the bereaved, asking, How does it feel?

The news was all that mattered. The story was all I cared about.

"You and Hinks have got a thing about the press," I said. "Must make for good pillow talk at night."

"Me and Hinks?" He laughed, genuinely amused. "Not so far, anyway—but she's doing her best to change that. She's got an old-fashioned crush on me."

"Tell me about her."

"Couple of things you should know. Hinks is the daughter of a local fisherman, and grew up poor. Professionally she is wildly ambitious. Edward Taggert, the Cape Cod county DA, is running for Senate, and he's going to win. For the first time in ten years the local field here is wide open for his job. Hinks is one of two official contenders. She's one of the best assistant DAs around, never lost a case. By all rights if merit were the deciding factor, she should get the job. But money's the thing, so she will probably lose this election."

"Money?"

"Campaign finance. She's running against Walter Blake, a Boston trust fund prep. He has a staff of thirty and is spending millions on television ads alone. Hinks has a staff of three volunteers—including me—and a stone-cold empty coffer. She's campaigning on her record the old-fashioned way—pumping flesh and charming the voters."

"She didn't exactly charm me out there tonight."

Wheeler chuckled. "You saw the personal side of Hinks," he said. "She's fiercely competitive. Gets her back up when there's another woman in the room—especially if I'm there, too. Beauty and money. Hinks has way more of one and not enough of the other. You've got a hell of a lot of both, not to mention fame. That would piss her off. She'll give you a hard time. Consider yourself forewarned. There is no fury like Hinks when she's mad—or jealous."

"But you like her."

"That is an understatement."

"Then why aren't you together?"

"I'll never leave this island. Hinks wants to get as far away from Nantucket as she can. She wants big-city success more than she wants me—she just doesn't know that yet. If she wins the election, she'll stick it out five years, then move on to bigger things in Boston. If she loses, she'll move on to bigger things in Boston anyway. There's no reason for her to stay in Cape Cod."

"Maybe that's just the point, Wheeler."

He glanced at me.

"Given a good reason," I said, "Hinks might stay."

"Enough about me," Wheeler said. "Let's talk about Jane Doe. Frankly I'd like you to forget you ever found the body, Ms. Wagner."

"Why?"

"You're a high-profile lady. The story's different coming from someone like you. A small-town reporter filing it wouldn't carry the same weight. You're part of the story and that's going to stir everything up, and the last thing I want on Nantucket's a national press feast. No thanks."

He stopped the Jeep in front of my house and set the brake. "Good night now, Ms. Wagner."

"I want to be there tomorrow for the same reasons you do. *'Never seen anything like it,'* you said. Well, neither have I. It's irresistible. Take me along."

"No."

"The way I see it, you have two choices. Shut me out and I'll file a story tomorrow live from McKenzie's lobby with the following spin: 'Nantucket officials may know more than they're telling about a shocking radiation-related death on the island.' The way you and Hinks are behaving could make me think you've got something to hide. How's this for a headline you'd hate to see on the national news: 'Nuclear cover-up on Nantucket.' If I spin it that way, you'll have a hundred reporters on your doorstep tomorrow afternoon. *Yours,* Wheeler."

"Are you threatening me?"

"Just making a promise. I want in. Take me along and you won't be sorry. I promise you that, too."

"How about if I get you an advance copy of the autopsy protocol?"

"Not good enough."

"Why?"

"All the critical elements don't always get into official reports. Facts can be concealed. Evidence can be suppressed."

"I'll fill you in personally."

"Reporters are born cynics. We believe one thing, and that's our own eyes and ears—just like you, Wheeler. Take me along."

"The Cessna's too small. You won't fit."

"I'll take the first commercial flight out in the morning."

"First flight leaves at eight. You'll get to Boston too late."

"The first high-speed ferry leaves at six. I'll be at the morgue receiving bay at quarter to nine sharp."

Wheeler eyed me, nodded, and said, "Do most folks have a hard time saying no to you?"

CHAPTER NINE

I hurried into my study and punched up the speakerphone, speed-dialing the number for Boston's NBC affiliate newsroom. The news director there was an old friend. Dan Cohen answered his own phone.

"If you're looking for a job, Lacie, the answer is yes."

"Just looking for some help. I've got a story for you."

I gave him a quick rundown, focusing on the radiation burns and sketching out all the possible implications.

"Nuclear mishaps," Dan mused. "Radioactive waste. Those two sentences alone push all the right buttons—

not to mention the fun of having WRC's star talent on my air. What do you need in the way of a crew?"

"A cameraman and a news van."

"I'll send you Ben O'Brian. He's young and talented. You'll like his work. Just tell me what time and where."

"Hyannis ferry, seven a.m."

"Consider it done. I won't be in tomorrow, but I'll give the desk a heads-up."

"What about WRC?"

"We can zap it over via satellite."

I called Harry.

"This tastes big," he mused, "hundred-proof military to me."

"That's what I'm thinking."

"I'm going to run it as the lead."

Dinner was a chopped salad at my desk picked at slowly while I sketched out a story "skeleton," a time-line of events, relevant phone numbers, and one-word notes to myself questioning the significance of elements I did not yet understand. At the start of a piece, I usually filled two or three pages with potential sources, witnesses, and long lists of phone numbers. Now I had only one page with two phone numbers—Tom Wheeler's and Hinks's—and two events noted: the date and time the body washed in and the date and time of the autopsy. The single page was symbolic of how much was not yet known.

Developing a news story is much like an investigator's work—taking known facts and lining them up against a seemingly infinite array of variables. It is a methodical way of bringing order to chaos. I loved the unpredictable nature of the process, how that which seemed most relevant at the beginning of an investigation might prove to be totally irrelevant at the end.

Stories revealed themselves in unique ways, and part
of the investigative process was having the patience to
let a piece naturally unfold, to not get ahead, push
sources that weren't ready, make clumsy moves out of
haste.

I surfed the Net, trolling for information on potential
sources of radiation burns, starting with the most obvious place first: the Nuclear Regulatory Commission.
The agency had an extensive site. Using the infrared
connection, I put it up on my home theater screen and
clicked my way through to a full-color map of commercial reactors licensed and operating in the United
States.

The country was divided up into four geographic re-
gions with small red pyramids marking the location of
each reactor. The highest concentration was on the East
Coast. Twenty-seven red pyramids dotted the Northeast
corridor, only one of which was on the coast in Cape
Cod, not far from Nantucket. I made a note. The proximity was significant.

There were hundreds of industrial reactors in the
United States, all monitored by the Department of Energy. The third type was a production reactor used to
manufacture nuclear weapons. All relevant information
was classified at the Department of Defense and unat-
tainable. The public's right to know did not outweigh
national security interests.

I searched nuclear waste sites flagged by the Environmental Protection Agency as hazardous and made a
list of everything on the Northeast coast. And I considered hospitals. Equipment used in nuclear medicine,
chemotherapy units, even X-ray machines all had powerful radioactive components inside. In the wrong
hands, cesium chips could be deadly and pack a hell of
a burn. They were easily obtainable on the black market, too.

The military was the most probable source. Five major units were locally based at the Massachusetts Military Reservation out on the southern tip of Cape Cod, including marines and the coast guard, both of which had divers.

The largest naval base on the eastern seaboard was in Bethesda, Maryland, too far from Nantucket to consider.

Little Creek Amphibious Base in Norfolk was even farther away. But according to the EPA summary I had just read, the base had a couple of lakes that were so radioactively hot they practically glowed. Little Creek was home base for Special Ops, and while there were no women in SEALs, I found the mix of military divers and nuclear waste too compelling to ignore.

If she was U.S. military, she would be identified in the next twenty-four hours. If she had ever been convicted of a crime or done jail time, her prints would be in the national database and I would know her name by sundown. If someone had reported her missing, the police might get a quick match and—again—I would know her name soon.

Her name was the most important piece of information. Once I had the *who,* I would be able to move forward, to ask the questions that needed asking, to wind my way deeper into the *where, what, why, when,* and *how.*

Upstairs in the bedroom, I looked out across the bluff at the house next door. The blue pool was lit, and despite the late hour, my neighbor's pool man was working. I had seen him on and off over the months, always at night, skimming methodically, carefully, obsessively cleaning the pool. Some nights he would stay out there for hours, and no matter what the weather, he was always dressed the same in long baggy cargo pants, a dark hooded jacket with long sleeves, and gloves.

I caught brief glimpses of his face—enough to see the black eye patch over his left eye and a shaggy black mustache. Mostly I just saw the hood bobbing up and down as if he were nodding, pleased with himself as he gripped the long-poled skimmer, skimming, skimming, skimming. Now he put the skimmer down and stretched out, belly flat to the ground, reached into the water with his gloved hands and scooped something out. A small creature, I guessed, a field mouse, hummingbird, sparrow, or frog.

I went to bed and lay in the dark trying to steer my thoughts back to the dead diver, but I thought of the pool man instead, wondering what he was fishing out, what tiny life he was saving, why he always worked at night, but mostly wondering why on earth I even cared.

CHAPTER TEN

The big glass eye of the scope caught her ghosting by the upstairs bedroom window in a black silk robe, moving back and forth with unspent energy, or so it seemed to him.

She stopped once for a long moment and gazed out at his pool, and he wondered what her view looked like from up there, if she could see detail in the tile work, and if she admired the vivid sapphire color, the bright gemstar gloss of the water, the serene beauty of his man-made sea.

She moved away, and her window went dark.

The glass eye stayed locked in place.

He imagined black silk falling to the floor, her long

pale body against bedsheets, blue eyes closing, slipping into sleep.

Vale had watched her all summer, on the beach and in her house, learning the cadence of her days and nights, her habits and small seasonal rituals like the way she dried her hair outside on hot summer afternoons.

She came out on the deck dressed in a short black silk robe, draped her lithe body across a chaise, and spread her wet hair out in a fan, an offering to the sun. She always drank a bottle of water, and he watched the arch of her neck, the way her throat worked, pumping in a sexual way as she swallowed. Mostly he loved the way she reveled in her sublime solitude, nearly naked and free, uninhibited and unashamed.

It was on those afternoons when her wet hair was slicked back off her face that he saw the pure beauty of her bone structure, learned the angles and planes. He studied her face with an artist's eye and came to know it so well he could sketch her quickly and perfectly from memory. Just for fun, he often did.

All the months she had lived there, Lacie Wagner was always alone. There was never a man walking, running, sitting, dining, or sleeping with her. She was so alone it moved Vale, made him want to go to her now, rap at the door, carry her away across the sand to his own empty bed.

Vale had watched her through the spring and summer into fall.

Now he knew it was high time they met.

CHAPTER ELEVEN

The alarm went off at 4:30 A.M.

Outside my window, the sky and sea were one color and texture. There was no way of knowing where water ended and air began.

I swung out of bed, showered, and dressed carefully in black wool slacks, a black cashmere sweater, and glossy calfskin boots with high stacked heels that put me over the six-foot mark. Height gave me confidence, and I knew I would need that later in the day when I faced the camera for the first time in ten long months. I applied makeup with care, tied my hair back, and studied my reflection in the mirror. For a split second I thought of Jane Doe with her ruined face and wide-open eye, and fear rolled through my body, prescient, intense.

I believed that somehow she was an omen meant for me.

A taxi pulled up in the drive. The horn sounded.

I considered canceling my appointments and heading straight back to D.C., to the bright hot studio lights I loved so much—to the safety of being nothing more than a voice in America's living room, a face on the screen.

Out of reach.

Then my hard news sense kicked in. I closed up the house and got in the taxi telling myself the dead girl was just a story, not an omen.

We drove past the aquarium-like house next door.

Lights burned brightly on the first and second floor. My dark-haired neighbor was up early. Stocks, I thought. The business of money never ends. European bourses are in full swing when America first wakes up. The pool, still lit, was a shock of color against dark moors.

The driver cut across the center of the island. The road curved north, spilling out on the west side of Nantucket where the shore was protected by a broad sweeping bay. Soon we were rolling over cobblestones through the cozy downtown.

Square redbrick captains' houses stood in trim neat rows. Wrought-iron streetlamps glowed yellow in the dawn, and the square was storybook New England lined with plane trees, antique shops, boutiques, and small cafés. The smell of fresh-baked bread filled the air.

We turned right into the harbor, past tiny cottages on stilts lining the waterfront. The driver let me out at the transport authority landing. The old-fashioned ferry carries cars. The crossing takes hours, and in high seas the pitch and yaw are fierce. The new high-speed catamaran does not carry cars. It is twice the price but twice as fast, and time was of the essence on this day.

There were few passengers aboard the first boat out. For most of the crossing I had the outside deck to myself. Then, as the sun slipped over the horizon, a stranger's voice startled me out of my thoughts.

"Do you like mornings, Ms. Wagner?"

A tall man next to me at the rail, cradling a cup of coffee in his hands.

"You know my name," I said.

"Correction. I know your face, and that's why I know your name."

His eyes were green, the color of tropical water, and bright against his tan. His hair was a glossy deep black, dead straight, clipped short, and swept back from his forehead in a sharp widow's peak. He was dressed for the sea in expensive clothes—heavy twill slacks, thick wool sweater, and a dark blue canvas sailing jacket with the collar turned up.

His hands were as tan as his face, with long graceful fingers, well-kept nails, and powerful wrists. An outdoorsman, but his sports were most likely refined. He had sensual lips and a strong carved chin. His age was hard to guess. From the crinkles at his eyes, forty seemed right. He exuded power and sex. A man used to getting his own way.

"I like the island off-season," he said. "It's a welcome change from the summer crowds in town, but I've got to admit, out on Siasconset where you and I live, it's pretty private all year round."

I put it together. The dark hair, the tall trim figure. He was the neighbor I saw casting at the tide line, the solitary man who lived in the aquarium house next door.

"You fish at three-thirty most afternoons," I said.

"And you run on the beach every afternoon right about then. Excellent form, good pace. Looks like an eight-minute mile."

"Seven."

"Seven! You're serious about your sport."

"Aren't you?"

"Yes and no. The best time for surf-casting is actually at high tide. Better shot of getting a bite."

"High tide's never the same time every day. So why do you always fish at three-thirty?"

"Because that's when you run. Fishing has been nothing but a pretense. I've been working up the courage to run alongside you and introduce myself properly."

"What held you back?"

"I guess I'm shy, Ms. Wagner."

"That's not the first adjective that comes to mind."

"I didn't want to intrude. You looked like you wanted solitude."

He was right.

"And," he went on, "you don't strike me as the kind of woman who's comfortable with strangers, not after all you've been through."

His fingertips gently brushed my cheek, sweeping over the shadow of a fading scar. I pulled away. He was dangerously close to having me shut down cold. One word about *it*, one question, and I would walk away.

He changed subjects, as if he had read my thoughts. "This morning I saw you standing up here alone and I decided to throw caution to the wind. So here I am."

"Here you are."

"There's a measure of solicitude in my intentions, a certain stolid New England pragmatism, old-fashioned neighborly goodwill. I thought it would be nice for you to know who your neighbor is, have a name and a number you can call."

"Why would I want to call you?" It came out more sharply than I intended.

He laughed outright. "Just wait until the first night your heat boiler goes out, or your water main goes bust or the electricity blows. The local tradesmen close down at five and don't work weekends in the winter. I'm a hell of a handyman, Ms. Wagner. I can fix just about anything."

Despite myself, I smiled. He was electric. Charismatic.

"See the eddies out on the water?" he said, squinting into the sun. "The way the swells are building and rolling? That's a sure sign a storm's coming in."

"There's not a cloud in sight."

"Storms blow up fast out of nowhere here on the Atlantic. If you're caught in open water, a winter nor'easter will leave you wishing you had never left the safety of shore."

"You say that as if you've been through it."

"I know the seas," he said quietly. "I've come to respect the ocean. I understand water the way men used to—long before they had compasses and barometers. Way back when, mariners had only the sea itself to guide them. They used the surface, the color, the patterns the wind made on the water."

"I thought they used stars for navigation."

"At night they did. But during the day they read the water the way you read words on a page—measuring the swells, the way an ebb tide runs, the shape of the waves, the height, the timing between sets. When the compass came along, man began to lose his intuitive connection with the water. Worse still, all those instruments tend to make a sailor feel overly confident, like he's smarter than the element he's sailing in. The water has all the power. To forget that is to jeopardize your life. Have you ever heard the expression *Never turn your back to the sea?*"

"Of course."

"There's wisdom in that old cliché."

His words stirred up a childhood memory from before the fire when my hands were whole. I was playing on the beach, skipping in and out of the surf. I waded out deeper, then turned around to check how far I was from shore. In that split second, the ocean changed. When I turned back a standing wave was towering in, polished gray green inside the curve, a hollow tunnel of breaking water. The wave crashed down, punching the air out of my lungs, roughing me over sand, sucking me up and turning me head over heels twice more before spitting me out bloody and bruised and weeping on shore.

The ferry horn blew announcing our arrival in port.

My green-eyed neighbor led me down the ramp to the dock, his hand warm and sure on my arm. "I'm glad we finally met," he said. "Feel free to knock on my door if you ever need anything. Now that we're not strangers, I hope you'll consider me a friend."

"You're still a stranger. I don't know your name."

"Vale," he said, smiling. "My name is Justin Vale."

Passengers ebbed and flowed around us. We were locked for a moment in our own world, separate and still, energy intense. The breeze ruffled Vale's hair. He reached up and swept at a lock of hair that wasn't there, a motion intended to tuck it behind his ear, as if he had worn his hair longer once and still had the habit. He hesitated as if to say something else, then changed his mind and ducked inside a waiting taxi. The dark widow's peak, sharp as a prow, turned my way; green eyes watched me as his taxi slid away from the curb and a white WBZ news van pulled up in its place.

I opened the passenger door and looked up at the driver. He had a mop of curly brown hair and a fresh, open young face.

"Ben?" I asked.

"That's me. Hop on in, Ms. Wagner. Where are we going today?"

"To Boston. The city morgue."

"Sad destination for a pretty day."

"Won't be pretty for long. A storm's heading our way."

I looked up at the bright blue sky and the strangest thought crossed my mind: I had often seen Vale fishing, but in all those days and nights of summer, in all those months that the pool next door was lit and open, I had never once seen him in it.

I had never once seen my neighbor swim.

CHAPTER TWELVE

Miles McKenzie was waiting in the receiving bay, an unmistakable rambling Irishman, six foot three with a long pale face, bushy red brows, and thick black frame glasses. He wore a heavy plastic apron over blue scrubs and a surgical cap.

"Lacie Wagner," I said, approaching. "WRC-TV. Washington, D.C."

"I know damn well who you are," he replied, glaring at me, blue eyes blazing behind Coke-bottle lenses. Neck flushed, arms crossed, lungs working, foot tapping, Miles McKenzie was not happy I was there. He threw the door open and waved me in. "A reporter attending an autopsy . . . highly unusual protocol."

"It's a highly unusual case," I shot back as we walked past the morgue and down the hall toward the autopsy suites.

"I agreed to this outrageous request of Wheeler's on a conditional basis."

"The conditions being?"

"You go out the way you came in, through the back door."

"Fine."

"And you do not under any circumstances tell Hinks that you attended. That goes for your driver out there, too. Should anyone in the building ask what you're doing here, you say you were just on your way out—tossed out by me. *Comprende?*"

"Yes."

"You may take handwritten notes for your background use only. Your visit's strictly off the record. You're here thanks to my benevolence."

"*Benevolence* is an intriguing word."

"*Idiocy* is probably more accurate." He stopped abruptly in front of the autopsy suite. "Is this your first or did you manage to worm your way into Dick Prince's morgue?"

Prince was the chief medical examiner in D.C. I knew him, but had never stood in for an autopsy there or anywhere.

"This is my first," I said.

"Well, then." He arched an eyebrow and smiled for the first time. "I hope you skipped breakfast. If you feel nauseated, like you're going to throw up, get yourself out and down the hall to the ladies' room. If you think you won't make it that far, please use the plastic trash can. It's there expressly for that purpose. You'd be surprised at just how often it's used—mostly by cops."

"Cops?"

"Tough on the outside, squeamish on the inside. The taller they stand, the harder they fall. The flesh-and-blood facts of death seem to disturb them more in here than out in the field."

He opened the door and ushered me in.

Wheeler was wearing scrubs and a heavy apron like McKenzie's. He nodded hello.

The body lay faceup on the steel table, her black wet suit partially unzipped. The tank pack, buoyancy vest, and weight belt had all been removed, tagged, and spread out on a counter. McKenzie pulled on his latex gloves.

"A body with no name and no face," he mused, looking her over, "symmetrical burns marking the torso. What's your first thought, Wheeler?"

"Radiation," he said. "She might be military."

"If she is," McKenzie replied, circling the table, "we'll know that by tomorrow. All military personnel now have DNA samples on file in Bethesda. One day we'll have more than that. One day we'll have *national* DNA ID banks. Your identity will be documented at birth. Faces and fingerprints can be altered, even eradicated, but an individual's DNA ladder cannot. Once the DNA profile is entered into the master data bank, wherever you die, however you die, under whatever name you have chosen, we'll know who you really are—who you were born to, on what day, in what year.

"The data bank will have your full genetic and medical history culled from those tiny ladders. All relevant genetically predisposed illnesses will be revealed in DNA profiles. We will know your past and your future the day you're born. The only thing we won't be able to foretell is your death. But once you die, you cannot do so without a name. There will be no more mysteries like this one, no such thing as a Jane or John Doe."

McKenzie pinched the bridge of his nose. "This morning, however, we have a Jane Doe and the burns notwithstanding, the cause of death *appears* to be drowning, but in my business you never ever believe your own two eyes. She might not have drowned at all. She might have been murdered first, and thereafter tossed into the sea by someone wanting to cover up the crime. She could have been shot or strangled or poisoned. That's my job today. Let's get started. Let's find out."

He pointed to a pile of clothing on a side table. "Put those scrubs on over your clothes, Ms. Wagner. You'll find a shower cap in the stack. The plastic face shield goes on last. If the latex surgical gloves are problematic for you given your manual limitations, you can keep your own leather gloves on. Booties over your street shoes are optional. The other items are not. They'll protect you against any fluids that might come your way. These days you can't be too careful."

Except for the booties and latex gloves that required a dexterity I did not have, I put on the protective gear as instructed. This was McKenzie's show, and I would play by his rules.

McKenzie moved to the dead girl's side. A morgue ID tag dangled off her right index finger. Jane Doe had a case number. For now that was her name. McKenzie wore a small tape recorder on a belt around his waist. A microphone was clipped to his collar. He turned the recorder on and looked at the tag.

"Case number 987865. Female." He went on to state the date and year.

The room reeked of formaldehyde. Fluorescent lights sputtered and flared.

"She was x-rayed last night," Wheeler said. "The pictures are here. There are no bullets or other foreign objects in the body. I measured and weighed her. She's five feet nine inches tall."

The same height as me.

"Weight?"

"Minus the dive belt, a hundred and thirty."

Twenty-five pounds heavier than me.

Wheeler picked up a Polaroid camera and tested the flash. McKenzie walked around the table again, looking at the body and speaking while Wheeler followed, taking pictures for the ME's record.

McKenzie's deep voice was calm. "The unembalmed, well-developed, and well-nourished Caucasian female body measures sixty-nine inches in length and weighs one hundred and thirty pounds. She appears to be in her early twenties."

Ten years younger than me.

"Her scalp is covered with blond hair."

A rich strawberry blond, wavy and short, brushing

her shoulders where mine is a deep red gold and falls to my waist.

"The hair is streaked lighter in places," McKenzie observed, "and the streaks appear natural, from salt water and sun. Some are tinged green, probably from chlorine."

Someone had thoughtfully closed her one open eye. McKenzie leaned over and lifted the lid. "The eye color," he stated for the record, "is deep blue."

Sapphire, I thought, *the same shade as mine.*

"The pupils are equally dilated and the sclerae are white. There are no signs of petechial hemorrhaging on the conjunctival surfaces or eyelids."

Meaning she hadn't been strangled to death or hanged.

He picked up a syringe and drove it deep into the side of her right eye. I flinched as he drew out vitreous fluids for the standard tox screens. He passed the syringe to Wheeler, who prepared and labeled the sample for the lab.

McKenzie inspected the wet suit. "The neoprene is one-quarter-inch thick and appears to be new," he noted. "There are no signs of heavy wear at the elbows, but there are numerous tears along both the right and left forearm sections of the suit, some of which go through to the skin. The right and left knees of the suit are also badly ripped to the flesh, jagged tears in all shapes and sizes."

With Wheeler's help, he rolled her gently to the right, then to the left, inspecting the back of the suit.

"There's some pitting at the shoulder line," Wheeler observed, "small tears that don't penetrate through to the body. The neoprene at the buttocks area, like the knees, is ripped through to the skin."

McKenzie drifted down to her feet. "The soles of the dive booties are ripped all the way through. Now, let's remove the wet suit."

"They're hard enough to get out of alive," Wheeler remarked.

They went back and forth, discussing options, and finally agreed to slice and remove the wet suit in multiple sections, marking each with references for the crime lab. It was time-consuming work, cutting and lifting pieces away from the forearms, thighs, abdomen, and chest. When they cut away the back, Wheeler read the label.

"The brand is O'Neil," he said. "The size is a woman's large."

He put the tagged sections of suit into a large brown evidence sack and set that down in the row of gear.

We all stood in silence, just looking at her. The vivid savagery of those red oozing wounds hit us full force. There was a violence to the burns, as shocking as the vicious work of a knife or shotgun.

"Good God," Wheeler softly swore. "How the hell did she get into the wet suit?"

I imagined the pain of pulling the tight wet suit over festering skin, the sting of salt water hitting raw open flesh.

"The internal examination will tell me how far advanced her radiation sickness was," McKenzie said, "but judging from the severity of these burns, I believe she was in the late stages and very near death."

"Then how could she stand, let alone swim?" Wheeler asked. "How could she dive if she was as sick as that?"

"That's what we're here to find out," McKenzie said. "Let's get on with it. The epidermal layer on her face is, for the most part, gone. The abraded quality of the underlying tissue and absence of hematomae tell me facial damage was sustained *after* death, most likely from high impact against rock or coral while the body was in water. You see this a lot in floaters that come out of the ocean. Lakes, less so because there are no tides. Pools, never."

Hands still sheathed in latex, he opened what was left of her mouth.

"The tongue is smooth," he said, "pinkish tan in color, and granular. There are no signs of swelling on the tongue or bite marks, the organ is normal in color and size, and is completely intact."

He noted details of her dental work and missing teeth, then picked up a penlight and inspected her nose. "The nostrils are both patent and contain a small amount of yellowish mucous material." He pointed the penlight into her ears. "The external auditory canals are patent and free of blood. The right and left lobes are pierced with one hole each and she is wearing diamond studs that appear to be about a half-carat in size."

I had not noticed them at the beach. Expensive jewelry did not fit a military profile.

McKenzie moved his hands into the thick mass of hair. Using the penlight, he inspected her scalp from the crown to the base of her skull.

"There are no premortem contusions or fractures on the scalp," he said. "The skull appears intact."

Meaning she wasn't shot in the head, hit with a blunt object, or beaten with fists.

"The neck is clean," McKenzie said. "There are no ligature marks, abrasions, or petechial hemorrhages that would be consistent with strangulation, manual or otherwise. Note that the flesh here is free from burns."

McKenzie moved down the table and picked up her right hand. "All five digits are intact. There are no rings. The nails are ragged and unnaturally short, painted with pink polish, and all five are torn down into the nail bed. The epidermis is covered with bruises of varying ages, some old, some new, and there are numerous puncture wounds consistent in size and placement with IV lines."

He turned the hand over.

"The flesh on the right palm bed is covered with lacerations, some shallow, some deep, all shapes and sizes. These are ragged flaps of tissue not consistent with the deep clean incisive slice wounds of glass or of a knife. Nor are the wounds the result of degeneration from long-term immersion in water. They're not from fish or other sea life feeding on the corpse. On this exposed extremity, there's no sign of postmortem tissue deterioration or bloating at all. The body wasn't in the water long following death. Note there are no ligatures or abrasions on her right wrist, no watch or jewelry of any kind."

The left hand was as beat up as the right with the same ripped nails, surface bruising, puncture wounds, and ragged lacerated palm flesh.

Wheeler snapped Polaroids of both, then reached for his magnifying glass and studied her fingers again.

"Take a look at this." He passed the glass to McKenzie.

McKenzie whistled.

"Her fingers are so ripped up," Wheeler said, "only two, the right index and the left pinkie, have enough skin left to tell. She has no prints. None at all. If you look closely, you can see the precise, surgical scarring from skin grafts. . . . The flesh on her fingers was removed down to deepest dermal layers, then rebuilt with smooth, ridgeless skin patches: the equivalent of my own bald head."

"Special Ops," McKenzie ventured, "something military or governmental, not necessarily U.S."

He examined the arms next, holding right, then left up for Wheeler's camera, rolling each slightly to capture different angles, and document all of the burns.

"Apart from the radiation burns," McKenzie summed up, "the arms appear normal and the skin clean. The chest is symmetrical, breasts fully developed and normal in appearance. There are no bite marks, no scratches, no bruising on left or right. Just burns, evenly distributed, five to each side, equal in shape and size."

The Polaroid whirred; the flash flared.

"The abdomen is flat and, other than the burns, contains no scars."

She had never had an appendectomy or a cesarean.

McKenzie laid his hands on her stomach and pressed gently, left to right and back again, feeling for lumps that might be tumors.

"There are no palpable masses," he announced. "The external genitalia is that of a mature adult female. Pubic hair is strawberry blond, the same as the hair on her scalp. Aside from the radiation burns, there is no visual evidence of trauma."

McKenzie continued down the right leg, then the left, documenting multiple contusions and deep bruising on both the right and left knees consistent with the location of the tears in the wet suit.

"Her lower legs have no body hair," Wheeler said. "She either shaved recently or waxed."

McKenzie worked his way down to her feet. He was quiet for a long moment, looking at the soles. "Multiple lacerations," he finally said, "on the right and left soles. Profoundly deep."

I stepped around and looked at flesh that was savagely ripped in a hundred different places.

"They're fresh," Wheeler observed, "but washed clean from the sea. I can't identify the source of the cuts, but they're similar in organic structure to the lacerations on her hands. That is to say they're ragged flaps, not the kind of wound you see from glass or a knife. I'm guessing she was running hard over sharp rock or shale."

A hundred and thirty pounds of body weight slamming down as she ran across rocks, splitting neoprene and slicing flesh. Wheeler was right. She had to be running hard to shred her feet like that.

"Her toenails appear to be well groomed and painted the same pink as her fingernails," McKenzie observed. "There are no ligatures on her ankles, nothing out of the ordinary except the lacerations and burns."

With Wheeler's help he rolled her over facedown on the table. Burns staggered across her back and shoulders, hips and legs. McKenzie went over her carefully, but aside from the burns, found nothing at all. There was no bloating to the body, no discoloration of the skin. No ocean scavenger had fed on her flesh. She could not have been out at sea for more than a few hours, McKenzie said, if that.

She was long-legged like me, but full and round at the hips, where I am slim and narrow like a boy. Her muscles looked powerful and were clearly defined. Wheeler noticed, too. He touched her lightly, as if taking mental inventory, sweeping his big hands over her swollen deltoids and the taut cords of muscle flaring along the dorsal V-shaped latisimus.

"Lats like these," Wheeler observed, "she must've been a strong swimmer."

He brushed the tight quadriceps, pumped and primed, the full heavy curve of her calf, alabaster skin satin where it was not burned. He helped McKenzie turn her over, and once again she lay faceup. His hands traveled the front of her as they had the back, touching the swell of biceps, hard ripple of belly, thigh muscles sweeping and carved. In life she had trained hard.

"An athlete," Wheeler said, "judging from the muscular development. Very low body fat, too. Less than fifteen percent."

He lifted her arms and inspected the skin in the cove of her armpits. "Smooth," he noted. "Recently shaved."

There were no tan lines. Her skin was alabaster and pale, as if it had not seen much sun. But the burns were red, riotous craters the exact size and shape of a quarter, festering open wounds that seemed almost alive, arranged in a way that seemed too deliberate to be natural. Something about the pattern made me think of tattoos.

Wheeler measured each burn carefully, noting depth and diameter, and location on the corpse, and calling out the numbers to McKenzie.

"The shape troubles me," he said. "They're all perfect circles, as if the source of radiation was an external organic object pressed to her skin."

"Quarter-size units of cesium 133 are used extensively in medical radiology," McKenzie pointed out. "They're routinely replaced with new ones. The old ones don't have enough juice for a radiology lab, but they're still hot and toxic. Press one on your skin, leave it there awhile, and you'd end up looking like this. A radioactive leopard."

"Cesium chips are accessible," Wheeler said.

McKenzie agreed: "Hospital waste management's a joke. There's no way to confirm the source, but cesium units are the most likely cause. And I'm inclined to believe those burns were deliberately made."

When Wheeler finished measuring the burns, he and McKenzie ran a rape kit.

It took them forty minutes, carefully combing for evidence, taking swabs for the lab. When they finished, McKenzie summed up his visual examination for the record.

"There's no sign of trauma to the vaginal walls, no evidence of forced entry. This isn't to say she did not have sex prior to her death, but the salt water washing through her bodily cavities could have carried most of the evidence away. We took swabs anyway. The lab might pick something up."

McKenzie and Wheeler pulled chain mail steel-Kevlar gloves over their latex gloves, followed by a thick pair of rubber gloves over the chain mail. They put on full face shields next, identical to mine, equipped with small motorized ventilation fans. McKenzie looked over at me one last time, eyes unreadable behind the face shield and thick prescription lenses. All I saw was my own reflection in the plastic—otherworldly in my strange mask, dark eyes open wide, large against pale skin.

He chose a scalpel, and the knife work began.

A reporter is part observer, part investigator. I suppose it was a mixture of the two in equal parts that kept me lucid as I watched.

"There's a splendid order to nature," McKenzie preached, "and nowhere is that more evident than in the ingenious construction of the human body."

He drew the scalpel laterally across the chest, left to right in one clean stroke.

"I've been at this for thirty-two years, Ms. Wagner, yet each time I open a subject my excitement and anticipation are as powerful as if it's the first time."

He centered the knife at the far right edge of the lateral cut and sliced down in a sweeping stroke, matching the left side to the right, until a perfect Y had been carved into the dead girl's skin. I felt light-headed, but McKenzie's factual tone of voice kept me grounded.

"No one ends up on an autopsy table because they expected or were expected to die," he said. "In its own spectacular way, nature leads to the truth nine times out of ten. The inconsistencies, conflicting facts tell me what's out of order in the body."

McKenzie gently pulled the triangular flap of freshly carved skin down, opening the body cavity with all its mysteries, folding back the flesh, opening it wide with his curious hands.

"Note that the anterior chest muscle is highly developed for a female," he said, dropping his gaze down to the ribs. "No sternal or rib fractures are identified. The bone structure is intact."

He and Wheeler emptied the body cavity of organs—one by one—carefully studying, weighing, and slicing samples from each, looking for something unnatural, some sign of trauma, or other evidence proving the cause of death. I felt as if the earth were spinning faster just then, and despite the ventilator in my face shield, I could not get enough air.

"Popular fiction and film would have you believe that water in the lungs is all the proof you need someone drowned," Wheeler explained to me as McKenzie began removing the lungs. "But a dead person cannot close his air passages. Water enters the lungs through these passages and also flows out. So if a man shoots his wife and dumps her body in the Atlantic, her lungs will be full of salt water, even though she did not drown. Or, if he drowns her in the bathtub, then dumps her in the Atlantic, her lungs will be full of salt water, not fresh."

I took notes as he spoke, happy to have a distraction from the wet work on the table.

McKenzie lifted the right lung out of the chest cavity and held it in two hands, pressing on it gently. "The color is red purple, and the organ feels saturated." He placed the organ in a metal scale. "An average female lung weighs between two hundred fifty and five hundred grams. This one weighs one thousand grams. The lung is wet, saturated with water."

He removed the left lung and placed it in the scale. "The left weighs in at nine hundred and fifty grams."

McKenzie sliced samples from both for the lab while Wheeler worked on removing the aorta and vena cava, thymus, spleen, adrenals, and finally the heart.

"As if we didn't know it from looking at her," Wheeler said, holding the heart in his hands, "she was in superb condition. The heart is larger than average for a female." He placed it in the scale. "Three hundred grams for a one hundred and thirty pound woman—evidence of an extremely efficient cardiovascular system. She was definitely an athlete or trained like one."

McKenzie continued his visual examination, commenting on the normal tan-pink color and appearance of the coronary arteries. He noted the absence of fibrosis, infarction, or arteriosclerosis and moved along, emptying her body of the remaining organs. Kidneys, liver, and bladder were inspected, weighed, and dissected. The GI tract fascinated him most.

"The lab work will give me the definitive answer," he said, "but it looks like she was in the advanced stage of radiation sickness. There are multiple holes in the gut, and the stomach itself is unnaturally shrunk."

I remembered articles I had read the night before on the Internet. If exposure to radiation is intense enough, two things will occur: The first is called GI syndrome, or more colloquially, "gut death," which takes place in the first two weeks following exposure. Holes appear in the stomach, the victim loses the ability to absorb nutrients from food, and without medical intervention will starve to death or die of infection, whichever comes first.

If the victim somehow survives the first two weeks, the latter stages of radiation sickness set in. The body will lose its ability to replenish red blood cells, which have a life span of 120 days. Red blood cells die off and are not replaced. Anemia sets in. The body loses its ability to fight infection, and ultimately the victim dies from infection.

"I'm estimating initial exposure at four weeks ago," McKenzie said, "not less than three. The substantial amount of fluid present in the stomach indicating she aspirated water into her stomach while she was still alive. This isn't evidence of drowning but compounded with other determining factors, it is critically important.

"The stomach is tubular in shape and shrunken as if she hadn't eaten solid food for some time—consistent again with radiation sickness, which makes the victim nauseated and incapable of keeping down solids. Her body tissue and muscles are still in good shape. There's no visible wasting or evidence of rapidly lost weight. It's as if she had been getting nutrients from an IV, consistent with the punctures noted on her hands."

He analyzed her reproductive system next. "She had a vaginal hysterectomy and, judging by the lack of notches on her pelvis, never had children prior to the procedure. Also based on the appearance and development of the pelvis as well as the gums and teeth, I'll put her age at somewhere between twenty-two and twenty-four. We'll examine the brain and skull next."

I knew what he meant, what was coming next, how he and Wheeler would literally peel off what was left of her face, open the cranium, and lift out the brain. I closed my eyes, but I could not shut out the sound of the precision saw slicing through bone. From time to time, McKenzie spoke directly to me.

"Until recently there's been no distinct pathology for drowning," he said. "No way to actually *prove* drowning was the cause of death. It's been a conclusion made from circumstantial evidence, witnesses if there were any, and the absence of other physical trauma or organic explanation for the cause of death. 'Wet lungs. No trauma or toxicological cause of death. Therefore the victim drowned.' Shaky medical reasoning at best."

"And now?" I asked.

"We have a new method for definitively proving death by drowning. It originated in Canada and is gaining wide acceptance here. It's called the diatom test. Do you know what a diatom is?"

The saw whined. He repeated the question. I said I did not.

"A diatom is a microscopic cellular skeleton of aquatic plant life that allows us to identify a source of water. Each body of water—lake, river, pond, ocean, quarry, even your home bathtub—has its own unique microscopic plant life. Put another way, different bodies of water are differentiated by their diatoms.

"Death by drowning is not instantaneous. When a victim is drowning, he breathes water into the lungs—water that's full of microscopic plant life; diatoms that are instantly absorbed into the lung walls and blood, then the marrow of the bone; a biological transformation that can't take place unless the victim is still alive and circulating blood. Diatoms in the lungs or marrow are definitive proof of death by drowning. And those diatoms definitively prove where the drowning actually took place."

"How's that possible?" I asked.

"Say a man is murdered—drowned in the Charles River—after which the murderer dumps the body in the Atlantic. The diatom test will prove that the victim did not drown in salt water—even though his lungs may be full of salt water. The diatoms in his bone marrow will not match the diatoms in the Atlantic. The test will prove he drowned in the Charles River. The diatom test is complex, and it takes a couple of days. If you'd like to see what a diatom looks like, help yourself to the microscope on the counter there."

The saw whined again, and McKenzie went back to work.

I sat down in front of the microscope expecting to see dull cellular forms, worm-shaped at best, but the diatom stunned me. It was a circular burst of beauty, an elaborate jeweled circle made up of every known geometric form. Triangles, rings, squares, ovals and stars, a riotous kaleidoscope as beautiful as a Fabergé egg, rich gold in color, the hue of Renaissance suns. Crystalline and stunning, a microscopic delight.

"Beautiful, isn't it?" Wheeler said.

I turned around. He was peering into the split skull, looking at the brain. I went back to the diatom, hoping the kaleidoscope would work magic, that it would spin me into another world far from flayed faces and burns.

"Removal of the skullcap reveals a normal cerebral hemisphere with no subdural hemorrhaging in view," McKenzie said. "There is no inflammation in either hemisphere, no contusions or discoloration. The brain stem and cerebellum are clean. The facial injuries were definitely sustained postmortem."

Translation—she hadn't been hit over the head or slammed face first into a rock while she was alive. She hadn't been beaten or battered by powerful fists, kicked down a staircase or thrown out of a moving car. Except for the rips on the palms of her hands and the soles of her feet, there was no evidence of physical violence.

"It's too early to make an official call," he went on. "We need to see the lab work and diatom test, but I'm inclined to believe she drowned."

If McKenzie found those Fabergé diatoms blooming in her bones, we would know for certain she had drowned but not how she came to be in the wet suit or in the water. Not how those booties were shredded or why the knees of her wet suit were torn out. Not why her nails were ripped, her uterus and fingerprints removed, or why despite her late-stage illness she cared enough to shave her legs and paint her toes. We would not know why or how she was exposed to radiation or even with what. And nothing would ever tell us her final thoughts before death.

"In all my years as an ME," McKenzie said, "there's one aspect of death I fear the most. That is the last seconds of life, when you know you are dying, when you know the end has come. There is no such thing as a 'quick death.' No such thing as a sudden merciful release. Death is a biological progression of systemic functions shutting down. Seconds must feel like eternity when you know you are going to die.

"Underwater, deprived of air, no matter how painful the burning sensation in your lungs, the survival instinct prevails, an inner command: 'Do not take a breath; if you breathe water you will die!' It takes on average eighty-seven seconds for your oxygen level to run low enough that your involuntary reflexes kick in, forcing you to take a breath. Eighty-seven seconds, fully conscious, then, that spasmodic involuntary breath floods your lungs with water and the drowning begins in earnest."

As McKenzie spoke, I saw how it was for the diver when her tanks had run dry, inhaling and getting nothing, spitting the hard steel regulator out of her mouth. Burning lungs, bursting lungs, the deadly phantom vise clamped down on her sternum, eighty-seven seconds and then that one spasmodic breath.

She was still conscious, panic-stricken, and very much alive when water swept into her lungs and the drowning began, her body shutting down one orderly biological step at a time until all that was left was the brain flickering sporadically, then not at all, and it was just the diver hanging suspended, filled with the Atlantic, eyes open but sightless alone in the black liquid vault.

"That's it," Wheeler said.

She was faceup on the table. Organs had been returned to the body, the incision sewn up. Part of me hoped she would be buried a Jane Doe, that no mother, father, or husband would have to view her dreadful remains—the obliterated face, the violent weeping craters, the black Y stitched into her skin.

CHAPTER THIRTEEN

Hinks was leaning against the WBZ news van, eyes invisible behind Ray-Bans, mile-long legs spread wide, the lovely shape revealed by a slim pencil-cut skirt. Her dark blazer flapped open in the wind. Under it she wore a conservative blouse that nonetheless did little to hide her body. Her clothes were inexpensive, but she wore them like couture.

"How did you talk your way in?" she asked, full of spite and ill will.

"Didn't," I said. "McKenzie's a real prick. Kept me waiting three and a half hours, then came out and told me he had nothing to say until the lab results come back. Two to three days, maybe more."

I reached for the door.

Hinks laid a hand on my arm. "You lie," she said.

"Why do you say that?"

"Most spectators in an autopsy neglect to put protective booties over their street shoes. They are under the misguided impression that standing well back, away from the table, they are out of range—that there is no risk of body fluid from the corpse getting to them. You are one of those misguided spectators, Wagner. Take a look at that fresh blood on your left shoe."

I glanced down. Hinks was right.

"Expensive leather," she said. "Italian, I'd guess. What does a pair of boots like that cost exactly down in D.C.? Four hundred? Five?"

"Five-fifty, plus tax. Would you like to see the receipt?"

I glanced at her shoes, carefully polished but obviously run-down, and I felt ashamed, regretted the low blow. It was a short trip by boat from Nantucket to the Cape, but a much longer, rougher one from fisherman's daughter to assistant DA—and even so, the pay was not good.

Then Hinks closed in tight, crowding my personal space, and my regret faded in the force of the animosity on her beautiful, icy face. "Don't fuck with my case," she said.

"Sounds like a threat."

"Barks like a bitch, it usually is."

"And I thought this was a standard little catfight, Hinks, good-natured verbal clawing going on here between you and me."

"Why don't you go get your hair done, Ms. Wagner? You look like shit."

With a flash of bright white teeth, Hinks was gone, striding across the parking lot in a hip-rolling, bust-bouncing gait, startling blond hair glossy and shining in the sun.

"Wildly ambitious," Wheeler had said. Running for DA.

We were at opposite ends of the ring but both after the same thing. Hinks might work with me—if I could help her.

"I'm on my way to tape the story now," I called out. "I'd love to have you give a statement."

Hinks paused in the center of the lot.

"WBZ's running the piece three times tonight—on the five-, six-, and eleven-o'clock casts."

She turned around.

"My station in Washington is running it, too. It would be great exposure for you, Hinks: a network affiliate in Boston, a network owned and operated station in D.C."

"You taping here in the parking lot?" she asked.

"Come on," I said, smiling. "We can do way better than that for you."

I chose a deserted stretch of beach north of Boston, wanting mood and mystery, a sense of foreboding and the power of the sea. Nature obliged. The day had completely changed, just as my neighbor had predicted. Ocean surf was angry and high. A hard wind drove black clouds across the sky. Drizzle came down in a mist.

Ben pinned cordless mikes to our collars and went through a series of audio checks.

"I'm getting some static from the wind," he said as he framed the shot, "but your voices are clear. Whenever you're ready, Ms. Wagner. I'm rolling."

Hinks was calm and collected at my side. She had a natural sense of the camera, looking straight into the lens as she answered my questions. She was verbally adroit, as well, skirting my hard-hitting inquiries with the grace of a born politician, serving up innuendo and inference, steering clear of statements and conclusions that would be inappropriate given the early stage of the investigation. Despite myself, I was impressed.

"You were good," I said when we wrapped.

"You think?" She eyed me suspiciously.

"You have presence."

"We'll see tonight. If it's as good as you say, then I owe you one."

She straightened her blazer and strolled away, strong back at attention, a smile lighting up her striking face. That was as close to a truce as I was going to get from Hinks.

"I'm ready to go with your solo stand-ups," Ben said.

We taped the open and close four different ways, giving us options if the body was identified before airtime.

I wrapped the last take just as the drizzle turned to steady rain.

Driving up Storrow Drive alongside the Charles River, I looked out at gray water. Trees lining the bank were bare as if a giant wind had stripped the branches in one great breath. It seemed that autumn had been short-lived here, that winter had already arrived. Drizzle turned to icy snow just as we pulled into the parking lot at WBZ.

Despite the colonial brick façade outside, the station was firmly planted in the twenty-first century. Tape and film archives were stored in a master computer data bank, and accessible through a variety of search methods. Put in GANG CRIME 1990 TO 1995 and the server would send back a list of stories that had run on WBZ or the NBC network. Ben settled in a digital editing bay and trolled the archives, looking for stock footage we could edit in with our own—nuclear reactors, scuba divers, radiation burns, WWII—subjects that were visually relevant to my story.

I took a seat at an empty desk and looked around the busy newsroom. Television news has changed over the years. Altruistic journalism has been tempered by business affairs, bottom-line pressures, and the fight for market share. Now, most evening news shows were entertainment judged by ratings and the price of commercials. Nonetheless, there was enough meat left to satisfy journalists like me.

I hit the phones. The dive gear inventory was first up in my notes. I called Cal's, the only dive shop on the island. The owner picked up on the second ring. I gave him a physical description of the diver and ran through the gear list: O'Neil wet suit, Mares buoyancy vest, Oceana mask and fins.

"Nope," Cal said. "She didn't get her tanks filled here, and she didn't buy or rent equipment here, either. I sell

Body Glove wet suits and Columbia vests. My fins are Dive-Tech, same as the mask, good quality, but not top of the line like hers. She could be from somewhere else. Most hard-core divers travel with their own stuff."

"You think hard-core divers travel to the East Coast to sport dive in late October?"

"Now that you mention it, no. Water's too damn cold now. The Caicos, Belize, Mexico, anywhere south of the equator—that's where I'd be headed this time of year. As for locals, I know all the divers round here as well as their gear, and I can tell you she's not from Nantucket. I promise you that."

I hung up, frustrated. I had guessed she wasn't local the minute I saw the burns. That left me with the eradicated fingerprints. Two explanations came to mind. She was a high-ticket mercenary: a jewel thief, drug runner, something illegal, or she was a Special Ops soldier, not necessarily U.S. military.

I put a call in to Max next. He was my uncle, my father's brother, and he loved me like I was his own. Max was a high-ranking officer in the Delta Force branch of Special Ops. His position gave him access, information, influence, and contacts government-wide, not just the Department of Defense. I left a message on his voice mail and checked in with Wheeler on the status of the ID.

"There are no missing persons reports for a woman like her," he said. "Not in Nantucket or Hyannis or New Bedford or anywhere in the state of Massachusetts. Even so, if nothing pops up, it doesn't mean it won't later on. Could be that it's still too early for anyone to be missing her yet. The military DNA bank run is another thing. We'll know if there's a match by tomorrow at the latest."

"If you get her ID'd, would you give me a call?"

"I don't have a problem with that."

"Hinks might."

"You didn't ask Hinks. You asked me."

I thanked him and joined Ben in the editing bay.

"Do you want the close-up here," he asked, "or should we stay with the wide shot on the open?"

"Stay wide. I want to see the rough surf and the black clouds in the background." Every detail to add to the mystery, every detail to amplify the fear.

He had a good eye and a practiced hand cutting in stock shots of Nantucket's picture-pretty harbor with images of nuclear nightmares. Three Mile Island, black-and-white stills from the Russian incident at Chernobyl, soldiers prone in grimy hospital beds, bodies covered with radiation burns.

I recorded my voice-over, speaking slowly with intimacy, using terms like "third-world nuclear weapons" with care, walking a fine line between fact and implication because the word *nuclear* in any context stirs up fear. The twin shadows of Hiroshima and Nagasaki are long and dark, spilling over from the past into our own present day. Time moves forward away from the past, but when we hear the word *nuclear,* a mushroom cloud is what we see—not clean energy plants, efficient power supplies—just billowing smoke, blotting out the sun, raining down death. And the images the word *radiation* brings to mind are always the victims, their ravaged bodies and long agonizing deaths.

My story was hard and tight. Benjamin and I watched it one more time, then passed it on to the desk.

I checked the clock.

Quarter past five. Time enough to catch the last flight back to the island.

CHAPTER FOURTEEN

Lacie, lovely Lacie, right there in his living room on his wide-screen digital TV.

Elemental Lacie, with fiery red-gold hair and eyes the shade of a southern sea.

Vale filled a flute with champagne, relaxed in his leather recliner, and turned up the sound.

"The body of a female diver washed up on Nantucket last night," she said, "and while the autopsy is over, the cause of death is still unknown. There are more questions than answers this evening, a young victim without a name."

Lacie Wagner, his solitary neighbor back at work after a long reprieve.

He admired her on-air cool, her natural composure, the way she broke down the third wall and looked into the lens with an intense intimacy, as if she were right there in the room, close, talking to him one on one.

He noted details. Her black clothes were couture cut, tailored to fit close to her body with an understated elegance. The open collar of her cashmere coat revealed delicate bones at her throat. Gusting wind lifted her hair, and he saw she wore no earrings; her earlobes were bare, and somehow that moved him. There was no watch or necklace or bracelet. She had no need for jewelry or cosmetic enhancement. Her own beauty was enough.

Vale sipped his champagne and remembered standing close to her on the ferry that same morning—recalled the fresh-washed scent of her skin, the rich low sound of her laugh—how she had been so aware of him then and spoke to him in a second silent dialogue of desire, leaning in close to him, as her eyes devoured his hands and lips.

Her body wanted his. Of this he was sure.

Now she was right there in his living room, larger than life on screen, sad and somber, relating a litany of tragic details as storm clouds collided and the ocean surged huge behind her, a towering, rolling, swelling, rising, cresting living thing.

Lacie the reporter, so caught up in the drama of her tale, she was oblivious of the changing weather, how the drizzle had turned to a steady rain.

The camera moved in for a close-up, and he saw the rain wet her lips, catch in her hair, dampen her cheeks in a light, glistening sheen. He saw the shadow of a scar he had touched that morning, a remnant of the fire. The irony struck him: Lacie telling a tragic story when her own had been so much more.

Then a second beauty filled the frame. A ravishing woman dressed in a suit, an assistant DA.

"Twenty-four hours into the case," the marvelous blonde said, "there is no hard evidence of foul play, and the state medical examiner has not yet ruled on the cause of death."

Vale rose and paced as he listened to the DA's statement, Lacie's follow-up questions, and her final wrap: "The only thing officials know for sure is that this young Jane Doe would certainly have died from radiation sickness if something else—or someone—had not killed her first. Reporting from Cape Cod, this is Lacie Wagner."

Vale emptied his glass and turned off the set.

Lacie the star back on the air after a long reprieve.

Back from the living dead.

CHAPTER FIFTEEN

Night falls fast in Nantucket in late autumn, and northern storms swallow land. When my Cape Air flight approached, the outline of the island was invisible, smothered by clouds and heavy fog, and when we touched down, airport lights were smudges in the drizzle, gray halos in the dark. I hurried across the slick, wet tarmac through the terminal and out, into a taxi.

Visibility was next to nothing on earth, as well. The center divider was a white snake in the night. The driver drove carefully all the way to Siasconset, a slow twenty minutes through the storm. Still, the cab fishtailed on curves and vibrated under the power of the rain, and slowed to a crawl going down my mud drive. The high-peaked roof of my house appeared in the mist. As we pulled in, the porch took form next, and so did the pumpkin-colored Jeep pulled up tight to the steps.

Wheeler waited inside, a powerful profile caught in the taxi's headlamps—the graceful curve of his bald head—and before I could open my door he was out and striding over to me, oblivious of the fact or not caring that it was pouring and he was getting wet.

Water drummed down on his suntanned skull, silver-gray pearls melting to a thousand tiny rivers running down his smooth, tawny face. His shoulders appeared broader and thicker than I remembered, revealed now by the wet T-shirt clinging to his chest. I paid the driver and got out.

"Evening, Wheeler," I said, moving up the porch steps out of the rain. "Thank you for a fascinating day."

"Forensically challenging," he said, following alongside. "She's a scientific puzzle."

"I couldn't help thinking she was someone's daughter lying there—someone's friend, lover, maybe even wife—how death goes on past the dying, grief taking chunks out of the living left behind."

"We all think about that," he said. "Even McKenzie, who does autopsies every day."

I tapped in the alarm password, opened the door, picked mail up off the floor, and went into the kitchen. "Would you like coffee?" I asked. "Something stronger to drink?"

"If you had a cold beer, I wouldn't say no."

I got one out of the refrigerator.

"The bottle's just fine," Wheeler said.

I tossed the mail on the counter, five catalogues pitching pool toys, vacuums, swimsuits, and chemicals. Wheeler noticed.

"You keep a pool on the property?" he asked.

"No. I don't swim. I think they're meant for the house next door."

I poured myself a glass of merlot and guided Wheeler into my study. Skyla's aquarium on the sill was lit and glowing, the king angel swimming circles with her long lovely fins. I shook a helping of food in and sat down in a deep armchair. Wheeler sipped his beer and looked at the gallery of framed photos on my desk.

"Your daughter?" he asked.

"Skyla," I said, "from this last summer here on the island."

"Where is she now?"

"Boarding school."

"Because of what she went through?"

"Yes."

"All the publicity, all those stories on the news about her kidnapping—you must be afraid of a copycat crime."

"I am. She's safe at the school. And, she feels safe there. You have children?"

"A daughter. Twenty-two. Hardly a child."

"Does she live on the island?"

"No, Rio doesn't come here at all anymore." He studied the aquarium. "King angel. Despite the name, this one's a female. You can tell by the markings on the body and the sweeping size of the tail. The female's more beautiful than the male. *Angelus imperator.* She won't breed in captivity, so don't bother trying."

"Something on your mind tonight, Wheeler?"

"Off the record?"

"Okay."

"Evil," he said.

"Evil?"

"I'm a simple man with a complex soul, a scientist with a superstitious side. I believe in the unseen ways of our natural world, in life forces we don't understand. If it had been me who found that Jane Doe, I'd have pushed her out to sea, let the currents that carried her here take her back, wash her all the way to the mainland. Hell, I might even have taken her there myself in a boat. Left her on the Hyannis beach or farther north, out of Massachusetts altogether. I wouldn't have given a damn about tampering with a crime scene. Even if she did die drowning, my gut tells me it wasn't an accident. It was much more than that. Accidents are one thing—part of the natural course of life. Evil's quite another. I don't want it visiting us here, not on this island, not in my paradise."

"It's too late, Wheeler, like it or not. You don't live in

a time warp or a bubble, and no matter how much you or I wish it, Nantucket isn't a world apart."

"Oh yes, it is," Wheeler said. "That's why you came here. Here on the island you might see a purse snatching, pickpocket in summer—stolen car maybe, local kids out for a kick. That's about it. Money buys privacy and peace in this small town, freedom to come and go as you please, no matter how high your profile. It's the Nantucket way. Back in D.C., you'll have drivers and doormen, layers upon layers between you and the sky. Here on the beach all summer you and your girl lived free. You feel so safe on the island you ran five deserted miles all alone yesterday."

"And now?"

"There's been an elemental change. Murder has come here, and one murder always attracts another. Evil in the universe just seems to work that way. It's a never-ending circle once it starts. I know you think what I'm saying is simplistic, and that you're surprised to hear such things from an educated man, but I'd just as soon the whole damn thing go away."

"It won't."

"Then drop the story."

"Dropping it won't change what happened."

"I didn't imply it would. What I mean to say is that I'm afraid for you."

"Why?"

"Chasing this is going to bring you nothing but trouble. I've got a strong feeling about that. Call it intuition or premonition or even paranoia. Forget this story, Ms. Wagner. Go on to something else."

"Sorry, Wheeler. Come hell or high water, I'm going to find out the truth about how and why that young woman died."

"Come hell or high water?"

"That's what I said."

"Strong words."

"And accurate."

Wheeler finished his beer and dropped the bottle in the wastebasket. "Night, Ms. Wagner," he said. "I'll see myself out."

CHAPTER SIXTEEN

Dinner was chopped chicken salad on whole grain toast and another glass of red wine. I ate standing up in the kitchen, thinking about what Wheeler had said, lining up facts against superstition, going around in circles until I ended up right back where I had started. I went back to my computer and worked the few facts I had like they were puzzle pieces.

Max called at nine. His call came in from his computer to mine, both of which were equipped with See-Phones that allowed us to see each other on screen while we talked. I clicked the infrared port, and his face filled the big home theater screen on the wall.

"Evening, Lace," he said, a smile warming his fierce, tan, grizzled face. "Got your message. What's going on?"

I settled back in my chair and told him about the dead girl in detail: the empty air gauge, the inflated vest, and water in her lungs. I described the burns, the deep injuries on her feet, shredded skin on her hands, and said I thought she might be military.

"You'll know soon enough when they run her prints," Max said.

"They can't." I described her finger pads, how the print-bearing layers of dermis had been surgically removed and replaced with smooth blank grafts. "Covert military's the only logical explanation, foreign or domestic."

"Maybe." Max scratched his chin. He had a strange look in his eye.

I had to ask the obvious. "Max, could she be one of yours?"

"Always fishing, aren't you?"

"That's your answer?"

"Delta has no female operators."

"*Officially* Delta Force has no female operators. *Officially* Delta Force doesn't even exist."

"Nice try, Lace." He smiled. "But officially and unofficially, Delta has no female soldiers."

Max knew I was fascinated by Special Ops, that I smelled a hundred stories in Delta Force alone. He was my best source for military exclusives, but he was a soldier first and an uncle second when it came to Delta. He didn't mind giving me the heads-up on stories coming out of other branches of defense, but Delta Force was taboo. The little that he had told me over the years was off the record, confidential, revealed in a privileged bond of trust, a bond I would not ever breach.

"She might be from one of the other Special Ops units," I said. "Can you make a few discreet calls?"

The smile disappeared. "I'm leaving soon for a training mission in one of God's more forbidding places. There's a lot to be done. My schedule's tight."

"Max."

"You're wasting your time thinking Special Ops."

"Why?"

"Our military isn't in the habit of misplacing divers or SEALs or Special-Ops soldiers. They don't lose track of them on active international missions, they don't lose track of them on training missions, and they sure as hell don't lose them off the coast of Massachusetts."

"As far as you know."

"As far as I know."

"You're probably right. Her dive gear wasn't government issue."

I read him the inventory list.

"Actually," Max said, frowning, "a Special-Ops diver always wears commercial brands. That way if something goes wrong and he—"

"—or she—"

"—gets killed, the opposition can't use the gear to track the soldier back to a home country. Standard practice the world over."

"The ME said the wounds on her feet could have come from running hard on dry land. If she was American, what or who was she running away from here? Or was she the one doing the chasing?"

"I don't know the answers to those questions, and I won't ask around. Best I can do is let you know if I hear of anything that might relate."

"If it doesn't involve Delta."

"Of course."

"Fair enough."

He blew me a kiss and disconnected.

The bells chimed midnight on my grandfather clock.

Talking to Max always made me want to talk to my daughter, too. They were the only family I had. It was too late to call Skyla, so I sent her an e-mail full of little nothings, steering clear of the story—an instinctive protective impulse born of the conviction that she had seen too much of death too soon in her life; she did not need to hear more about it now.

Outside, the storm had hit with gale-force winds and hard, driving rain, whipping the Atlantic into twelve-foot walls of breaking water that battered the shore. Foam striped the sand with iridescent streaks. My cottage creaked and moaned from the full frontal assault, and I worried that the roof I hadn't gotten around to fixing would suddenly spring leaks.

I went around closing shutters and checking locks. Upstairs in my bedroom I looked across the moor. Lights in the big house blazed in every window. My neighbor was home. The square pool was lit and glowing in the hard falling rain. The water level had risen too high and the overflow had begun, seeping over the edge, running in fingers down the bluff. A white fork of lightning split the night, blue water went black as the pool lights went out, and both my house and his went dark at the same time.

I sat at the top of the stairs listening to surf and rain, then to the heavy footfalls on my deck and a solid, strong rap at the front door.

"Ms. Wagner? It's me."

The green-eyed stranger had come calling, and I was more than happy to let him in.

"Told you a storm would hit," Vale said, shaking water off his white rain slicker, sweeping wet black hair back off his forehead. "I came home not too long ago, noticed lights on as I drove by your house. When the power went out, I worried about you here all alone. County lines must have all gone down."

"They'll get fixed."

"Nonetheless, here I am. There's an old stone path cutting across the moor, linking our two properties. Perhaps I'm overly superstitious, but I like to believe it's symbolic of how we were destined to meet."

He smelled fresh and good. The air between us was electric. My physical reaction scared me. I didn't know this man, but my body wanted to. Vale didn't ask why I had no candles lit or a fire burning in the grate. He didn't ask to come in or for something to drink. He simply leaned on the deck rail in the wind and watched the surf.

"Have you ever seen the whale migration?" he asked.

"No."

"It's something. Like radar, they know exactly when to start swimming south. How do they know when to go? How do they even know where it is they're heading? Instincts. Amazing instincts. Make ours seem pitiful in comparison. I swam alongside a whale once, down in Belize. The water was crystal clear, hundred-and-twenty-foot visibility. I swam right next to him and looked into his eye."

"You like the water."

"Yes. I remember swimming before walking. Diving before running. I'm a man of the sea. I love the ocean and couldn't bear to live far from it. That's why I came here, to the island. It's nothing but a tiny scrap of rock and sand in the middle of the ocean. We ought to feel hemmed in and trapped. But we don't, do we? Having all this water around makes us feel free, as if there are no boundaries to our lives, our souls, ourselves. The four elements feel bigger here than anywhere else. The sky, the sun, the wind, the ocean herself. I don't know you, but I'd guess you came here for the same reasons, because it makes you feel free."

I sidestepped the question and came back with one of my own, all reporter, collecting facts, trying to stay objective and override the very subjective energy pulsing in my veins.

"Where do you live when you're not here?"

"Boston."

"What do you do there?"

"Not much these days. I had a software company, Geostar—ocean mapping for oil drillers, satellite-assisted nautical navigation systems, and so forth. I carved a nice little niche out for myself in the computer world. Patented proprietary technology and no competition. I was a sitting target for a buy-out. Big fish eat the little fish. That one aquatic truth is the way of the world. The big fish came along earlier this year and made an offer too good to refuse. So I sold."

"And now?"

"I do what pleases me." He stood abruptly. "It's late, and I've been rude. Chattering on while you're standing here, freezing. I've forgotten my manners. Please accept my apologies. Something about you makes me want to talk. I'm sorry." His easy smile contradicted his words. He wasn't sorry at all. "Truth is, I'm really working up the courage to ask you to have dinner with me."

"I'm on a story. My days aren't my own. The way it looks I'll be spending a lot of time away."

"But you'll be here tomorrow."

"Maybe not. In news you never know."

"Then leave it this way—if you are, we'll have dinner tomorrow night and I promise you it will be a light evening of friendly conversation about this and that. I'll tell you more about the whales and the things I've seen. There will be no talk of the past. We will look only forward, Lacie. May I call you that?"

"Of course."

He had moved away from the rail and was standing close. His smile was brilliant, his eyes intense. He was glib, but I didn't believe Justin Vale was a lighthearted man. I believed he had a very strong will running hard and high like the tide.

"No prying questions," he said softly, touching my cheek. "I promise you that."

His eyes locked with mine. My body was aware of his, of how close he suddenly was, the heat of his breath on my skin, and the fresh smell of him, all rain and wind and sea.

A gust ripped across the beach, picking up wet sand and tossing it in the air.

Gold glitter at night.

Gold glitter in the rain.

My skin tingled, and it wasn't from the cold.

"Lacie?"

"Yes."

"I'll come by for you at eight."

He went down the steps. His slicker flashed white in the darkness; he cut across the moor on the path and was gone.

I went to bed wanting Vale in a way that frightened and excited me.

I wanted him and knew he wanted me, too.

I tossed and turned alone in my bed as rain hammered my windows and wind shrieked through the eaves. My heart raced and adrenaline surged, the way it did when I woke from a nightmare, but it wasn't fright or the fury of the storm that kept me awake that night.

It was desire.

Raw, naked, pulse-pounding lust.

CHAPTER SEVENTEEN

Morning dawned crisp and bright, the sky scrubbed blue and not a cloud in sight. I wondered if I had dreamed the storm and Vale's visit, as well. I lingered on the porch with my coffee, watching sandpipers play. Waves were tame, spilling to shore in long lazy sets. Harry checked in from the station at ten.

"Great piece last night," he said. "We're running it again today at noon. Ad sales is jumping up and down. They see how great you look, and now they're jacking up the November commercial rates, tagging on a ten percent premium."

"For the 'Lacie Wagner effect'?" I asked, loving it.

"Yes," Harry said. "I got a call this morning from a guy who says his name is Preston. Don't know if that's a first or last. He claims he may know something about the body. He wouldn't say what, only that he wants to talk to you. If you decide to see him, maybe you ought to do it with the police."

Harry's subtext was clear. He was afraid for me. With all the crazies out there and the media blitz my imminent return had stirred up, security was an issue. I took down the number. The area code was 617, Brookline, Mass. I used the mobile so my home number couldn't be traced, but no one answered.

I tried on and off throughout the day, feeling he was my only live lead. At three-thirty, I went for my afternoon run. When I got back, I tried again but listened to the same long, unanswered rings.

Wheeler was next on my list.

"I came on a little strong last night," he said. "I love this island. It's my past, present, and future. I've had plenty of offers to move along to Boston, even New York. But I'm rooted here. Nothing will ever drag me away, not money, not greed, and certainly not love."

"Don't jump to conclusions," I said. "The heart has no logic."

"Mine does, and it's been put through the test. I'll tell you sometime. Anyhow, as far as I'm concerned, Nantucket's the last little pocket of peace in the country, and I'm downright paranoid about anything that's going to change that."

"Like evil."

"As a medical doctor and ME, I'm grounded in the physical, in the here and now. But you've got to remember that way back Nantucket was a Quaker colony. The

Quakers were a superstitious bunch in their own way. I come from pure Nantucket stock. So the way I figure it is some of those Quaker feelings are in my blood, and the thing they feared most was change. I'm that way about this island, and my feelings aren't out of line, all things considered."

"What do you mean?"

"A place goes on for decades safe and comfortable, then suddenly a murder occurs and a short time later everything peaceful has turned bad. Look at Colorado, the last great wilderness, God's country, Rocky Mountain High. First you get JonBenet Ramsey, then the whole state comes tumbling down. The Rogers killing, the Columbine High massacre. Convinces me that we've got to do everything possible to keep evil out of here in the first place. I guess by turning it over to the state, that's what we've done. Sent the problem to Boston. Maybe, just maybe, that'll be the end of it here."

"Does that mean you're closing down on me, Tom?"

"No, ma'am, it does not. I respect you. If you want information, go ahead and ask."

"Missing persons?"

"Nothing's come in. Maybe tomorrow something will pop up."

"McKenzie?"

"Waiting on the lab. Tox screen comes in first, and that's due in tomorrow."

"Her gear?"

"At the state lab. They're backed up, so it might be a couple of days before they get to it."

"What about the point-of-entry issue?"

"Kiri Hannover's constructing a computer simulation of the tidal and current activity at the time you found the body. She's working backwards from there, trying to figure out if the diver went in the water here or if she washed in from the Vineyard, the Cape, or the waters right off the mainland. Might help us. Might give us nothing at all."

"When will she have it done?"

"I sound like a broken record."

"Tomorrow?"

"That's right. At the earliest."

"I know I'm out of line asking, but I'd appreciate a duplicate set of the crime scene photos you took out there on the beach. They'll never go on-air or show up in print, I promise you that. I just have a feeling they're going to be useful in some way. I can't say how or why yet, only that I have a strong feeling they will be."

There was a long silence.

"That'd be a pretty clear breach of protocol here," Wheeler finally said. "I couldn't justify doing it on an official basis."

"Unofficially?"

"Who's to say you didn't take your own shots out there, Ms. Wagner?"

I thanked him and tried Harry's mysterious caller again, but got the same long, unanswered rings.

CHAPTER EIGHTEEN

Slap.

He was in, arms milling, feet kicking, in wild aquatic flight.

Sometimes—not often—he swam during the day.

It was not as peaceful as at night. The water did not

have the same magic as when it glowed in the dark, but still, the good wet work of stroking and kicking, the powerful grace of amphibious flight gave wings to his imagination—and it was there in the water his finest thoughts came bubbling up from his subconscious, whirling out of his solar plexus.

When he felt desire building to the breaking point, when he felt the red-hot fire of need, he swam to cool off, to dream, to plan, to think himself down from the giddy high of his carnal craving.

Night or day, he wore the wet suit.

Night or day, he swam hard.

Intense exertion cleared his mind, took him beyond conscience, beyond hunger, thirst, or lust, to a place where yesterday and tomorrow did not exist—only the moment, the here and now, the split-second present, where he heard nothing, not even the splashing water from the fury of his sprints.

The sound of swimming was drowned in the roar of his pumping heart as it shot his pulse past 160 and up right through 180; driving blood was thunder in his head, as was the great whooshing noise of his bellowing lungs sucking in air to feed the body, oxygen to feed the swim.

When the fury was spent he drifted down to the drain, closed his eyes, and held his breath. The utter silence filled him, and he knew what it sounded like to drown: the quiet, the profound deep liquid hush.

He thought of Houdini and his amazing water tricks: locked in a box and thrown from a bridge into the river, a certain death for any mortal man.

Then he bunched his thigh muscles and sprang. Shot up through the water at the speed of light. Houdini, he thought, miraculously freed from the box!

He took a deep breath and dropped back to the bottom and imagined the great magician unlocking the box. Once again, he bunched his thighs and sprang, up to the surface, up to the air.

Drop, unlock, spring.

Houdini in flight, a hundred times over.

CHAPTER NINETEEN

Restless with undirected energy, feeling frustrated that my story had stalled, I spent the balance of the day on the Net researching my dinner date instead.

Justin Vale. Accomplished and wealthy. Very well-bred. *But who is he?*

I typed his name into a search engine and got 512 hits.

Geostar's own Web site was first up on the list. I used the infrared connection and put it up on the big home theater screen on the wall facing my desk. The site was impressive, with multimedia, real-time streaming audio and video demonstrating portions of Geostar's product line. Product did not interest me. I clicked my way into an option titled "News Archives" and accessed a full complement of articles from the *New York Times,* the *Wall Street Journal, Fortune, Forbes,* and more.

Details substantiating Vale's story were all there, documented in the press. Stories of the buy-out, staggering figures of Vale's newfound wealth. There were photos, too, of Vale standing with the president of Exxon, Bill Gates, Al Gore. Vale was larger than life right there in my home office, on the big screen with his unmistakable black widow's peak and unforgettable eyes.

Call it a security check. Vale checked out. An hour on

the Internet told me he was a gifted, driven, self-made man who moved in impressive circles. Vale was solid. Vale was safe.

It's just dinner, I thought later, changing from jeans and boots into a black jersey dress and glossy high heels. *It's just a date.* I let my hair fall loose at my shoulders, pulled on black silk gloves, and grabbed my coat as Vale rang the front doorbell.

He was casually elegant in a charcoal sweater and cashmere slacks. His smile was easy, his eyes bright. The wind ruffled his hair.

"Beautiful," he said, "stunning, in fact. I made a reservation at the best restaurant on the island."

A dark blue Lexus sedan sat in the drive, engine idling. I got in thinking we were going to the Wawinet or McCabe's, both of which were miles away. Our trip was surprisingly short. He made a right turn out of my drive and then a right turn into his.

"I asked Ann Gamble to come out and cook for us tonight," Vale explained. "She's one of the best chefs on the island."

"Excellent," I said, meaning it.

The truth was, I was never comfortable in restaurants wearing my gloves through dinner. Here there would be no sidelong glances, no curious diners waiting to see if I would take them off.

Inside, Vale took my coat and led me through double doors into a wide open living room with vaulted ceilings, skylights, and those huge glass windows I was so used to seeing from the outside. A brass telescope on splayed tripod legs stood in front of the deck, aimed at the sea. Floors were polished oak covered with thick dark blue rugs. Two plush sofas squared out the living area, and a leather recliner faced the extraordinary view of the windowless north wall.

Aquariums were displayed on deep, built-in shelves.

There were eight tanks, each three feet long, two feet high, all dramatically lit. One was empty, the other seven were full and teeming with life: striped angels, violet parrots, riotous red tigers, deep blue medusae, cobalt clownfish, rainbow-striped dragon fish.

"Amazing," I said.

"My passion," Vale said, guiding me close. "The seven full tanks are symbolic of the Seven Seas. The ancients coined the phrase for the bodies of water known to them then. They were limited in their ability to travel. Their world was defined by that which they could access. The original Seven Seas were all near or around the cradle of civilization: the Red Sea, the Mediterranean, the Persian Gulf, the Adriatic, the Black Sea, the Caspian, and the Indian Ocean. I'm a romantic at heart, and have sailed them all.

"Today the Seven Seas are considered to be the seven major bodies of water covering the earth's surface. I've sailed those, too. Each of my aquariums holds a fish unique to one of those seas. *Fellinas solaris,* a cadmium-crested fighter from the Mediterranean. Go on. Look at her close up."

Fellinas solaris glowing tangerine orange, three inches long in the body, eight inches tall from dorsal to basal fins, with a five-inch diaphanous tail.

"*Amphiprion ocellaris,*" Vale said softly at my side. "Indigenous to the South Atlantic and very rare to find."

Amphiprion, a cobalt kite, a ten-inch triangle with lateral spinning fins and bright lemon lips.

Vale moved on. "*Thalassoma lunare* from the Indian Ocean. Ancients believed *Thalassoma* was a deity in the form of a fish. To swim with *Thalassoma,* have her tail touch your skin, bestowed karmic good fortune for lives not yet lived."

Thalassoma lunare, an emerald ribbon twelve inches

long. *Thalassoma,* the color of Vale's eyes, almost too intense to be true.

"*Naso volitans* likes her water cold," Vale said, moving along to the next tank, "ten degrees Fahrenheit, matching her native Arctic habitat. *Naso* is pale, almost transparent. Look there in the front of her chest, that small dot moving is her Arctic heart. Next is *Holanthus ciliarus,* from the North Pacific."

Holanthus, a rare ruby cloud in the shape of a perfect circle, eight inches in circumference with sheer spinning fins.

"And finally, *Hippocampus imperator,* the rarest species of sea horse known to man. Habitat, South Pacific—Fiji, in fact."

Hippocampus was a magical creature, one inch long with a tiny curving tail and fast fluttering fins. His head was long-nosed and horned, eyes the same bright blue as the body.

"They're a delicate, endangered species," Vale explained. "I don't feel guilty keeping them. They're safer here."

"Why?"

"The ecosystem in their natural habitat is their worst enemy. Virulent algae flowerings from polluted waters is killing them off. The few that are left are prime targets for poor locals who know how much collectors will pay."

"By buying them aren't you simply encouraging the black market trade?"

"I didn't buy them. I caught them myself and brought them back. They are fascinating creatures. Did you know they are notoriously bad swimmers? They spend most of the day with their prehensile tails wrapped around reef coral so they don't get swept away by strong ocean currents. Their love lives are interesting as well. Sea horses mate during the full moon, and when they do it is for life."

"Why is the eighth tank empty?" I asked.

"Ah! Back to the ancients again. There was much talk and speculation of an Eighth Sea and belief that the mariner who found it first would be blessed with immortality. It was a legend and prophecy rolled into one. My eighth tank is symbolic of the Eighth Sea—a promise that there are still wonders to the world to be discovered. A reminder that if we look beyond the confines of our own world there are amazing things out there in the great unknown. I keep the water at a steady eighty-six point five degrees. The temperature never changes."

He spoke persuasively with passion, conviction, and a deliberate double meaning I did not understand.

"Come," he said, as he poured me a glass of champagne. "Enough about fish. I'll show you the rest of my home."

Piano music played softly from hidden speakers, lights were low, and the sound of pots and pans clanking in the kitchen assured me we were not alone.

Upstairs were two guest rooms, and the master bedroom with a bathroom en suite. The bathroom was enormous, with skylights and a sunken tub. Walls were decorated with old whaling pictures. Towels were sea green, and robes were Japanese.

Vale showed me the study next and his impressive collection of model ships, a dozen vessels displayed on pedestals. Some were small, the size of a hand; others were three and four feet long and had masts as tall as a five-year-old child.

"This is a reproduction of the Venetian galley sailed by the great explorer Marco Polo in 1298," Vale explained. "Venice battled Genoa that year, and Marco Polo was taken prisoner. He was the first European to cross the entire Asian continent and leave a full record, complete with maps. He's one of the explorers I admire most."

He moved to the next pedestal.

"Angela Dorado," Justin said, caressing the figurehead on the largest ship. "Norwegian built in 1850 and bought by an Englishman who crossed the Atlantic under the power of her sails. Eighty feet long, thirty feet wide. She went down in the winter storm of 1923, just off the coast here, not far from the Weymouth shoals. Eighteen men died at sea that night. They drowned in swells the size of buildings, in water that was cold as snow."

"You sail."

"Nothing as big as this," he said, patting the prow. "I sail one-man vessels the old-fashioned way. No satellite tracking or twin turbo engines for me. I use the sun and stars and the power of the wind. Catch the wind just right, tack over to a thirty-degree pitch with all the mainsails tight, and it's a flying feeling, free and fast, skimming over the ocean like a bird. I'm a once-upon-a-time modern capitalist with a mariner's old-world heart."

The walls around us were filled with photos of Vale, many of which I had seen on the Internet.

"The capitalist was quite busy at one time," I said, stepping close to the wall.

"My vanity shots," he laughed, sheepish and at the same time proud. "Can't help it. I started out in life with nothing. And the truth is, I'm damn impressed at where I ended up. Dinner with Dan Rather, for crying out loud. Coffee once with Al Gore! People ask me how I did it, and I say if you want something bad enough, you get it. Simplistic as it sounds, the basic philosophy's rooted in the ancients—in their belief that we can determine our own destiny. The mind's a powerful thing. I'm a terrible host. Here I am boasting, and your glass is empty."

He led me back downstairs. I drifted over to the telescope while he poured more champagne.

"Eighteen fifty," he said, joining me. "Hand-hammered brass. I love the purity of antique navigational equipment, but in this instance I rebuilt the inside with modern opticals. This glass can pick up the rings of Saturn as easily as if they were pelicans right over there in the sand. You won't see much tonight, not with the heavy cloud cover."

I leaned into the eyepiece, looked at the black sea, then right and down, at the square of pool glowing blue in the raw red ground.

"I see your pool man from time to time," I said. "Does he always work at night?"

"He works only at night. He said he sees the surface better, the bugs and so forth that float on top. I leave him be. He's dependable and thorough—that's what counts. Come. Dinner's ready." He touched my elbow and guided me into the dining room.

Two sides of the room were windows and the ceiling was glass. It was at once intimate and open, as if we were dining outside, but the air was warm. Sconces on the wall cast an inviting soft golden glow. A round oak table was set with silver, china, and crystal and an ice bucket with champagne. Vale pulled back a chair.

"Please," he said.

I sat.

Ann Gamble came in from the kitchen. She had a motherly face and gray hair piled up in a bun. Her cooking was a local legend around town, and when I tasted the food I understood why. The first course was a delicate squash soup infused with ginger and exotic spices. Next, she brought in plates of steamed lobsters. As she set mine down, Vale instantly understood his mistake. I could not eat lobster from the shell with my gloves on. He came to my side and carefully, delicately, pulled the meat out of the claws and tail and back with a fine silver fork.

"I saw your story on WBZ last night," he said as he worked. "You have a gift. And, you obviously love what you do."

"How can you tell?"

"Intuition."

"A trait reserved for women and journalists."

He smiled. "A man can't have that?"

"Only if he's a journalist," I teased.

"How much do you rely on intuition?"

"I depend on it."

I did not go on to say that intuition was the radar that guided me through the investigation of a story. I did not expound on the intricate facets of my reportorial approach, how I looked for conflicting information to guide me to the truth. Nor did I go on to talk about the story. The truth was I wanted to forget about McKenzie's saw and Wheeler's warning. I was a woman in a black dress at dinner with a wholly alluring elegant man. And my woman's intuition said he wanted me as much I wanted him.

"Would you like extra lemon?" he asked, offering me a forkful of succulent white lobster meat.

"No," I said, taking it. "This is wonderful just the way it is."

Vale wished me a *bon appétit* and sat back in his chair. He went on to tell me about the champagne as he poured it, the unique qualities to the vintage, and the unforgettable beauty of the château.

Ann Gamble moved quietly around us, serving side dishes of truffled potatoes, offering fresh bread, tossing crisp romaine salad, and finally flaming souffléd crepes for dessert. Her presence was constant, and I knew Vale had orchestrated that. Having her there made me feel safe.

"A Rossetti face," he said, studying me in the soft light. "Dante Gabriel Rossetti. English painter with an

Italian name. In 1870 he was at his peak. Do you know his work?"

"He painted portraits."

"Of women. Once you see them they are hard to forget. The women were all different but of a distinct type with alabaster skin, high fine cheekbones, and wide sensual lips—like yours, Lacie. I could sketch you in my sleep."

"Have you?"

"Guilty as charged." He laughed.

Vale was the perfect companion, attentive and true to his word. He didn't ask me a single question about my hands or my past or my private life—not even anything more about my work. He stayed on neutral ground, talking politics and art, revealing bits and pieces of his own life along the way. One short-lived marriage when he was twenty-two, no children, no living parents, no ties, and, since the sale of his company, no formal occupation.

From time to time as he spoke, his right hand brushed at his hair, as if he were tucking an errant strand behind his ear. It was a mannerism I had noticed when we met on the ferry—the habit of someone who once had longer hair. I had the same habit, and somehow I found it touching, watching it in a man.

"I'm free," he said, stretching his long legs out. "Free to do as I please, go where I want, sail when the wind is right. Some say forty-six is young for such freedom. I believe the contrary, that success has come much too late."

Vale. Elegant in cashmere, swirling his glass, stirring up bubbles in the gold liquid, watching me with a meaningful smile. Captivating and entertaining, telling tales of the ocean, the history, the lore. The meal and champagne worked magic, leaving me feeling floaty and light, free of fear.

"It's midnight," he said when the second bottle was empty. "I promised to be a gentleman and that means it's time to take you home."

We took our shoes off and walked home on the beach, toes curling in the night-chilled sand. The wind was high, the black Atlantic streaked white with iridescent foam.

"Water is beautiful," he said quietly when we were on my deck looking out to sea. "Never the same. Ever changing and endlessly wild."

What was the arc that pulled me to Vale that night? Loneliness? Libido? Lust? The convenience of him there—rich, romantic, and willing? I had spent nine months alone healing, a lonely gestation. January to October, winter snow to summer solstice, and on through autumn leaves. I was scarred but healthy, a woman in her prime, sleeping alone too long with nothing but books to fill the bed. Every night there were a half dozen tossed like anchors across the sheets; I fell asleep with books all around me wishing paper could turn to flesh. My close brush with death and the long time alone had left me with a huge hunger to feel alive. Passion coursed through my dreams, desire so intense I would often wake up damp and warm, wishing I could lose myself in the luminous curves of a man's hard-carved arms.

Vale was right there, the champagne still strong in my blood. The hour was late, and my defenses were down. We were very close. He had each arm up on the doorjamb, his body blocked the wind.

I leaned into him and brought my lips up to his ear. "Don't go," I said.

"Say it again so I know you're certain."

"Don't go."

His mouth came down on mine.

The kiss killed control, set us both loose. His hands traveled my body, wild and bold, anything but shy trav-

eling over my breasts, my waist, my hips, my silk briefs—
testing me there.

Somehow, sometime, we moved inside and upstairs.
My gloves stayed on, but our clothes came off and we
were together again, driven by a deep hunger and
strong shared need. We drifted down onto the bed—
down, down, down we went, out of this world and into
another where his long fine fingers and silky voice were
all around me.

"Let me take you there again, Lacie," after each wild
rush. "Let me give you more."

Good as he was, high as we flew, wild as we rolled
through those hours between midnight and dawn, when
the moon was fading and the sun was lifting over the
sea, I couldn't help but feel a twinge of regret and guilt.
Despite the fine feline contentment, and the languid
beauty of his body, I could not help but think I was cradled in the arms of a stranger, lying skin to skin and
limb to limb with a man I did not know.

He woke at sunrise, glorious green eyes intense and
close to mine.

"What do you want, Lacie?" he softly asked. "Tell me
what you want."

Uncertainty fluttered in my heart. I thought I should
ask him to leave. But when he smiled that lazy smile and
asked the question again, I answered with one strong
word.

When he asked what I wanted, I just said *more*.

CHAPTER TWENTY

Vale slowly walked his wall of aquariums, carefully doling out portions of tropical fish food. He leaned close to *Amphiprion* and tapped the tank glass.

The small fish watched him.

What do you see? Vale wondered. He thought back to the summers of his youth when he was boy.

"Such a beautiful boy. Smart and good."

Vale had heard those lines for a lifetime, from his parents and even Callista, his father's lovely niece.

"He's a beauty." Callista laughed in her silvery voice.

Callista looked after him in the summers. Summers on the island, summers by the sea. Summers spent with Callista the Olympic swimmer, who taught him to swim.

"My tiny fish!" Callista laughing and kissing, splashing with him in the water in her red swimsuit. "My flying fish! Look at him go!"

And up she tossed him, high in the air. Up, up, up into the blue, only to fall back down to her wet, waiting arms.

The soapy warm bath and the cool blue pool.

Splashing with Callista, to the sound of her sweet warm voice. Callista, holding him, teaching him to swim.

"You're so pretty in the water, baby," she said. She had one hand on his tummy, holding him up in the water, so he could breathe. The other hand caressed his back in long, leisurely strokes.

"You've got what it takes," she said, tickling his lats. "Look at the big muscles growing strong back here! Wings like this, my water baby can fly."

He loved the pool water but always felt cold.

"My sensitive little baby," Callista said. "We'll fix you up right."

And she did. It was not his mother or father but Callista who went out and got him his first neoprene wet suit when he was four. Custom made, a half-inch thick. His magical rubbery warm second skin. Each summer she bought him a new one. When he was five, she gave him a plastic action toy she called Diver Dan. He had twin tanks loaded on his back, flippers, a mask, and a hooded black suit.

"Diver Dan is fearless, little baby!" Callista tossed the toy in the water and together they watched him paddle around.

Callista suddenly grabbed the toy and plunged it underwater and held it there. The tiny black legs kept right on kicking. After a minute she let go and Diver Dan shot to the surface.

"Diver Dan's a commando," Callista explained. "Nothing scares him."

Callista was a swimmer, and a great one at that. She had trophies on her dresser and a framed Olympic medal on the wall. Every morning, she swam laps for one full hour and let him sit on the side and count.

"How many?" she would ask.

"Ten."

And minutes later, she'd ask again.

"Twenty."

She used the pool to teach him numbers, and she used it to tell tall tales. When the swimming was done, she would open her arms wide to him and he would jump right in.

"Let's make up a story," she'd say, sweeping him around the shallow end. "Look at the pretty pictures carved on the pool tiles here. Pick one out and we'll imagine wonderful things."

He pointed to the mermaid, the girl-fish combing her hair with a shell.

"That's a siren," she said, stroking his baby fine hair. "Some were good, some were bad."

"Why bad?" he asked.

"They sang to sailors on the wide wild seas. They sang so the sailors steered right into reefs. When the boats sank, they grabbed the sailor men and swam them away, down into the deep where no man could breathe."

"Why didn't the sirens die, too?"

"They were part fish, baby. Don't forget that." She held him up close to the siren etching. "Look at her face. She looks like me, don't you think?"

She shifted him from her right hip to left.

"You're getting heavy, little baby," she whispered. "You're growing up fast."

He held his arms around her neck tighter and buried his face in her hair, breathing in the good summer smell of her skin, her hair, and the light scent of chlorine.

Callista cared about him. Callista loved him right to the end.

He remembered that last summer day, when he was a legal adult in his late teens.

"Marco?"

"Polo!"

It was a classic pool game, so much so, the encyclopedia had a special dedicated listing explaining the rules:

> The one swimmer who is "It" must be blindfolded and must shout "Marco?"
> The other swimmers in the pool must answer by shouting "Polo!"
> The blindfolded swimmer must "catch" one of the Polo-shouting swimmers to win the game.

Callista, blindfolded, side-stroking around the pool. He in his wet suit, slipping from one side to the other. "Marco?" Callista called.

"Polo!" he replied.

"Marco?"

"Polo! Polo! Polo!"

Then she was on him. She had won.

"I've got you!" she cried.

He laughed and splashed her, then leapt forward and gave her a dunk. She came up laughing, but before she could take a breath he dunked her again.

She came up coughing water.

He looked at the fear in her eyes, put his hands firmly on her shoulders and dunked.

Callista came up screaming, shrieking, crying. "What's wrong with you?"

Big and strong and fit, virile in his black wet suit, he took her under again—felt the red rage rising, and along with it something new, a real-time aquatic high holding her down while she struggled for air. He felt like a commando.

Callista! Callista!

The sound of her. The feel. The wiggling. The high-pitched keening cry.

Callista in the cool blue water, silent and still, drifting up from the bottom, red swim skirt fanning around her in that sublime aquatic hush.

Callista drowning calmed his rage—and the sun took on a new dimension for him that day.

He kept detailed notebooks of the investigation that followed—cut out news articles from the papers and photo spreads from weekly magazines—paged through them every night for months.

The coverage made him high—almost as high as had the kill.

Vale now picked up the remote and turned on his wide-screen color TV, to a tape cued up and running. Lacie on the shore, wind in her hair, standing in the rain, telling the story of a drowning, of the strange, sad death of a young Jane Doe.

CHAPTER TWENTY-ONE

I awoke late in the day, alone in my bed.

It was after two, the sky outside was gray and hard, the house quiet. Justin Vale was gone.

I showered and dressed and found him in faded jeans and bare feet at the tide line fishing, casting with a natural athletic grace.

"I'm using live bait," he said. "Striped bass can't pass it up. I caught two, enough for dinner. Or was I too optimistic? Will I be eating alone?"

"No."

"Excellent."

He planted the pole in the sand and pulled me in close with a hard, hungry kiss.

"It's cold," he said. "And rain is coming."

"Then let's go in."

We worked our way back up to my house in a heated embrace. Suddenly Vale stopped and dropped his arms.

Tom Wheeler was on my porch, leaning against the rail, watching.

"I'll be at home," Vale said to me. "Come by when you like."

He left us alone.

"Should've called first," Wheeler said as I went up the steps. He had a thirty-five-millimeter camera in his hands and was fiddling with the long lens.

"What's on your mind today?" I asked.

"Thought I'd take you for a ride. There's something I want you to see."

I locked up and followed Wheeler out to his Jeep.

He turned on to the dirt access road and drove down to the beach, then north, out along the deserted stretch of Siasconset toward the rock where the body had washed in. Clouds were gray sheets sliding in from the north. Wheeler stopped from time to time, opened his window and took a shot.

"Hobby of mine," he said, "taking pictures of the island storms. We've had more rain in this one October than we usually get in three full months. But then again the weather's turned strange all around the globe. Hot where it should be cold. Wet where it should be dry. The glacier on Mount Kilimanjaro started melting a while back. Twelve more years at the current rate and Kilimanjaro will be as bald as I am. Good thing Hemingway didn't live to see that. Storms here are good as teeth, eating away at the shoreline. Kiri Hannover tells me we may lose a whole foot of beachfront this winter alone. Isn't usually this way, Ms. Wagner."

"Lacie, please."

"You like the island in autumn?"

"Love is a better word."

"My wife, Brinn, hated it here summer, winter, spring, and fall. I make a decent living, but the island's small. I'll never have the kind of practice here that pays like the city would. Money splits Nantucket right in two, and I fell on the wrong side—at least I did for her. She was always eyeing the weekenders, men with big houses and fancy cars. I have a good life, the best I think, but I could never give her those things. Brinn wanted me to go to the mainland, to Boston, where I could make more money."

"Did you?"

"Wouldn't have lasted a day. The city suffocates me. Except for college, med school, and my hospital residency, I've always lived on Nantucket like my dad before me and his dad before him. I need this island. I felt right here, so I stayed and she left. Moved to Boston and married a high-flying heart surgeon. She got her million-dollar country club, gated community, the works."

"Regrets?"

"Not over her." He gave me a rueful smile. "But I've got to admit, I envied your neighbor back there. What is it you see in him?"

"Personal question."

"And out of line." Wheeler laughed. "I know the answer anyway. It's a physical thing. That's why I fell head over heels for Brinn. Later I learned she wasn't at all the woman I thought. Fire on the outside, but pure hard ice on the inside. Mean, too. I never saw it until we split. She felt she had wasted the best years of her life stuck on this island, as she put it."

"Who left who?"

"Personal question," Wheeler quipped.

"Out of line?"

"Not at all. Brinn just up and went to Boston one day, took our daughter Rio and filed a fat lawsuit full of lies she called grounds for divorce. Rio was ten at the time. Brinn was gunning for custody, knowing she could take my money and I would not care. Take my daughter and I would weep. I fought hard, ran through most of my money and guess I finally won something. The court granted me summers and every other weekend. Holidays were split."

"Standard arrangement."

"Maybe, but Brinn didn't like that, not one bit. Soon as she married a rich man, she plotted a buy-out on my girl's love. She used that man's money, spoiled Rio something awful. Bought her everything under the sun, then signed her up for Boston's most prestigious debutante social club. Imagine that! A daughter of mine coming out as a deb.

"The money thing worked, and next thing you know Rio dropped my last name, became Rio Haverfield. As in Henry Haverfield, her new dad. By the time summer rolled around, Rio didn't want to come to the island. She wanted to go to camp with her debutante friends. And pretty soon after that, she didn't want to come here at all. Said Henry Haverfield was her father. One was enough. She didn't want two. Court decision's worthless when those are your little girl's words."

"What did you do?"

"Wasn't much I *could* do. If I'd tried to force my rights, Rio would've just hated me more. I had to wait for her to come back to me on her own time, of her own free will. That doesn't mean I wasn't there for her. I was an absentee father, but never absent. I was the invisible dad, watching her over the years from a distance—at the school, across the street. I'd write long letters to Rio, give them to another kid to pass along. She'd look up, look around, and sometimes she'd look right at me, but never approach. I'd nod and blow her a kiss. She'd tuck the letter in her pack and walk away. Didn't know then that she was reading them, but the hope was huge inside me that she was. Huge enough, I kept writing them."

"What did you write?"

"Whatever was on my mind. Stories about wildlife, creatures I've seen in the sea. I talked about her new dad, too—I had to do that. How our values were just plain different as black is to white. I sent her my philosophy, my feelings, my heart—everything I wanted her to learn from me. I'd paste in photos of me just so she wouldn't forget my face. Treasures I'd find walking the shore. A sand dollar, a purple rock, a pink shell. There was always something pretty. A daffodil in spring. Rose in the summer. A leaf from my oak tree in October. Handful of berries from the local cranberry bog. The colors of the autumn. Winter I'd send her snapshots of the shore here covered in snow. Tell her the story of how I brought her into this world one snowy day. We didn't plan it that way, but a blizzard hit, closed the island down cold. No way to get to the hospital so I delivered my girl Rio at home.

"All those years passed and I never heard a word—until this last January. She called me out of the blue. *Daddy,* she said. I didn't know her voice, but that word was the giveaway. *Daddy.* Not Hello, Father; Hello, Tom; Hey, Wheeler; Son-of-a-Bitch; or even plain old Dad. 'Daddy. It's me.' Across the years and a lifetime, just like that. And with those three words my daughter began the long journey home."

"Why did she call?"

"Said she wanted to get to know me again, but she wasn't ready yet to come back here so she took a room at an inn over in Hyannis Port. Stayed for two full weeks. I rode the ferry across every day, and we'd have lunch and dinner, and take long walks together on the shore, swim together in the sea. She and her mother and Haverfield had had a huge falling out. They weren't talking. Rio wanted to go med school, be a surgeon like me. Brinn went ballistic. She wanted Rio to marry a pedigree prep, stay home, have babies, polish silver, and buy couture. Good old Henry Haverfield agreed. He refused to pay a dime of tuition. Rio said it was a revelation, and that's when she decided to come look me up.

"She had never told Brinn about the letters I wrote. Rio brought them all when we met, hundreds tied up in neat little stacks. She told me she was coming to understand how everything good in her had come from me. Her love of the outdoors, the spiritual completeness she felt there. Her compassion for all living creatures, her aptitude for athletics."

"What's her sport?"

"Swim team. Rio loves the water. Five-hundred-yard

freestyle. That's her event. Speed and endurance. The optimal mix. She swam her way through undergrad. I love the irony in that. There was Henry Haverfield with all his millions, and my girl went to school on scholarship, went to school for free because she was a fish in water like me. I just loved that! The DNA screaming the truth. I was in the bleachers for all the meets. I was there for graduation, and I'll be there when she finishes med school. She started Harvard this fall. And she's there on scholarship again. Rio's riding through med school on her own rich brain."

"Do you talk to her often now?"

"She calls every month or so. Her dime. She wants it that way. I haven't heard from her since before Labor Day, but I can't push. I've got to let her come back on her own terms, in her own time. She's feeling her way into it slowly. The dynamic's different when you're twenty-two. Her last close memories of me were when she was still a kid. The huge guy who taught her to swim. Huge, laughing guy who rode her around on his shoulders, took her kayaking and hiking, taught her to pitch a tent. The big bald guy who coached the summer swim team here on the island. Matter of fact, I still do. Displacement, the shrinks would call it. The satisfaction I get teaching other folks' kids. Still, it filled up a tiny bit of the black hole in my heart. I must say it did do that."

We reached the rock. He stopped the Jeep and looked at me.

"You must miss having your daughter here with you, Lacie. Must've been hard sending her away."

"More than words can say."

"So many ways to lose our children. So many ways they just disappear. You thought your daughter was dead, murdered, lost to you for all time. And it was some kind of miracle how she survived. You got her back, all in one piece. Crazy as it sounds, despite the years that have flown by, I'm hoping for that with my girl, that one day I'll meet her at the ferry, she'll come walking off right back into my life here. Hope is huge inside me. I won't deny that."

He pulled a wallet out of his jeans pocket and dug two snapshots out.

"Rio," he said. "In the first one there she was eight. Captain of the island swim team."

Rio in a racing suit the colors of the flag. A wild mass of honey-colored hair, a birthmark on her shoulder in the perfect shape of a heart. Wheeler touched it with his big hand.

"Symmetrically flawless," he said. "She asked me once what I thought it meant. I said God gave her a second heart because I had too much love to give her to fit it all in one heart. She could dye her hair, change her face, but that heart's a dead giveaway. Nature's way of telling me that's my little girl. This second shot here we took this summer, on the mainland, at the shore."

It was a close-up of Rio and Wheeler at the beach.

"She doesn't look much like me or her mother," Wheeler said. "DNA's the damndest thing. I was down in Key West once and saw a bartender there looked so much like me my own heart stopped cold. I took a closer look, realized his nose was longer, chin rounder, eyes smaller and spaced closer together. But at first glance, I tell you it was enough to shake me up. Just last night NBC aired a Lucille Ball look-alike contest. Hell, there were *thirty* gals looked just like her. All the infinite possible combinations of DNA and two total strangers can look so much alike, and still your own offspring can look as different from you as night is to day." He pocketed the pictures. "Okay. Enough about me, now. Let's take a walk."

Wheeler slung a nylon backpack over his shoulder and we got out.

"For two miles in either direction," he said, "this path is the only beach access."

It was nothing more than a steep hard-packed channel gouged into the earth. We hiked up it to the top of the bluff where the path opened into a dirt road just wide enough to accommodate a car. Scrub oak all around us was waist high and thorny. Wheeler sat down cross-legged and looked out at the high-running surf. I folded down next to him.

"That was a smart move, putting Hinks on the air," he said. "It'll pay off for you down the road."

"Have you known her long?"

"Since she was a little girl here. I taught her to swim. She still competes. Butterfly's her event, the roughest stroke in the pool. Kiri Hannover swims butterfly, too. For Kiri it's an intuitive thing, like she takes herself right out of the earthbound world and becomes a part of the element she's in.

"Not Hinks. Her form's technically right, but it's raw power that fuels her swim, the single-minded burning desire to win. There's no real grace. Hinks's work is a lot like her swimming. She goes flat out on raw energy when she could go a lot farther with gut intuition.

"She has good instincts—excellent, as a matter of fact—but she moves too fast. Hinks moves when she should be standing still, thinking. She doesn't have the patience to take a good, long look and see information that's all around. And I tell you there's evidence all around us. Just takes a good eye and careful mind to figure it out. I've been thinking about it good and hard. I believe there's only so much chance that can happen at one time, and it seems a long stretch to me that a girl washed up when the tide was going out, on this particular beach at *the precise moment* you were walking by."

"But that's what happened."

"Is it or is that what you *think* happened?"

"What do you mean?"

He pulled a map out of his pack and unrolled it on his lap.

"I drew this myself," Wheeler said. "There isn't an inch of this island I haven't mapped. This one's a topographic detail of ten miles of Siasconset shoreline here." He put his finger on a red-inked *X*. "This is your house. Two and a half miles down from you is the Old Whale Rock." He tapped another red *X*. "See this little gray squiggle here on the bluffs, straight up from the rock? That's where we're sitting now. There are hundreds just like it zigzagging all through the scrub. None of them are marked. You'd have to be local to know this one's here. Like I said, it's the only beach access for two miles in each direction."

He rolled the map up and put it back in the pack and looked out at the sea. The sun was low in the sky and the cool breeze light.

"On Sunday," Wheeler said, reliving the day, "the wind was blowing pretty steady, about fifteen knots offshore, and the tide had been running out since two o'clock, a good hour and a half before you passed by. That's where the facts just don't add up. How come the body washed *in* when the tide was going *out*? That's scientifically inconsistent—especially since she hadn't been in the water very long.

"Remember, her skin wasn't even shriveled the way it might be when you spend too much time in the tub. She wasn't bloated, and the fish hadn't started to feed on her flesh. I did some checking around. She didn't fill those tanks on this island, she wasn't staying in any of the hotels, and none of the locals have reported anyone missing. All that got me to thinking."

"And?"

"I took a ride on out here yesterday and poked around. Remember we didn't do that Sunday night. It was getting dark, and there didn't seem to be any reason because we thought she had just plain drowned and washed in. I walked a grid on the beach down there, five hundred yards to either side of the rock, and I found this washed up on the sand."

He rummaged in the pack again and pulled out a child's toy: a twelve-inch plastic scuba diver in a black wet suit with a pair of flippers, mask, and twin tanks.

"This little guy runs on two double-A batteries," Wheeler said. "Turn him on, drop him in, and he'll swim around underwater for hours. Going back to what I said about coincidence—seems pretty far-fetched to me that a toy diver and a dead diver wash up on the same chunk of beach by accident."

He flicked the power switch, and the little diver began to kick. It was so innocent in Wheeler's big hands and at the same time deeply disturbing.

Wheeler turned the diver off. "When I finished combing the beach yesterday, I went up the path to the access road here. I poked around some more, and found this caught on a branch of scrub oak."

Wheeler pulled a plastic evidence bag out of his pack. Inside was a knot of tangled strawberry-blond hair.

"Like finding a needle in a haystack," he went on, shaking the little bag. "I'm betting this hair I found matches the hair on our girl's head."

"You're saying she made a beach entry right at the rock?"

"Yes, but not by herself. She would've left a car parked up here if she had walked into the water on her own." Wheeler rose. "Stand up."

I did.

"You and the girl are roughly the same height, right?"

"Yes."

"The scrub oak here comes up to your thigh."

"So?"

"Pretty hard to catch your hair in it if you're walking. She wasn't walking, and she sure as hell didn't wash up in the surf. I figure someone parked right here at the end of this road, carried our girl out to the beach, and put her in the water at the Old Whale Rock so you would find her."

"But if I had run by five minutes later, I might not have. She could have drifted away in the outrunning tide."

"The tide had been running out for *two hours.* She would've drifted away long before that. You're forgetting one important fact."

"What's that?"

"Her gear was tangled up in the kelp. I had to cut it off with a knife."

"That's right." I remembered the thick, slippery seaweed wound tight around her tank valves and how I couldn't unwrap it with my own hands.

"I took close-ups of the tangle," Wheeler said. "I don't believe the kelp was tangled at all. Looks to me like it was in knots. Someone used the seaweed to anchor her there, to make certain she didn't get carried out to sea. And I don't think they were timing the dump by the tide at all. They were timing it by you."

I knew exactly where he was going next.

"Lacie," he said, "I'm betting that body was put there, intentionally, so that you'd find her on your afternoon run. It was put there by someone who's been watching you, who knows your routine. How often do you run?"

"Seven days a week."

"Same time every day?"

"At three-thirty. But what if I had left the island and flown back to D.C.?"

" 'What ifs' don't count. Fact is you were here."

"But how could anyone possibly know I would still be here?"

"Pretty easy to figure out if someone cared enough to try. I did some checking on my own. You had a sizable grocery delivery Monday morning, isn't that so?"

"Yes."

"You had an appointment in town set up for early Tuesday morning, just as you always do, at the local salon. You're booked on Cape Air to D.C. a week after that because you're due back on the air the following Monday. Until then, you're here. Simple deduction based on fact."

"Our private lives are not private at all. If you're right, why me?"

"Can't say. I don't have answers for the rest of it, either. Not for the burns or the ripped-up feet or the who, what, why, or how. I don't feel good about how you're involved in this. When I came by last time, it was just superstition talking, a gut feeling, but now I've got physical evidence."

He gave me the toy diver.

"Someone's talking to you, Lacie, just not using words. I'm going to say what I said again: Drop the story. Let Hinks do the job. Let her do the rest. Leave the island until it's over. I feel danger for you here. You'll be safe in the city."

"That's ironic, Wheeler, coming from you."

We rode back down the beach at sunset.

Packs of gulls roosted in the sand. Wheeler slowed as he approached, and blew the horn. The birds scattered in an explosion of wings and guttural complaints, white triangles beating the darkening sky. Eight packs later, we arrived at the shore fronting my house.

"I'm sending the hair straight out to McKenzie," Wheeler said, turning up the access road to the bluffs. "Luckily it's forensically good."

"Meaning?"

"The roots are intact. A simple strand of hair isn't enough to make a positive ID. You need to have the root. If the roots on these match Jane Doe's, we'll know for a fact this hair came from her." He pulled into my drive. "You should have someone with you tonight, while you think things over. I'd be happy to stay. Just say the word."

"I won't be alone."

His face closed down, and he gave me a manila envelope. "Your set of crime-scene photos," he said. "My mobile number's inside, too, if you change your mind."

"Thanks, Wheeler."

He just nodded and flicked on the wipers.

Water was misting the windshield, a gentle drizzle drifting down like dew.

I went inside and opened the envelope, flipped through six eight-by-ten glossies documenting the body and gear, the featureless face and ripped-up feet.

Two more calls to Harry's source went unanswered. After I showered and dressed for dinner, I tried again.

He picked up. His voice was rich with the music of the South, sweet-timbered and young, a little afraid.

"I've never talked to a reporter before," he said. "You aren't recording me now or anything like that? You aren't going to use what I say on the air without telling me?"

"That's against the law."

"Still, you might do it and it'd be my word against yours. I'd feel better if we met in person. I'm on my way to D.C. tomorrow. It's the anniversary of my brother's death in the Vietnam War. I go every year and leave something at the Wall. We could meet there."

"I won't be back in town for two weeks." I was testing him, to see what he had, if it was worth my time and the effort of travel. "We'll meet then."

"Too late. She'll be buried; she'll be long gone."

"Who?"

"Your Jane Doe."

"Do you know her name?"

"No."

I waited out a long pause.

"But," he finally said, "I think I know where she's from."

"Can you tell me the name of a town?"

"Not exactly."

"You don't know her name or her address, but you know who she is."

"I know what she *was.*"

"That's a strange way to put it."

"The truth is stranger still."

"When you can be more specific, call me at the station. We'll talk then."

"Wait!" he said so quietly I almost didn't hear. "Here's something they didn't report in the news. Did the police find a sonar tracking device on her tanks?"

I said nothing. I didn't know. I had looked at the gear in a superficial way, as had Wheeler, McKenzie, and even Hinks.

"Find out," he urged. "And if there was one, you'll want to meet me at The Wall. October 26, 1968. That's when my brother was killed. The last name is Porter. I'll be there tomorrow from noon till five, whether you come or not."

I looked out and saw Wheeler's battered old Jeep still sitting at the end of my drive, glistening and wet.

Stubborn man, I thought.

I called Hinks on her mobile. She was in a speedboat. I heard the hull slapping water and the whine of engines.

"Good piece last night," I said. "You came across real well."

"Calling to collect on our deal?"

"I understand the state crime lab is backed up."

"Like a clogged drain. Why do you care?"

"The tank pack's there. I need to know if it's fitted with a sonar tracking node."

"What makes you think there's something like that?"

"Long-shot thought. I'm trying to rule something out."

I wandered the house while I waited and looked out at Vale's from my bedroom window. The pool was lit and the pool man was on his knees, driving long iron stakes into the earth at two-foot intervals. I left the window, changed my clothes, and looked out again. He was unrolling a big black stretch of canvas and methodically covering the pool, feeding rope through rivets on the sides and tying the rope down around each stake. When Hinks called back fifteen minutes later, the black canvas was stretched drum tight and the pool was closed.

"Your long shot was dead-on," she said. "A Fathom Five sonar tracking node is soldered to the underside of her tanks. It's the size of a nickel—that's why no one noticed it right off. Crime lab tells me the Fathom Five's a state-of-the-art chip with big range. It can track a diver fifty miles out and is accurate up to a hundred and fifty feet down."

"How?"

"It emits a high frequency, an ultrasonic *ping*. The sound is pitched specifically to the Fathom Five master unit. No one else can hear it. It's a high-priced device."

"What's the customer profile?"

"Seventy-five percent military."

"The other twenty-five?"

"Industrial clients like deep sea oil drillers, where the foreman up top needs to keep track of his workers. The lab said the node's been customized in interesting ways that makes him ninety percent certain it's a military piece. Thing is, Defense isn't missing any divers."

"None that they know of."

"Meaning?"

"The diver was definitely military."

"Not a chance," Hinks said. "Let me tell you why. The run on Jane Doe's DNA was comprehensive for all departments in Defense. It came up a big fat zero, but I didn't stop there. We've got the Massachusetts Military Reservation right here on the Cape—eighty-two prime acres dedicated to a multi-unit defense commune with coast guard and air force, pararescue jumpers and SEALs. They've got divers coming out the kazoo. I spent the day over there, personally talking to the commanding officers of every division, and came up empty-handed. I had a team of five state troopers on the phones, working over the rest of the military installations located on the Northeast coast. None of them is missing a diver. If she was U.S. military, why don't they step up and claim her?"

"I don't know the answer to that yet."

"But you intend on finding out."

"We're both after the same thing, Hinks."

"Can I talk to you off the record here?"

"Yes."

"Understand this: The Cape has its share of crime, but rarely if ever does something really big come along. This case feels like it could make my career—win the election for me. I know there is no hard evidence yet, but my gut tells me this diver was murdered, and that the circumstances behind the crime, once revealed, will leave every last one of us shaken. It will be my personal and professional glorious privilege to prosecute the guilty party or parties, and I will not let anything or anyone—you included—preempt my investigation, take from me the opportunity to stand on the steps of Justice and bask in prosecutorial glory."

"Hell of a speech, Hinks. Evangelical, in fact."

"Just stating the facts," she said. "You come across something relevant to my Jane Doe, you call me first. I come across something, I'll call you. We can work together. Mutual effort for mutual benefit, as you yourself proposed. Don't preempt me. Don't piss me off. Believe me, you don't want to do that."

She disconnected.

I looked outside. The pool lights were out. The pool was black, and Vale's pool man was gone.

I booked the first flight off-island, packed a bag, closed the house, and went out on my deck.

Wheeler.

Still there, at the end of the drive, ready and willing to sit through the night, close to me. I thought of his fine strong profile, the intensity in his eyes and sobriety in his voice. *Drop the story. Leave the island. Go back to the city. You'll be safe there.* Uncertainty fluttered inside me, and along with it the first stirrings of fear.

I opened my umbrella and took the shortcut across the moor.

Vale was waiting at his front door, casually elegant in black cashmere.

"You closed the pool," I said.

"Season's over. It's too cold to swim."

I passed him my bag.

"Moving in?" he asked, smiling.

"Just catching an early flight out in the morning."

"The story you're working on."

"I finally got a break. With a little luck the whole truth could fall right into place tomorrow."

"Do you want to talk about it?"

"No," I said softly, touching the sharp V of his hair. "Talk is not what I want tonight."

We dined on caviar and champagne in the center of his bed.

The taste of Vale was better than both, the smooth cool surface of his flesh, his lips sweet and strong, but it was his hands that did me in; warm hands pressing my shoulders into the pillows, cupping my hips, and later, at midnight, those same hands leading me out of bed, through sliding doors to the upstairs deck, out into the night and the storm; hungry hands sweeping wet hair off my face, running down my back, around my thighs, hungry hands parting me, then holding on tight while he rocked in and our heated flesh became one, oblivious of cold or wind or the hard driving rain.

And then he was drifting down, and I saw him from above, the lovely proud line of his nose, the curve of his cheek, his fine dark head slick and wet, pressed against me there, and all I knew was his sensual mouth and the heat it roused in me there with the pure cold water of Heaven falling all around; Vale's oral ceremony in the rain, driving me up time and again, I was lost in pulsing need, drowning in abject desire.

CHAPTER TWENTY-TWO

My taxi arrived at 6:00 A.M.

Tom Wheeler was still slouched in his Jeep at the end of Vale's drive. He got out when he saw me. "You're leaving the island," he said.

"But not dropping the story."

"Where are you going?"

"D.C."

"How long will you stay?"

"That all depends."

"You'll let me know when you're coming back."

He glanced up at the house, at Vale standing barefoot in the open doorway, fresh out of bed in jeans but no shirt, showing off the hard table of his stomach and powerful spread of his chest.

"You don't like him," I said softly to Wheeler.

"He dyes his hair," Wheeler replied. "Why do you suppose a man would do that?"

"We'd best be leaving now," my driver called out.

I ducked inside. As the taxi pulled away I looked out the rear window at the two men standing in the early morning light.

Vale the lover. Sated. At ease. Lounging against the doorjamb, warm breath smoking in the cold island air.

But it was Wheeler who held my gaze.

The fierce lips. The sweeping forehead and fine broad skull. Chin lifted and set. Feet parted, shoulders squared, arms crossed at his chest. Combat stance.

Who's the enemy, Wheeler? Can you tell me that?

On the drive into D.C. from the airport I passed fifteen huge WRC billboards with my own airbrushed face: LACIE WAGNER'S COMING HOME! Home was the station, not my new condo on the twenty-eighth floor of a high-security building. Home was the news desk, the set, camera, and lights. The condo was just expensively decorated cement, a place to sleep—not a home at all, not without my daughter to share it with.

I arrived at the Wall at quarter to one. The granite was a black mirror in the midday sun, reflecting the

Washington Monument in Constitution Park. A white obelisk celebrating freedom, a dark wall commemorating grief.

As I approached, a wealth of statistics ran through my mind.

Cost of construction—nine million dollars, not a penny of which came from federal funds. Designer—Maya Ying Li, a native-born American citizen whose parents fled China when Mao took control. One generation from oppression to freedom, the American way. Names—58,132; only eight of which were women. Military nurses. The rest were men. America's sons.

It was an autumn weekday, and although it was still early, offerings had piled up: American flags, floral bouquets, stuffed animals, snapshots set up in altars. It was always this way. Each night the National Park Service collected the offerings and tagged and stored them in a Maryland warehouse—a cavernous space filled floor to ceiling with tokens of grief, gifts for the dead.

"Fathom Five sonar tracking?" a voice asked.

I turned around.

Preston Porter looked nothing like he sounded except that he was young. The soft southern voice was at odds with the physical man. He was six feet of rock-hard muscle. Despite the cool air, he did not wear a jacket, just a tight turtleneck the color of stone. He had a strong square face, dark brown eyes, crew-cut blond hair, and huge hands.

"I knew it," he said. "A month ago I heard she was missing, that something got fucked up. I was staying with a friend here in town and saw your story on WRC. I waited an hour before calling the station because I wasn't sure what to do."

"About what?"

"An oath. A promise. If I talk to you, I'd be breaking my word."

"Does anyone get hurt?"

"No. I kept on going over it in my head all night long, first thinking it's right to speak up, then thinking it's wrong."

"And you finally decided it was right."

He looked up at me, and his eyes filled with tears so fast it startled me.

"This is a confidential meeting," I said. "What you say to me here will never go on record with your name. I promise you that."

"It'd be my life if you broke that promise." He sat with his back to the Wall and openly wept. Emotion is expected at the Wall. To any casual onlooker, the outburst would not seem out of place.

I sat down next to him, understanding the vertigo of emotions on free fall, the struggle for control, the fear that a dam has opened, one that might never be shut.

"What happened to you, Preston?"

His expression changed, and I knew he was remembering my own sad face on the news when I was the story, not the anchor. The memory of what I had lived through must have given courage, as if we were bonded.

"I almost died once," he said.

And with those four words his story began.

"I almost died once, and sometimes when I think of it I can't believe I'm really here, that I survived at all. My brother died a hero in Vietnam. I never knew him. He was killed before I was born, but he was around me my whole life, his spirit, his memory, his ghost, and I grew up expecting I'd pick up where he left off. Make my family proud. My folks don't have money. My dad worked his whole life driving a rig. He had no education and no choices. I was a good athlete, and the way I added the world up, I had two choices: carry the ball for

Old Atlanta and try to go pro after that, or carry the flag for Uncle Sam. Uncle Sam won. The navy wanted me, and once I was in, they asked if I would make a run for Special Ops."

"SEALs?"

"That's how it started. I was right there in training with all the other recruits doing just great, top of the class. Then suddenly I was pulled out."

"Kicked out."

"No, pulled out and moved up."

"Delta."

"Higher than that."

"There is nothing higher in Special Ops."

"Nothing you or John Q. Public knows about."

He was holding his hands out toward me, palms up, body language for sincerity that anyone could fake. But no one could fake the expression in his eyes. The huge sadness I had seen earlier, welling up, threatening to take him under. Right along with it was regret and a flicker of fear.

"They told me it was a test cell," he said, "an experimental platoon, the only one of its kind, and the pay was big. And they promised it would pump up my record, make going for officer grade later an easier thing. 'You are chosen,' they said. How could I say no? We numbered five hundred, pulled from every branch of Defense. All of us were smart and way above average in athletic form. Damn smug to be picked, too. Pardon me for saying this, but the media has hurt the military."

"How's that?"

"The press prints everything, every detail. The Internet's the last straw. Log on, and you can get the army's classified manuals, read about the navy's tactical training strategy, learn how to build a friggin' bomb. It's all there for anyone who wants to look. There's nothing much secret in the military anymore.

"SEALs are so popular they do exhibitions now at county fairs. Delta was created as a top-secret Special Ops division. No one was ever supposed to know about it, and the Pentagon still won't publicly admit it exists. But you know it does, I know it does, and John Q. sure knows it does, thanks to Hollywood. Delta and the SEALs are too exposed, so Special Ops created SEATEC—a completely invisible unit that gets kicked into full operation next year. Right now they're still in the training phase. Operatives have been excised out of the military DNA database. If they die in the field, on enemy turf, there's no direct link back to Defense. They are invisible men. Soldiers of fortune. SEATEC missions are designed to go five steps beyond SEALs, and one or two beyond Delta. Think of a CIA agent in a wet suit who can rappel down a mountain and kill with his bare hands, whose job it is to kill."

"A platoon of government-sanctioned military assassins?"

"SEATEC isn't *government sanctioned.* That's the whole point. The President and the Congress have no idea it exists. SEATEC was created by elite military commanders who have so much power and authority and freedom they think they're above Congress, the President, and the law—the kind of officers who think the military has *no accountability* to anyone other than itself. That's not the way the U.S. military is supposed to work. We have a system of checks and balances in this country to keep the military clean."

"What's SEATEC's tactical objective?"

"Political assassination where it serves the best interests of the United States."

"That's against international law."

"I know. It's the damndest thing. War's okay. Tactical covert assassination isn't."

"So what happened, Preston? You had a moral problem with the job? Wake up and decide you couldn't be a killer for hire?"

"No, I woke up and realized I couldn't stand by and do nothing but watch when teammates died in training. In Special Ops, the commanding officers use real tactics to prepare recruits for field conditions and toughen them up. The COs are good. They know how far they can push. A recruit might get pushed to the limit, beaten to a pulp, but in the end, the CO will scoop him up and make sure he lives. Recruits who can't cut it are kicked out. They leave the military alive."

"And SEATEC?"

"There are no commanding officers in the training field. Exercises are run by outside consultants, brought in because they are world class in their individual specialties and hard-assed sons of bitches to boot. The objective in training is to achieve perfection, the theory being that in the field, in an active mission, there is no margin for error. SEATEC can't afford for an operative to screw up out there. The stakes are too high. SEATEC believes it's better for an operative to go down in training than in enemy hands."

"Give me an example," I said.

"In standard naval pilot training there's an exercise that simulates an open water crash. The recruit's catapulted to the bottom of a swimming pool in a real jet cockpit. He has to free himself from the cockpit and swim to the surface. Rescue divers are standing by. If he doesn't make it out in a set amount of time, the divers go and get him before he drowns. In SEATEC no such rescue takes place. The fellow recruits and tactical supervisor wait poolside. If the recruit is stuck, if he can't get out, if he panics, no one helps."

"But teamwork is the foundation of every military operation. How could they convince you to compromise that?"

"Money. Upon successful completion of a mission, each member of the operative cell will get a million dollars. One thing all SEATEC recruits have in common is that they're poor. The chance at that kind of cash buys total obedience from guys like me.

"SEATEC's doctrine is never compromise the operation, never jeopardize the goal. In the field, going out of your way to save a teammate who screws up might put the mission at risk. The million's hanging out there like a carnival prize to make sure that doesn't happen. They give us code names. No one knows anybody else's real name, just the tag. Mine was Bingo. It's a way of desensitizing and dehumanizing each of us so we can stand by and do nothing if one of our buddies makes a mistake."

"How could you?"

"I couldn't, and that's why I'm here. But let me explain something about how our minds work, something a lady like you might not understand. Deep down, all of us young healthy soldiers believe we're immortal. The man in the black hood isn't going to get us. No ma'am. We're faster and stronger and wilier by far. Try as he may, old man death doesn't have a chance.

"Suspension of reality's a necessity in military life. You watch an F-18 explode midair and it's your buddy sitting in the pilot's seat, you don't have the luxury of grieving, not in a normal way, because grief makes you weak when you're paid to be strong. So you make jokes about how old Slammer bit the dust. You drink an extra beer with the boys, tell morbid jokes, sleep late the next day—and when you wake up, you've got to move on. You've got to get in a plane yourself and fly into combat, and you can't do that if you're thinking about how old Slammer felt when he burned to bits. Much as a soldier doesn't believe he's ever going to die on the job, he sure as hell doesn't think he'll die in training. Even in SEATEC when they tell you up front, you think it's a joke. No one will die. Not with people watching."

Tears rolled hot and fast down the freshly shaved face.

"Those are the rules, Ms. Wagner. I stood there— once, twice, three times—and watched my buddies die when they screwed up a training exercise. I watched, did nothing, and went to sleep at night thinking: 'Death won't get me. I'm a better soldier than he was, stronger and smarter by far.'

"But two weeks ago we were on location off the coast up north of Boston. It was a foggy night. In open water exercises like that, the tactical trainer in command stands watch up top in a Boston Whaler. He keeps track of us using Fathom Five sonar trackers soldered on our tanks.

"I was up first going through a new underwater ob- stacle course. I had to dive without lights. It was so damn dark down there, I miscalculated and ended up stuck in one of the traps. My tank ran dry. I've never felt anything like it, sucking on the regulator and not getting any air. If I had stayed cool, I might've figured my way out of the training trap, but I panicked. All I thought about was a teammate who had drowned in a similar course, how he used up the last of his oxygen on panic, and I believed it was my turn. I had fucked up. It was my turn to die."

"But you didn't."

"One of the recruits topside broke down. Operative went by the tag of Blitz. He was a better man than me. He told the trainer to go fuck himself, then jumped in. He came down with a full twin set of tanks that be- longed to the trainer. There was no sonar device on the pack. He got me out, ditched my pack, and the two of us sharing that one regulator swam as far as we could. Came ashore way north and stripped off our wet suits.

Lots of houses were nearby. We went round through yards swiping shorts and T-shirts off clotheslines, anything that fit, and then we hitched rides. Along the way, Blitz told me his real name. Jimmy Sanders from Memphis, Tennessee. Here's his picture. I carry it to remind me what a real man is."

He dug a Polaroid out of his wallet. Jimmy Sanders, short and wide and strong. Bulldog legs, a wrestler's chest, and long, hanging arms that made him look like a cartoon. His hair was jet black, and a long pink scar ran lengthwise across his forehead.

"Where is he now?" I asked.

"Six feet under. He made a big mistake, Jimmy did. He went back home. Two days later he died in a car wreck. Police say the cause of the wreck is unknown. But I know. SEATEC cleared the slate. They don't like loose ends, and I'm a walking, talking loose end. I've been in D.C., but I've got to move on soon. My stuff's packed. I'm going to disappear."

"Did SEATEC have female recruits?"

"Special Ops view women as nothing but trouble. But the architects of SEATEC thought women could be real assets in covert tactical work. So they were trying it out. They had one."

"Had?"

"I think she's your girl. I think she's the Jane Doe who washed up on the beach at Nantucket."

"Do you know her name?"

"No. Her tag was Siren. Like a mermaid. She definitely went down in training, because those Fathom Five tank packs are controlled gear—not personal—and it gets inventoried and locked up when it's not being used in the field. Jimmy and I knew we couldn't go public with our story. No one would believe us. We had no proof—no body. You have one now. You have the Siren."

"What do you know about her?"

"Nothing. I can't tell you where she lived and I don't know her real name, but I can tell you this. I saw her from time to time driving a big old Cadillac El Dorado. I'm nuts about cars, and this one was a beauty—a 1972, two-door gold convertible. More like a boat than a car. Nine feet long. Bench seats. And a monster V8 with 235 horsepower. Had a bumper sticker on the front fender that said DIVERS DO IT DEEPER."

"What did she look like?"

"You tell me."

He turned me to the smooth mirror of black granite. I saw our faces side by side reflected in the high gloss of the stone. He gently pulled my hair back with one hand and traced my reflected image with the other.

"In training," he said, "we learned how to look beyond changeable physical variables like weight, eye color, hair color, style, and cut. We learned how to use bone structure to effect an ID. The Siren was younger than you, Ms. Wagner, but if you had short strawberry blond hair, you could be mistaken for her. She had your face."

A Rossetti face, I thought, shaken, turning away.

"Why do you think SEATEC didn't recover her body?" I asked. "Why did they let it just wash up on shore?"

"I don't know, but I can tell you who does. I'm going to hand you the head of SEATEC on a silver platter. That's the reason I called you. Jimmy avenged me. He not only risked his life for me, he also *died* for me. Now I'm going to avenge the Siren, even if it's too late. I want you to blow SEATEC out of the proverbial water, but let's be clear about one thing."

"It's your deal, Preston. I'll play it any way you want."

"You've got to make the colonel think I'm dead. Everything I've told you is off the record."

"So I have a body but no witness, no source I can quote. Makes it hard for me to be credible with allegations like this."

"If you say a SEATEC survivor stepped forward, there's only one of those and it's me. They'll find me like they did Jimmy."

"There are people who can protect you."

"No, there aren't. You're one smart lady, Ms. Wagner. I figure you'll find a way to do this on your own. Agreed?"

"Yes."

"Okay. Bastard by the name of Spivak runs the whole damn thing. Richard Spivak, Dick to his friends. He's a five-star colonel in Special Ops."

"Which is headquartered at Little Creek Amphibious Base in Norfolk."

"You won't find him there. SEATEC home base is set up in an ancillary military installation between Cape Cod and New Bedford. It's buried in the woods and hard to find. It's not listed in any government directories. If you stumbled on it by accident, you'd think it's just a satellite naval post, but the compound is maximum security inside and out." He handed me a map. "SEATEC doesn't like loose cannons, Ms. Wagner. You start asking questions, stirring things up, you might put yourself in a tight spot."

"If I do my job right, I won't."

"Okay. Consider yourself warned."

Preston was totally credible, the story media rich, and I was ready to run hard with it.

Then I heard Max's voice, our heated debates in the past. The relationship between the government and the press has always been adversarial at best. Journalists like me believe the First Amendment set us up to be political watchdogs. But Max argued the rights to secrecy in national security issues so persuasively sometimes I saw things his way. When Preston left, I walked the Wall as if those dead soldiers were a jury listening to Max and me debate.

Max's rationalization for SEATEC would be compelling:

"A few men and women die in the name of a higher good. How many more would die if another Milosevic emerges from the Balkans? How many more if Hussein carries on? Isn't the sacrifice of a few American soldiers worth the greater gain—especially if they volunteered and knew the high stakes at the start? If Jane Doe is SEATEC's Siren, then what right does the press have to break the story and take from Defense the very thing it needs most?"

"Every right," was my unspoken reply.

I sat on a bench next to the long reflecting pool. The water was alive with imagery, the Capitol Rotunda, a silver jet, white puff clouds drifting by. I sat there until late afternoon when the sun rolled right over the Washington Monument, a blazing red globe stabbed by the sharp obelisk stone.

SEATEC wasn't sanctioned by Congress or the President, and as such existed outside the framework of the Constitution, operating with a mandate that broke international law. Responsible news is grounded in a governing ethic all its own: the public's right to know when the built-in checks and balances in the constitutional framework are compromised.

That alone gave me the right—the duty—to play a part in bringing SEATEC down.

CHAPTER TWENTY-THREE

I went across town straight to WRC, the first time I had been back in almost a year.

The lobby was still the same, old-world conservative and drawing-room cozy with fine dark polished wood and overstuffed chairs. Poster-size pictures filled the walls, showcasing NBC television stars and the *WRC Action Six* news team. I breezed by my own portrait, tapped the wood frame once for luck, and wound through a maze of corridors to the newsroom in back.

Reporters and camera crews were out in the field taping stories. A couple of researchers slouched at computer terminals, trolling the Web. Fax machines hummed, telephones rang sporadically, a WRC custodian swept the floor.

Harry was in his glassed-in corner office, standing over his desk, phone in one hand, cigarette in the other, shouting and smoking, fueled by his usual high-octane mix of nicotine and caffeine. He was dressed in a pale pink Egyptian cotton shirt, gray custom-cut suit, and red silk tie. Although his feet were under the desk, I knew he wore white silk socks and that his loafers were polished to a high shine.

He was sixty-odd years of age, and on Harry age looked good. He was long and lanky and lean. Sharp brown eyes missed nothing; lips were full and expressive; and thick silver hair, glossy. His voice was memorable with a low resonant timbre suited to broadcast.

I smiled watching him, and suddenly realized how

much I missed him. Harry had brought me in from Norfolk when he came to D.C. Together we took WRC's news from last place to first. I considered Harry Worth not only my news director but a caring friend, as well, and I knew the feeling was mutual. A year in the news business is a lifetime, yet he had held my anchor slot open until I was ready to come back. There were a half a dozen big-city anchors who would have come running if Harry had just asked. But he had not. He had anchored the news himself—something he hadn't done for twenty years—and waited for Lacie Wagner to come "home."

I rapped on the glass partition.

Harry looked up, smacked the receiver down, and waved me in. "Wagner! God bless you! Is my calendar wrong? Is it November first?"

"Nope. Six days to go. How do I look?" I asked, wanting to know if he thought I was ready for the hot lights of the studio, the unforgiving close-ups natural to my work.

"Damn great." Harry grinned. "Miraculous, in fact, considering how you were six months ago. You looked amazing on air the other night. What brings you in?"

"The story."

He dropped into his chair. "What've you got?"

I laid it out in detail, including my guarantee of confidentiality to my source and how I believed every word he had said.

"In some ways," Harry said, "his story leaves you with more questions than answers—like how SEATEC lost a soldier with a sonar tracking device on the tank pack."

"Right. They could have recovered the body easily. And when you consider the forensic evidence, the list of questions grows longer still. How was she exposed to a lethal dose of radiation in training? Why was she left untreated all that time?"

"Those are questions you'll have to ask SEATEC."

"Easier said than done. The Department of Defense doesn't acknowledge Delta, which everybody *knows* exists. I have no witness, no proof, nothing I can use. There's no way Defense will cop to this."

"Yes, there is," Harry said, smiling. "You just haven't found it yet."

I went back to my spacious private office, switched on the lights, and looked around. It was as I had left it so many months ago. A library of videotapes filled one entire wall—my special reports, multipart series, interviews with the President, the sum total of my career. Framed pictures of Skyla filled the facing wall. She was, I thought, the sum total of my life.

I left the door open, loving the sounds of the newsroom drifting in: field teams angling for time in the editing bays, producers roughing out the story lineup for the early cast, arguing over which piece would lead and which would close, tech crew hauling cables and cameras in from the vans, reporters blowing by, rumpled and frenzied, eyeing the big clock, feeling pressured and late.

My private line rang. I picked up.

"Had a feeling I'd find you there."

"Hello, Max."

"What are you doing back at the station?"

"Working on my story."

"Your Jane Doe."

"SEATEC's Jane Doe."

There was a long silence. I waited for him to speak. When he didn't, I tried again. "Ball's in your court, Max."

"I have nothing to say."

"You know about SEATEC."

"I've heard talk."

"So have I. Shocking allegations." I laid them out. "Does that line up with what you learned?"

"I can't say."

"Can't or won't?"

"Steer clear, Lacie. It's not your place to pass judgment on matters of national defense."

"It is my place to report on those matters—if what I've been told is legit. Will you at least look into it, validate the accuracy of my information?"

"If I do, it will be on my own behalf. Covert military operations are sacrosanct. I will not be a party to any actions that may compromise that."

"I'll nail it down on my own."

"I have no doubt you will, and that's what worries me most."

"Good enough," I said. "And Max? I'm sorry."

Sorry not for going forward but for drawing a hard line in the sand between us.

"I'm sorry," I said again.

But I was talking to a dead line. Max was already gone.

I focused now on the hard work that lay ahead. I had a name and number for SEATEC. I needed one for Jane Doe. A name was what SEATEC's Spivak would fear most because the minute I had one I could get facts, trace paychecks, interview relatives, draw a thousand little lines in the sand that would lead straight to him.

All I knew about the Siren was that she had been seen on occasion driving a 1972 two-door Cadillac El Dorado. I started with the Massachusetts Department of Motor Vehicles. My source there promised to fax through a list within the hour.

Miles McKenzie had promised lab results by the end of the day. It was still early, but I went ahead and gave him a call while I waited.

"You're one step ahead of Hinks," he said. "The first reports are in, and Wheeler asked me to answer any and all questions you might have. He also said you'd be wanting a copy of the autopsy protocol when it's complete."

"I do. What did the blood work tell you? Was she drugged?"

"No, the tox screens are clean."

"What about the hair sample Wheeler sent in?"

"The bulbs matched up. The hair on the bluff came from her head. Traces of chlorine residue deep in the shaft don't tell us much. Just that she spent time in a pool. Nothing out of the ordinary about that."

"What *was* out of the ordinary?"

"Her blood cell count was dangerously low, in keeping with the usual progression of radiation sickness. Her immune system was highly compromised, nearly defunct."

"You still stand by the timetable?"

"I do. The results are consistent with an exposure date of four weeks ago. It's also my opinion that had she not drowned first, she would have died from the radiation sickness in a matter of days. To cut right to it, Ms. Wagner, aside from the diatom test, which I'm still waiting for, only one thing came back that was a surprise."

"What was that?"

"Heart cell blocks had been destroyed prior to death by an adrenergic response—a physiological phenomenon that is triggered by intense fright. Put another way, fear has its own pathology. Enough psychological duress, and your heart will essentially burst. Our Jane Doe was terrified when she died. If she hadn't drowned first, the adrenergic response would have killed her— she would have literally been scared to death."

*　　*　　*

The physical facts squared with Preston Porter's description of SEATEC tactical training methods. I wanted to sit face-to-face with Jane Doe's commanding officer and ask what went through his sick mind when he allowed her to drown. That it was a good riddance? A weak link pulled from the chain? Did he feel a flicker of remorse, a shred of guilt? Did he? Would Max have? I wanted to believe Max would not have stood by and watched, but in my heart I was not sure. I would never completely understand the military mind or the moral chasm between man and soldier that allowed for a cold calculation of acceptable losses. Death was part and parcel of defense.

In the newsroom, a young metro reporter had her police scanner turned up loud. The 911 voice floated in through my open door, a disembodied clipped recitation of urban chaos. Shots fired, bodies down, blood spilling. Another day in D.C.

The metro desk was a hard but rewarding place to start in television news. I envied the young reporter all the emotions she felt as she raced out the door—excitement, frustration, exhaustion, exhilaration—wanting them all to myself.

Hard news exhilarated me. It always had from the day I started at a station in a no-name town in Alabama. There wasn't much action to cover outside of zoning disputes, but I covered them like they were congressional budget battles and the local mayoral race like it was the American presidential campaign.

A news director in a bigger town nearby liked my hard news on-camera style and offered me a hundred dollars a week more than I was making to go to work for him. The station was still relatively small. I had to horse my own camcorder around and tape my own stand-ups, but I did it with gusto and a work ethic that got me promoted up through four more cities in a straight line up the eastern seaboard—Knoxville, Asheville, Raleigh, and then Norfolk, where I anchored the midday cast and finally got my first big break in the form of my first dead body.

He washed ashore two miles south of the station in Norfolk. If the bloated, naked, white-bellied male floater with a rope noose still around his unlucky neck had drifted down to the next town, I would have lost out. There were signs of torture. Cigarette burns on the feet. The victim was a navy officer. I stayed one step ahead of the police, interviewing every enlisted man who had been under his command, working tenaciously until I figured it out.

A young recruit had cracked in training, and I got his full confession on tape. The monstrous crime earned him a life sentence, and I snagged the one and only interview with him before he was sent away. Not Geraldo or Barbara Walters, but Lacie Wagner—because the killer liked me. He said he trusted me. The interview got a network pickup, and suddenly I was hot enough to land the lead anchor slot in Washington, D.C.

History was repeating itself: a dead body in the water then, a dead body in the water now.

The big white clock on the newsroom wall clicked over to twelve straight up. The fax from Massachusetts DMV rolled in. There were not many of those gas guzzlers left on the road, and even fewer that were gold. The list was short, whittled down to eighteen current registrations spread all across the state. Of those, three had outstanding moving violations, and one had an unpaid parking ticket and tow fines from an outfit called Leeds Towing dated thirty days back. That El Dorado was registered to Tina Delmar, 1250 Tiverton, Falmouth, Massachusetts.

Thirty days sitting in a tow lot a stone's throw from the SEATEC compound.

I called my DMV source back, angling for a copy of her driver's license—but he had stepped out for a late lunch, and I was in no mood to lose time.

That nine-foot old gold Cadillac was waiting for me.

CHAPTER TWENTY-FOUR

When I landed in Boston the sun was a watery silhouette behind gray-sheeted clouds. Men in suits the same color gray swirled around me, checking watches, hurrying ahead into the business day. Death was my business here.

I rented a car and soon was heading down I-95 toward the coast with a strange sense of vertigo, headlights on high, holding tight to the yellow center line. It was the only thing I could see in the thick swirling fog. The road would dip down, sink into the belly of the mist, then rise again, lifting me up on a crest, the fog settling under me, a wide silver lake, a table of smoke.

Somewhere out to the left and right were the rolling New England hills, a riotous rush of autumn color, trees weeping fire-colored leaves, but all I saw were yellow slashes on black pavement urging me forward in my story, always forward.

Falmouth is perched at the southwest tip of Cape Cod, bordered by a triangle of water: Buzzards Bay, the Vineyard Sound, and Nantucket Sound. The whaling and shipbuilding center of Cape Cod in the 1800s, it is still the nautical center for the Upper Cape, with a bustling port, classical downtown, and fifty miles of spectacular beaches.

Leeds Towing was located inland on a small lot out near the small local airstrip. I pulled up at ten and went inside. A young clerk lounged in a chair, feet up on the counter watching a tiny TV. The office reeked of stale beer.

"Make, model, license number, driver's license, and registration," he said, yawning and dropping his feet.

"A 1972 Cadillac El Dorado," I said. "Massachussetts tag THY 873, towed from the village Friday night October fifth."

"Took you long enough. Must have been some kind of party night." He dangled a set of keys. "You left these in the ignition. That's sixty-five for the tow plus ten bucks a day for storage. Cash or credit card, and I need proof you paid the ticket at Town Hall before I can release the vehicle."

"I'm not the owner." I offered him a hundred-dollar bill. "I just want to look inside."

The hundred disappeared.

"It's in the back row of the lot," he said. "You can't miss it."

He was right. Even unwashed and crusted with dirt, the car stuck out. The sheer size of it was memorable, the length, the width, the whitewall tires. A bumper sticker plastered to the front fender matched Porter's description: DIVERS DO IT DEEPER! The convertible top was up, doors unlocked.

I got in and sat down in the half-light, gloved hands resting lightly on the wheel. The seat was adjusted perfectly for me; Tina Delmar was my height. The air inside was musty and smelled of salt water and musk perfume. The car was old, but the stereo system looked new, top-of-the-line Alpine CD. A pair of plastic scuba fins dangled from the rearview mirror. My dead diver had no fins, just shredded booties and lacerated feet.

The passenger seat was a jumble of belongings, as if a

purse had been turned inside out. Two tubes of May-belline lipstick, one pale orange, the other bright pink; powder compact; black eyeliner; Ultra Lash mascara; eye drops; and a travel-size bottle of hair spray. A lady in a hurry who wanted to travel light.

The driver's-side sun visor was down, tiny mirror open. She had touched up her makeup and spritzed her hair. The last face she saw before leaving the car, I thought, was her own.

I felt around under the seat and came up with a hair-brush, bristles twined thick with strawberry blond hair. I slipped it in my bag, then checked the glove compartment and found a laminated white card with a simple black bar code. There was no photo ID, no name or rank or serial number, but I had a feeling it was a base pass. I slipped it in my pocket and checked the backseat. She had left a Little Creek baseball cap and a pair of sun-glasses on the rear dash. I put both in my purse, got out, and popped the trunk.

Nylon bags lay open and empty. They were sandy and smelled of brine and salt like the sea.

I had no doubt that Tina Delmar was the Siren who had washed up at my feet.

I sent the hairbrush to McKenzie via overnight courier and drove on up the Cape to Hyannis. 1250 Tiverton Avenue was a battered old white cottage in a low-rent neighborhood. The drive was empty. I went up the walk and rang the bell. Drapes were drawn, the porch light on. There were no old newspapers stacked up, but then again I did not expect a SEATEC operative to have a subscription to a daily, not when assignments pulled her out of the country for months at a time.

In Special Ops the standard habits of daily life ceased to apply. Phone, cable, water, gas, and electric bills all went on prepay from secure bank accounts held at the base. Credit cards and mortgages, too. 1250 Tiverton had not been home to the average renter. Now it was home to no one, I thought, looking at the peeling paint, missing shingles, broken bricks on the front walk and the deep carpet of autumn leaves covering the small yard. Still, the porch light troubled me. The fact that it was on. As though someone was coming back. Driveways to either side of the cottage were empty. This was a working-class neighborhood in the middle of a working day.

I went back to my rental car and worked the phone, angling for a copy of Tina Delmar's driver's license, but my source was unavailable. Next I called Reese Manson, a tech wizard who tested security systems government-wide.

"Lacie!" he said, delighted. "What piece of the puzzle is puzzling you today?"

"A laminated white card the size of a standard business card," I said. "It has a black bar code on one side and nothing at all on the other."

"Base pass," Reese said without missing a beat. "We came up with it this year."

"How does it work?"

"Assume the pass is yours and you arrive at the base entry gate. The sentry swipes the bar code with a handheld scanner. The bar code's linked to your digital biometric dossier in the master mainframe. Next the sentry takes a digital shot of your face. The system runs one hundred twenty-eight facial characteristics for a match with the mainframe."

"Facial biometrics."

"Exactly. D.C. Metro Police have installed it in all government buildings. NYPD uses it, too. So does Super Bowl security. Surveillance cameras positioned at entry points scan faces of the people entering a building, running a hundred twenty-eight characteristics from each face against a master database of criminals looking for a match. The system's ultraefficient, works in a split second, but the accuracy is not one hundred percent."

"Why?"

"Because there are literally thousands of people walking around with the same *type* of face! Even one hundred twenty-eight characteristics aren't enough to be a hundred percent accurate. So here's what happens: Run-of-the-mill Joe Blow walks into the U.N. and—wham!—feet back and spread 'em, because the system matched his face to that of a bomber in Oklahoma. Department of Defense wants infallible, not accurate, and there's only one biometric for that."

"Fingerprint."

"Right. The scanner for that bar code pass has the pad for the fingerprint element built right in. The intent is simply to protect the integrity of the pass. Even if the card is forged or stolen, only the true authorized holder can get through the base entry."

Not necessarily, I thought, thanking him and hanging up.

At the tow yard, the same sluggish attendant was sitting behind the desk. Another hundred and the keys to my Hertz rental bought me his copy of the local yellow pages and more time with the Cadillac, this time behind the wheel and rolling. He was so happy with the cash, he even held the door while I got in.

"Get it back here before eight," he said. "My shift's over then."

The army/navy surplus was close by. I bought brown desert combat fatigues and boots, wore the ensemble out, and went to Headhunters, a wig and makeup shop downtown.

"What do you need?" the middle-aged counter woman asked.

"To be a twenty-four-year-old strawberry blonde."

"Don't we all. What's the look?"

"Wavy and full."

"Long or short?"

"Shoulder length."

"I've only got long and straight in stock, but I can cut and curl right here."

She asked dozens of questions while she worked, and when the wig was right I put it on. The hair changed me dramatically; the light color intensified the blue of my eyes, the short cut emphasized the high contour of my cheeks.

"You look five years younger blond," the counter woman said. "But you want ten, so we got another five to go."

She applied foundation and blush, working brushes and sponges with a quick, firm hand.

"That's it," she said, stepping back. "Sexy and hot. Have fun. Stay up late. Hell, stay up all night. The makeup will last."

Shadows were long and the sun low when I turned down the narrow road leading to SEATEC's installation in the woods. A pair of white signs flanked the road, stating that this was government property and restricted to authorized personnel. Speed bumps forced a slow approach. I put on sunglasses and the Little Creek baseball cap and rolled ahead.

Security cameras mounted in trees at fifty-foot intervals monitored my arrival. High, electrified chain-link fences circled the compound. A dozen more red-and-black signs posted voltage warnings. Through dense woodland I caught glimpses of cinder-block bunkers, dark gray, chunky and square. Some had narrow slits for windows set ten feet from the ground. Others appeared to have no windows at all. Roofs were flat fields of white satellite dishes.

A small cinder-block hut sat off to one side behind the compound entry gate. Two soldiers stood sentry. They wore desert camouflage like mine and carried rifles in addition to standard sidearms at their waist. A third sentry emerged from the hut. He looked at the bumper sticker on the front fender, slapped the hood lightly, and leaned down at my open window. His smile was bright, his manner casual and familiar. His name tag was stamped CRUZ.

"Haven't seen this big gold boat in a long time," he said. "You haven't been around."

"Nice to know you noticed."

I offered up my pass. He carried a wireless tablet with a whip antenna that fit Reese's description of the scanning unit.

"That dinner offer's still open," Cruz said. "Doesn't expire."

"Thanks!" I said.

He scanned the bar code, held up a small cube that was the digital camera, and entered my face into the mainframe. The biometric matched, and he held out the tablet for the final ID. Cruz was too busy checking out my body to notice my hands. I slipped my right glove off, quickly pressed my index finger on the biometric pad, and replaced the glove.

The LED glowed green. The ID was good.

The dead diver had no fingerprints. Hers had been surgically removed. My fingerprints had been burned off long ago in the fire that crippled my hands. Our biometric was theoretically identical.

A shrill shriek sliced the woodland quiet, a high-pitched squealing alarm.

Cruz glanced at the LED screen and dived, jamming his nine-millimeter sidearm into the base of my throat.

"Hands up where I can see them! Now! Now! Now! Good. Cut the engine with your right hand—slow now—keep it slow. Good. Pass the keys to me—slow now. Good! Both hands up now—good!"

The two gate sentries had raised rifles, locking me in their sights.

Cruz jerked my door open. "Out of the car! Out of the car! Now! Now! Now!"

I got out and Cruz took me down hard, slamming me facefirst into the ground. The baseball cap flew off my head, the sunglasses broke. My teeth cracked. I tasted oily asphalt and petroleum grit. Cruz jacked his knee into my back as he shackled my wrists.

"Rhineholt!" The word was a gunshot.

A pair of combat boots came in close to my chin. The cold rifle barrel kissed my ear.

"Foster!"

A second pair of boots appeared next to my cheek.

"Search her," Cruz ordered.

Foster did, hard and mean. "The subject is clean," he said.

"Search her bag," Cruz ordered.

And Foster did. "The bag is clean."

Cruz yanked me up and passed me off to Rhineholt. "Take her in," he ordered. "She goes to Spivak. B-6, Quadrant 18. Her name is Sinclair."

The car belonged to Tina Delmar, but the dead diver's name was Sinclair.

Sinclair with her high-flying cheekbones, pale skin, and wide full lips.

Sinclair with Lacie Wagner's features and missing fingerprints.

I smiled as they marched me to their Jeep and loaded me in.

*   *   *

Cruz opened the gate and we rolled through, into the compound.

Rhineholt drove. Foster kept his nine millimeter jammed in tight to my throat. Both men were stone-faced and silent. The night was cold, smelled of moss, burned leaves, and gunpowder. The sound of crickets and wind rustling trees was all around.

At Quadrant 18, Rhineholt slowed to a crawl in front of a row of single-level cinder-block bungalows. A parking space out front was marked RESERVED with Spivak's name in fluorescent yellow glow in the dark paint. He had a silver Jag with vanity plates.

Unit 6 was low and square with a flat roof and long narrow windows that looked like slits. Even a trained eye would not see the differences I knew were there: the piezoelectric oscillator that prevented laser surveillance of conversations taking place inside, the infrared surveillance transmitters that prevented covert picture taking from the outside, and as a backup, white noise generators that blocked electronic audio surveillance.

Foster ushered me out and passed me off to a steel-faced soldier in combat attire waiting at the door. He led me through a maze of computer workstations and on in to Spivak's private office.

I faced a broad walnut desk and the back of the colonel's high leather chair. His hand was all I saw, poised in midair, thick fingers curled around an unlit cigar.

"Long time no see," he said, dripping danger and malcontent. "Where you been?"

"Beachcombing up north," I said. "It's a nice time of year."

Spivak swiveled around. He looked like he sounded: a hard-driven pit bull of a man with a round face, small colorless eyes, and dirty blond hair buzzed down tight to his skull. The skin on his hands and face was thick and leathery from the sun. Against that dark tan, his full dress whites almost glowed. He wore the traditional colonel's insignia on each shoulder: a proud eagle holding dead prey in sharp talons. The image was a warning, I thought as he rose, reached across the desk, and ripped off my wig. Recognition flashed on his face.

"Wagner," he said. "Where the fuck did you get the pass."

"What you really mean is, why did I bother?"

"What the fuck are you doing here?"

"Your security sucks."

He waved at his yeoman. "Pat her down, Driscoll, and just because she's female doesn't mean you should be less than thorough. She's a reporter, famous one, too. The media has a nasty reputation for playing below the belt. Wires and so forth, putting off-the-record conversations on tape. They're an unscrupulous bunch. Why, just look at how she snuck in here like a thieving dog! Keep that in mind when you do the honors, Driscoll. I'll keep my eyes averted, spare *Ms. Wagner* the indignity of suffering a Peeping Tom while she's searched."

Driscoll went through my purse, opened my lipstick, checked dollar bills, eyed my cell phone, and rifled through an envelope full of crime-scene shots.

"Arms out to your sides," he ordered.

I complied.

He was quick but thorough, running a metal detector over my body first and following up with his hands, taking his time with my hair, feeling his way methodically through the mass of it, searching for some minute device.

"Take off your shirt," he said.

I did.

He inspected every inch of my bra in a purely professional way, feeling for hidden mikes, adjustments in the wires, modifications that could conceal a recording device. When he was satisfied, he stepped back and nodded. "Boots and pants now."

I pulled the boots off, stepped out of the cargo pants, and stood bare-legged in black silk briefs staring at the back of Spivak's shaved head. My graft scars were clearly visible, streaking up and down the inside of my thighs, terrible channels of white waxy flesh where parts of my own body had been dug out to rebuild my hands. There were fresher pink scars from the more recent harvest, when strips of my legs had been used to rebuild parts of my face.

Driscoll patted my underwear down with the same cool, professional hands. My pants were next. He turned them inside out checking the pockets, hem, and seams.

"Remove your gloves," Driscoll said.

"I won't do that."

"Standard security procedure."

"The gloves stay on."

He looked toward Spivak for guidance. The colonel nodded once, waved his cigar.

"The gloves come off," he ordered.

I peeled the right glove off, then the left, and passed them to Driscoll. For a split second his impassive expression cracked. The scars from reconstructive surgery were as ugly as burns. He flushed as he inspected my gloves carefully, turning each black leather finger inside out, feeling along the seams. When he was satisfied, he passed them back.

"Sorry," he whispered under his breath, a look of pity on his hard face.

And I hated him most right then, preferring ridicule to pity.

"The subject's secure," Driscoll said out loud when I was dressed.

"Thank you, Private," Spivak replied, waving the cigar one last time. "That will be all."

Driscoll saluted and marched out.

The door clicked shut. We were alone. Spivak spun around.

"I'll ask you one more time," he said. "What the fuck are you doing here?"

"Interviewing you."

"The fuck you are."

"All the things I thought you might be, hasty and stupid weren't among them. Refusing to talk to me's not your best option."

"I don't appreciate threats."

"And I don't make them."

"Then just what are you saying, Ms. Wagner?"

"I have a damning story the network will run, one that could wreak havoc around here. The way it looks now, you'll personally take the fall. I'm giving you the chance to talk off the record, set the facts straight."

"About what?"

"You missing any Special Ops soldiers?" I said. "Anyone go on leave and not come back?"

"You're fishing."

"No, I went beachcombing, and guess what I found."

"A pass."

"Better than that." I leaned across the desk. "I found the Siren."

Spivak was good. A cheek muscle fluttered; that was all.

"Your verbal games confound me, Ms. Wagner. First veiled inferences of military shame and now talking to me in riddles, making vague allegations of a havoc-wreaking scandal. Those are strong words."

"Murder's even stronger."

"Murder!" His pale eyebrows shot up. "Why, I'm afraid you've come to the wrong place. There's never been a murder in Special Ops. Sergeant Collins in Media Relations down at Little Creek headquarters will confirm the fact. Feel free to call him and ask."

"What if I ask him about SEATEC?"

His eyes narrowed; he leaned back in his chair, the cigar forgotten, a sixth digit in his right hand.

"My story's about SEATEC," I went on. "The American public still has a soft spot for women. Dead boys in uniform might not stir up our cynical citizens, but a *girl*, Spivak? A beautiful young woman who dies in training while her own commanding officer and teammates stand by and do nothing? How will the public react when they learn about the agonizing death of the beautiful Siren—SEATEC's guinea pig, the first female Special Ops soldier in your new platoon of elite combat-trained commandos. And what on earth will Congress and the President say when they hear about SEATEC for the first time?"

His neck muscle was working, giving away his unease. I had hit him dead center and hard.

"Talk is cheap," he said, "and conjecture's free. What've you got to back up your wild allegations?"

I picked a shot of the beached body, slid it across the desk, and watched his face. I guessed he had won a hundred poker hands with that blank expression. But when I slid the next shot over of the graphic burns, he paled considerably under his leathery tan.

"Those are radiation burns, Spivak. Stage four."

The cheek muscle fluttered again. His jaw clamped down tight. He looked from one picture to the other and then up at me. "Nothing here to prove she's military, let alone Special Ops. What makes you think your floater's either?"

"The pass."

"Funny, base security told me the unauthorized pass you used belongs to an African-American male sergeant, very much alive and present here in the compound. Sergeant Collins in Media Relations will be more than happy to confirm that, and he'll thank you on behalf of Special Ops for bringing the pass back to its rightful home." He leaned back in his chair. "What else have you got?"

He was testing me. Information was currency. I had to give to get.

"Her fingerprints have been removed."

"That so."

"Last I heard, nose jobs and breast implants were a woman's first choices for cosmetic surgery—unless she's Special Ops."

"What makes you think she's mine?"

Much as it would have won me instant credibility, I wasn't going to compromise Preston Porter. I could give up his partner—Jimmy was already dead.

"Blitz dropped by to see me a few weeks back," I said, "on his way home to Memphis."

"Blitz?"

"Nice kid named Jimmy Sanders. He's dead now, like his teammate Preston Porter, who died in the water under your watch. But that's another story for another day—at least that's what my news director has decided." I was letting him know others knew and that sending me on a joy ride like Jimmy's wasn't going to make the story go away.

Spivak leaned across the desk. "Where did you find her?" His interest was genuine.

"Nantucket," I offered, "Atlantic side of the island. She washed up in the surf."

"When?"

"Three days ago."

He couldn't hide his surprise. "Three days?"

"That's right."

"Autopsy?"

"Done."

"Where?"

"Boston."

"And?"

"She drowned. SEATEC let her die in a training exercise. Your bad idea of performance sports."

"Wild allegations with no basis in fact. Let's stay general for a moment, Ms. Wagner, and talk journalism. About how it works. This compound here is a legitimate naval satellite operation used for Special Ops tactical training. By your own admission the two so-called witnesses to the terrible practices you allege are dead. Without a witness there's no story—nothing but unsubstantiated hearsay, and we both know a story based on hearsay hardly lives up to the journalistic standards one would expect from a big-city network affiliate. Short of that, it's a piece for the *National Enquirer*. Credibility runs real low there, now isn't that so?"

"I've got a body that belongs to you."

"If she does, then the military DNA bank will come back with a match."

"Not if you don't want it to."

"More conspiracy theory?" He grinned and shook his head. "Next you'll be telling me you believe everything on the *X-Files* is true. Without a witness, I'd say you're washed up, excuse the pun." The grin disappeared. "Unless your Jimmy isn't Jimmy at all."

His closing point was implied not stated, but I heard the message loud and clear. He was gunning for Preston, to find out if he was still alive.

"The Jimmy I met had dark hair and a scar on his forehead. Short but power trained. Long arms out of proportion to the rest of him, almost dragged on the ground, as a matter of fact."

"We're back to wild allegations unsubstantiated by fact. If you don't have a witness, why did you bother to come here?"

"Eyes are the windows to the soul, someone once said."

"A reporter schooled in the classics." Sarcasm dripped. "Imagine that."

"I'm not here as a reporter today."

"No? Then what are you?"

"A self-appointed avenging angel," I said, matching his sarcasm word for word. "Searching for the truth."

"And you thought you'd find it here."

"I did, Spivak. It's in your eyes."

I pushed the photos back across the desk. He snatched them up and spun around in his chair, giving me the high leather back, an impenetrable wall. I waited out five minutes in silence while he decided what to say.

"*If* this unfortunate young lady was under Joint Special Operations Command," he finally said, swiveling back around, "I assure you her death would be a surprise to us all. The radiation burns would be an even bigger surprise."

"EPA has Little Creek on the Superfund National Priorities List as a contaminated, hazardous waste site. You've got three hot landfills and contaminated soil. She was exposed down there."

"If she was one of ours and those burns occurred on base, your Jane Doe would be in ICU at the medical center on the naval base in Bethesda getting state-of-the-art care. She sure as hell wouldn't have been out swimming in Nantucket. Off the record, that is all I am going to say: Your victim didn't die in the course of naval training or naval work, Special Ops or otherwise. Do you read me?"

His words were couched but the message was not. The body was his, but her blood wasn't on his hands—or so he wanted me to believe.

He flipped the crime-scene photos across the desk and punched up the speakerphone. "We're finished here, Driscoll. Ms. Wagner's on her way out. Give her a ride back to the gate. See that she makes it safely off base."

I gathered my photos and stood. "I'm not easily placated, Spivak. If you're lying to me, I'm going to find out."

He leaned back in his chair and sucked his cigar. "I remember your first big story down in Norfolk," he said. "The Tristan Worth interview that got you your hot job in D.C. Funny how it started a lot like this. Dead body washes up on shore and the lovely Lacie Wagner turns into a star. Now here you are stirring things up because dead bodies in the water equate with big things for your career, gold rings and ratings, offers to move up."

"I'm gunning for the truth because that's my job."

"And I thought you got paid all that money for the sight of your pretty face on TV. So far your investigative reporting stinks. You attempt an unauthorized entry on a restricted compound using stolen ID, then come waltzing in my door, spouting off wild allegations you can't back up, and all you've got is a stack of dime-store snapshots."

I held back, let him go on.

"Yeah, that's right," he crowed, grinning satisfaction, the Cheshire cat in full dress whites. "All you got is a picture of a Jane Doe diver. No name, no face, no positive ID. Isn't that so?"

"I've got her face and fingerprints, and thanks to your boys at the gate and by your own admission right here when I walked in I've got her *name.* My Jane Doe is now Jane Sinclair. It won't take me long to put a first name with the last. And there's one other fact of interest: Sinclair had a Fathom Five sonar node soldered to her tank pack. It was activated, and according to the state crime lab, had been modified in ways unique to U.S. Special Ops."

Spivak could not hide his true emotions this time. I had him.

"A SEATEC diver's training gear is not personal," I

went on. "Recruits are never allowed access for personal use. Isn't that right? When the gear isn't in use in the field, it is under total lockdown. How would Sinclair—your Siren—get access off duty? More important, Spivak, why?"

I turned my back and walked out.

Driscoll was sitting in the Jeep, waiting to drive me out.

We were pulling away when I heard it, the knuckle-cracking sound of Spivak's rage. I had left the door wide open, and now his fist pounding wood and angry words carried loud and clear into the night:

"Goddamn . . . motherfucking pricks . . . how did this happen . . . damage control . . . shit!"

Sinclair was his—and I was certain she had died in active training.

CHAPTER TWENTY-FIVE

I returned the Cadillac, changed clothes at a gas station, and went back to the cottage on Tiverton, where windows were dark, the drive still empty, the porch light on. I pulled out my phone and called Harry.

"Got a fax for you here," he said. "Driver's license in the name of Tina Delmar."

"Run through the stats."

"Address—1250 Tiverton. Vitals—twenty-two years old, five-two, brown eyes, black hair."

"What about her picture?"

"A young Asian woman. Does that help?"

"Maybe, Harry. Maybe more than I think."

The porch light at 1250 was now a beacon in the dark, teasing me with the promise that someone would soon be home.

I spent an hour adding to my notes and listening to jazz. Exhaustion from my sleepless night pulsed through me in waves. The last ferry to Nantucket left Hyannis at eleven. I planned to be on it.

At 8:00 P.M. the drive was still empty and the porch lamp still lit. I craved a warm shower, a hot dinner, and my own big bed. I pulled out my phone and dialed Wheeler's number instead.

"Have you heard from your tidal expert?" I asked.

"Kiri checked in today. Judging by the weather conditions and the way the currents were running, she said the body didn't wash in from the Vineyard or the Cape or the mainland coast. The entry point was local. She was damn sure of that."

"Anything else?"

Wheeler paused. "You know what AFIP is?"

"Armed Forces Institute of Pathology, the Department of Defense's group of medical examiners. Why do you ask?"

"They came down hard on McKenzie tonight with a pile of federal orders, then flew the body out on a military chopper along with all the forensic evidence that went with it—yanked the case right out of state's jurisdiction. McKenzie's not happy—not to mention Hinks."

"Hinks is out?"

"I am, too. Won't be of any help to you now. Once AFIP moves in, none of the usual protocol for interagency cooperation applies. They're under no obligation to disclose or apprise the public; hell, they don't have to tell state police or McKenzie—or you—anything at all. Defense runs by laws of its own, especially when it comes to Special Ops. An investigation doesn't get more shut down than this."

*   *   *

Spivak.

I had jumped too fast.

"You screwed up, Wagner," I said to my reflection in the rearview mirror. "You didn't let the story reveal itself. You got all riled up and jumped ahead, and now you are quite possibly completely, royally screwed."

McKenzie was my next call.

"They took full jurisdiction?" I asked, after apologizing.

"Hinks is so mad she's ready to pop. It's a territorial thing. I don't have to tell you."

He didn't. I had worked enough multidepartmental cases to know how it went. The local cops hate the state cops. State police hate anything federal, including the Bureau and the Department of Defense.

"Hinks is a pit bull," McKenzie went on. "She's not giving in. Swears she's going to fight the jurisdiction issue to the bitter end."

"On what grounds?"

"She claims the death occurred off-base while Jane Doe was off-duty in Massachusetts—Hinks's state. Technically, she's right. But the navy doesn't care, and somehow they got federal paper to back them up. Never seen anything like it, the military doing headstands to take over a murder case that technically isn't theirs."

"What happened to the forensic samples?" I asked.

"They pretty much cleaned me out, too, everything except diatoms and hair. The diatom work is still at the lab. They've got an agent there ready to confiscate that when it's done, but the lab specialist is a longtime friend. He'll send me the results. And they missed the hair sample Wheeler sent in. I've got that right here in my office."

I told McKenzie about the hairbrush I had sent him.

"I'll run it against Wheeler's sample just as soon as it gets here," he said.

"What about the autopsy protocol?"

"I'm writing it now. Bethesda wants the whole document sealed, but they didn't get a federal order for that yet."

"Can you fax me a copy when you finish—background only?"

"Technically, no. Ethically, yes—so long as I cover myself. I have more faith in you than Defense. There won't be an investigation. AFIP's going to bury the whole damn case right along with the body. The only time they go nuts like this is when there's something there they don't want anyone to know about.

"You'll get an unofficial document from me in plain white sheet form, no letterhead, signature or seal. Won't stand up in a court of law, but it might help out somehow. The fax won't come from my office. I'll use an alternate source. What's your number?"

I gave him one that would send the document straight through to my e-mail and hold it in cyberspace until I picked it up.

We said good-bye, and I went back to watching the house.

She turned up at eight-thirty, on foot: a tiny young woman with a long black braid, dressed in a pink parka and nursing whites.

"Tina Delmar?" I called out, moving quickly to the drive.

Her face was pretty. China doll lips and pearls for teeth. Recognition flickered, and along with it suspicion and hate.

"Lacie Wagner," I said. "WRC-TV."

"What do you want?"

"To talk."

"It's late, and I'm coming off back-to-back ten-hour shifts."

"Tomorrow morning, then."

"No."

"When?"

"You're wasting your time. I have nothing to say of interest to the press."

"How about state police?" I said. "You want to answer questions cold from them tomorrow without knowing why they came? I'll leave now and let you do that."

She waited until I was at the curb, then called out: "Questions about what?"

I took that as an invitation and moved back up the drive. "A 1972 gold Cadillac registered in your name, towed from the waterfront a month ago."

Surprise flashed across her face, but her voice stayed flat. "So what," she said.

"Any crime associated with that car's going to send the police right to your door."

A cold wind blew dead leaves across her feet.

She shivered.

I waited.

"The car's mine," she finally said.

"I know that already. Why did it get towed?"

"It's my own damn fault." She backed out of the truth and into the lie. "I went out partying at the clubs one night, ended up going home with a guy in his car. We left mine there. It got towed. That's all."

"You let it sit in the tow yard for the last four weeks racking up a monster bill?"

"That's right."

"Why?"

"Double shifts and a low energy level."

"How do you get to work without it?"

"I take the bus."

"You take the bus when you could just go get your car out. Doesn't add up."

"Doesn't have to. It's my car and my life."

"You didn't loan the Cadillac to a friend."

"No."

"A friend named Sinclair."

"No." Dark eyes stayed flat and hard. She was digging in. "It's my own damn fault the car's there. Good night, Ms. Wagner."

"Do you dive, Tina?"

"No."

"The truth's a welcome change."

"I think you should leave now."

"I think I should stay."

"Give me one good reason."

"Your friend is dead."

"If anybody I know died, I'd be hearing about it straight from the family or police, not the press."

"You trust Special Ops to give the family the truth?"

"Is that what you're here with? The *truth?*"

I took Wheeler's photos out of my bag and held them up in a fan.

They hit her hard. But there was no other way. Good friends of Special Ops soldiers understand the importance of their work. They are wildly overprotective and will walk through fire to protect the privacy of a Special Ops recruit. Classified friendships, Max used to say. Stand-up friends. Tina was one through and through. Her jaw tightened, but she held her ground.

"You got a positive ID?" she asked.

"Not yet."

"So the body's still a Jane Doe."

"Officially."

"Cause of death?"

"Drowning."

"Then you've got the wrong girl."

"Why?"

"My friend's a hell of a swimmer. No way on God's great earth she drowned diving at sea."

"No way on God's great earth?"

"Where did you find her?"

"Nantucket. Two and half miles out from my own front door."

"Your floater's still a Jane Doe."

"Officially. I believe her name is Sinclair."

"So that's what you came looking for. You want to know her name."

"It's more complex than that."

"Death's a pretty straightforward thing."

"Not this one. The victim was Special Ops. That mean anything to you?"

"If it did, I wouldn't be at liberty to say."

"A classified friendship with Sinclair?"

She did not reply.

"The privilege ends at death," I said. I plucked a shot out of the fan and held it up, one with a close-up of the torso and head.

"Shit." She flinched, banded her arms around her stomach. "Your bedside manner sucks. What happened to her face?"

"The surf tossed her against the rock. She was already dead."

"And the burns?"

"She was alive for those."

Tina started to say something, then twisted around and dropped to the ground, vomiting into the deep carpet of leaves.

"I'm sorry," I said, feeling bad, but there had been no other way.

Tina swiped a hand across her mouth and made her way up the front steps. She fumbled with keys, cursing softly, opened the door, and paused.

"Her name is *Ashley* Sinclair," she said. "She lived here with me. The car's in my name, but we shared it. It's still sitting at the tow lot because they never sent me a notice. I thought Ashley was off in it somewhere. I thought she was coming back. You'd better come in."

Her living room was furnished in early American pine, matching pieces sold in sets on time payout deals. The kitchen was an open pass through, old but clean.

"I need a drink." She poured herself gin, straight up in a tall glass. "Want something? Beer, wine, vodka?"

"Water, thanks just the same."

"Ashley's drink," she said, filling a glass from the tap. "Water. That's all she ever had. Bubble water, flat water, tap water. On the rocks, straight up, and sometimes in a martini glass because she said she liked the way it looked. She's a health nut. *Was,* I mean."

"You knew her for a long time?"

"Eleven years. Half my life. We went to the same high school in Boston and became roommates after that right through college and the military. Ashley always liked the boys' games more than the girls': climbing trees, digging trenches to hide in. While the rest of us played Marco Polo at the school pool, she played commando all by herself, sitting underwater with a waterproof stopwatch, seeing how long she could go without coming up for air. She was nuts about the water from the start. Swam her way through college on a sports scholarship."

"Did she have family?"

"No. Her parents died in a car wreck when she was nineteen. Her dad was a commercial fisherman in Boston like mine."

"Boyfriend?"

"No."

"What about close friends?"

"Chris Preata. She was on the BU swim team with Ashley. Still lives in Boston. Chrissie spent Labor Day weekend here when Ashley had a few days off. Chrissie and me. That's it. Ashley can't have many close friends, can't—couldn't—have a normal life."

"You knew Ashley was Special Ops?"

"Of course."

"Did she tell you what she did?"

"Some. Ashley was proud. Said she'd been hand picked—yanked right out of SEALs training and put into something brand-new. 'The Ironmen of Special Ops,' she bragged, 'and I'm the only girl.' More guts, more glory. The Ashley way. She said her work had a globally important mandate, a big prestige factor and an even bigger paycheck. She never gave specifics. She couldn't. And I didn't push. I dated a guy from Special Ops once. I know how it goes.

"Ashley was always getting pulled out at the last minute on assignment. Once, in a restaurant, she took a call on her mobile and walked right out. Didn't come back for months. This time I didn't think it was any different. One day she was here; the next she was gone. Looked like it was business as usual—only she took the car. That's what I thought until last week. I came home one night and the place was a wreck, like a hurricane blasted through. They tossed the house and tossed it good."

"They?"

"Special Ops. Had to be. Everything that had anything to do with Ashley was gone. Her personal files. Mail. Checkbooks. Computer. Cleaned out her bathroom and closet. They even took her toothbrush. And they went through my things the same way. Took every damn snapshot I had of Ashley. Every videotape, too. Like they had wiped her off the face of the earth. I figured then they took the car, too. Ashley kept her gear in the trunk. You can't exactly go to the police and accuse Special Ops of stealing a car."

"When was the last time you saw her alive?"

"A month ago. At my birthday party. She gave me a pair of pearl earrings." She held up a small hand and closed her eyes. "Please go now, Ms. Wagner. I've told you everything that counts. Now I just want to be alone."

I called Harry as I walked down the drive and brought him up to speed.

"Your ID's tasting a hundred proof," he said. "We have to walk a fine line here, Lace. We can't go all out on SEATEC yet because we can't use your one eyewitness. But the documented facts you do have so far are strong enough to put on the air. How far are you now from Boston?"

"An hour and a half out. It's nine-thirty. I can make it in time for a live spot on the eleven o'clock news."

"I'll call over and set it up," Harry said. "I'm going to take you on a simulcast here. It just doesn't get much tastier than this."

But it could get hotter, I thought, dialing Hinks on her mobile.

A DA presence would add heat and pressure, make Spivak squirm.

Hinks was ready and willing and more than happy to go back on the air.

CHAPTER TWENTY-SIX

Lacie, serious Lacie, filling his wide-screen TV.

So controlled, Vale observed. Hard to imagine the woman in his arms the night before had been one and the same. He smoothed a crease in his dark cashmere slacks and leaned forward in his chair.

She was in a studio now, not on the beach, and instead of that gorgeous fire-colored hair blowing wild in the wind, it was twisted back in a neat glossy chignon. She was cool and sophisticated, her voice silky smooth. Only her eyes gave away her excitement, the rush of the story, the thrill of the chase.

"Despite the fact that Colonel Spivak claims that Ashley Sinclair was not in the military's employ, I learned today that Ms. Sinclair was stationed at a Special Ops training facility on Cape Cod and was part of an elite tactical unit reporting directly to Colonel Spivak.

"Spokesmen at Special Ops headquarters in Norfolk refuse comment tonight. The Department of Defense declines to comment on why the Armed Forces Pathological Unit forcibly removed the remains of Ms. Sinclair and all collaborative forensic evidence from the State Medical Examiner's Office in Boston earlier this evening. And, spokesmen for the navy at the Pentagon refuse to comment on the victim, her identity, or the circumstances surrounding her death."

The camera panned over to the assistant DA.

Vale watched, riveted.

"Without a full and vigorous investigation of the very troubling circumstances surrounding Ms. Sinclair's death," the blond DA said, "we will not know where the ultimate jurisdiction for prosecutorial and judicial relief resides. Until then, we believe the investigation should be conducted by the Massachusetts state police with the full and enthusiastic cooperation of Department of Defense. The total lockdown that AFIP has perpetuated on the state medical examiner and investigative unit of state police is unacceptable, unprofessional, and unethical.

"We do not have faith that AFIP or Defense will be forthcoming with the results of a closed independent investigation. Their behavior thus far has shown they are all too willing to issue false statements to the press and public, and there is no reason to believe that will change now.

"Someone's daughter, friend, and possibly spouse died in a terrible way under suspicious circumstances. It is the state's mandate to find out if criminal action was involved, and if so to administer the best and full remedy in the appropriate court of law, be that a state, federal, or naval court—a jurisdiction only the factual truth will determine. We will not be silenced on this matter."

Lacie and the assistant DA.

Scylla and Charybdis, Vale decided, thinking of the two mythical sea creatures who lured sailors to their deaths in the Strait of Messina.

Scylla and Charybdis, right there on his screen.

Two posing beauties who were really dangerous beasts.

Lacie was doing much more than report the story. She was stirring up a high-profile investigation.

Vale moved quickly, back rigid and straight, good shoes sinking into wet earth and not caring.

Fury filled him, but he kept it tightly locked down as he walked purposefully, a heavy bucket in each of his two strong hands. He took them out two at a time, until there was only one left to carry, and then the row of buckets at the pool edge numbered seven.

They were filled with water from each of his seven tanks.

Rain splashing in now made aquatic cocktails with colorful cubes.

Vale dipped his hands in a bucket and let the colors wash over his skin. Silky soft, feather light, they were the tiny bodies of his flamboyant fish wriggling and swishing over his wrists, slipping in between his fingers.

Vale caressed fins and dorsals and tiny fluttering gills.

They swam in his palm, flapped and swished against his flesh.

Kneeling on the wet ground in the dark, he knew their genera by feel—the round belly of the fighter, the diaphanous fan of the angel. He brought one tiny fish close to his cheek, felt the heaving side, the thrashing tail, the rolling dorsals, the fluttering gills.

He held it against his cheek, his chin, his ear, and lips as he tasted the panic of his brightly colored tiny captive.

Then Vale thought of Lacie, smug there with the DA, and his tightly contained anger burst. He hoisted buckets, tossed the contents into his pool—flinging, spilling, pouring water and fish and gravel and sand and filters and shipwrecks and tiny plastic mermaid busts until the buckets were empty.

He covered the pool and walked away from the pool and the house to his waiting car in the drive. His shoulders were squared, hands curled at his sides.

Vale was humming. He was pleased with his work.

CHAPTER TWENTY-SEVEN

Back at Hyannis, Hinks and I walked the harbor piers too wired from the day to call it quits. The sky was on fire with white diamond-studded constellations, the surf drummed against pilings, seabirds roosted on the docks. Low-slung chubby fishing ketches rocked next to sleek sailboats and commercial trawlers. Winches were high-necked and white against the night sky, nets piled up on deck were rolling jute dunes.

Hinks had her hands jammed deep in her pockets and her collar turned up against the night cold. "Ever been to Kodiak, Alaska?" she asked.

"No."

"Good. Don't go. Coldest goddamn water on the face of the earth."

"The Bering Sea."

"Right. On a calm night there, open water waves are the size of Tom Wheeler, and a seventy-mile-an-hour wind is considered mild. Storms blow up out of nowhere, flip boats in ten seconds flat. It's a remote, brutal, extremely isolated place."

"What makes you think of Kodiak?"

"My father drowned out there when I was a kid. More fishermen die there than any other place on the planet. It's dangerous water but rich with snow crab, swordfish, and salmon. Fishermen who brave it are paid top price. My dad couldn't make enough on Nantucket running one small private boat. He left me here with my mom, went to Kodiak, and made five times more. One night, a monster wave swept him right off the deck and he drowned. I think that's probably why I swim so much—as if it will help me save someone's life one day, maybe my own."

Hinks put a foot up on the rail, looked out at the boats, and inhaled, taking in damp salty air that smelled richly of fish. I stayed quiet and let her go on.

"People trip all over each other to get a place out on the island," she said, "and I've spent my whole life trying to get the hell away. Well, I am twenty-four miles from the Nantucket shore and am still surrounded by the same sights and smells: fish. Can't seem to get away from the goddamn fish. Maybe I should go to Boston and join a private practice. Be a defense attorney instead of assistant DA. Boston's a good city. Pay will certainly be better than here."

"What if you win the election?"

"Then I'll go to Boston in five years anyway and with a hell of a good credit to boot."

"What about Tom Wheeler?"

She looked at me and carefully said, "What about him?"

"Where does he fit in?"

"He doesn't, at the moment. His choice. Not mine."

"Maybe it's because he thinks you're going to Boston, one way or another, like his ex-wife did."

"He told you about that?"

"The subject came up."

"Wheeler doesn't usually open up to strangers about his personal life." She dropped her foot off the rail and straightened, regretting the momentary slip of her own personal guard. "District Attorney Taggert called tonight after the cast. He formally pulled me off the case and shut the investigation down."

"Why?"

"I got some high level uniforms at Defense stirred up by what I said, and they have found ears in the Senate. That in turn has run straight to Taggert. Everyone knows he's going to win his Senate race. Hell, he has already picked out furniture for his office on Capitol Hill. Quid pro quo: 'Help us now, Taggert, we'll help you out down the line.' That game means more to him than anything local now here."

"What if you were in his shoes?"

"I would do the same damn thing, but I'm mad at him anyway."

Hinks took her heels off and leapt down on the burnished deck of a sleek red cigarette boat berthed at our feet.

"Hop in," she said, patting the rim. "There are no more ferries or planes running to the island tonight. I'll give you a lift. *Ruby* here is one of my few perks. The state confiscated this rocket ship in a drug bust. She'll ride us across in twenty minutes flat in this kind of calm. Fresh cold air will do me good. I can't sleep anyway, I'm so pissed off at Taggert."

Hinks offered a hand.

I took it and stepped in.

It was the right thing to do.

CHAPTER TWENTY-EIGHT

At two-thirty in the morning, on the taxi ride home from Nantucket's main dock, I wanted nothing but sleep—until I saw all the lights blazing in Vale's aquarium house, his empty drive, and wide open front door.

The driver let me out at the front steps. I rang the bell, waited, rang again, then walked on inside.

The big sliding glass doors fronting the deck were wide open, too.

Two bodies in the rain. His seductive words in my ear.

Now, all I heard was the wind and waves.

No rain. No Vale.

Something else was missing. The whoosh of the aquatic air-filter systems. I turned around.

The aquariums were gone. There were no sea horses, no angel fish, no water, nothing but the empty wall—an ominous symbol I didn't yet understand. The living room was neat, the dining room orderly, kitchen wiped clean.

Upstairs guest suites were immaculate, as if a cleaning crew had just been through. Model boats were gone from the study, the pedestals, too. There were no photo-

graphs of Vale, no framed clippings of Geostar's mete-
oric success, nothing now but plain white walls. I went
down the hall and opened the master bedroom door.

Two hungry bodies twining sheets into a sweaty heap.

The bed was stripped down to a plastic-covered mattress. No sheets, blankets, or pillows. The open closet
was empty, the bathroom bare. The sea green towels I
used after my shower, the Japanese robe I had worn,
Vale's handheld razor, his toothbrush, shampoo. Every
trace of Vale was gone.

As if I had dreamed him.

As if he had never existed at all.

Just then my cell phone rang.

There was no voice, just the sound of water—the
whisper light music of waves brushing sand.

Someone's talking to you, Wheeler had said, holding
the little toy diver. *Someone's talking to you Lacie, just
not using words.*

My body registered the implications a split second
ahead of my brain.

My breath turned shallow, my heart raced as my pulse
kicked up.

I felt used, abandoned, cheap, and then something far
worse.

I felt chosen.

Targeted, suffused with a wild racing dread.

What had I done? What in God's name had I done?

I fled the house, cut across the moor on the old stone
path, and waited the night out asking questions of walls.

As the sun was first rising, I called Wheeler.

A half hour later, he was on my front deck.

"Things are happening," I said. "Things I don't understand."

My voice caught. I couldn't go on.

He circled my shoulders with his big arms. "Come.
Let's walk awhile."

He took me far down the beach to a curve in the bluff where it was warm in the sun. We sat down side by side, Indian style, facing the waves. The Old Whale Rock was a black pinprick in the distance, a granite mirage.

"Take it slow now," Wheeler said. "One step at a time."

I told him about SEATEC and all I had learned. I chose my words carefully, clearly delineating conjecture from fact, leading up to the description of Vale's stripped aquarium house.

"Ashley Sinclair looked like me," I said, summing up. "What do you think, Wheeler? What does your scientific mind say about that?"

"Wheeler the scientist chalks it up to pure random chance."

"And the superstitious Wheeler?"

"Believes it's powerfully symbolic. Intimately tied into why Ashley Sinclair was planted where you would find her."

"And what about Vale? Why did he leave? Where did he go? Who exactly did I sleep with?"

"The wrong man." Wheeler's blue eyes bored into mine. "Tell me what you feel."

"Targeted."

"Explain."

"Like I was chosen for a purpose and reasons I don't yet understand."

"And?"

"I can't begin to explain who or what Vale is, but my instinct tells me to be afraid of him now. I'm not going to be a victim. Not again. Not ever. I will not sit here with unanswered questions. I have to go after him. I have no choice. But I can't do it alone. I need resources, access, the weight of the law."

"Christ," he said. "What I really want to do is airlift you out of here and hide you away."

"Not an option. Think proactive."

He looked at me, reluctance brimming in his bright eyes.

"Hinks's investigation has been shut down by the DA," I said. "It's one hundred percent AFIP's now. I can't go to the Bureau. Defense has got the body, and as far as the Bureau's concerned, AFIP's a four-letter word. The feds will smile politely and throw me right out the door. There's no one left, is there?"

Wheeler ran his hands over his smooth head. "Not necessarily," he said. "There's one man. . . ."

"Who?"

"Nick St. James. He's been a lot of things in his life. A rescue swimmer with the navy, a parachute rescue jumper, a SEAL, a U.S. marshal after that."

"And now?"

"St. James is retired. He's got a license, but he's not a full-on private investigator. He only takes cases no one else wants or that can't be cracked. The feds hate him, not to mention the state police, but that doesn't stop them from calling him in when they're stuck. He's the last resort, the guy the law turns to when the law runs headfirst into a brick wall."

"How do you know him?"

"I don't. I just know of him, through McKenzie. St. James has worked a couple of federal cases that involved the state ME. He can turn a cold case to hot like no one else, and he's a legendary man-hunter, top-notch at finding men who don't want to be found. And, he has access to federal and state resources. You'd best be prepared, though. Nick St. James won't fit your idea of a standard investigator."

"Good. This is anything but a standard investigation. I want him."

"McKenzie has the relationship, not me."

We called McKenzie on Wheeler's mobile, passing

the little phone back and forth, briefing the chief ME. He promised to get back to us as soon as he had something to say.

We waited out the full day.

Wheeler's phone rang at five, as we were sitting on my porch steps.

"You'll have to go up and see St. James," McKenzie explained. "He wants to hear the details from you in person. Then, if he agrees to take the job, he'll discuss his fee."

"Where does he live?" I asked, thinking of Boston or New York, some major urban metropolis close by.

"Way north. Twenty miles off the coast of Maine, on Rams Island. That's St. James's place."

"He owns the island?"

"St. James is a wealthy man," McKenzie said.

"Why does he bother to work?"

"Ask him. It's late now. He's expecting you tonight. Pack a bag. He said he'd take care of finding you accommodations. You'll need a private plane to get there. He'll have someone meet you on his landing strip."

I already liked St. James. He was a man of action. He didn't waste time.

"One other thing," McKenzie said. "The hair in the brush you sent me is a match. Jane Doe is Ashley Sinclair."

CHAPTER TWENTY-NINE

Wheeler drove me out to the Nantucket airstrip, and I hired a young pilot with a Cessna to fly me point to point. Wheeler loaded my suitcase in the belly of the plane.

"Take care now," he said, hands heavy and warm on my shoulders. "Take good care."

I boarded and settled into my seat. Looking out the tiny window, I saw Wheeler standing on the side of the runway, arms clasped behind his body, the smooth orb of his skull picking up the late afternoon sun.

The Cessna started to roll. "Fasten your seat belt," the pilot called out over the whining props. "It's going to be bumpy."

We flew over a long narrow sandy finger of shore, the Sankaty lighthouse perched at the end, and out over the shallow shoals gliding at such low altitude the opal-colored ocean seemed close enough to touch.

"This clear sky's deceptive," the pilot shouted back at me, over the engines. "Higher up, winds are so strong we'd get bounced around something fierce. It's slower going down here, but smoother."

He flew a straight shot across Massachusetts Bay, then north, skimming the rocky coastline of Cape Cod.

I counted lighthouses—two in Boston Harbor, one just past Salem, four at Cape Anne alone, one in New Hampshire, one just opposite at the Isle of Shoals, and after that we crossed over into the wilds of Maine. It was lonely country where summer was a short eight-week reprieve in ten months of cold.

North of Bar Harbor, past Jonesport and fifty miles beyond, the plane veered right in a hard half roll out to open sea. The tiny Cessna window framed minute details of the seascape: a pelican gliding low hunting for prey, wind stirring water to a greenish gray, a school of fish running south, the wake of a speedboat pearling out in a wide white tail.

"That's Rams Island below us now," the pilot said.

Money buys privilege, and privacy is one of the priciest privileges around. An entire island up north in the wilderness, with no neighbors for miles. I wondered what kind of man would choose to live in such isolation, surrounded by glacial water and dense dark forest.

We started our descent over a long piece of land running north to south, a densely wooded teardrop in the Atlantic green. A single black sweep of tarmac was carved out of the trees.

"There's not much length to the runway," the pilot said. "Hold on."

We dipped in over the pines and touched down hard. Shrieking engines wound down, and the Cessna stopped. I unbuckled my seat belt.

The pilot came out of the cockpit and opened the cabin door.

The sound of growling dogs drifted in. Three Great Danes crouched on the tarmac, ears flat and teeth bared. Someone whistled sharply. They backed off and sat at attention, heads cocked, waiting.

"It's okay," a man's voice called out. "Don't pay the dogs any mind."

My pilot lowered the staircase. I followed him down.

Cold wind slapped me in the face, cut right through my coat. There was nothing at all left of summer and little of fall. Snow was in the air, the promise of winter creeping down from Canada. The sun hung low in the west and was speared by the tops of looming pines. Shadows fell in long dark columns across the strip. The pilot passed me my bag.

"I'm going to take off before it gets dark," the pilot said. "Looks like your ride waiting over there."

He pointed to a lone figure in the shadows, a man sitting ramrod straight astride a chestnut stallion. A smaller honey-colored horse waited alongside. I waited out the Cessna's turnaround and takeoff. When it was gone, I crossed the tarmac and approached.

The rider dismounted. He wore a long, black cowskin coat and black leather riding boots. His straight silver hair was combed back, revealing a high forehead and aristocratic face. Brown eyes studied me behind wire-rim glasses, and although his pale skin was lined, it was hard to know his age.

"Mr. St. James?" I asked.

"No," he said. "I'm Hathaway. I'll be escorting you back to the house at the opposite end of Rams Island. There are no roads here. I hope you don't mind horses."

His stallion was stamping and snorting, pawing the earth.

"I have ridden," I said warily, "but it's been a long time."

"Don't worry," Hathaway said, "the mare's docile and slow."

A black wool cape lay across the saddle. Hathaway pulled it off and passed it to me.

"Your coat's not heavy enough for the cold up here," he said. "These are old-fashioned but functional. Heavy Irish wool. Keeps the damp out and your body heat in."

He draped the cape around my shoulders. It was ankle-length and heavy. The high collar touched my jaw. Hathaway was right. The wool was a barrier, shutting out the wind and the wet chilled air.

Although I had not been on a horse since I was a child, my body remembered the moves. Since mounting was mostly legwork, I had no problem getting on. Hathaway lashed my overnight bag to the pommel and mounted his horse.

"Ready?" he asked.

"Yes."

He pressed his boots into the stallion and we were off, the three Danes trotting alongside. The reins rested lightly in my hands. The mare knew the way and needed no guidance from me. We went down a rough-cut riding trail, in through the trees.

"All this land here is a nature preserve," Hathaway

politely explained. "The main house and staff quarters were built a hundred and ten years ago. Zoning laws forbid further development."

"Do you live out here year-round?" I asked.

"Yes," Hathaway said. "I take care of things for Mr. St. James, look after the house and the island when he isn't here."

"He's not married?"

Hathaway smiled slightly, amused. "No," he said. "Mr. St. James doesn't have a wife."

"What about children?"

"Kids?" Hathaway laughed. "None that he knows of."

"What kind of answer is that?"

"An honest one," Hathaway said seriously, looking back.

We rode side by side, sometimes through forest so thick and dark it was hard to see, other times skirting the rocky shoreline. From time to time Hathaway pointed out something of interest: the oldest tree on the island, the Indian graves, and a sad sight, a small cove where a baby whale lay washed up dead on shore.

Beyond the cove, the house appeared on a promontory, an imposing two-story white colonial with six chimneys and a sweeping flight of front steps.

"Come," Hathaway said, dark eyes shining like polished onyx. "Mr. St. James doesn't like to be kept waiting."

He picked up the pace, and my horse naturally fell in.

A quarter mile on, I saw detail in the house, how the white paint was peeling, and the garden was overrun with weeds. Hathaway glanced over, and satisfied I was well seated in the saddle, he kicked his stallion into a canter. My mare followed suit, and soon we were dismounting at the main entrance. Brick steps were covered with dark lichen and moss, the brass door knocker tarnished and dull.

Hathaway took off his coat, and I saw he was wearing formal butler attire underneath. He guided me through an entry hall and across the main floor. As run-down as the outside of the house was, the interior was immaculately well kept. St. James was wealthy, McKenzie had said. Judging from the furniture and paintings, that had been an understatement.

We walked through rooms with burnished wood floors and oriental rugs. Most had massive stone fireplaces. There were wonderful old grandfather clocks, polished antique silver, and dark oil paintings of classic seascapes, ships tossing on high angry seas.

Hathaway opened a set of French doors. "Mr. St. James is waiting for you."

I stepped out onto a wide deck that faced west, looking over shimmering water.

St. James was leaning against the rail. The way Wheeler had described him, I had pictured a genteel silver-haired man military in bearing and certainly past his prime. I had expected a suit-and-tie federal Moses, a crew-cut miracle worker, the ultimate superagent. I never expected the man who stood before me.

"Mr. St. James?"

"City manners to go with the city dress," he replied, moving away from the rail. "You're in the woods now, so Nick will do."

He was six two, long and lean and all male, a wholly primal creature. His hair was the same color as mine but longer. He wore it loose and wild, spilling over his shoulders, an auburn tangle framing a battered, deeply tanned face. Wolf gray eyes smoked out at me. The carnal attraction was so strong it reminded me of Vale, and I stepped back, afraid.

At first glance, there was nothing formal or genteel about St. James, other than the house he lived in. He wore scuffed leather hiking boots, old black jeans, and a frayed black polo shirt. His hands were covered with scars from knives and hooks and white half-moons that looked to be marks from other men's teeth.

His lips were full, his nose aquiline, and his cheekbones were Dakota Plains, wide and high and flat. There was Indian in St. James mixed with something else. The Indian was in his face, the rich tawny cast of his skin, and the way he carried his body, the graceful way he moved, prowling the porch. The something else was in his light eyes and the wheat gold streaking his fire-colored hair.

And then there were the scars, one running north to south on his forehead, two east to west across the Dakota cheeks, and a small lightning fork split his lower lip. He wore his scars like prizes, proof of adventure, life lived, lives taken: St. James's courage measured in channels of injured flesh.

He took his time lighting a cigarette, cupping the match flame against the wind, breathing it to life, squinting at me while he exhaled as smoke curled up into his eyes.

"Lacie Wagner," he said. "Miles McKenzie didn't tell me you were a beauty."

"My looks are hardly germane to the case."

"Aren't they?" White teeth flashed, dark brows arched. "What makes you so sure about that?"

The wind had picked up, blowing cold on my face.

St. James in short sleeves, oblivious of the temperature, was watching me.

"Can we go inside?" I asked.

"Not yet. Sunset's the prettiest time here. Hate to miss one." St. James dropped into a slope-backed Adirondack chair and patted the chair next to his. "Have a seat."

"I prefer to stand."

"So formal, pretty Lacie. A day or two around me and you'll relax."

"You don't know what the case is yet. You haven't heard the details. You may not want to take it. In a day or two, I might not be around."

"You will be. Let's talk about my fee."

"I'm not convinced I should hire you."

He laughed again, a big, full-throated laugh. He was genuinely amused. "You want me to prove my worth?"

"I'd like you to hear the specifics; then I'd like to listen to your game plan, St. James."

"You dropped the *mister.* We're making progress, and the night's still young."

"Save it for another time and another woman."

"Save nothing, for tomorrow may never come."

"Well, I've come a long way," I said, standing in front of him, blocking his view. "I'm tired and cold, and I don't have time to waste."

He smiled, lazy and content. "I like women and wine too much for my own good," he said, "but I pretty much swear off both when I'm working."

"Is that your idea of an apology?"

"Close as I can come."

"Let's talk about the case."

"And you'll decide if I'm qualified, isn't that where we left off?"

"Yes."

"Tell you what," he said, looking up at me with those pale wolf eyes. "Lay it all out for me, and *I'll* decide if I'm qualified."

Hathaway appeared with a steaming cup of hot tea. "Mr. St. James thought you might be cold," he said.

"Thank you." I took the cup. Hathaway disappeared inside.

"See?" St. James said. "I'm not as uncivilized as I look. A man's face reveals nothing of his soul. Most folks haven't learned that yet. Until they do, my appearance has its advantages. It's easier tracking criminals if you look a little lawless yourself." He patted the chair next to him again. "You're missing the sunset."

I sat down.

"How long were you with the marshals?" I asked.

"Five years even."

"Short stay."

"Too true."

"They throw you out for bad behavior?"

"No, I quit."

"Where were you before that?"

"Navy at the start. Rescue swimmer for a few years; then I went into the paratroopers for eight glorious years and Special Ops for five after that."

"Why?"

"Because it was fun. Blowing up the bad guys, sneaking in on foreign beaches at midnight, sabotaging enemy subs. A grade-A rush. I loved it."

"Why did you quit?"

"I said I quit the marshals, not the military."

"Why did you leave Special Ops?"

"They threw me out. I had a problem with authority. Still do. But the *official* reason was different. I took a bullet in the head and spent eight weeks in a coma. That gave them a chance to toss me out with an honorable discharge. The navy shrink was afraid I had posttraumatic stress syndrome from the incident, that I'd blow up at the wrong time in the wrong place."

"Was he right?"

St. James laughed. "Probably. Anyway, I kissed Defense good-bye and signed up with the Department of Justice."

"Why do I think it wasn't out of an altruistic sense of law and order?"

"Good detective work." He grinned again. "I'm a thrill seeker. I live for the rush."

"U.S. Marshals is a branch of the Justice Department

with a traditional chain of command, top-down authority. What made you okay with that?"

"They let me run solo. I was a one-man bounty hunter
who happened to stand on the right side of the law. Out
in the field, success is the only thing that counts. My job
was hunting men, and I was the best the marshals ever
had."

"How do you work now without your old support systems?"

"Come. I'll show you."

He strolled through the open French doors. I followed him in.

"One thing you'll learn about me," he said, leading
me down a steep flight of stairs, "is that when it comes
to the tools of my trade, I'm state of the art. The outside
of my house is run-down on purpose. I don't want to attract attention from the wrong kind of people. Not that
my security here would be easy to breach. I've got cameras and infrared fences circling the island. Animals set
them off all the time, but the security's worth the hassle.
When a site in the fence is breached, Hathaway checks
it out."

He stopped in front of a large metal door and tapped
a code in on a keypad lock.

"Why not just use house alarms?"

"By the time a man's close enough to trip a house
alarm, he's close enough to kill me. I've made more than
a few enemies along the way."

He opened the steel door and stepped in.

A six-foot-by-six-foot flat plasma screen hung suspended from the ceiling at one end of the room, and a
bank of computer monitors and keyboards lined the
other. In between was a walnut conference table ringed
with six leather chairs. A climate control read-out on
the wall said the air was a comfortable seventy-two degrees.

St. James walked me through a door into a second room as large as the first, packed with digital, video, audio, computer equipment, and a wraparound three-sided work bay. There were two rolling swivel chairs and a three-foot-square ultrathin plasma screen that rose up out of the desk like a strange flower. The screen saver was a custom job—full-motion video of the Atlantic in a storm. Rolling white-capped swells, breaking waves in open sea, raging wind and surf the size of small buildings. It made me seasick. I turned away.

"In an investigation," St. James said, "information is power. And when it comes to gathering and analyzing information, technology is king. I have everything I need here. Part of my agreement with the feds. Cell phone triangulation, digital audio recording, digital imaging analysis and processing, and so forth. The nerve center of my computer system and my mini-lab is there."

He pointed to a wall packed floor to ceiling with computer hard drives.

"Everything down here runs on a dedicated generator," he said, "and there's a backup to that. I have my own network and server through which I have full access to the Bureau resources, including credit and DMV records, fingerprint database, state and federal tax information, the works."

"What don't you have here?"

"My own lab. I've got some rudimentary equipment—scanning electron microscope, Poli-light, evidence collection, things like that. I use the FBI crime lab when I need to, but frankly the standards have slipped, so I go private. That kind of expertise comes at a high price, but if you're willing to pay the bill, you can buy the experience and cognitive power of some of the best forensic analysts in the country."

He rolled a swivel chair across the floor to me. "Have a seat."

I did.

He straddled his own and wheeled over next to me, facing the floating screen.

"I'm not a beer-drinking illiterate howdy-doody boy who works with nothing but gut instinct, a big gun, and a six-pack. I do have a traditional weapon, a beautiful Sig Sauer that I never leave behind. I've discovered that as handy as a gun is for face-to-face combat, technology's a far more effective weapon for hunting a man. I'm set up here with a wireless satellite Internet connection. There's really nothing I can't find if I put in the time."

He touched the mouse and the raging seascape changed into a full color news photo, one that had run in the national press. It was a tabloid shot of me taken leaving the hospital the previous January. My face and head were wrapped in white gauze like a mummy. St. James touched a key and the photo dissolved, revealing a solid page of text.

"This is a brief summary of your life," he said. "I compiled it from a variety of sources, some on the Net, some buried deep in government databases. Uncle Sam kept track of you because your father, technically speaking, was a DOD employee with top-level security clearance."

"That was a long time ago."

"Uncle Sam never forgets." He turned to the screen and read out loud. "Lacie Wagner. Born thirty-five years ago to Richard and Cynthia Wagner. An only child and a normal one until the age of ten."

I closed my eyes but I couldn't shut out his voice. He went on reading my life story in a clipped, emotionless way. For a life that had been filled with so much emotion, it was painful to hear. He knew everything about the first fire that killed my father and destroyed my hands, my mother's subsequent suicide and how I spent my teenage years with Max after that.

He had hospital records describing the injuries to my hands—medical descriptions five pages long detailing the handicap, the depth, degree, and result of the burns. He had sketches, details of skin grafts, documentation of muscle loss, results from my dexterity tests.

"Ten years old," St. James said, "and it was hell to hold a pencil, a challenge to write your name. Edward Beane killed your father and last fall he killed your daughter's father, too. He held your daughter hostage for eight long weeks. With the help of a rogue agent at the Bureau, you hunted Beane down and killed him, setting your daughter free."

He hit a key and ran the CNN national news clip of federal agent Jack Stein, my daughter, and me surrounded by police and mountain rescue and ambulances after the final deadly confrontation with Beane.

He froze the frame, leaned back in his chair, and studied the screen.

"Jack Stein," he mused. "Federal legend. FBI gem. He saved you once. How is it you're not back on his doorstep asking him to go one more round?"

"He's on another case."

"A little white lie." The screen flashed over to the *New York Times* shot of Jack, tired and drawn, ducking into a patrol car, pulling away, out of sight. "Stein just closed a case. If we're going to work as a team, you have to be straight with me now. Word around the Bureau is that you and Stein were lovers."

"The answer to your question is implied in the tense."

"The affair's over. But that doesn't mean he wouldn't help if you asked. Are you too proud to go back for round two?"

"No. I don't want to put him in the line of fire, figuratively or politically."

St. James nodded, leaned back in his chair and put his feet up on his desk, giving me his full attention.

I laid out the events of the last week in detail, then gave him a file with all my notes including my interviews with Spivak and Tina Delmar. For the next half hour, St. James went through them carefully while I waited. Finally he looked up, eyebrows raised.

"Spivak!" he said.

"You know him?"

"Six degrees of separation. I'm still trying to figure out if he was hatched or born."

"And?"

"I'm leaning toward hatched. He's one hard-assed son of a bitch. He started out as a parachute jumper same time I did. You're saying *Spivak's* running SEATEC?"

"That's right."

"Holy shit. God help the recruits. There's a man without a soul. He's got to be monumentally pissed off that you're digging around on his turf. Spivak could be your mysterious caller. He's mad. I'd say when it comes to motive, the colonel's got the upper hand. He could be threatening you."

"Ashley was clearly planted so I would find her. Spivak didn't do that."

"When I start an investigation, I go after the conflicting facts, the pieces that don't fit together, inconsistencies that don't add up."

"What's your deal?"

"A one-time fee, fully refundable if I don't succeed."

"How much?" I asked, ready to pay anything even if the station wouldn't because I needed his skills. I could not do this alone.

"One U.S. dollar. Cash. No checks, no credit cards, no promissory notes. A buck up front. Can you handle that?"

"I'm not in the mood for jokes."

"I'm as serious as can be, Lacie. I don't give a damn

about money. I don't keep track of what or when or how much I spend. I was born with more than my share of hormones and cash. My goal in life is to use up both before I die."

"Then why the dollar?"

"It's a genetic thing. St. James men have always been capitalists, banking and industrial commerce. They never ever did anything for free. And, contract law stipulates that a contract must have two things to be valid: a meeting of the minds between the parties and material consideration. There is one other point that is nonnegotiable: I work alone. No state police. No DAs. No feds. Just me. I work alone. If you agree, then pay up, and we're signed and sealed."

I couldn't help but laugh. "You're crazy."

"I've been called worse."

I took a dollar bill out of my bag and gave it to him.

He tucked it in his pocket, leaned forward in his chair, and worked the computer keyboard.

"We have three major conflicts staring us in the face," he said. "One, Spivak. He swears Sinclair isn't his, but then does a turnaround and sends AFIP in to confiscate the remains. He's acting like a guilty party.

"Two, Ashley Sinclair was wearing SEATEC-controlled gear. If she didn't die on their watch, how and why did she get the gear?

"Three, Vale. Ashley Sinclair washes up dead at your feet on the beach where you and Vale live. The next day Vale makes a move on you and then suddenly when you nail Sinclair's ID, Vale disappears. What kind of car did he have?"

"Dark blue Lexus. Four-door sedan. Smelled new inside."

"Plates?"

"I'm not sure. Massachusetts, I think. He said he lived in Boston."

"Assuming he told you the truth. Did you take any snapshots of him?"

"No."

"Did he rent the house?"

"He never said. From the way he talked I thought he owned it."

"What's the address?"

"I'm 2048 Clifton Way. Vale would be 2050."

"That's enough to keep me busy tonight. Leave me your cell phone. I should have some answers for you in the morning."

"Meaning what?"

"It's late, and pretty as you are, you look wiped out, like you haven't slept in a few nights. Hathaway will bring you dinner in the dining room. You'll find your suitcase upstairs. This old house has eight bedrooms to choose from, including mine if you like."

"How thoughtful. The ultimate host."

"Rejection noted," he said, smiling easily. "I'm a direct man. I say what's on my mind. So let's leave it like this: Consider my interest stated. The rest is up to you. And don't lose any sleep over my so-called reputation. I never go where I'm not invited."

He turned his back and went to work.

I put my cell phone on his desk and went up to the dining room.

A single place was set at the end of a mile-long table lined with fourteen straight backed chairs. Old silver, a heavy linen napkin, a cut-crystal wineglass, and one white candle burning. Fire of any size unsettled me. I blew it out and sat down. The empty chairs reminded me of how alone I was. Hathaway appeared at my side, elegant in his English butler attire. He filled my glass with red wine.

"A 1985 Lafite," he said. "Mr. St. James made the choice."

He showed me the label and waited as I tasted it.

"Superb," I said. It was.

"Mr. St. James prefers red wine with fish."

Hathaway served. "Filet of sea bass," he said, "grilled with olive oil and lemon. Baby potatoes are roasted with rosemary, and the bread is home-baked sour-dough."

I tasted the fish. "It's excellent."

"Mr. St. James will be pleased. He cooked everything for you himself."

Hathaway stood off to one side, white-gloved hands behind his back, eyes focused politely on the wall while I ate. Eight massive oil paintings were hung around the room.

"Who are they?" I asked.

"The patrimonial gallery," Hathaway replied. "That's Mr. St. James's great-great-grandfather there at the end. Crossed the Atlantic from England in 1710. The works are displayed in chronological order, starting to your left."

The first seven faces all looked much the same: white-haired and stern, with icy pale eyes set like stones. They glared out at me across the years, righteous and prosperous, as if they were not yet dead.

"Is that St. James's father at the opposite end?" I asked.

"Yes."

He had the same fine-boned features as the rest of the St. James males, but his smile was the only one out of the group that seemed genuinely soft and welcoming. A gentle-eyed dreamer, a romantic among steel-mongering ancestors.

"Is he still alive?" I asked.

"No. Mr. St. James lost his mother and father in a plane crash twenty years ago."

"He must be very proud of his patrimonial heritage."

"On the contrary," Hathaway replied. "With the exception of his father, he keeps these up to remind him of the kind of man he never wants to be."

After dinner, I made my way up the big oak staircase. All the doors were closed, except one at the end of the hall. I looked in and knew this was St. James's bedroom. It had a stone fireplace, four-poster bed, and white-framed windows looking out over water. The air smelled of cigar smoke, Bordeaux, and old leather. Sheets and blankets on the bed were a tangled mess. Two wing-back chairs were buried under piles of jeans and sweaters. Books were stacked up ten high on the end tables and floor. Forensic pathology, satellite technology, computer programming, and poetry, too— Browning, Barrett, W. B. Yeats. A collection as eclectic and puzzling as the man.

Framed photos crowded his fireplace mantel. A strikingly beautiful woman was the same in each. She had heavy black hair, full lips, and high cheeks, sparkling eyes and a confident smile—beautiful bone structure, St. James's tawny skin, and high, arching brows. His mother, I guessed. His own face echoed clearly in hers. In every shot, she wore doeskin pants and a matching shirt. In one, she carried a bow and arrow and stood proud over a kill.

I chose a bedroom at the opposite end of the hall, white-walled and airy with a canopy bed and crisp white sheets. There were brass lamps on beautiful polished antique end tables, fresh flowers in a cut crystal vase. I stripped off my clothes and crawled between the sheets. Sleep came in fits, broken with nightmares of raging fires and towering seas, tumultuous dreams of two coupling bodies in the pouring rain.

CHAPTER THIRTY

The Atlantic was a fucking bucking bronco, Vale thought, grinning, legs spread wide, riding the hard pitching roll of the boat with the ease and grace of a man born to the sea.

Twenty-two miles off the coast of Cape Cod, speeding along in a Boston Whaler customized with two million dollars of Special Ops electronics, conditions were ideal: The wind was high, the sea furious, and visibility was dead zero.

"Fucking heaven," Vale said under his breath, glancing back at the men sitting at attention, under his exclusive command. They knew him as Andreas Villard, special training consultant to the Special Ops tactical unit SEATEC. Villard, whose white-blond hair and amber eyes were as memorable as his training style.

Vale smiled. These men were at his mercy. And he had none. Not on this night or on any other.

Vale checked the bank of sonar and LCD screens lining the instrument console. GPS coordinates were locking in. They were getting close. He eased back on the throttle and slowed. The sonar pinged, locking in his target fifty feet below.

Vale cut the engines and spun around.

Ten divers suited up in hooded black wet suits and full face masks sat on hard slats watching him. Against the dark sea and moonless black sky, they were almost invisible. Only the whites of eyes flashed in the night.

Vale was a human beacon, his phosphorescent orange

wet suit strobing color every time his lean powerful body made a move. The hood glowed with the outline of his skull. His long white-blond hair was hidden underneath. He wore no mask, and his face was blacked out with grease. Only the spectral whites of his eyes and the white enamel of his teeth showed in that void. The effect imbued him with an intimidation factor of the highest degree.

Vale wanted it that way: the recruits seeing pleasure in the white split of his smile and glittering eyes, and he in turn measuring the fear in theirs.

At this moment, the ten divers were highly tense and alert. They wore Interspiro face masks fitted with Lar-5 microphone and earpiece adapters enabling two-way communication with Vale during the dive.

Vale wore a mini boom mike on a neckpiece and a CDK-6 sonic communication pack belted at his waist. He dropped the sonic transceiver in the water, paid out a generous thirty feet of cable from the pack, and ran through audio checks. The system was ready. He was pleased.

"Hooch!" he barked.

"Sir!"

"Are you prepared for entry?"

"Yessir!"

"You have five minutes of air. Now get your ass in the water and swim!"

Hooch slapped his hand across the dive mask and rolled. He dropped off the side of the Whaler and hit black water in a hard tight ball.

Vale punched a stopwatch and flicked a switch, activating the Fathom Five tracking system. A high-pitched sonar ping sounded at steady intervals, in unison with the green blinking light on the console in his right hand.

Down under, Hooch had no light to guide him, nothing but the glowing compass strapped to his wrist. He had location coordinates memorized, and he kicked hard now approaching the long tubular structure he could not see but knew was there: a precision underwater obstacle course jury-rigged from cutter hulls and airplane scrap, a five-hundred-meter medusa loaded with sadistic traps, a sinuous twisting carapace designed to challenge mechanical dexterity and psychological balls.

Hooch touched the open metal grid of the narrow slit entry and checked his watch. He had four minutes fifty left to swim through the carapace and out the other end. Sliding in, metal from the slit scraped his tanks, and he felt like Jonah slipping down the gullet, sucked into the belly of the whale.

The entry grate slammed shut and autolocked behind him.

The unmistakable voice of Andreas Villard filled his head. "You're in, boy. Now there's only one way out."

Hooch laughed, full of himself.

Up top, Vale tingled with anticipation. They always thought it was fun at the start. "Four minutes twenty!" he shouted.

The green light moved steadily, blinking in time with the sonar pings, tracking Hooch's progress fifty feet below. Big Bose speakers rigged at the skiff's central command dash broadcast audio from down under to Vale and the nine divers aboard. The sound of Hooch's regulator working was rhythmic and relaxed. He was inside the Rabbit Hole, the first trap of the course.

"How you feeling?" Vale asked.

"Like Alice in fucking Wonderland," Hooch said. "I'm out of the Hole and heading for the Cocoon."

Vale stood at the prow, peering down at the water as if he could see into the cold, murky depths. Three-foot swells rolled dead on, hitting the hull and exploding, drenching him. He was oblivious of the cold salty spray, counting down time that was elapsing fast.

"Exiting Trap Two," Hooch said, "with the grace of a butterfly."

"Getting cocky there, boy?"

"Yessir. I'm approaching the Web and feel like fucking Charlotte."

Each time Hooch sprang a trap below, a square on the sonar tracker lit up. Three now glowed pink with six left to go.

Goddamn he's fast, Vale thought. *He's fucking excellent, the best of the bunch. Hooch is going to ace this and come up grinning with tank air to spare.*

"Looking good, Cock Robin," he crooned into the mini mike. "You're a friggin' knife through butter, boy."

"Melted butter," Hooch crowed. "I'm out of the Web and inside the Nest."

Hooch's breathing was rhythmic; he was dead calm and in total control.

The course is too easy for him, Vale thought. *He won't even break a sweat.*

The fifth square flashed pink.

Hooch giggled. "Shit, this is fun."

"Three minutes fifty!" Vale shouted. "Hooch is in the sixth trap." He held up the console so they could witness the progress of Hooch's swim.

The sixth square pinked.

Hooch hooted.

"Three minutes fifteen," Vale announced. "Is this what we call good work?"

"Yessir!" the nine divers shouted in unison to the man they knew as Villard.

Pink seventh square.

"Is this what we call fucking awesome work?"

"Yessir!"

"Is this the way you should all fucking swim down there?"

"Yessir!"

At two minutes ten, the roving green blip went dead still, signaling that Hooch had stopped moving.

Vale grinned. "Something wrong, boy?"

"Just stopping for a martini, sir, two olives, straight up."

Trap Eight, the Coop, Vale noted, the toughest in the course. Hooch had a huge head start. He had time to spare. He had a month of Sundays left in his tanks. He would keep his shit together.

Vale was wrong.

Down under, Hooch was wedged inside a tight steel cylinder. The access door had slammed shut and autolocked upon entry. The exit door was a thick metal frame of barbed chicken wire secured with a lock far more complex than all the rest. He had aced this lock easily on land a dozen times. But down here in the dark, up against the wire, racing the clock, it was different. He thought of Villard up top, the grin that he knew was on Villard's face. His hands began to shake. He glanced at his watch.

One minute fifty.

The trap after this was called the Blender, a Plexiglas cone where turbo props beat water to a white rushing froth creating maximum churn in which he would have to trip multiple locks. If any one of them were as tough as the single one here in the Coop, Hooch knew he would never make it out. Black water around him felt like a cold, wet tomb.

Topside, the green blip was frozen in place.

Well, well, Vale thought, surprised. *Chicken Little has met his match.*

Down under, Hooch fumbled with picks, driving them in hard and twisting without grace or feel or finesse. The lock was heavy—heavy as his own heart that was a rock now in his chest.

"What's the sticking point, boy?" Vale was on the two-way, coming in loud and clear in Hooch's earpiece. "What's got you fouled up? Your air's running low."

Teeth clamped around his mouthpiece, Hooch sucked hard, knowing he was breathing faster than he should—but he needed air to cool the hot, rising panic. The glow of his dive watch was right in front of his nose, ticking down his life: a minute thirty of air left in his tanks.

"Hooch is no Houdini!" Vale shouted, walking the length of the skiff. "He can't trip the lock!"

Nine divers looked at him, and Vale saw fear in nine sets of eyes. "How you feeling, Hooch?" he whispered into the mike. "Scared yet?"

"No, sir."

"Yes, you are, boy! You're fucking afraid! Fear has gone and squeezed all the cock right out of your voice, Cock Robin! Fear's your enemy. It can kill you down there."

Vale listened to the sound of the regulator working ten times too fast. He nodded, pleased, and raised the console high. "Fifty seconds of air left, and Chicken Little is still sitting in the Coop!"

Down under, Vale's voice slammed into Hooch's head. "Whadd'ya been doing in topside class, boy? Thinking about football, fast food, getting laid? Locks, Hoochie Koochie. You should'a been thinking about locks. Houdini did these blindfolded, and he wasn't ever in a freakin' million-dollar nursery school funded by the U.S. of A. Thirty seconds to go, boy. I'm beginning to think you've fucked up."

Hooch exploded, ripping at the barbed wire with his bare hands, slamming into it headfirst, twisting it in his teeth—he swore he could chew his way through. Thirty seconds of air left, and goddamn if he was going to die like this.

"Two traps left," Vale said. "The Coop and the Blender. Can you do both in twenty-eight seconds? Are you good enough for that?"

The big black speakers shuddered from the explosive sound of tanks slamming against the metal cage.

Vale went on and on, filling Hooch's head with the taunting, the time left, the count—only to croon then like a lover, talking Hooch down into death. "Ten seconds left—you ready to beg for help now, son?"

Hooch wet himself, and the warmth of his piss heated the thin layer of water between the wet suit and his skin. But he would not—could not—verbalize his fear.

"Ready to call it quits?" Vale said. "You want to come on up to Daddy? What's the sticking point, boy? What the fuck's going on down there?"

Tanks slamming metal, barbed wire scraping steel, the low howling, the grunting of superhuman effort. Nine divers watched the rolling swells—as if the green blip was wrong and Hooch would miraculously break surface.

Vale watched the clock and counted out loud. "Five seconds, four, three, two! Hey, Hooch? You are now officially out of air."

Nine divers shifted on the slats. The big speakers were twin grim reapers broadcasting the terrible sound of Hooch trying to suck air out of dry tanks.

"Hell, boy," Vale said in mock disgust, "hang in. We're coming to get you."

A diver rose. Vale shoved him back down on the slat.

"Just kidding," he whispered, grinning into the mini mike. "No one's coming, Hooch. You fucked up."

Out of the speakers came the high pitch of Hooch shrieking, a long wail louder than the hull slapping surf or lowing north wind.

One of the nine divers bolted from his slat.

"Back off!" Vale ordered.

"But Hooch is out of air, sir!"

"He fucked up!"

The diver grabbed the rim of the skiff, tucked and

ready to roll. Vale kicked the diver back down on the slat.

A second diver shot over the side of the boat, hitting the black water in a tight hard roll. Vale grabbed a long fishing gaff, hooked the diver deep in the shoulder, and pulled him in close to the pitching skiff. Blood swirled, a black stain on dark water.

"Insubordination will not be tolerated in this unit," Vale said. His mini mike was still on, the speakers broadcasting every word in stereo. "Insubordination is treason. Are you a traitor, soldier?"

"No, sir!"

"Then why did you disregard orders and jump in?"

"Hooch needs help."

"He fucked up, and there is no margin for error in this unit. There is zero tolerance for less than perfect performance, understood?"

"Yessir!"

"Are you ready to get back on this boat now and perform?"

"Yessir!"

"Sorry, soldier. That is not an option. You hit my zero tolerance button, and you hit it hard." With his free hand, Vale reached down and slashed the diver's air hose. "Take a deep breath—you are going for a swim."

Vale put his full weight on the long gaff. The diver went under, kicking and bucking, trying mightily to free himself, but the barbs were jagged teeth buried deep in his flesh, and with Vale driving the gaff mercilessly down, there was no way he could get free.

Vale shouted at the remaining eight divers as he manned the jerking gaff.

"You all agreed to the rules when you signed on! A million bucks is hanging out there for each of you once you successfully complete a mission. Wall Street's at work right here inside the DOD. But you'll never get a chance to nail the million if you screw up in training. In training, as in the field, you are on your own. No one steps up to help you. Those are the rules. If you break the rules here, you will never see the field, never go out on a real mission—never earn that million. So don't even think about helping Hooch now. Each man for himself. That's the way it is."

The wild splashing had stopped. The gaff had gone still. Vale was holding dead weight. He counted out an extra five minutes just to be sure, then hauled the body up and dumped it on deck. Vale marched the length of the boat, wet suit glowing orange as his own fury, molten lava in the black of the open Atlantic.

"Zero tolerance. Is that understood?"

"Yessir!"

"Is this the fucking Boy Scouts here?"

"No, sir!"

"Is this a fucking zoo here? Are you the fucking SEALs?"

"No, sir!"

"What the fuck are you, then?"

"SEATEC, sir!"

"Operatives who can't cut it in training don't belong in the field. Operatives who fuck up get fucked. Two things will kill you: fear and overconfidence. Either one turns you sloppy, and when you get sloppy you make mistakes. Irreparable, deadly, intolerable mistakes. Do you understand?"

"Yessir!"

Vale stepped over the dead body, put one foot on the prow, and worked the console, electronically resetting the course below. He idly wondered what had happened to Hooch, if he had gotten claustrophobic and freaked out in the dark. Black water did that to a lot of men. Black water was heavier than earth for some, a living internment that cracked their cool.

Vale wished he had been down there watching Hooch lose his bravado and struggle, buck and kick inside the cylinder, try to twist his way to freedom. He wished he had been right there up close watching him drown when help was just seconds away—and withheld by Vale's own steel-willed order.

Vale spun around and crouched in front of a diver he called Trigger. "You're up next," he said, palming the smooth arc of the young diver's hooded head.

Trigger's eyes were wide and wild with terror.

Vale pressed fingers on his throat, felt the rocketing pulse. "Shaking like a bunny." He grinned. "And appropriately so. The Rabbit Hole's waiting, boy. Now get your ass in the water, and show me you know how to swim."

CHAPTER THIRTY-ONE

Deep in the night, my cell phone rang.

I woke disoriented, certain I had left it with St. James, but it was there right next to me. When I finally answered, all I heard was the faint sound of living lungs drawing in air and a whisper of flesh like a cheek brushing the receiver—a sigh that blended into the sound of waves stroking sand; then it was all ocean, waves rolling, cresting, breaking, shore pounding surf that built in climactic momentum and force so loud I had to hang up.

I slept fitfully after that and woke again at dawn to sunlight bouncing off white walls and spilling gold on the polished wood floor. The sound of the ocean was close. I pushed sheets aside and went to the window.

St. James was in the water, a lunatic without a wet suit in a frigid sea, swimming five hundred yards out, parallel to shore. He had a powerful kick and high arcing strokes. Two fat yellow buoys were set fifty meters apart. St. James used them as markers, swimming back and forth between them.

I showered, dressed quickly, and went downstairs.

Hathaway was in the kitchen brewing coffee. I carried my cup out to the deck. St. James was still in the water.

Hathaway appeared next to me, holding out a plate with steaming scrambled eggs and four slices of lavishly buttered toast.

"No, thanks," I said.

"With all due respect, you need to eat more," Hathaway said. "Mr. St. James will leave you behind if he thinks you're not up to the hunt."

"It's my hunt, not his."

"All the more reason for you to eat."

The eggs smelled good. The butter even better. I took the plate. Hathaway left me alone.

Out in the cove, St. James swam to shore and stood. He was totally nude. I should have turned away, but the sight of him held me. As battered as his face was, his body was beautiful, with long limbs and smooth, sun-stroked skin. Grace and power. Eden's exile wading out proud and unashamed. He shook his head hard. Sparkling water droplets sprayed out like a halo, but I knew St. James was no angel. His face was nicked and pitted, burned from the sun. Still, when those white teeth flashed, St. James was undeniably striking, tempestuously appealing.

He looked right up at me as he toweled down slowly, deliberately, watching, grinning—white teeth flashing—waiting for me to react.

I turned my back, walked inside, and waited for him there.

He appeared twenty minutes later dressed in old gray sweatpants slung low on his hips and a faded gray polo shirt the same color as his eyes. His hair was still damp, cheeks flushed from a warm shower. His feet were bare, and I couldn't help but notice that he walked without noise, moved without disturbing the air.

"Come," he said simply.

We went downstairs. He punched a code in on the office door lock, opened up, and led me in.

St. James sprawled in the rolling chair. "Do you always wear only black?" he asked.

"Makes traveling easier," I said. "Everything matches."

"Reasonable explanation but probably untrue."

"Think what you like."

"I think color reminds you of fire, and you choose black because that's what's left when the flames are gone."

Bull's-eye. Score one for St. James.

"Don't you get cold out there," I asked, "swimming at dawn with nothing on?"

"I swim every morning. The colder the water, the better. Builds stamina and good health. Do you ever swim nude?"

"I don't swim at all."

"Why not?"

"I can't."

"You can; you just won't."

"I got another call last night."

"I know. I cloned your phone."

"And put it back in my room while I was sleeping."

"You had kicked the sheets off. The view was something. It's reassuring to know you sleep in the nude. Beautiful topography. Your gloves add an interesting mystique."

My face flushed, but my voice was cold. "I value my

privacy," I said, "same as you value yours here. In the future, please respect that about me."

"Reprimand duly noted. I'm sorry."

The sparkle in his eye gave away the lie. He wasn't sorry at all.

"The cell phone, St. James. Let's talk about that."

"I cloned it and tried to trace the call. But the caller's technologically bright. He redirects the signal so I get a bogus feedback. Next subject—Vale. Justin Vale as you know him does not exist."

"That's not possible. I got over five hundred hits on the Internet, stories about Geostar, pictures of him in the press."

"Take a look at this." He pushed a stack of paper over to me, copies of dozens of search requests for information about Geostar. In every instance the search came up blank.

"There is no Geostar," St. James said, "not anywhere on the Net or in the IRS records for corporate taxes."

"But I found articles in the national press and a dedicated Web site."

"What you found were a bunch of articles that *appeared* to have run in those magazines and newspapers."

"They had magazine and newspaper logos, and issue dates."

"Manufactured images to make you think they were really there."

"But I saw pictures—on the Net and originals in his home. Justin Vale with Al Gore, for Christ's sake."

"And those pictures gave him credibility."

"Yes."

"They made you feel safe."

"I suppose."

"Listen to me carefully: Justin Vale manufactured an identity. He created a false history of an entire company that does not and never did exist. He planted the articles on the Net, knowing any casual search of the Web would lead to those. He took a gamble, and he bet right. You did what we all do when we're mildly curious about something. Log on, type a name into a search engine, and see what comes up."

I shook my head, but I knew what he was saying was true. "The photos . . ."

"In the right hands, anything can be created with digital imaging. Anything. A picture of you hugging Hitler. Me kissing Marilyn Monroe. When they're done right, even the best forensic labs out there have trouble proving that they're fake. We live in a new era, Lacie. We can't trust our own eyes and ears. Our voices and faces aren't our own anymore. They're free for anyone with the technical know-how to appropriate. That's why I call technology the new king—the new God. It's capable of creating entire worlds where none existed before. Justin Vale was a master of illusion, and you bought the illusion: the money, the high-level connections, the pictures on the wall all made you trust him. You let every one of your defenses down because you instinctively equated stature with safety."

St. James was right.

"A fake name, a company that never existed," I said. "Why did he go to the trouble?"

"I don't know yet. I will tell you what I do know. Day one, Ashley washes up dead on Nantucket. Two days later Justin Vale takes you to bed. Three days after that Vale disappears along with his complex manufactured identity. Three events taking place in five days. A triangle, two women, one man. Sex and deception and death. Vale's smack in the middle of both.

"Anyone who went through such elaborate measures to create an identity has resources. We'll find that he paid for the car in cash and has it registered under a false name. You don't know the plate number, and even if you did, it would be a dead end. What we do have is a very expensive rental house. I got into Nantucket's City Hall records. The house is owned by Sherman and Nancy Stillwell of Boston, Mass. He's an investment banker. She's his ex-wife. I read the court documents. She got the house."

"And rented it to Vale."

"Right. He would have filed credit references with the Realtor, and that would be Sheila Gaines."

"How do you know?"

"Utilities and phone bills were paid through her office on his behalf. The phone records are a white out. There was a phone in the house, but he didn't use it. There were no calls going in or out for the last ten months. Vale used wireless. Sheila Gaines will be able to fill in a lot of the blanks. Her home phone's listed in the directory. I tried it, but a machine picks up. The office doesn't open for two more hours."

St. James went to the door. "Come," he said.

"Where are we going?"

"To show you a higher art form of the hunt."

I followed St. James across the big field fronting the deck, striding through knee-high grass misted with dew. He was still barefoot, and I wondered if his feet were cold or if he cared. The smell of the wild was heavy; loam and moist earth, pungent pine and rotting wood.

St. James worked a black leather glove, a falconer's gauntlet, over his left hand and thrust his arm over his head, and whistled three times sharply.

Something soft rustled the pines. The sound of tiny bells followed, sweet high notes on a northern breeze. St. James, anything but sweet, stood rooted in place watching the trees, black fist raised tight and high and hard, waiting.

He whistled again.

A hawk answered with flapping wings and silver bells. It sailed out of the shadows and floated overhead in a long lazy circle before drifting in and settling on his glove.

"This is my falcon," St. James said, easing the fisted raptor down to eye level. "She's a peregrine and a beauty."

Her body plumage was a deep glossy slate blue; her throat, creamy white. Black feathers capped her head, and a slim collar of tiny silver bells circled her neck. Yellow feathers ringed dark eyes, and her bright yellow feet curled around St. James's gloved fist. Long talons were sharp black sickles digging into the leather, sharp black beak a matching sickle, a hard shiny curve the texture of horn.

"I found her when she was young," St. James said, "injured in the woods. I cared for her and, when she healed, trained her to hunt for me on command."

As he stroked her back with his bare right hand, I looked at the white half moon scars scything his flesh.

"She did that to you?" I asked.

"I was full of myself at first. Tried to handle her without gloves."

"Why do you keep her out here in the wild?"

"That's where wildlife belongs."

"Don't you worry that she'll leave the island and never come back?"

"That's the test of love."

"You believe a bird's capable of love?"

"This one is."

"Does she have a name?"

"Henry."

"A man's name?"

"A *king's* name because Henry the Eighth was so passionate about the sport of falconry he nearly drowned once chasing a hawk. Back then, falconry was a metaphor for war."

"Is that why you practice it, St. James? As a testament to war?"

"No. I'm intrigued by the way the peregrine hunts and the fact that it kills its own kind like men do."

"I thought hawks hunted rabbits and mice."

"True, but a peregrine is a separate genus of the hawk species, the only one to hunt birds, slaughter them right in midair."

St. James transferred the falcon to his shoulder. She roosted obediently, tucking her huge yellow feet and savage killing talons under her body, out of sight. St. James walked us away from the forest and down to the cove. A birch wood canoe sat on shore. He carried it down to the water line.

"Get in," he said.

"Where are we going?"

"To a place where the falcon can fly."

I settled on the rear slat seat. St. James rolled his pants legs up and pulled the canoe off the shore into deeper water, then high-stepped in and sat on the front slat seat.

"Peregrines were almost wiped out in the eastern U.S. and western Europe," he said, paddling away from shore. "DDT nearly killed them all off. They were taken off the endangered species list just this year. You'll be surprised to learn that as hard as I am on mankind, I'm gentle when it comes to creatures of the wild. I give generously—both time and money—to conservation groups."

"Conservation?"

"I don't look like the charitable type?"

"No."

He laughed. "I'm deeply committed to the fight for survival of endangered species. Does that make you like me a little bit more?"

"It's an admirable cause."

"You've lived in D.C. too long. You answer questions like a politician."

He maneuvered out to open water.

"Why the canoe?" I asked.

"Can't walk on coastline like this." The shore banks were steep and rocky, covered with green algae and moss. "Rams Island's almost pure forest, but on the leeward side I've got a big wide-open field. It's easy for Henry to land there and easier still for me to find her when she brings down her kill."

St. James worked the oar, powering us through water.

"These islands were originally settled by Penobscot Indians," he said. "Little by little they were driven out by the English. The Indians that stayed became God-fearing Catholics. They gave up hunting and forsook the wild, spending their days tending missions in the name of the church. They traded deer skin for muslin and offered up their souls to the white man's God."

"Was your mother Penobscot?" I asked, thinking of the pictures on his bedroom mantel.

"You know anything about the tribes, Lacie Wagner? You ever do a story on that?"

"Not much—and no."

"My mother was Iroquois—as different from the Penobscot as a hawk is to man. The Penobscot were a docile people. The Iroquois were not. The Penobscot gave up when the English came in. They didn't fight for their birthright. The Iroquois did—in a battle that lasted a hundred years. The invaders drove all the Iroquois up out of the Americas into Canada, where they lived freely again."

"How is it your mother came to Rams Island?"

"My father met her when he was deer hunting in Canada. They fell in love. She had a university education, a Ph.D., but still the spirit of her people burned strong inside her. She wore only her own native clothes." St. James laughed and glanced back at me, delight dancing in his eyes. "My mother scandalized proper Boston."

"Why?"

"She hated conventional, socially correct WASP life and all that went with it—the class caste system, the stiff-necked dinner parties, the matronly women, the partners of the bank. She liked to show up at black tie dinners dressed in doeskin threaded with beads. My father loved her and didn't give a damn what she did or how she did it. They were the talk of the town. Michael St. James with his injun bride."

"And his half-breed son?"

St. James paddled in silence for a moment.

"There was plenty of that," he said. "Racism passes from father to son. I was born with a wild streak, and the verbal abuse I took from my peers made it worse. That's why I always liked it here on Rams Island. It was—and is—my own nonestablishment world."

He pulled the paddle out of water.

St. James and I, at opposite ends of the rocking canoe, were eye to eye and equal in height but different in every other way.

A swell rolled in, tilting us far left. I put a hand out to each side and hung on. Water sloshed over the edge; a cloud rushed by overhead, speeding a black streak over the sun, casting us in shadow. The air smelled sharply of wet plumage and male sweat. St. James. His skin, his hair, his bird.

"If we tip over," he said, "you'll have to swim to shore."

"I can't swim."

"What do you do for sport?"

"Run."

"Why?"

"To stay healthy."

"Just when I thought we were making progress, the lie sneaks in. That's your one bad habit, Lacie. You don't level with me. The truth now, please."

I told him I ran because it set me free, took me outside my physical self, as if one day I might run into a new body unmarked by fire.

"That's better," St. James said. "The truth is good. Look at me, covered with scars, and I don't give a damn. The difference between you and me is I accept who I am and you don't."

"That's not true."

"Then why don't you take off your gloves? Why do you wear them when you sleep?"

I did not reply.

He answered for me. "You're ashamed when you should be proud."

I couldn't help myself. I laughed out loud. "Proud."

"Your hands are symbolic of all you've been through. The one action that destroyed them was like a rock thrown in water, sending ripples out long after the rock has disappeared. Your life will never be peaceful, Lacie. Your hands are a promise of that. It's your destiny, your fate. Proof of your courage and spirit is right there in your fingers. There's no shame in that. Back to the question now. Why don't you swim?"

"I can't."

"You can; you just won't. Runners have strong hearts, powerful legs. A swimmer needs that."

"A swimmer need hands."

"Not true. Legs like yours, strong enough to run like the wind, legs that strong can sure as hell swim. All you have to do is fall in and kick. Don't think about the water, what's under you that you can't see. Start with a pool or a lake or a summer-lazy sea. Wade in knee-deep, let yourself fall back, and then kick like hell."

The falcon gave me a long slow blink, stretched her wings, and opened her beak.

"Your bird looks hungry," I said.

"She's anxious to hunt. Enough of fire and water, let's take to the air."

He picked up the paddle and worked us in, shoulders rolling with each strong pull. The belly of the canoe scraped shallows. St. James stepped out and pulled it up on shore. He helped me out.

"Your heels are too high," St. James said, leading me into the dense forest. "Not practical for walking. Surprisingly frivolous for such a practical girl."

"I wouldn't expect you to understand why women wear heels."

"Because I'm a man?" He laughed. "The sexes are elementally different. I'm the first to agree. You'll appreciate the differences in the peregrine breed. The males are high-strung and nervous. Females are calm. The females are also bigger and far more powerful—superior hunters in every respect."

We broke free of the trees and came out on a vast clearing the size of a football field. The falcon roused her tail. St. James pulled off his gauntlet and passed it to me. "Put this on," he said.

It was large enough to slip over my black leather glove.

"Offer her your hand," St. James said.

I did.

The hawk stepped gracefully from his shoulder to my fist, heavy on my undersize hand. I had trouble holding her on my own. St. James moved in close behind my body and reached around supporting my wrist with his hand.

"Extend your arm," he said. "Move nice and easy along with me."

His breath was warm on my neck, his voice soft in my ear. And together like this, we flew the hawk.

St. James guided my arm backwards, gracefully rotating it through forty-five degrees as if casting a fishing line, but now he was casting the hawk, literally throwing her into the air. She shot out, and her chunky body was instantly transformed into a swift, streamlined missile burning over the field, skimming tall grass, soaring up to fly a spiral in the sky. She worked the wind, turning in wide circles, higher and higher until she was a black triangle against blue, looping hundreds of feet above our heads.

"She's found her pride of place," St. James said. "She'll wait there for her prey. Could be five minutes. Could be two hours. When you watch her up there, think of her eyes. Each one is larger than her brain and far more sophisticated than our own. We have two hundred thousand cells to each square millimeter of fovea; the peregrine has over a million. Her field of vision is binocular in front and widely peripheral to the side so she can see everything but a narrow strip directly behind her. Her head has a gyroscopic design that allows it to stay steady while her body rocks in the wind. She can see me flash a white handkerchief from a mile away and home in. When she dives to kill, her air speed can reach a hundred and eighty miles an hour.

"She has two methods of killing her prey. In the first, she'll fly with her talons closed, using them to literally 'punch' the target dead right in midair. Her second tactic is to descend on her target at that same hundred and eighty miles an hour and open her middle toe, using that talon to rake or slice her prey. She may make a second pass, raking again until the prey is dead. Look. See that duck flying to the left there below here? That's going to be her kill. It's too big to punch, so she'll probably rake it."

The falcon zeroed in, folded her wings, and dropped straight down, falling from the heavens in a high-speed vertical dive. Wind rushing through her bells sounded like shrieks. She hit the duck hard, then circled away and came around for the second deadlier strike that bloodied the air and knocked a cloud of feathers into the sky.

When I saw that peregrine drop like a bullet from the sky and strike, I felt that I was the quarry and the falcon was fate; that I was the unwary prey destined to die the same violent death, attacked without warning. We were both targets. And savagery bound us.

Wings spread wide, the falcon grasped the duck in her deadly talons and rode her kill down, landing twenty-five yards away from us. She perched on the prize, plucking feathers and ripping flesh from bone with her sharp curved beak.

"Blood lust," I said, watching her feed.

"You don't understand the natural world."

"What I don't understand is death as sport."

"It's not sport to the falcon."

"She's a killing machine, and you fly her for sport, to celebrate death."

"You've misunderstood completely. I fly her to celebrate strength. The difference between you and me is that I accept death as part of life. Natural and unnatural. My falcon hunts for food. Today man hunts for pleasure."

"Do you?"

He looked away, gray eyes hooded.

"Is that what your manhunting's all about, St. James? Have you given yourself a legitimate license to kill?"

St. James walked away, bare feet quiet on the loam. He disappeared into the trees, leaving me alone on the forest edge with the wet sound of the peregrine feasting—the unimaginable noise of skin ripped from bone, the sucking, tearing, swallowing, the guttural groan of satisfaction, silvery killing bells ringing all around.

Standing at the forest edge, heels digging in to the soft mossy ground, I felt a hundred pair of eyes on me from above and behind. I was a tall, fire-haired intruder, unwelcome in this place. Then I laughed out loud at myself: to be afraid of wild creatures when it was man who had brought all my pain.

I cut back through the trees, to shore. The canoe was sitting in the shallows with St. James in front, motionless and straight, looking east, away from me. I stepped in carefully and settled on the slat. St. James whistled three times. The falcon flew in, roosted on his shoulder.

St. James held the oar in a two-handed grip, dipping and pulling, changing sides with a quiet elegance. The motion of oaring did not disturb the hawk. She rode the roll of his deltoids like a human rides the swells of the sea, curling bloodied talons around his collarbone; the black beak wet with blood nuzzled his shirt, his neck, his ear.

When St. James looked at her he saw freedom.

When I looked at the falcon I simply saw death: my own, inevitable and close.

St. James paddled back into the same cove where he had swum at sunrise. I followed him out onto shore. He stopped short and turned to face me. The falcon's eyes glittered black, contrasting with St. James's pale lupine gray.

"You didn't answer me back there," I said.

"The answer is yes. I have given myself a license to kill. And that's why you're here."

"I hired you to help me find Vale, not kill him."

"Two women, one man," he said, moving close, crowding my space. "Sex and deception and death. Picture the triangle, Lacie. Vale is the apex, with you and Ashley at his feet. The geometry alone is compelling. You might come to find my self-granted license useful. Now, tell me this: You're a young woman with an old soul who's seen too much of evil far too soon. Can you hold a lit candle without fear? Or does the element still rule you?"

He looked at me intently, listened to my silence.

"Until you can," he said, "that element will own you. Be careful of fear. Are you certain you're not so afraid of dying that you've forgotten how to live?"

I took a step back.

"Don't ask hard questions of me," St. James said, "unless you're prepared to answer a few in return."

He picked the falcon off his shoulder and walked away, leaving me in the cold next to the soft lapping tide.

CHAPTER THIRTY-TWO

I found St. James in his office, on the phone with Sheila Gaines.

I checked in with Harry while I waited.

"We're taking some heat," he chuckled. "I've got three press offices going ballistic on us this morning. Little Creek, U.S. Navy, and AFIP. They're running into each other like bumper cars, giving so many conflicting statements I can hardly keep track. But one thing's clear. You've got someone high up out there pretty mad."

As soon as I hung up, St. James filled me in on what he had learned.

"Sheila Gaines took out a big ad in the *Boston Globe* back in February. Vale was on her doorstep the first day it ran. He said he was willing to pay 'whatever it takes.' Those were his words. He said his family summered on the island when he was a child, and that he had good memories. Sheila charged him top dollar—twenty-five thousand a month for high season, May through August, ten thousand a month for the off season. Twelve months in all, plus another twenty-five for the security deposit. Vale didn't even want to look at the house, just gave her first and last month's rent plus the security deposit *in cash* right then and there. And, he paid the rent in cash every month."

"Why did he move out early?" I asked.

"Sheila doesn't know. It took her completely by surprise. He had a professional cleaning crew in yesterday morning. Sheila did the walk-through yesterday afternoon. The house is in tip-top shape. Vale is entitled to a full reimbursement of his security deposit. I asked her to let me know if she hears from him."

"What about his credit references?"

"He gave her names and numbers of three bankers at Citibank. The first is Mr. David Morgenstern, Senior Vice President."

St. James punched up the speakerphone and dialed.

A recording played: "*You have reached a non-working number at Citibank. Please check your number and try back later.*"

"Mr. David Friedman," St. James said, reading off the next name. "Executive Vice President, Corporate Finance."

He tapped in the number. We listened to the same recording.

"Mr. Fred Poltrak, Managing Director."

The recording played again.

St. James disconnected.

"Bogus names," he said.

"I bet they weren't when Sheila Gaines called," I said. "Someone answered and gave her the information she needed."

"Vale set this up."

"Citibank? Come on, St. James."

"In every big company ten percent of the allocated extensions to the main exchange typically remain unassigned. Vale figured out which were unused."

"How?"

"Actually, you could program a computer to do it for you by simply asking it to dial every conceivable combination of numbers using the Citibank prefix. Anytime you got a recording like the one we just heard, you'd know the number hadn't been allocated. It's child's play to intervene with an automated call-forwarding command. When Sheila Gaines called those three numbers, the calls went straight to Vale. He gave his own references. Simple but smart."

"You don't think she would have noticed that she was talking to the same voice three times?"

"A voice is the easiest thing in the world to change. All you need is a ten-dollar device like this." He rummaged in a drawer and pulled out a black round component. "Mail order, ten ninety-nine." He twisted it on the receiver of a traditional telephone. "Pick up your extension."

I did.

"Now," he said, speaking into the receiver. "What do you hear?"

His voice was pitched an octave higher and had a different tone. I never would have guessed I was speaking to Nick St. James.

"You have to understand your opponent to beat him," St. James said in his new strange voice. He unscrewed the device and hung up. "Vale's technologically accomplished, to say the least. And now he has cut and run."

"He left a twenty-five-thousand-dollar cash security deposit."

"Which he won't bother to pick up. Money and technology are the great enablers. If you have enough of both, you can do any damn thing you want—including disappear. A man who runs like he did does so because he has something to hide."

St. James touched a key, and the big suspended flat screen lit up with something called Face Pro.

"This is a program that allows me to put together a composite sketch without an artist," he said. "We'll go through, feature by feature, and try to re-create Vale's face."

He double-clicked, and a virtual sketch pad filled the screen. A question blinked in the center of the empty pad: CHILD OR ADULT? St. James clicked ADULT. A second question popped up. MALE OR FEMALE? St. James chose MALE. He went on in this manner, clicking options, narrowing the field to a male Caucasian thirty-five to forty-five years old. The screen flashed and a generic male face filled the "sketch" page.

"Face Pro uses a data bank of digital images," St. James explained, "photographs, of thousands of variations on facial features we can choose from and digitally refine until we have a customized face that fits our man. When we're done, the picture will look like a photograph. The feds have learned that photographs are a hundred times more effective than sketches. Good as they are, police sketches don't look real. They're not flesh-and-blood faces. Face Pro's are."

We worked together for an hour, carefully refining each element, piece by piece, building a reproduction of Vale's face.

I had to close my eyes several times to try to picture him. The color of his eyes was the only detail I was dead certain of. I remembered the way they looked, half open, glittering and bright as he drove his body into mine on that first reckless night. I knew his eyes, but had

trouble remembering detail in his face. Although I
could remember the feel of his lips on my skin, I could
not remember if they were full or thin. How high did his
brows arch? What was the shape of his nose? I remembered the way his cheekbones felt next on the small of
my back, but I could not describe them well enough to
get the sketch right.

St. James was patient. "Like this? Or like this?" He
clicked the mouse, switching back and forth, giving me
choices, until we had it pieced together.

"What do you think?" St. James asked of the finished
sketch.

"It's close."

St. James hit PRINT.

"Time to have a chat with Spivak. It's Sunday. Odds
are he's at home."

St. James tapped a key on his computer.

"According to the Department of Motor Vehicles, the
colonel owns two cars. A three-year-old white Carrera
and a new silver Jag XJ6. He lives at 5040 Windjammer
Road in Hyannis Port. Waterfront. Exclusive and expensive. Let's go say hello."

"What about your cell phone clone?"

"The mainframe here is set up for remote access. If
your caller calls again, the desktop will make a digital
recording. Everything in my system's available to me
from anywhere in the world through wireless digital
satellite. Are you ready?"

I said yes, but I was talking to his back. The question
was really an order. St. James was already taking the
stairs two at a time, calling out for Hathaway, closing up
the house.

I lingered and watched the first composite roll out of
the color laser printer. St. James was right. The overall
finished effect was like a snapshot, not a sketch, and because of that, the face was eerily real, almost alive.

Who are you? I wondered, tracing lips that had kissed mine.

"Was he good?" St. James said, back at my side, reading my mind. "Did you live a little, then?"

CHAPTER THIRTY-THREE

Vale entered the auction room and strolled down the center aisle—wonderfully out of place.

Men seated around him wore suits of fine Italian wool, ties had the sheen of good silk, socks were cashmere, and shirts, custom-cut. A few women were sprinkled through the crowd, dressed in refined couture: wrists and fingers and necks and ears loaded with gold and diamond pavé.

He heard the hiss of whispers and felt the appraising glances. His combat fatigues made for good camouflage in the desert perhaps, but here at Boston's most prestigious auction house they were a red flag in a bullring. As he made his way to the front row he felt the contempt rising like corrida dust.

Soldiers did not mingle with the wealthy—unless they were high-ranking Pentagon colonels, which he clearly, obviously, unquestionably was not—not with hair hanging down to his shoulders, half moons of sweat staining his shirt, and mud caked thick on his high, laced boots. So why didn't security throw him out?

Because security had been advised by management.

Vale was a valuable, albeit eccentric client, a connoisseur and avid collector rich enough to indulge any desire, which he did enthusiastically and often at this very establishment. They did not know his true identity—or even his true name. Management knew wealth frequently fosters eccentricity. Vale bought enough each year for management to forgive his war game folly.

He took a seat in the front row, stretched his long legs out, and smiled, amused at the visible stir his entrance had made.

The women were staring at him openly now, despite themselves intrigued. The soldier had a strong face and intense amber eyes, the color of a tiger's. His hair was white blond, bleached from the sea, salt, and sun. He wore it long, to his shoulders, in a straight glossy curtain—at odds with the combat attire, but he owed no one an explanation, least of all the people gathered in this room.

The men were fops, the women not his style. They were too studied, too false, too old. Vale loved women, and chose them as carefully as he did his art. He had huge appetites, one of which he would satisfy here. Today it was not a woman he desired, but an object.

The object of his desire.

He had inspected it several times before the auction; triple-checked the provenance, run his loving hands over the smooth aged wood, the fine old glass, and metal detail. It stood as high as he was tall, a perfect square in mint condition, as if it had been crafted yesterday and not a hundred years ago.

The auctioneer moved to the microphone and tapped the podium with his slim gold pen. "We open bids tonight for item number forty-six in your catalogue," he said. "Provenance is cited in the listing. The original Water Torture Cell introduced, used, and owned by Harry Houdini."

Two gray-suited attendants wheeled the great tank in and slowly turned it around. The top opened on hinges and was inset with a pair of thick ankle shackles from which the lucky tank occupant would be secured and suspended, hung upside down, then submerged. All four sides were glass reinforced with strips of metal and wood, allowing for excellent multi-angle viewing of the captive hanging inside.

Vale had paid special attention to the master locks at the top: strong sliding bolts to the right and left, and a fat standard padlock front center. And, he had studied the wood girders, confident they were strong enough to withstand blows from a captive in panic trying to escape. Vale smiled at the thought.

Bidding opened, and the soldier patiently waited for the low-ballers to drop out of the game. Vale did not carry a numbered paddle. He had no need. A simple, almost imperceptible nod signaled his bid. The frenzy slowed. Two men battled it out in fifty-thousand-dollar increments, until there was only one left. Then Vale nodded and upped the last bid by another hundred thousand.

"Are we done here?" the auctioneer asked, scanning the room. "All finished? Yes?" He tapped the podium sharply with his gold pen. "Sold for one million two hundred thousand dollars."

The tank was his.

The crowd around him buzzed, surprised that a soldier caked in mud and sweat had just dropped millions with the tilt of his head. Vale smiled at the irony—his appearance so at odds with the act. But then again, appearances were deceiving. Vale was living proof of the power of that one simple fact.

Vale as Villard was not a government employee—he was not even U.S. military. He was a consultant. An agent for hire. An independent contractor. And he certainly was not working for money. He had truckloads of his own.

There were many thrills money could not buy, and frankly Vale enjoyed those the most.

CHAPTER THIRTY-FOUR

We were retracing my own steps, St. James and I, through the same rolling New England countryside I had traveled alone and fresh out of Vale's bed. Billboards flashed by: McDonald's, United Airlines, and a tourist welcome from the Cape Cod Chamber of Commerce: CAPE COD IS FOR LOVERS!

"See that?" St. James said with his sly tomcat smile. "My luck with you might change here today."

"Blind optimism?"

"Reasonable hope. I keep thinking your bad taste in men might just spill over to me."

"Rolls right off, St. James."

I glanced at his rugged profile, the way he was slouched in the seat, lazy body language that could not hide the workings of an agile mind. His long fingers drummed the wheel, keeping time to some inner beat. The window was cracked, and a breeze blew in, lifting pieces of his long streaked hair. A strip of belly showed between his shirt and belt revealing the Sig Sauer tucked at his waist. His skin there was dusky dark from his heritage and sun, feathered with black hairs and rock hard with muscle from those 6:00 A.M. swims. He caught me looking and flashed a devil-may-care grin.

"Want me to pull over?" St. James asked. "Are you finally ready for me, here and now?"

He was a totally dissolute creature at that moment. It was so at odds with the meticulous, painstaking work of tracking a man that I laughed.

"That's better," he said softly, nodding approval. "It's good to hear you laugh."

The grin vanished, drumming fingers stopped. Eyes fixed on the highway, the carefree bad boy was suddenly gone, an intelligent hunter materialized in his place. It was a side of St. James I had glimpsed when he was focused on work, a different St. James, sexier than the rogue he played, and I thought it was too bad he didn't realize that.

I stole another glance at that bare strip of skin and wondered if I would ever want a man again, or if my libido was as wrecked as my hands.

"Evil attracts evil," Wheeler had said. *"I'm afraid it will find you here."*

And later, my own damning words. *"I feel targeted."*

I still did.

St. James must have felt it in me when we flew his falcon. The mute acceptance of a premature violent death, sometime, somewhere. The chill intuitive understanding that that *sometime* could have been in the sheets or on the terrace, and the fact that it hadn't already happened didn't mean it wouldn't.

It occurred to me that his constant teasing had a more serious intent; St. James was daring me to stay in the living flesh-and-blood world, not to let fear freeze me, not to live like I was already dead. Violence was as natural to him as the rising sun and the phases of the moon. He had managed to integrate life and death, and I was certain he wondered why I couldn't do the same.

"Tell me why you divorced your husband," he said, out of the blue.

"Tell me why you never married."

It was his turn to laugh. "Just like a reporter. Turn the tables. Answer the question with a question to deflect attention from yourself."

We traveled on in silence, but the tension was there, a

tight wire strung between us: St. James watching and waiting for his next chance to test me while I burrowed deeper into myself. We stopped once at a strip mall. St. James left me in the car. He came back with a gift-wrapped box.

"A little something for Spivak," he said. "To help break the ice."

We drove out along the shore in Hyannis Port, where estates were big and private. Spivak's was a two-story New England beauty with sweeping wood decks, a three-car garage, and custom landscaping, Japanese waterfalls, and pretty koi ponds. His Jag was parked out front.

St. James whistled. "A four-million-dollar piece of real estate miraculously attained on G-10 government pay," he said. "How do you want to play this?"

"Any way you want. This time he's all yours."

St. James slung his computer bag over his shoulder, picked up the gift-wrapped box, and we got out. I rang the intercom at the iron fence.

The colonel answered.

"Spivak!" St. James exclaimed. "Who would've thought a devil like you would end up living behind Heaven's own gate."

"Who is it?"

"Don't you have a camera rigged up? Can't you see who's at your own front door? You're falling behind the technological curve, Dick. Wouldn't have expected that from you."

"Give me a name or I'll send security out and have you forcibly removed."

"They'd have a hard time doing that. Don't you remember you once said I was the best fighter in your class? You chalked it up to 'Injun blood'—yes sir, those were your very words. 'Injun blood in a half-breed boy.' I never forgot that, Dick. Fate works in funny ways. The one dog I never wanted to lay eyes on again, and here I am come-a-calling for Sunday tea."

Spivak was silent for a long moment, then he said, "St. fucking James."

"Mind's still sharp as a tack. Be a gentleman now and unlock Fort Knox. It's in your best interests, I promise you that."

"Damn you," Spivak cursed, but the buzzer rang.

St. James pushed the gate, and we went on in.

Spivak's yeoman Driscoll was waiting at the front door in full dress whites, sidearm drawn. He acknowledged me with a curt nod and waved us into the foyer.

"No guns or cameras or mikes," St. James said, holding out the package. "Just a gift for the colonel."

"I have to pat you down just the same," Driscoll said.

"Dick thinks I'm wearing a wire?"

"Standard security procedure."

"I lied." St. James gave him the Sig Sauer. "I pack a gun, but that's all." He put his computer bag on the ground, shrugged out of his shirt, removed his sneakers, peeled off his jeans, and did a full turn in the hall. "Nothing here but prime flesh."

"Your hair," Driscoll said.

St. James bowed his head. Driscoll inspected his scalp the way he had done with me, then moved on to the clothes, running a metal detector hard to the seams.

My cell phone rang.

"Take it," St. James said.

It was Tina Delmar. She said she had something I needed to see. I told her I would drop by later in the afternoon.

Driscoll was carefully opening the gift, checking it out, and when he was satisfied he wrapped it back up and gave it to St. James.

"You can dress now," Driscoll said, "but your computer stays with me."

"What about the lady?"

"There are no exceptions to the procedure."

"I know the drill," I said, handing him my bag. "St. James, would you please turn around."

He had the courtesy to comply.

I stepped out of my shoes and held my arms out at my sides. Driscoll searched me thoroughly, inspecting my clothes, my bra, my hair, but this time he did not ask me to remove my gloves. He simply felt each digit and the palm of my hands, nodded once when he was done, flushing just the same.

"Your bag stays with me," he said. "This way now."

He led us through double entry hall doors into an airy living room with white carpet, white couches, and white marble carvings that passed for sculpture if you knew nothing about art. The far wall was all window fronting a deck, five big glass sliding door partitions, one of which was cracked. The ocean breeze blew in, salty and strong.

Spivak in swim trunks and a tennis shirt was leaning on the rail, watching the waves, the ever-present cigar clutched in his right hand. His legs were thick muscled stalks covered with fine blond hair. When he heard our footsteps on the teak, he turned around. His eyes locked on me, and an expression of bitter contempt soured his hard face.

"St. James, the Trojan fucking horse," he said. "I have nothing to say to the press. Driscoll! See them out."

His yeoman made a move.

St. James held up a hand. "Haste makes waste," he said. "Think of me as damage control, Dick. You've had some bad television publicity, and it's about to get worse. I'm here to broker a peace treaty between you and Ms. Wagner, save you a very public humiliation. She's ready to roll with full disclosure on SEATEC. I'm counseling restraint for a variety of reasons, one of which is my deep-seated respect for the U.S. military and its tacticians."

"Never know you were a soldier once," Spivak said. "Goddamn hair like a hippie. Bet you wear an earring in your nose and you took it out just out of respect for me."

"Don't flatter yourself," St. James replied. "If I had one, though, it'd be five fat carats, square cut, and flawless."

"No doubt."

"Diamonds and puppies and money. If you have any of the three you're sure to get the girl. It's just a matter of time."

"You come here to talk dating technique?"

"No. I came to talk about death," said St. James.

"Morose subject for a beautiful day."

"Ashley Sinclair was a beautiful girl," I said. "If the world were right, she'd be taking a walk by the sea right now. I've got enough on SEATEC to trigger a congressional investigation."

He looked at me with hard glittering eyes. "Driscoll?"

"Yes, sir!"

"Step inside. I'll be spending some time alone here with my *guests.*"

Driscoll saluted and left the deck.

I sat down. St. James sprawled on a chaise longue and toyed with the wrapped gift.

"Nice house," he said. "Private-sector lifestyle on military pay. How do you afford it, Dick?"

"Had a rich uncle."

St. James laughed. "The only uncle you ever had was named Sam."

"You know shit about me," Spivak said.

"On the contrary. I've got you nailed down tight to the board. Character and history are the two things a man can never change about himself. You were born in

South Carolina, downwind of the paper mill. Can you still smell it, Dickie? That godawful stink? Playing in the salt flats in your grimy BVDs. The only family you had was a father who beat you, and when he drove his truck headfirst into a tree one night, you were glad. You told me so in those long, lonely nights at boot camp, don't you remember? You hated the military, resented having to enlist, but that was the only option for a poor boy like you.

"Your mother ditched out the day you were born, and you don't have any uncles or aunts, rich or poor. You're alone, Richard L. Spivak, isn't that right? Full of spite and feeling pretty big in your colonel's shoes—feeling righteous, in fact, slicing down heavy cash for running a top-secret tactical unit in Special Ops. They waved a stack of greenbacks and said, 'Jump.' You said, 'Yessir, how high?' Money for murder, a mercenary wearing the American flag."

"You finished?"

"No. One thing they never taught you was how to deal with the press. You blew it big time. First you told Ms. Wagner for public attribution that Ashley Sinclair wasn't yours; then two hours later you sent AFIP in to take custody of the remains."

"Special Ops has venues of its own for crime investigation and is under no obligation to divulge details to the press or public. Nor is Special Ops obligated to divulge the names of operatives to the press or public. If it turns out that the diver was military, rest assured that naval officials are moving ahead with a full and competent investigation of the death."

St. James opened the box and took out a plastic toy diver, identical to the one I had told him about Wheeler finding on the beach. He flicked the switch and the little diver began to kick. St. James held the toy up, cocked his head, and frowned.

"Did you do it, Dick?"

Spivak flushed, veins bulged thick and purple, rooting down his neck.

"C'mon," St. James taunted, "it's a yes or no question. Did Ashley die in one of your SEATEC exercises while you stood by and watched? Doing nothing's the same as murder in the eyes of the law. Did you kill Ashley Sinclair? Were you watching while it happened?"

"You goddamn . . . "

"Careful now, Dick, you've got the press right here." Spivak slapped the rail.

Driscoll floated on the other side of the sliding glass, watching the colonel, ready to move.

Spivak screwed his eyes shut and forced his temper down.

St. James put the kicking diver down on the deck. "How much does it cost these days to train a Special Ops soldier, Dick? A million dollars? One and a half? More?"

"Fuck you." Spivak turned his back. Lit his cigar. Looked out to sea.

St. James didn't let up. "Okay, I'll give you the benefit of the doubt, say you had nothing to do with Sinclair's death. But she is yours. We know that for a fact. One of your soldiers washes up on a beach, and I got to believe you're shitting bricks trying to find out what happened to this grade-A piece of ass."

"That kind of talk is disrespectful to a female operative."

"We're making progress now, Dick. You admit Jane Doe was Special Ops. Must be rough for you to do that without spitting. Remember how you said women don't belong in the military? The 'Spivak Doctrine,' the Redneck Chauvinist Spivak Doctrine. It went like this: 'A woman in Special Ops is a target, a weak link in the chain. Sooner or later the chain's going to break right at the G-spot.'

"The modern world's passed you by, Dick. Women wanted in and proved they could do it just as good as or better than men. Must burn you up having to train girls. But now you're close to getting proof that you were right all along. If you weren't the one who killed Sinclair, I've got to believe you're trying to find out who did—not because you give a goddamn about her dying. You're worried she was hit because SEATEC was the target and she was the weak link in the chain. You're worried that she caved, did too much talking under duress."

Spivak stayed silent, looking out to sea.

"I've got enough now to break the full story," I said. "You've got the body, but I've got the ID locked down solid and backed up with forensic proof AFIP missed in their Boston sweep. If Ashley Sinclair didn't die in training, then our mutual interest is in finding out who did kill her. We can make a deal now, Spivak. Something that works for both of us—if you'll talk to me off the record, give me something germane to the case."

Spivak studied me, weighing the sincerity of my words.

Truth was, without Preston Porter, I didn't have enough hard evidence to make outright accusations about SEATEC's training practices or even prove the unit existed—not as a responsible journalist. But Spivak didn't really know where I came down on the issue of integrity. He watched me now, trying to guess.

"Maybe you're barking up the wrong tree," he said. "Ever think this all might have something to do with you? After all, she washed up on your beach, in your proverbial backyard, and with the exception of the hair, the two of you could pass for goddamn sisters. Now, there's a lot of *coincidence*, Ms. Wagner. You ever consider that?"

It was the one thought I was trying to repress.

"That wasn't the question," I said. "Do we make a deal or not?"

"Time's a-wasting," St. James called out. "Three minutes more basking in the sun, then Ms. Wagner goes straight to Boston in time to break SEATEC on the evening news. Don't miss your cue."

Spivak paced the length of his deck, left to right and back again, hands jammed in his pockets, forehead glistening in the sun.

The sliding glass doors opened. Driscoll marched out.

"Sir!" He passed the colonel a fax. "This just came in."

Spivak sucked on his cigar as he read it. A slow, satisfied smile split his lips. He moved forward and stepped on the little toy diver, crushing it.

"So much for your fucking deal," he said, holding the white fax paper up like a kite in the wind. "The diatom report is in. The diver drowned in fresh water, not salt. The chlorine content was consistent with a swimming pool. Now answer me this: If she died in a pool in Special Ops training, why on earth would we have dumped her body in the ocean? Does that make sense to you, Ms. Wagner? St. James? Is there a modicum of logic on any level in that?"

There was not.

"If she was off-duty and off-base," I asked, "why was she swimming around in a pool with an activated Fathom Five on Special Ops–controlled gear?"

Spivak ignored me.

"The following statement is official," he said. " 'On behalf of the United States Navy, I regret to announce that the Armed Forces medical examiner has concluded that the cause of the death of Private Ashley Sinclair was a homicidal drowning. Navy investigators will maintain full investigative and judicial jurisdiction in a single-minded commitment to find the truth.' You can broadcast that verbatim, Ms. Wagner. This is our soldier and our case. Now get the fuck out of my house."

At Tiverton, the gold Cadillac sat in the drive. Tina Delmar was slouched behind the wheel. Her eyes were closed, the windows rolled up.

"Tina?" I said, tapping the hood.

She opened her eyes and cracked the door. "It's weird in here," she said. "I can smell Ashley's perfume. It's like she's all around me and nowhere at the same time."

St. James looked at the jumble of makeup on the passenger seat. "Are these her things?" he asked.

"Yes. I can't bring myself to clean the car out. Everything is exactly as she left it, right down to the CD in the deck. Who are you?"

"St. James."

"Cop?"

"Quasi-fed. Did Ashley always leave her personal effects in such a mess?"

"No. She was a hyperorganized neatnik. She must have been in a hurry to dump her bag out like this—or just plain nervous."

"Over what?" I asked.

"That's why I called."

Tina got out. She wore a pink jogging bra and tiny Lycra running shorts that rode up high, revealing a lot of backside. St. James liked what he saw. We followed her into the house.

"I had a big birthday bash here a month ago," she said, flopping on the couch. "That was the last time I saw Ashley alive, and she didn't look anything like a soldier that night."

"The way she was dressed?" I asked.

"The way she was *undressed* is more like it." Tina shook her head and smiled. "I've hardly ever seen her in anything but ripped-up Levi's and sneakers, but there she was, wearing a skirt that barely covered her butt, a top cut down to her navel, and nothing but a G-string underneath it all—on a girl who always wore waist-high white cotton briefs!

"And her shoes! Three-inch strappy sandals. She laughed when I noticed and said they were her fuck-me shoes. The best part is this: Ashley had a pedicure. I swear to God, her toenails were red. Never have I ever seen Ashley Sinclair paint her nails, and that goes for her hands as well as her feet."

"What about her diamond earrings?" St. James asked.

"A full half carat each set in white gold, on a girl who never wore jewelry. I never saw those before either. I thought she was dressed up for my party. But a friend of mine, Billy Zane, came by this morning with a video he took that night, and I learned why Ashley dressed the way she did."

"Did she have a date?" I asked.

"Not when the party started. Take a look at the tape. It's in the deck, cued up and ready to go."

She tossed St. James the remote. He hit PLAY.

Party time. Fifty young people milling through the house, hoisting drinks, popping champagne. Footloose and carefree. A night off and something to celebrate. Ashley stepped into the frame, dressed in a short black skirt, high-heeled sandals, and a backless silk halter top cut deep in front. Her hair was slicked back with gel. I instantly saw the uncanny similarities in our faces—as if I were watching a younger version of myself in an alternate life. I was not ready for the flesh-and-blood incarnation, for the revelation I saw there, and the striking resemblance shook me.

She blew a kiss at the camera. "Come on, Billy, get out of the goddamn doorway and let me by."

"Where you going, Ashley? Aren't you going to dance with me?"

"In my next lifetime, Zaner. And maybe not even then."

It was good-natured kidding between close friends.

"Your best friend will want to know why you're sneaking out on her party before the cake's cut."

Ashley put her hands on her hips and smiled sweetly into the lens. "I'm going on a date."

"With who?"

"None of your business. He's not military, which is a damn nice change. Sophisticated, elegant, and rich. Drinks at Ortell's. Dinner after that. Dancing, too. Did I mention sexy, Zaner? He oozes sex. If I'm lucky I'll get laid tonight, which is more than I can say for you!"

"Cut me some slack, Sinclair."

She elbowed by, he went on taping, bantering a fast-paced commentary as she skipped down the front steps and into the night.

"Ashley Sinclair," Billy Zane said, "resident babe and navy poster girl, exits stage right for a romantic rendezvous with a mysterious Don Juan. Will she get laid or won't she? Stay tuned."

"That's it," Tina said. "Ashley walked out, drove off in the Cadillac, and never came back."

St. James popped the tape. "What's Ortell's?" he asked.

"High-priced jazz club down on the waterfront in Falmouth. The car got towed from the parking lot there."

"Do you have any idea who she was going to see?"

"No. Just that it was a hot date. Had to be for her to dress the way she did. The sum total of her social life was having a pizza here with me. Said she just never met anyone who gave her the big thrill. Not that she had a chance. Ashley was working most of the time. She was on leave that weekend of my birthday when she disap-

peared. Before that she had three days over Labor Day.
Chris Preata came down and spent the holiday with us
here."

"Have you told Chris about Ashley?" I asked.

"Not yet. Part of me is in total denial."

"We need her number."

She wrote it down and gave it to me.

"And we need your car for a few hours," St. James
said.

"Okay," she said. "The keys are in it. Hey. I almost
forgot this."

She gave us a snapshot of Ashley at the party, smiling
and very much alive, very much like me.

I held out the composite of Vale. "Do you know
him?" I asked.

"Never seen him," she said. "I would remember.
That's not the kind of man you forget."

The drive out to the waterfront in Falmouth was surreal.

St. James sat in the back so the jumble of makeup on
the passenger seat would not be disturbed. Ashley's
flowery perfume was still heavy in the air, the flacon
rolled around on the floor. L'Air du Temps and saltwater brine. A heady mix. The soldier and the seductress. I
was at the wheel as Ashley had been on her final trip
from the place she called home, and slipping through
the night, I felt a shiver of her anticipation, as if it were
my own.

We traveled in silence, lost in our respective thoughts,
and did not speak until we were parked at the wharf.

"Flip the visor down," St. James said.

"Why?"

"It's what she did."

The visor makeup mirror lit up, and I went through

the moves instinctively, glossing my lips, brushing on fresh blush, palming my hair back, and smiling at my reflection. My hands were unsteady as I imagined hers had been. Love unnerved her, I thought. Ashley the woman was far less secure in love than in war. I believed she must have become frustrated rummaging through her bag, digging for the small bottle of perfume—so nervous that she emptied the bag out on the passenger seat to find it.

So nervous she forgot to take the keys when she got out of the Cadillac.

Nervous—and preoccupied with the hundred small motions of a soldier unaccustomed to seductive clothes. Tug the skirt, check the sandal strap, adjust the top. One more sweep of the hair and she was off, striding across the lot tall and confident, walking fast, heels tap tapping in counterpoint to her heart.

Tap tap, toward the heavy wood door of Ortell's, where he is waiting inside.

He didn't pick her up because she was proud. Didn't want him to see how and where she lived. He is rich. She is not. Tap tap, tug the skirt, and check the watch. She is on time, hyperpunctual, on the dot.

I pulled the door open and with St. James close behind, walked on in.

CHAPTER THIRTY-FIVE

Ortell's Dinner Club had dark-paneled walls, wood floors, deep leather chairs, and candles on every table. The décor was upscale mariner and intimate, geared for seduction, with soft lighting and a tight dance floor. We made our way to the small cozy bar. A jazz trio played softly in a corner.

Men and women were paired up, energy running electric between them. This was a hunt of a different kind, and it made me feel old. The gentle teasing, flirting, the fun of mating with none of the pain.

The bartender dealt out cocktail napkins, good linen embossed with a gold *O*. I ordered a glass of merlot; St. James had a gin and tonic with a twist.

St. James paid up front, flashed ID, and placed the picture of Ashley on the bar. "You ever see this woman in here?"

"Yes, sir," the bartender said, nodding. "One time. Coupla weeks back on the weekend. The way she was dressed, it took me a while to forget her. Real pretty young thing. Tall and built, and the outfit she was wearing showed it all off. She sat right here at the bar with her Mr. Wonderful."

"Anyone you know?"

"Not a regular."

"But he's been here before?"

"Couldn't say. Maybe, maybe not. Thirty years working the bar I usually remember the girls, not the guys, you know what I mean? She was something special. A lot like you, ma'am, if you don't mind my saying."

"How about Mr. Wonderful?"

"Dark hair. Early forties."

"Do you remember how he was dressed?"

"Low-key but rich. Long enough in this business, you get to know who folks are."

"Tall?"

"Not short."

"Was this the man?" St. James slid our composite across the bar.

The bartender looked at the photo long and hard.

"Could've been. But I wouldn't stake my life on it. Sorry. Like I said, money and girls, that's what sticks in my mind."

"He paid cash?"

"Lemme think." The bartender closed his eyes, sucked in his cheeks, thinking, and then nodded three times. "Cash. Not plastic. I remember that because he ordered a bottle of the most expensive champagne on the card. They each had a glass, danced one number, and left the rest. I capped it and drank it myself with a friend after we closed. Roederer Cristal. Vintage. Couldn't bear to think of it getting poured down the drain." He opened his eyes and shrugged. "That's all I know."

"If he shows up again, give me a call." St. James slipped him a hundred wrapped around a card with his cell phone number.

"Sure thing. Mondays we're closed. I'm here the other six nights. Hey, stick around for a set. The music's good."

We stayed at the bar where Ashley had a glass of champagne with an unknown man on the last night she was seen alive. St. James looked at the wine list and ordered a bottle of Roederer Cristal, pushing the drinks we had ordered but not drunk off to one side.

"Why champagne?" I asked.

"It's what they drank."

I sipped the expensive bubbly. It was iced and good.

"A cash customer with a million-dollar date," St. James mused.

I thought of the tape, Ashley's bright smile and easy way. She was a soldier trained to kill. But if the chronology was right, if medical science did not lie, she died twenty-eight days after she raised her glass with a stranger, off-duty, out of uniform in circumstances that had nothing to do with her job, with a date who was not military in a sexy bar that was not cheap.

Something happened after the clinking of glasses and

mutual toast. She walked out in strappy sandals and a thigh-high dress, and something happened. Four weeks later that something had her running for her life with fifty pounds of dive gear on her back. That something scared her so much her heart cells burst and even so, she managed to push through a debilitating late-stage radiation sickness with a superhuman strength born of the singular overwhelming need to escape.

Who, Ashley? Who were you looking at that night? Who did you walk out with? Where did you go? What were you running from?

St. James, in the stranger's place, running his battered hands over my arm, the polished bar top, the chilled glass, touching things the stranger had as if tactile connection would transport him back to that night.

"What are you thinking?" I asked.

St. James leaned in close to me, his lips next to my ear. "How he felt looking at her, what was in his mind, how she smelled to him, and felt when he took her hand in his. How he was charming, persuasive, elegant."

And dark haired and well dressed and rich. The room was full of tall, dark-haired well-dressed men. I watched the animated faces around us, shining eyes, healthy hair, and clean scrubbed skin—the mating dance, the flirting and smiling and subtle touching, and I knew what Ashley had felt that night. Excitement. Anticipation. The thrill of sitting close to a man, knees touching like mine did with St. James, hands brushing, fingers interlacing, a thousand quiet signals, flesh waking flesh. I felt her youth, her hunger, her need. *Love me, even if it's just for one night. Let me leave the soldier outside, let me live like a woman for one night.*

I looked up at the decoration on the wall behind St. James. An antique figurehead, a siren carved in wood. Back arched, chest thrust out, chin tipped high to the heavens.

Ashley, supine on the beach, Ashley in the sand.

Back arched high and unnatural, like a classic figure-head come unlashed from the prow.

Nausea rolled through me, a physical manifestation of the dreadful conclusion I had to make.

The composite of Vale was faceup, green eyes almost glittering, widow's peak dramatically black.

"Could it have been Vale?" I asked.

"I don't know yet," St. James said, "but there's a perfect symmetry to it that way."

"Tom Wheeler told me he thought Vale dyed his hair," I said. "He wondered why a man would do that."

"A man who does that has something to hide. Might have been him, Lace, sorry to say."

The memory of her savage burns flashed in my mind.

Did you, Vale? Did you? How could I have misjudged you so badly?

It must have shown on my face. St. James gripped my shoulders.

"Don't blame yourself, Lacie." His voice was hard and eyes, bright. "It's a flaw in our human construction that we can't know who someone really is right off, see the raw truth about what lives in a man's soul."

"I can't help thinking how Ashley felt when she was with him. That she must have felt like I did. Swept away. Out of control. And I wondered how he really felt, where the line was between the actor and the lie."

St. James handed me my glass. "Drink," he said. "It's what she did—what they did together here."

"You try to go into the killer's mind, like profilers do."

"Some of our tactics might be the same, but our fundamental approach is radically different. I don't believe in the holy scripture Bureau profilers preach—explaining away a man's violence because of what his childhood was like, using behavior to try to unravel motive, come up with a nice neat explanation about what makes a man tick."

"What do you believe?"

"That some men are born evil, and nothing in their environment or upbringing's going to change that. I try to put myself in the killer's frame of mind—not because I want to know what made him the way he is, but because by imagining what he felt I will slowly get to know him. I try to become him, and once I do, I can figure out where he's going next.

"It's an Iroquois hunting technique. They believe transference is elemental to the art. 'As long as you stay a man you'll never hunt the stag.' When you become the deer, you think like he thinks, you hear sounds in the woods with a deer's ear—and they are different, Lacie. You step out of yourself into deerskin; then and only then—when you are the creature you are tracking—do you have a chance of winning. It's the same hunting man. And that's the only true way."

"You ever lose yourself?"

"I've come close. Couple of times." He held up his glass. "A toast."

"To what?"

"To you."

"Why?"

"You're missing your cue. It's what he said to Ashley that night. Or something like it."

I touched my glass to his and took a sip.

"He watched her throat work as she drank," St. James said, narrating the imagined scene. "Her perfume was sweet and good, but not as sweet to him as her sweat would be. Her eyes were shining with anticipation, and all the while he knew they would soon burn with fear. He liked the prelude, the courtship, how she flirted shamelessly with him, not knowing she was flirting with death."

St. James rose and guided me through the crowd to the dance floor. "He saw the admiring glances from other men," St. James said, "the way they clearly envied him his trophy." St. James danced well. He drew me in close and smiled, beautiful in his own strong way. "They danced to long, slow songs like this one," he said. "He held her close, like I am holding you now. He breathed in the smell of her clean hair, and liked the way her body gave in to his, the way she was so easy to lead."

St. James was fluid and graceful on his hunter's feet, turning me in tight circles under the swirling pinpoints of strobe lights. His cheek brushed mine; he held the back of my head. His thighs pressed in against me. I felt him rise, the hardness between us, and I tried to pull away.

"No," he said, holding me tight, his voice warm in my ear. "That's what she felt. Be Ashley now. How does it feel to her?"

"Hungry. It's been a long time."

"And?"

"Pleased. That she did that to him right here in public."

"See what you do to me?" St. James was speaking words the stranger might have spoken in his seduction that night.

I broke away and threaded through the crowd back to the bar, putting a no-man's-land between us.

St. James followed, slid onto his stool. "Lacie?"

I would not look up, could not meet his eyes.

"You're in deep with me," St. James said. "I just hope it's not over your head."

I left the bar, and waited for him in the backseat of the car.

He slipped in behind the wheel. "If it was Vale she met in there," St. James said, "he wasn't worried about being remembered because the widow's peak and green eyes were both illusions, manufactured, fake. His natural traits are too general to help. He's an average man of average height and average weight. His facial structure is nice but not memorable aside from the details he puts there, the things he wants to stick in your mind."

St. James opened his laptop and talked while he worked the keyboard.

"If the widow's peak was waxed in," he said, "and the eye color from green contacts, then I'm certain he has changed the way he looks by now. We don't know Vale's true face any more than we know his true name. He is memorable only in the atrocities he commits. Those acts give him his one and only true face."

He put the laptop on the dash, angled so I could see the screen. The Face Pro full-color composite was on display. St. James tapped a key. The widow's peak and raven black hair melted away, green eyes turned brown, facial hair sprouted. I was looking at a bald man with a light brown mustache and beard.

St. James tapped a key again.

Red curly hair covered the scalp, eyebrows were full, eyes turned blue. The facial hair disappeared and the tan skin blanched pale.

St. James tapped again.

The hair was close cropped and yellow blond, the eyes stayed blue, but a blond beard grew in, concealing the jawline. None of the basic architecture had changed in the composites, not the line of the nose, or the shape of the eyes and lips. Still, each rendition looked totally different from the last. And the men were all strangers to me.

"We don't know who we're looking for," I said. "He could have been any of the men in Ortell's tonight."

"That's right. The composite is useless. We wouldn't know Vale if we passed him on the street."

St. James started the engine and turned on the stereo. A preloaded CD kicked in, filling the car with the sound of waves sweeping sand; then it was all ocean rolling, cresting, breaking, shore pounding surf that built in a climactic momentum and force so loud I instinctively reached out to turn the volume down.

St. James held me back.

"Listen," he said. "The killer's talking to us, telling us he was in this car."

Our eyes met, and although no further words were exchanged, volumes were spoken in that one long locked look.

CHAPTER THIRTY-SIX

We arrived at my house in Nantucket at midnight to a full moon burning a white hole in black clouds. St. James carried our bags from the taxi to my front door.

"I'm interested to see how you live," he said, "what kinds of things you surround yourself with."

"You'll be disappointed," I replied. "There's no personal history in this house. Everything's new."

"Still, your home is a reflection of your character. Do you fold your towels in half or toss them on the floor? Do you have frozen food in the freezer or is everything fresh? Do you prefer cotton sheets to synthetic? What books are on your shelves? You can learn about a person by knowing what they read. Your closet will tell me a lot about you, the way you keep your bedroom even more."

"I thought the trip here was about Vale, not me."

"Vale was in your house, in your bed, in your body," he stated simply, as if that gave him a warrant to search my life.

I disarmed the alarm, opened the door, and switched on lights.

"Sleek like the lady herself," St. James noted, taking in the expensive rugs, furniture, and oil paintings in my living room. "No frills or flounces. No ruffles or polka dots or chintz. Clean lines, neutral colors, and mint-condition Biedermeier, fawn-colored wood inset with black. Black oriental carpet on a polished oak floor, brass lamps with black shades. A muted room. Lots of black like your wardrobe. No white. No red. No orange."

Indian and aesthete rolled into one. He drifted into my office.

"The desk is neat," he observed, "hyperorganized, right down to the mail." He flipped through the stack. "Pool-supply catalogues. Toys, chemicals, covers, pumps, filters, skimmers, the works. You have a pool here?"

"No. At first I thought they were for Vale's address."

"And now?"

"They were sent here deliberately."

"I agree." St. James strolled over to the home theater and adjacent bank of full-size color TVs. "Quality installation. State-of-the-art electronics. Infrared capability with your laptop?"

"For the big screen."

"Handy device." He turned to my library wall. "Books shelved in alphabetical order. Contemporary works. Biographies and memoirs, the stories of other people's lives."

I had devoured them over the summer like a literary voyeur, reading about strangers and feeling terribly relieved when I found someone who had suffered pain the way that I had. I felt connected to their sorrow, a cousin to their tragedy. It was part of my healing process, traveling through another person's pages of grief.

"No Shakespeare, no Poe, no Flaubert or

Wordsworth," St. James said. "Classical literature is represented only by one Hemingway novel. *The Old Man and the Sea.*"

"That's not mine."

"Your daughter's?"

"No."

We left it at that.

He turned back to the library shelves.

"Contemporary political affairs," St. James went on. "Brokaw, Clinton, Walters."

Beyond that, everything I read related to my work—the profession of journalism itself, or subjects I wanted to explore as research for potential stories.

"No horror, no ghost stories, no supernatural stuff," St. James noted, dragging a finger over the long line of spines. "No mystery, no thrillers. No poetry, either—none of Elizabeth Barrett Browning's love sonnets to Robert. Not even a down-and-out raunchy love story, for heaven's sake. Black clothes and nonfiction. You're a restrained woman of decided taste, and that doesn't jibe with the kind of woman who would spend a night with a stranger on a first date. Why did you sleep with him?"

St. James was deadly serious. I preferred his mocking tone, his spicy verbal gibes.

"Why did you sleep with him, Lacie?"

He really wanted to know.

"Satisfaction with minimal emotional commitment," I said.

"You're holding back. What else?"

"Lust," I admitted. "Raw, raunchy, full-blown lust. Base animal instinct. I couldn't help myself."

"You invited him in?"

"Invitation is too formal a word for what I did."

"Which is?"

I closed my eyes, tried to shut out the memory. *Take me, please, right here, right now.*

"Beg," I said, opening my eyes. "I begged him to take me."

"Show me your bedroom."

"I'd rather not."

"You and Vale were together there. I want to see what he saw and where he slept."

I led him wordlessly up the stairs, flicking on lights, chasing darkness away.

St. James swept battered hands over my dresser, rough palms over my silk duvet and fat down pillows stacked three high. He studied the art on the walls and the built-in stereo unit next to my bed.

"What do you listen to up here?" he asked.

"Violin sonatas. They help me sleep." I opened the windows and storm shutters, looked out at the white curling surf. "Why does man kill, St. James?"

"Where does evil come from?" he said softly, coming to my side. "Is that what you're asking? No one can answer that. No one ever has, no one ever will, unless of course you take the Bible literally. Then the answer's easy. Simplistic, even. Evil is the work of the Devil."

"Do you believe that?"

"If I did, I would forget about finding Vale, knowing he'll get his justice come judgment day. Oh, yes—come *judgment day,* the final sentence comes down. I believe our world's more complex than that. What about you, Lace. Are you a religious girl?"

"Not anymore."

Truth was, I had lost God first when my father went up in flames; then I found him again when I held my newborn child in my arms. But in the last year I had lost him again, wondering what kind of God would let my young daughter be held hostage for eight long weeks, at the mercy of an evil man. I did not want a powerless or passive God. Now, thinking of what Ashley had felt in the long unknown days and weeks before her death, my spiritual blackout was complete. I closed my eyes, hoping I might feel a divine presence, but I felt St. James instead: his hand on my shoulder, his fingers on my cheek.

"What hurts you most, Lacie?"

"My daughter. What she went through. That I couldn't protect her against that."

"So beautiful and so troubled," he said, his warm body close to mine.

"Damn you." His hair smelled good. "The guest room's across the hall. Please go now."

"You have your own language, Lacie. You really mean stay. I saw you in the bar. You envied the women there. You're afraid that after Vale you'll never be able to give yourself to another man."

"Leave me alone."

"Remember the dance. You liked it in my arms."

"We were role-playing."

"Were we? Wasn't there some truth in our bodies there? The more you think about death, the more it makes you want to live. Isn't that so?"

"Get out, St. James. I'm tired, and it's late."

"Just two more reasons why I should stay." He tipped my chin up. "Eye to eye in stocking feet. Imagine how nice we would fit lying down."

He was daring me, and despite myself, it was hard to say no. I felt so alone. "Why on earth do you want me?"

"I've never met a woman like you."

"Oddity wins."

"No. I said it wrong."

"Say it right."

"I've never met a woman so much like me."

I laughed. "We're night and day."

"We're loners." He traced a scar on my cheek. "The fire?"

"Yes."

I touched the scars on his face one at a time, gentle

but curious—deep channels of waxy white flesh, carved out by bullets or knives or a raptor's razor talons. I had a dozen just like them channeling my thighs, my calves, my feet.

"Man or bird?" I asked of the lightning fork splitting his lips. "How did you get that?"

"A bow and arrow, learning to shoot. Got it all wrong that day, but believe me, I finally figured it out." He kissed my hair. "Lovely Lace hiding the scars on the outside when the worst are inside, raked across your soul, carved right into your heart. I could cure you if you'd let me."

"I hired you to find Vale. That's all."

His eyes went flat. He dropped away, gave me his back. Across the scrub oak and sand, the aquarium house was dark against a black sky. "That's Vale's place?" he asked.

"Yes."

"Don't wait up. I'll be out all night." He left, loped down the stairs, and out the front door.

I followed, locking up after him, resetting the alarm. My thoughts churned. My nerves were raw. Tired as I was, I could not imagine sleeping. I checked my e-mail and found a video message from Max. He used a sophisticated security encryption, a system that "recognized" my hard drive before allowing me to open messages from him. It ran through the check; then the video popped up. His face filled my screen, as if he were live on the other end, talking to me right then and there. His cheeks were sunburned, but I saw the high collar of his parka, and knew he was somewhere cold.

"Lacie," he said, scowling out at me. "I assume you're working flat-out on the story we discussed. I've looked into it and am now giving you four solid reasons why you are now ethically obliged to drop it.

"Number one, Spivak is no longer in the military's

employ. He's been retired as of this evening, and will be relocated from Hyannis Port to housing more appropriate to his new station in life. You won't find him.

"Number two, the training profile of the unit in question has been altered to conform to methods employed by all other branches of Special Ops. Compensation will be made to families that endured untimely losses, not that price tags can be put on lives.

"Number three, the Commander-in-Chief has been informed, and he has given the reorganized unit his personal blessing in the form of a sealed executive order.

"Number four, the covert nature of the unit's operations is essential and of the highest national priority. Any action that compromises that would be technically deemed an act of treason—no different from reporting U.S. strategic intent in times of war. In the eyes of the law, you have no right to report on SEATEC now. You are, in fact, forbidden to. This video file is programmed to self-delete at the end of the playback to you.

"When I'm back stateside, I expect that we will have dinner and talk of many things, but not of this. It will be an uncle-niece evening rather than soldier versus journalist, and I look forward to that, to the warmth we lost during our skirmish over your story. I love you, my girl. Good night."

He blew me a kiss. The image shrank to a pinprick of light; then the file flashed once and disappeared. I checked the cache on my hard drive and the recycle bin out of habit. There was no trace of the file, no sign it had ever existed.

There was one other message in my box, McKenzie's autopsy protocol on Ashley Sinclair. His conclusions squared with AFIP's, listing the cause of death as freshwater drowning, and the manner of death as a homicide. Spivak had shot straight with us on the diatom report.

I left a message for Harry on his voice mail, filling

him in. Special Ops had rolled SEATEC right out of our reach.

"Sinclair was murdered off-duty, off-base, and it may be that her death had nothing at all to do with her work," I said. "I'm chasing that angle now, and I'll let you know where it takes me."

I snapped out lights, went upstairs and looked out my bedroom window at the dark silhouette of Angel's Reef. St. James was sitting cross-legged on the bluff in front of Vale's house, face tilted up to the sky. I imagined his eyes were closed and he was focused on Vale.

Don't travel there, I willed him. *Don't go into Vale's world, his heart, his mind.*

I crawled into bed and lay wrapped in my thick duvet, thinking of Vale, fearing the worst. *Vale and a Special Ops soldier. There's no connection,* I reasoned. *No common ground.* I had slept with a man who had cut and run for reasons of his own that had nothing whatsoever to do with me. I was just a passing fling. That was it. We had absolutely nothing concrete to link him to Ashley, nothing to prove that Vale was the man she met that night, the man for whom she dressed to kill.

My mobile phone woke me at daybreak.

There was no voice, no words, no one speaking, or saying my name, just the sound of water, a shower running, a stream rushing over rock, cascading falls, then silence.

I slipped into black sweats and sneakers, pulled on a coat, and went out into the cold drizzle to the house next door. St. James was stretched out on Vale's front deck, flat on his back, arms straight at his side. A fallen saint or totem, that's what he looked like to me. I knelt down and touched his damp cheek.

"Ever sleep under the stars, little Lacie?" he asked without opening his eyes.

"What was the point in spending the night out here?"

"This was Vale's environment. I'm learning about him, traveling his sensory universe, discovering the sounds he heard, the smells he smelled."

"I had another call."

St. James's eyes opened. Clear gray and shining. Slate after the rain.

"No words were spoken," I said. "It was just the sound of water again, and the ocean. The sound of the surf coming down—exactly as we heard it in Ashley's car."

St. James rose. "I found a front door key taped to the top of the porch lamp," he said. "Come inside with me."

"A cleaning crew went through the day he left. What do you think you'll find now?"

"Your memory," St. James said. "The cleaners didn't take that."

Despite the fact it was morning, as we walked in, I felt I was back on that first night having dinner with Vale.

"How does the house feel to you?" St. James asked.

"Too quiet."

"What's missing?"

"The sound of the bubbling tanks." I went to the empty shelves. "This is where he kept his aquariums."

"How many?"

"Eight. One for each of the Seven Seas. The eighth was symbolic of the Eighth Sea. Vale said ancient mariners believed that the man who found the Eighth Sea would be blessed with eternal life."

"How big were they?"

"About three feet by two. Seven were full."

"And the eighth?"

"Empty."

St. James went to the tall brass telescope and looked out to sea.

"There are many reasons to rent this house," he said,

moving the scope in a slow 180-degree arc. "Paramount are the view and location. The island was important to him. I don't know how or why yet, just that it was."

He stepped back, and I looked through the eyepiece. The window of my bedroom filled the optical round.

"He watched me," I said flatly.

"Yes." St. James sat in the recliner, pressed a lever, and the footrest drifted up. "Why did he put the easy chair facing the wall?"

"He wanted to look at his aquariums."

"What were they like that night?"

"Dramatic, a living tableau of color and sound." I described the fish, the sea horse from Fiji, the model shipwrecks, the tiny figureheads, full-bodied females perfectly carved and arched like tightly strung bows. I told him that was how Ashley looked to me the night I found her.

"He told me he had sailed the Seven Seas," I said, "and there was an Eighth Sea as well. 'Eighty-six point five degrees,' he said. 'The temperature never changes.' What did he mean?"

St. James looked at me. Something stirred in his wolf gray eyes. That something made me afraid again—of him and of Vale, and of every wild thing who lived by rules I did not understand.

CHAPTER THIRTY-SEVEN

Vale went often to Woods Hole Institution at the far western tip of Cape Cod, and when he did it was always as Andreas Villard.

He found the science of water fascinating, and the

oceanographic laboratories there an endless delight. On this day, he sat alone in the auditorium, watching a special screening of an educational film. The giant cinerama screen was filled with his favorite subject: water.

Serene ponds, glassy blue glacial lakes, soft spring rains, lazy brooks, tranquil tropical seas, icicles slowly melting. Serenity masking power and force. The imagery was scored with the classical music of Vivaldi. A voice narrated in a reverential baritone.

"Consider the creation of the universe," the orator said. "Earth began as a ball of raging fire hurtling through space. Galactic elements converged, cloud cover wrapped the fiery ball, and a hundred-year rain came down in waves—showers so hard and wet and endless they beat the fire down, drove the flames underground until Earth's surface was a smoldering burnt crust wrapped around that molten core.

"And still the showers fell.

"Meteors now whirled out of the galaxy, flaming white bullets, slamming into Earth's new damp and tender crust, exploding on impact, gouging massive craters, great galactic wounds that were filled then with water from the hundred-year rain. Craters became lakes, ten-thousand-mile-wide valleys turned to vast oceans and seas. Over time the showers slowed to a drizzle, and that soon slowed to a trickle that melted then to mist, and the rain stopped and the clouds lifted and the sun embraced the earth, warming the oceans and lakes and ponds and seas.

"Water was the source, and out of it crawled Life, amphibious earth-roaming hybrids. Planetary rotation gave us time. As Earth whirled so did the centuries, spinning forward, turning the past into the future, creation into today, and now water remains the life-giving omnipotent, bottled and filtered and chilled to drink, warmed to cleanse, boiled to disinfect, harnessed to fuel energy creation in hydroelectric and nuclear plants. But even as man captures water behind dams and in reservoirs and bottles and tanks, he is helpless in the face and force of wild water unleashed."

The images on screen changed to ferocious aquatic destruction and the music to Mahler. Cyclones, typhoons, hailstorms and blizzards, tidal waves and squalls, hurricanes, floods. It was that fury of water that captivated Vale, the elemental beauty of a perfect weapon: a power he claimed for his own.

When the film was over, Vale walked to the end of the harbor pier and ate a lunch he had packed in his military rucksack. His camouflage field uniform was fresh; he was not due in at the SEATEC compound for another hour. His long white-blond hair was clean and combed. He leaned on the rail as he ate, watching pelicans do the two-step on pilings, sea bream schooling, fishermen mending nets.

When he finished, he tossed the plastic wrapper in a trash container, careful to not litter the sea. Vale was strolling back down the long pier when he saw an ethereal tiny angel coming his way. *Tinkerbell*, he thought, taking in her diminutive size and white-blond hair. He smiled, hungry for her—and then he spied the big one.

The lush one.

The body made for his bed.

A tall ravishing Swede with goddess curves. Her razored hair tapered to a point, revealing a graceful arch of neck, long column of throat, and a marvelous face.

Vale wanted her, and quickened his step.

She was instantly aware of his gold eyes on her, devouring her. She turned wary, raised a hand, and with long, pretty fingers raked her white hot hair as she looked him over, taking in his height, confidence, confrontational stance, the virile pelvic thrust that promised pleasure, adventure, deep primal satisfaction. He was at once refined and wild, the elegance of his body carriage at odds with the desert combat fatigues.

Most women went right for him without carefully analyzing their physical response. The rush of danger felt so much like lust. But this one was smarter than that, and highly tuned to her inner flow. As the distance between them closed, her pace slowed and her hand brushed her belly, sending him mixed messages so subliminal he was not sure she was even aware.

The belly brush was lust.

The slowdown was fear.

And her eyes were the dead giveaway, wide and fixed, locking on detail, the shape of his chin, the arch of his brow, measuring the forehead sweep, the stretch of lip, arc of cheek. Mentally snapping a shot.

Quid pro quo, Vale thought, noting the muscle twitching in her cheek. She was adding him up and not liking the sum. He knew who she was. He had seen her on the news. She was a local assistant district attorney, the one running for DA.

Still, he moved forward.

She was something electric, drawing him in.

Despite all her nonverbal warnings, he walked right up, close enough to smell her skin and see her nostrils flare as she read the wild in him, the savagery in the hard shine of his eyes. The Swede instinctively knew the bitterness she would taste going with him after the pleasure: the fear, the danger, the pain.

Desert fatigues were hiding nothing from her; she looked beyond the brown boots to the predatory stance, hands curled lightly at his sides, ready to make the grab, knead her breasts, grip her waist and pull her down into the dark place promised in his eyes.

No way, no how, the Swede swore with body language of her own. *I will kill you first, you son of a bitch. I will strip you of your camouflage, show the world your true face.*

Vale felt danger more than lust.

Not this one, he thought, regretting the fact he would not have her in his bed, riding her, owning her. Not this one. Not today. Maybe not ever. She was smart and strong and dangerous, and risk was never his thrill.

He backed off.

The Swede relaxed some, but not much.

Time and experience and intuition must have taught her—she must have known—that men like him come around and around and around.

The retreat was never final. And his retreat now was a stiff-backed promise. "I will be back," the stiff spine said.

Vale nodded once sharply at the Swede and smiled at Tinkerbell, then rapidly moved away, boots toeing the soft weathered wood, eyes cast down at the gaping spaces in the pier, at the rich emerald water thrashing pilings below, the white foam and dark kelp.

Vale walked swiftly and hard, careful to not step on the cracks. He felt the Swede fierce behind him, marble blue eyes drilling holes in his neck.

CHAPTER THIRTY-EIGHT

Down at the pool, the black netted cover stretched tight as a trampoline, slick and wet, funereal in the gray drizzled dawn. St. James sat on his heels at the rim of the shallow end. The long-poled skimmer lay off to one side.

"Vale liked to look at the pool, too," I said. "It was lit every night, even after he covered it."

"You ever see him swim?"

"No, but he must have."

"What makes you think that?"

"He had a swimmer's body."

St. James tried to pinch the cover back, but it was anchored tight, roped to steel tent pegs staked deep in the earth. He freed the rope at the corners of the shallow end and peeled the black canvas back, revealing a narrow strip of murky green-brown water. Algae bloomed thick on the surface and crawled up tiles above the water line.

St. James wiped a window in the green fungal fur, revealing a six-inch-high tile frieze inset as the pool's border.

"Beautiful," he said, wiping again. "Absolutely beautiful."

And they were.

Asymmetrical white stones were inlaid into six-inch squares of blue glazed ceramic tile, and finely etched with oceanic motifs: a fan-shaped shell, a classic mermaid, twin dolphins with their bodies entwined, a three-masted schooner, Neptune with his trident, a three-headed nymph.

"These are old," he said, touching the frieze. "The tiles are hand cast and colored, the white pieces laid in are whale teeth. This is scrimshaw. The workmanship is first-rate. I want to open the pool and see the rest of it. Can you manage the rope with your hands?"

"Yes," I said, testing one. The ropes were attached with basic slipknots and easy to untie, even with gloves.

We worked in tandem, peeling the cover back until it was neatly rolled up like a black carpet at the rim of the deep end. The pool was a rectangle of sludge, and on the surface was a floating armada of dead tropical fish: the violet dwarf angel, a magenta koi, the turquoise sea horses, too. Flotsam from one man's private storm. Seven Seas tossed into one.

St. James got the skimmer and gently gathered the litter of tiny corpses. He picked the cobalt angel out of the net. "Vale's?" he asked.

"Yes, from the tanks."

"*Amphiprion ocellaris,* found only in the South Atlantic, off Argentina. It's illegal to bring *Amphiprion* into the U.S. Commercial aquariums can get permits. Collectors can't. The species is almost extinct, wiped out by a black market of exotic fish collectors who will pay upwards of ten grand for a specimen. Argentina has been good about locking down the commercial trade. *Amphiprion* doesn't breed in captivity. Given the level of depletion, it's going to take decades before the population replenishes. Transporting the specimen is complicated. The fish is so delicate, it has to be shipped in tanks replicating their exact natural environment—water salinity, temperature, food, plant life. If not *Amphiprion* will die. This isn't the kind of fish you can sneak through customs in a jar."

I touched the body of a tangerine-breasted fighter.

"*Fellinas solaris,*" St. James said, "from the Mediterranean. The violet sea horses, *Hippocampus imperator.* The lime-finned ribbon here? *Thalassoma lunare* from the Indian Ocean. All endangered, expensive, and illegal."

"Why kill fish he went to so much trouble to get?"

"The answer is in the contradictions, the conflicting facts."

St. James was quiet as we crossed the shortcut in the moor back to my house. He went straight to my study and took *The Old Man and the Sea* from the shelf.

"You say this edition of Hemingway isn't yours, yet it is in your library. How did it get here?"

"I don't know."

He turned to Skyla's tank on the sill. "A starfish, a needle-nosed goby, and two king angels. One male and one female."

"Skyla only had one," I said.

"How did the second get there?"

"I don't know."

"You do, you just aren't ready for the truth."

"The truth."

"It's all around us. It has been from the start. You thought you found Ashley's body by accident, but we know it was planted there for you to find. You said you met Vale by chance on the ferry, but it really wasn't chance at all. He planned to meet you. You say you seduced him, but the truth is he seduced you—with his manufactured identity and two bottles of vintage champagne. Come upstairs."

We went into my bedroom. I paused by the window and looked out at the stripped pool.

"He gave the impression that he loved his fish," St. James said, "but he didn't love them at all. The thrill was in the calculated vicious total destruction of beauty."

"All we have is pure speculation," I said, beating back the dreadful admission. "We have no proof, no point of convergence that puts him with Ashley."

St. James went to the entertainment unit. A CD was preloaded.

"Violin solos," I said quickly. "Chopin."

He punched PLAY, and the sound of the ocean swelled filling the room. I reached out to turn it off.

St. James caught my hand. "Listen," he said. "The killer's talking to you now."

Breaking water roared around us, and as the final brutal conviction shuddered deep in my bones, St. James laid out the undeniable metric of guilt: the ocean sounds were from the phone calls—the caller was the killer who was in Ashley's gold Cadillac with the ocean CD—the same ocean CD the killer put in my bedroom.

And there was only one man that could be.

The caller, the killer, the lover were one and the same.

"Vale did it," St. James said, "and he wants us to know. He feels invulnerable now."

CHAPTER THIRTY-NINE

The shower was not strong enough, even though I had the taps open full blast. Two soapings were not enough, and neither were three. I scrubbed my body down a fourth time, doubting I would ever feel clean. The hands that had caressed my breasts had held Ashley's bucking body under water. The eyes that had stirred me so had glittered with satisfaction while he watched Ashley drown. Vale's guilt was no longer imaginative speculation. It was a heart-chilling fact.

I stumbled out of the shower and crouched at the commode, giving myself over to the nausea twisting my gut.

You slept with a killer. You invited him in.

I hugged cold porcelain as my insides came out, and when I thought there was nothing left, I threw up again.

"Don't go."

"Say it again so I know you mean it. That you want me to stay."

"Don't go. Make love to me tonight."

Two teeth brushings, and my mouth still tasted sour.

My stomach was empty, but I still felt sick.

Hair was a wet, long tangle snaking down my back. I didn't care. I pulled on black jeans and a sweatshirt and walked barefoot downstairs out to my deck. The wind was carving white lines in the sea. Rain blew down in sideways sheets. My heart was stone.

You slept with a killer. You invited him in.

Judgment is the guiding compass in news reporting. How could I work if my judgment was this bad? How could I be a mother, a journalist, a woman?

"You can't see a man's soul when you look in his eyes," St. James had said. "You can't know what lives in a man's heart."

Vale's glittering green eyes had promised elegant passion, pulse-pounding lust, great living emotions—everything but torturous death.

St. James appeared at my side. "You found Ashley because Vale wanted you to," he said. "You aired the story about that because he wanted you to—but then you went further, you ID'd the body, and Vale did not want that. He ran. His thrill is in the killing and the aftermath of the killing. The news story is his celebration. You went beyond the story. You investigated. You went too far too close to him here. He could not—will not—risk capture. But we will find him. Don't look back, Lacie. Move forward."

"Forward," I said, my mind a total, numbed blank.

"Always and only forward."

St. James guided me into my office. "Get information," he said, "look for inconsistencies, facts that don't add up, conflicts. Conflicting information inevitably leads to the truth." He gave me a sheet of white paper, a neat list of the fish in Vale's tanks. "These specimens require permits for importation into the U.S.—permits that are granted only to commercial aquariums—yet somehow the fish ended up displayed in a private home. That's a conflict. Start with that."

Keep moving ahead.

*   *   *

U.S. Fish and Wildlife.

I faxed over the list of species and hit the phones, requesting full disclosure of the import permits issued in the last five years for each of Vale's species.

"We don't have permits computerized yet," the media relations officer said. "They'll have to be pulled manually, and that will take some time. I'll get back to you just as soon as I can."

Don't look back, Lacie. Keep moving ahead.

Gaines Premier Properties. Sheila Gaines answered the phone.

"Vale contracted with us for domestic work," she said, "daily house cleaning, laundry, monthly window washing, and so forth."

"And the pool?"

"Oh," she said. "He had the option of using the company that services all our rentals, but Mr. Vale said he would take care of it himself. When we did the walk-through, I saw he had even put the cover on for the winter, saving us the trouble. He's a thoughtful man."

But Vale had not maintained the pool himself.

He had hired someone to do it.

Nantucket had seven pool service companies listed in the book. I spoke to each and still could not lock Vale's service down. All negative responses. I called the three shops that sold pool supplies off the shelf. I described Vale's pool man: the hooded jacket and black swatch over one eye that looked like a patch. No one knew him.

A one-eyed pool man skimming—spring, summer, and fall, working under clear skies and cloudy, in the wind, the fog, the cold, and even the rain—but always and only, alone at night.

* * *

Conflict—the pool tiles were old, but the house was new.

I called Gaines Properties again.

"Well," Sheila Gaines said, "the original house at Angel's Reef was built around the same time as yours. But when the Stillwells bought last year, they tore it down and built brand-new, from the ground up."

"What about the pool?"

"Oh, the pool was there. They didn't change that."

Keep moving ahead, Lacie.

Wheeler knew everything about the island. I wanted to ask him about the frieze. I called his mobile. He answered, and I heard a lot of background noise, music and talking, a crowded lively place.

"Glad I got you, Wheeler. I need your help."

"Lacie!" he said. "I'm sitting here at the Anchor downtown, sharing a platter of oysters with Hinks. You want to join us?"

"I need to talk to you privately when you've got a chance."

"Good enough. I've got to swing by the hospital; then I'll touch base with you later after that."

Wheeler hung up.

Keep moving forward, Lacie.

I called Ann Gamble and asked if she had worked for Vale often.

"No," she said, "that one night was the only time. But he had a cleaning woman in five days a week. I know that for a fact. She's a friend of mine. Said Vale was always alone there. He never entertained."

I called the cleaning lady, wanting my information firsthand.

She confirmed what Ann Gamble had said.

Don't look back.

Ashley's college roommate and friend, Chris Preata.

I tried her work number and got voice mail. I tried her home number and got another version of the same message.

A black state police cruiser screamed up my drive, running lights blazing bright in the storm-darkened day. Hinks dropped out, poured into jeans like cotton was paint. I met her at the door.

"Evening, Hinks. What brings you out my way?"

"Haven't heard from you in a few days."

"Haven't had anything to say."

"Why were you calling Tom Wheeler?"

"Ask him."

"I did, and he told me it had nothing to do with state police affairs."

"Wheeler's a truthful man."

She ran a long fine-fingered hand through her short hair.

"How's the swimming?" I asked, not quite knowing why.

"Good," she said, eyeing me, suspicious.

"Butterfly's your event."

"That's right. Singles competition and relay for the town master's team."

"Nantucket?"

"No, Hyannis Port. Big Olympic pool there. Good people. Great sport."

"Train hard?"

"Four nights a week, including tonight."

"It's not too late?"

"Hell, no. Pool stays open until ten. Getting lane time's not easy. Everyone wants to swim after work."

"Wheeler said you were something to watch."

"Tom said that?" A big smile lit her face, then quickly faded as she eyed me carefully. "Are you seeing him socially?"

"No."

"If you get the urge to, think twice. Tom's a good man who got a bad deal. Anyone hurts him again, they answer to me."

"Our relationship isn't like that."

"Then what is it?"

"Professional."

"You're working the case together, aren't you. You're working on the drowning that happened here. You're both shutting me out."

"We're doing you a favor, Hinks. Taggert pulled you off the case. It's not state business."

"So I've been told."

Her boots came down hard on my deck as she spun around sharply and headed back to her car.

I found St. James at my kitchen table, finishing scrambled eggs and a mug of coffee. He had showered and changed into his idea of fresh clothes: the same battered Levi's with a different polo shirt, this one the color of zinc. He was working on his laptop, scrolling through McKenzie's autopsy protocol. I knew the words by heart, the cold medical terminology, death's own iambic pentameter.

"Ashley was missing for four weeks before she

washed up," St. James said. "As her radiation sickness progressed, the nausea would have made it impossible for her to eat. But McKenzie remarks on the fact that her body was remarkably fit."

"McKenzie found puncture marks on the tops of her hands consistent with IVs. Vale could have kept her pumped full of nutrients if he wanted her strong."

"Yes," St. James said thoughtfully. "And then there arc her nails. In the protocol McKenzie notes the polish was fresh, and the color pink. In Tina's video her nails were red."

"Vale changed the polish."

"And shaved her legs. Her underarms, too, McKenzie says."

"He took care of her for four weeks?"

"Yes."

"Why?"

"It takes that long for radiation burns to manifest after exposure. I believe Vale burned her, then waited four weeks because he wanted the burns to be visible—he wanted you to see them, Lacie. He saw them as tattoos, birthmarks that bound you, making you sisters in a way. They are part of his dialogue with you. He's been talking to you all along without words."

My cell phone rang.

"Wait," St. James said. He tapped into the clone on his mainframe so he could listen in. "If it's Vale, talk to him. Draw him out. I'm ready now. Pick up."

I did.

"Ms. Wagner?"

A stranger, not Vale. A young woman, tentative and unsure.

"Who are you?" I said, skipping social pleasantries, steeling myself, afraid it was Skyla's school, her security detail with foreboding news.

"Kiri Hannover at Woods Hole marine biology lab over in Falmouth." She hesitated, undone by the hostility in my voice. "We met last week on the beach. I'm the oceanographer, tracking the tides on that drowned diver. I got a package in the mail today addressed to you care of me here at the lab. Instructions on the outside of the box say to call you at this number. It was sent yesterday, postmarked Hyannis Port. There's no return address. I haven't opened it yet."

St. James took the phone out of my hand. "Kiri," he said, "I'm a federal investigator working the case. I want to open the package myself."

"Woods Hole has a couple of different buildings," she said. "I'm in the lab on Water Street."

"Sit tight. We're leaving now."

CHAPTER FORTY

Vale powdered the insides of two wet suits. When the dusting was complete, he feathered his fine long fingers over the suits in a tender caress. Cool neoprene against his skin was as erotic as a lover's hot rousing touch.

Once suited up, Vale moved quickly, packing the van with essential gear. High-voltage underwater lights, twin sets of digital Nikonis waterproof motion-picture cameras, two weighted tripods, and generous lengths of heavy-duty white sailing rope.

Vale picked up his Interspiro full face mask and ran through audio checks on the Lar-5 mini-mike and earphone adapters fitted inside. Next, he inventoried the extra set of gear, double-checking payload on the extra dive belt, size of the dive gloves, and blacked-out Interspiro full face mask, then took the air reserve on the extra tank down to five minutes.

A small Zodiac inflatable craft was lashed to the roof of the van: transport for equipment and passengers.

In addition to himself, Vale would be traveling with a party of one.

Hands curled lightly at his sides, Vale looked at her and shuddered with anticipation.

She was crouched in the corner of the van, dripping wet and shaking, terrified beyond belief. He tossed the extra wet suit at her, crept up, touched her hand, her breast, her lips, her cheek. She was very grown up, yet cowered like a little girl.

"Hey, pretty baby," he said. "How did you get so pretty like that?"

Her body was wrapped in a soft fluffy beach towel, a pastel shade of coral pink.

"You'll be warmer soon, little baby, when we get you into your wet suit."

She blinked at him. Her mouth moved but no sound came out.

"That's right, sweetie. It's a fine night to make a movie. An even better night to go for a swim. I brought you something to help pass the travel time of the drive."

He held out a twelve-inch plastic toy diver and flicked on the switch. The tiny legs began kicking, black flippers flipping, and the little diver head turned rhythmically left to right. Vale set the kicking diver in her lap, tucked a stray curl behind her ear, and kissed her lightly on the forehead.

He was taking her to the dark water, still water, dead water that would be the water of her death. He was going to tape the whole event, from start to finish, add it to his private collection, and post it on the Net.

Vale opened a thermos and offered her a drink. "Want some, little baby? Are you thirsty sitting there?"

When she didn't respond, Vale shrugged and took a long slow drink of ice water. His throat worked, easing the liquid down. Nothing—not the best wine or champagne—refreshed like this. Ice rattled in the thermos, and the sound reminded Vale of how he had almost died in an avalanche once, almost drowned in the snow, how he rolled head over toes over knees and rode the monstrous towering frozen white wave, only to be sucked into the fulcrum, the centrifugal force of the slide, snow and ice swamping every bodily orifice, frozen water burning his lungs.

Drowning in winter on dry land was the closest to drowning Vale himself had ever come.

CHAPTER FORTY-ONE

The bay crossing on the hydrofoil was an hour-long bucking, pitching, wet rolling ride, slicing up out of the storm-frenzied waves only to slap down again, flat-bellied and hard. A half dozen passengers huddled miserably below deck, heads in laps, moaning, every last one of us feeling seasick—except St. James. He stood at the window, feet spread wide in a solid stance, eye to eye with the Atlantic, working the case over in his mind.

I kept my eyes closed and did not open them again until the ferry horn blew and we had pulled up next to the Hyannis wharf.

Dry ground felt good even in the hard-driving icy rain. Soon we were off in a rented car with St. James at the wheel, and I felt sick all over again as he pushed the four-cylinder Honda as if he were driving a Carrera. His right hand drifted off the wheel often, feeling for a stick shift that wasn't there. I fiddled with the radio and tuned in the news. A typhoon in Malaysia, a hurricane in the Bahamas, a flood in New Orleans, subway bomb in New York. Nature was wreaking havoc, and man went on creating natural disasters of his own. Death tolls followed by sports scores followed by commercial jingles, and all around us in the car was the sound of pounding rain the wipers could not keep up with.

Woods Hole sat out at the far western tip of Cape Cod, bordered on two sides by water. The Chemical Oceanography building was of red brick and three stories high, dramatically positioned overlooking the sound with a clear view to Martha's Vineyard. We parked out front, and as I followed St. James inside, I could not help but think of the lives lost in those local waters—Mary Joe off the bridge at Chappaquiddick, John-John and Carolyn off Gay Head, 310 passengers on the Egyptian jet two months after that.

We found Kiri alone in her lab. The room was huge, with twelve-foot ceilings, a gleaming white floor, and white waist-high lab tables laid out in a neat grid. Computer terminals were strategically placed in workstations, linked to digitizing equipment. Deep steel sinks were built into two walls, and the remaining two were lined with aquariums, seven six-foot-tall tanks. They were four feet wide and brightly lit. Big digital gauges at eye level glowed with the water temperature in each. There were no fish or plant life inside, just water.

Kiri was perched on a high rolling stool, peering into

a microscope. She looked up as we walked in, surprising me again by her startling ethereal look, the pale perfect skin, white-blond halo of hair, and delicate white diamond on the left side of her nose. Her lab coat was open. Under it she wore leggings and a tight Lycra top that showed off her tiny but perfect athletic physique.

Kiri held up the package she had called me about. "Does this have anything to do with the drowning last week?" she asked.

"It might," I said.

St. James examined the package carefully, smelling it and holding it close to his ear before opening it. The box itself was plain brown and addressed with a standard white computer printed label. Inside, Styrofoam packing bubbles made a protective nest for a little toy diver like the one Wheeler had found at the beach—but where the air tanks belonged was a simple glass test tube labeled with a typed note: *Go to this place where nothing lives. Your next story is there.*

St. James picked up the test tube and rocked it from side to side.

"Colorless liquid with traces of gray-silver sediment," Kiri said. "That's all you can tell from a visual examination. There are a hundred things it could be."

"Start by telling me what it's not," St. James said.

Kiri took the tube and removed the cork. "Gasoline, acetone, chloroform, organics like that have characteristics smells." She gently sniffed. "This has no odor at all."

Using an eyedropper, she transferred five drops of the liquid into a beaker of water.

"They mix perfectly," she observed. "Methanol or ethanol don't mix with water, so we know it's not either of those." She squeezed a drop of the sample on a small strip of paper. "The pH is seven—right in the norm for water. Drāno, soap, anything alkaline or lye would give us a pH of fourteen. Diluted acid, a pH of one."

She stepped down the lab table to a large piece of equipment that looked like a dishwasher tipped on its side.

"The mass spectrometer identifies the atomic structure of water samples," she said. "It will give me enough information to tell you exactly what kind this is."

"Why didn't you put the sample in there at the start?" I asked.

"I had to make sure it wasn't flammable first. If you put ethanol into an MS, you'd blow the whole place up." She inserted a tube into the vial and pressed a button. "The MS is sucking liquid from your sample into a nebulizer, which breaks the liquid down into very fine particles that look like a mist. The mist gets forced through a ten-thousand-degree quartz torch that dissolves the particles into atoms. The MS then analyzes the atoms to determine the elemental composition. You can't see that part of the process with the naked eye, but it's happening now."

She moved to a computer terminal and watched the results come up on the screen.

"This is fresh water," she said, "far too complex to be distilled water. The sodium level's too low for bottled mineral water. Chlorine level's too low for city tap water. It appears to be from an outdoor source that has an overabundance of silicate and aluminum-iron compounds."

"Which means?" St. James asked.

"The water has had long-term exposure to granite. My best guess? This came from a body of water in a granite quarry."

She prepared a slide with a sample of our water and studied it under the microscope.

"Weird," she said. "Abandoned quarries fill up with

rainwater and melted snow. Sometimes an underground spring acts as a source keeping it fed with fresh water, but usually not. Nonetheless the quarry water's alive, teeming with microscopic life—diatoms, amoebas, bacteria, free-formed floaters. Look in my microscope here and tell me what you see."

St. James went first. "Nothing," he said, standing aside to make room for me.

"Nothing at all," I agreed.

"There are two other classifications for water aside from salt and fresh," Kiri said. "Entropic, which is water that can support life, and atropic, which is water that cannot. Acid rain, an underground ore vein leaching toxic geological compounds, run-off from agricultural waste—there are dozens of possible reasons water turns atropic. You can swim in it, swallow small amounts, and be okay. But nothing can live in it, not even the most basic single-cell life-forms. We call it dead water."

"Is that what's in your big tanks?"

"No," Kiri said, moving to the giant aquariums. "These waters are full of life. You just can't see it. We're crossbreeding microscopic organisms hoping to create a hybrid that's naturally resistant to certain toxins. If we do, we'll farm the organism in mass quantities and use it to cross-pollinate the oceans, introducing a front-line defense against pollution and toxic waste. In layman's terms, we think we can create a kind of organic oceanic immune system before it's too late."

"Why seven aquariums?" St. James asked. "What's the significance?"

"For the Seven Seas," Kiri said, framed by glass and clear water as she walked the line of glowing tanks. "The ancients used the phrase to identify the bodies in the world as they knew it. To oceanographers today, the expression represents the most important bodies of water on earth—all but one of which are oceans, not seas. The water in each aquarium here comes from one of those Seven Seas."

St. James looked at me. We were both thinking of Vale.

"Do you know anything about the Eighth Sea?" I asked.

"Sure," Kiri said. "It's an old joke from college science class."

"What does it mean?"

"Eighty-eight percent of the human body is water—and the water's quite high in salt content. Technically, the human body fits the scientific definition of a sea: a self-contained body of salt water that has no currents or tides."

"The Eighth Sea is the human body?"

"That's right," she said, tiny against the wall of tanks. "Back to your sample. We have a national database of water sources here. If it were from a river, lake or ocean, we could match it using diatoms as markers. But we don't catalogue quarries."

"Which means you can't nail down the provenance."

"Not necessarily. If it's from the Northeast coast, we might be able to. Bruce Rickman is the resident geologist here. He knows more about Northeast rock than anyone."

We followed her down the hall.

Unlike Kiri's pure white gleaming lab, where everything was organized and perfectly placed, Rickman's was a mess. Papers and books were stacked three feet high. Old unwashed beakers were piled up in a sink. Dirty tools and rock samples cluttered every surface.

Rickman himself, tall and skinny, was just as unkempt, in a faded flannel shirt spotted with dirt and wrinkled chinos stained dark at the knees. Black wiry hair stuck up on his head. Kiri made introductions, but the geologist didn't seem to care who we were. His sole interest was in the rock. He removed sediment-filled fluid with an eyedropper, placed the sample on a slide, and studied it under a microscope.

"American granite," he announced. "No question in my mind. Definitely East Coast and high north. You get striation like this when the rock's stressed from extreme cold."

"What if it came from a quarry?" St. James asked.

"Then there are only two possibilities. Smyth's up in New Brunswick, Ontario, or Nelson Pitts, in Lowell, Massachusetts. Smyth's is still operating. The Lowell site was closed down ten years back."

"Why?" I asked.

"They ran out of granite. Happens all the time. Man goes in, strips the earth bare, then leaves. The dig site fills up with water, and poof. You've got a nice big swimming pool. All the fun, none of the bills. Problem with Lowell's is that something killed the water. Nothing can live in it. Not even a single-cell amoeba. The water's dead."

"You have divers on staff," St. James said to Kiri. "Where do they keep their gear?"

"Wet suits and tank packs are considered personal. The divers take it all home. Anything else—all the tools used for underwater work is kept here."

"Including lights?"

"Sure," she said. "The divers work a lot at night collecting nocturnal sea life."

"I need one of those lights," St. James said. "Now."

CHAPTER FORTY-TWO

We had nothing more than guesswork, and our assumptions derived from Vale's own words. There was no singular overt threat, but we raced on nonetheless, through rain that came down in waves, washing over the highway, turning asphalt to rivers, beating the roof so hard raindrops sounded like stones.

"Vale told you about a mythical eighth sea," St. James said.

"The human body."

"He sent the quarry water because he wants us to go to the Lowell quarry, where we'll find his next victim—another body, another eighth sea."

"We have to call the state police," I said. "Send them there now, ahead of us."

"There's no point. His victim is already dead."

"How do you know?"

"The note promises that. Vale's not interested in pitting us against the clock, in risking a survivor. Risk isn't his thrill."

"What is?"

"Media attention. He wants—needs—to show off his work. He is a highly organized, meticulous, controlled killer. I think Vale perceives the television coverage as part of his kill. He wants maximum control of *who* tells his story—and he has chosen you."

I didn't want to do this, to find another Ashley. I wanted to turn back, but I sat in silence instead, knowing I had no real choice.

An hour and a half up the coast to Boston, another hour traveling north, where we took the exit for Lowell and traveled east along a narrow twisting road. We were two and a half hours from Falmouth, and the storm was still with us as we went deep into the Massachusetts countryside.

We hit the turnoff for the quarry at four-thirty. A NO TRESPASSING sign warned visitors away, but St. James rolled right past it, down a muddy access road crowded by overgrown scrub on both sides. Low-hanging tree branches swept the hood. Old leaves tumbled in the wind, sticking to the radio antenna and gathering against glass, rust-colored and wet, the size of hands. The road came to a dead end at a broad rock plateau. St. James cut the engine, pulled off his shirt, and opened his door. Rain gusted in. He took the underwater light and went out into the night, to the quarry rim. I followed.

In front of us, granite walls rose thirty feet high, encircling a pool of water. Rain needled the surface, silver pricks dancing on liquid obsidian.

He toed his sneakers off and removed his jeans and holster.

"St. James!"

He dived. A splash flared white, and he disappeared. Ten feet out, he surfaced, took a deep breath, and jackknifed under again. He went on like this in a methodical way. He was swimming a grid, conducting an aquatic search, listening for the sound of regulator bubbles, fanning through the dead water searching for the eighth human sea, hoping against hope that she might still be alive, but knowing she was not. The underwater light barely penetrated the black night water, making his work impossibly hard.

I went to the car, turned high beams on, then paced the quarry rim, and waited.

St. James. His deal with me was to work alone.

After fifteen minutes, the diving and splashes disappeared.

St. James was drowning out there, a girl dying or already dead.

Bad deal, St. James. This wasn't the way to go.

I flipped open my cell phone wondering where on earth a 911 call would fall and how far away help was, but the call did not go through. Satellite blackout zone or maybe it was the storm. I tried again and got nothing but crackling static.

I called out even though I knew he could not hear. "St. James!"

Rolling thunder ate my words.

"St. James!"

Talking to the wind, Lacie. Talking to the sky.

In a split-second strobe of lightning I saw him sidestroking in, towing a body alongside. It was facedown, sheathed in a wet suit and loaded with tanks. He hoisted himself out first, then lifted and laid her out on the shore.

She looked exactly like Ashley had, arched unnaturally high and supine over the tanks, every detail revealed in our high-beam lights. Her wet suit appeared to be three sizes too big. There was no weight belt at her waist. Her hands were tied behind her back, and her bare feet were bound with the same thick white rope.

The glass of her dive mask was blacked out with paint. A neoprene hood covered her forehead and most of her cheeks. The little skin of her face that remained exposed was blue gray, the color of stone—except for a strange oval around her mouth that looked raw and fresh, blistering red.

If it was a radiation burn, it was unlike the round oozing craters on Ashley's body or any thermal burn I had ever seen. Her lips were hugely swollen and colorless;

chunks of flesh were missing as if she had been attacked by a fish. Eyeless and pale, branded with that savage red oval, she looked inhuman.

"She was loaded with a hundred-pound weight belt," St. James said, "to keep her down. I had to ditch it to bring her in."

I checked the air gauge on her tanks. The needle was on empty. I rocked on my heels, hyperventilating—letting the tears spill down.

"We couldn't have saved her," St. James said, "no matter what. Her body's rigid. Full rigor's set in. She died twelve hours ago, maybe more. McKenzie will lock down the time of death when he does the autopsy."

"McKenzie?"

"He did Ashley. I want forensic continuity. He might pick up something here someone else would miss."

"Tom Wheeler assisted."

"Then I want him there, too."

He laid the dead girl on her side in the backseat, mask and tanks intact. After he dried himself and dressed, he got behind the wheel and turned the heat up to high. His hands shook, and his skin was pale under the tan. St. James was chilled to the bone.

As we drove slowly away I felt a dreadful sense of déjà vu: the clinking of tank steel in the backseat, the presence of the body right there close to mine, the smell of water, the sound of the beating wind—just like the night I had ridden in Wheeler's Jeep, after taking Ashley's body off the beach.

When we were a hundred yards down the road, free from the high quarry walls, I dialed Wheeler's number and the call went through.

CHAPTER FORTY-THREE

McKenzie was waiting in the receiving bay.

"Highly unusual procedure taking delivery of remains like this," he said, tapping the hood of the Honda.

"It's a highly unusual case," St. James replied.

"Why isn't this one going straight to AFIP?" McKenzie asked.

"There's no military ID on her," St. James said, "and no reason to think we'll find any. Ashley Sinclair's military status had nothing to do with her death. I'm certain that the man who killed her tortured this woman, too. AFIP has no claim here tonight."

"What about the Bureau?"

"Technically this body belongs to the state right now."

"And you believe this death is directly related to Ashley Sinclair's."

"Yes. The same man killed both women."

"You removed the body before the crime scene unit could move in. That's going to ruffle some feathers over at state police, and if those feathers belong to a DA named Hinks, God help you."

"This body wasn't found in her county."

"Doesn't matter. It is directly linked to a body that was—and that gives her investigative clout. She'll go ballistic, slap you both with a pile of lawsuits—keep you locked up in depositions and legal red tape so long it'll be the same thing as shutting your investigation down."

"I'm the one who fouled protocol," St. James said.

"I'll take state's heat, whoever and however it's ultimately dealt out."

"Good enough," McKenzie said. "I've got no support staff working graveyard tonight, and I'm finishing up another body. Wheeler came in on a chopper. He's in suite two, ready to go. Get her on the gurney. Take her to Wheeler. He can start without me."

St. James loaded the gurney and we rolled her inside, down long deserted halls to the autopsy suite where Wheeler was waiting, suited up and ready to go.

Introductions were brief. We skipped social amenities, focused as we were on the solemn ritual about to unfold. Wheeler gave us each a set of protective clothing. I knew the drill. St. James did, too.

Wheeler moved the body to the steel table and measured her height while we dressed. He loaded a Polaroid, fired off a test shot. The flash popped loud in the cavernous suite. He turned on the small tape recorder strapped to his waist and looked up at me. A bright blue surgical cap covered his skull, his eyes of the same color seemed brighter just then.

"Case number 98789," he said. "Female Caucasian . . ."

As Wheeler spoke, I could think only of Vale and the pleasure he had taken in the kill.

White rope bound her hands tightly to the back of the tank pack, running down to her ankles, looping back up between her knees, and finally up—circling tightly around her neck.

"Sadistic bastard," Wheeler said. "Every effort to break free would have created tension on the neck rope, increasing pressure against her windpipe. If she fought to break loose, she would strangle herself. If she did nothing, she would drown. Hell of a choice."

He went over the rope system with a high-power loupe, looking for human hairs, bits of fingernail, skin scrapings caught in the twine, any physical evidence that could be traced back to her killer, but found nothing at all.

"Water's hell on forensics," he said, shaking his head.

Wheeler removed the rope and tank pack, then turned the body over so she was lying faceup.

"Is that a burn around her lips?" I asked.

"No," he replied. "This isn't from radiation or any thermal source. Scavengers didn't do it, either. The oval's too symmetrical."

Her blackened mask was still sealed on tight.

"He wanted her to feel trapped," St. James said, "without a sense of direction or time, focused on nothing but the dying."

Wheeler slipped a finger under the mask and broke the seal. He eased the mask off over her head, revealing the full face.

"What in God's name?" St. James said, uncharacteristically undone.

Her eyes, locked in a stare, were shrouded with a filmy yellow caul. Underneath, so many capillaries had burst the whites of the eyes had turned a bright bloody red.

"It's almost as if she suddenly underwent an extreme change in pressure," Wheeler said. "As if she plunged too deep too fast, and the air trapped inside the mask, which was pressurized for sea level, didn't have sufficient time to adjust. How deep was she when you found her?"

"Fifteen feet," St. James said. "Twenty at most."

"Too shallow to induce that kind of injury."

"What happened to her skin?" I asked.

The oval area under the mask was deeply wrinkled with a spongy texture that reminded me of soggy white bread. Chunks of sponge had fallen out, leaving open infected wounds. Her face was totally unidentifiable, as even male or female.

"I don't know." Wheeler probed the spongy flesh on her upper cheek. "I can't explain it any more than I can explain the caul. I've never seen anything like it."

He studied the facial injuries carefully with a magnifying glass, taking pictures as he went, for the record.

"The neoprene hood is tight at the neck by design," Wheeler said. "There's no way to remove it in one piece without my creating pressure on her face, which I'm not sure her deteriorated flesh will be able to withstand. I want those facial injuries intact for now, so I'm going to cut it off."

He made two incisions, one ear to ear over the top of her skull and a second cut from the back of her neck up to the crown. The hood peeled away in four sections. Underneath, her blond hair was a tangled, matted mess. Parts of the scalp were bald where patches of hair had been ripped out.

"Signs of a struggle," Wheeler said.

She wore dive gloves. He stripped one off.

Her right hand was swollen twice its natural size. Chunks of flesh were missing like the skin on her lips.

"The bones in all five fingers are broken," Wheeler observed. "Flesh is bruised, and judging from the varied colors, the bruising took place at many different times. Some are old, yellowing and fading, others are deep purple and quite fresh. The remaining epidermis on the palm beds and tops of the hands has the same spongy consistency as the skin on her face."

Wheeler studied the flesh with his magnifying glass.

"There appear to be small puncture wounds consistent with IV lines, similar to the wounds I found on Sinclair's hands. Unlike those, however, the degree of maceration indicates this corpse was in water for a very long period of time."

"Maceration?" I asked.

"Technical term," Wheeler explained, "used in

floaters to describe the deterioration of flesh from long-term exposure to water."

Wheeler appeared perplexed.

"What are you thinking?" St. James asked.

"Can't say just yet until I examine the rest of the body."

He removed the glove from the left hand and held the bruised, swollen appendage up for us to see.

"We've got a matched pair," he said. "Bruises sustained at different times, each of the five fingers broken, from the feel of it, in numerous places. The X rays will show just how many and where. I'd like to get her out of this suit right now, finish my visual examination; then I'll have her weighed and x-rayed."

The wet suit itself was loose on her body, three sizes too big, as I had noticed when St. James brought her out of the water. Wheeler slid down the front zipper and carefully peeled off the suit bit by bit. He worked slowly, turning the body left to right, front to back to front again, until she was fully stripped.

Water dripped from a sink faucet.

Fluorescent lights hissed.

We stood rooted in place, stunned into silence.

Like Ashley, she was nude under the suit, but the resemblance stopped there. Although there were no burns on her skin, she scarcely looked human. Her body was neither muscular nor fit. Body fat had been eaten away and muscles had withered, leaving only bone and tendon for flesh to hang on and her skin was frightening to behold. It had the same consistency and color as her face: white bread soaked in milk, yellow where chunks had fallen out, leaving infected craters. Breasts were withered, flopping to either side, deflated party balloons. Her belly was a concave valley, pelvic bone rising up in two high sharp arches, straining through the thin layer of skin, two peaks overlooking the deep crevices of her ruined torso.

Loose flesh sagged around her neck as if she were a hundred years old. I could see each rib from five feet away. Her legs were sticks, fragile-looking twigs, white knee bones poking through. Her hands looked more obscene next to that devastated body, swollen and battered, evidence of hopeless self-defense in a terrible lost private war.

"I've never seen or read about anything like this," Wheeler said, shaken. "The condition of her skin is one big medical contradiction. We usually see deterioration like this in corpses that have been at sea or in water for a long period of time. It's called the washerwoman effect. The water destroys the flesh. When you stay in the bath too long, for example, your skin wrinkles. If you stayed in long enough that wrinkling would progress and eventually your skin would disintegrate, fall off in chunks, which is what we have here.

"What troubles me is that she's not even slightly bloated. The body gases haven't begun to break down. This body is fresh. From that forensic point alone I'd put the time of death at twelve to fourteen hours ago, not four weeks, which is what the maceration suggests. The time of death is completely inconsistent with the degree of tissue decomposition. It is forensically inexplicable. Both timetables should align.

"And look here. Places where the skin has fallen away are infected. Dead bodies don't get infections. Only live ones do. We have conflicting pathologies. You couldn't spend enough time in the water alive to get degenerated skin like this. Even in a wet suit, you'd die of hypothermia first. Yet you would have to be alive for the degenerated skin to infect. It's as if she was dead and alive at the same time."

Wheeler picked up her hand.

What were you beating against? What and where were your prison walls?

We were all thinking the same thing.

Wheeler picked up a cutting knife, ready to make the big Y incision. He hesitated and leaned in close to the right shoulder.

"I almost missed this because of the bad condition of her skin," he said. "There's some sort of marking on her deltoid."

He put the knife down and inspected the marking with his loupe.

"Tattoo?" St. James asked.

"I don't think so. The color appears to be uniform and solid. Under normal circumstances, I would cut the marking out and preserve it as forensic evidence, possible proof of ID. But the epidermis here is too degenerated to withstand cutting." He passed St. James the Polaroid camera. "I'm going to stretch the area carefully, and when I get it back as close to true size as possible, take a shot for the record."

Wheeler worked gently. St. James leaned in close.

"Now," Wheeler said.

The flashbulb popped. The camera whined and whirred, and a print came rolling out.

"It's a birthmark," St. James said. "A perfectly symmetrical birthmark in the shape of a heart."

Wheeler. Motionless. Silent.

Then he exploded, ripped the picture out of St. James's hands. He roared, incredulous, and crashed out of the suite just as McKenzie came walking in.

"Holy shit," McKenzie said, eyes riveted on the body. "What the hell is that?"

"Rio," I said. "Wheeler's little girl."

I went after him.

Halls were empty, the men's room, too. In the receiving bay, the night clerk was asleep. Automatic doors hissed open and then shut again as I stepped through, leaving the morgue and all its dead.

A square white Boston ME van streaked by, wipers slapping, lights on high, Wheeler at the wheel.

"Wheeler!" I shouted as he shot out of the parking lot.

Rain and wind hit me hard in the face.

Nature mourning his cold wet loss.

Tears from the heavens for Wheeler's long-lost girl.

I locked myself in the car and wept, as torn apart as if it had been my own sweet daughter on that cold steel slab.

Fifteen minutes later, Wheeler's white van crept back into the bay, and he stumbled back into the building, shoulders curved, head bowed in misery.

I stayed in the car. As much as I wanted to go to Wheeler, offer him consolation, I could not will myself to go back to the suite and bear witness to the rest of the sad gruesome work: the Stryker saw screaming, the heavy thump of organs placed in the scale, the final dreadful excavation of his girl.

I peeled off my leather gloves and thought of how Rio's hands must have been brutalized in the act of self-defense against her killer, a man I had once reached for and begged to stay, a stranger I had slept with thinking lust was a replacement for love. I had used mine to pull his body close. She used hers to try to beat him off. I imagined her beating and beating until her hands were as broken and useless as my own.

Are there more than four elements? Is evil the fifth? *"Evil begets evil,"* Wheeler had said. Now a killer had taken an element and turned it into a weapon all his own. Water. More creative than a gunshot, more painful than a knife, each drowning meticulously planned and terribly drawn out. Vale's sick sweet pleasure blissfully indulged.

Grief settled over me, a lead weight rounding my shoulders, curling my back, squeezing my heart.

Two young women viciously drowned.

I had once killed a man. In the eyes of the law mine was an act of self-defense, but in truth it was so much more. I reveled in the agony of his death, tasted a deep primal satisfaction in my revenge. In the dark now, in the night, Wheeler's pain cleaved my soul as deeply as if it were mine, and I wanted the same satisfaction for him. Vale would suffer, I vowed. We would track him like the animal he was, and somehow, sometime—soon I hoped—Vale would die.

He had drowned two young women, but how many more had come before and how many more would follow?

St. James had left the keys in the ignition. I started the car, cracked a window, and turned on the heat.

As terrible as that sight of Wheeler's grief-curved body was, the knowledge that my daughter was alive and well filled me with a giddy, guilty joy. I called Skyla, but she was not in. I dialed the number five more times just to hear her voice on the answering machine tape.

A thousand-pound fatigue filled me. I fiddled with the radio and settled on jazz. A walking bass and a weeping sax. My eyes closed. The dark and the music and the rain were drugs lulling me into a foggy half-sleep.

The thud of car doors woke me.

An engine jumped.

Headlights blazed in my rearview mirror. The white van rolling fast, Wheeler soldier straight at the wheel, St. James sitting alongside. I leaned on my horn, but the van tore by. I followed it out, racing through the empty streets of Boston and up to the highway.

Nantucket was behind me, an hour and a half south; Wheeler was heading due north and fast, at eighty-eight miles per hour, recklessly fast in the fog over asphalt slick from the rain. The van had four-wheel drive. My rental did not, and the car was skittish on wet pavement, the back sliding out around the curves. I could not keep up, and soon it was out of sight.

Green signs strobed by overhead. The order was familiar. There was only one place they could be heading.

By the time I reached the quarry, the ME's van was parked at the rim, keys in the ignition, two piles of men's clothes stacked on the seats.

I looked at the dark pool and called out. My own voice bounced back. The water was eerily still, but somewhere down under were Wheeler and St. James. I paced the edge.

A patch of water glowed in the distance.

St. James, I thought, drawing my coat tightly against the cold.

A white funnel of light was moving my way.

Wheeler, I hoped.

They broke surface fifty yards out and finned to the rim using the beam of an underwater light to guide them. They were both wearing wet suits and dive gear. Wheeler wore a hood.

St. James climbed out first. The ME's official seal was stamped on the front of his suit. Wheeler crawled out next. The wet suit was too short, falling three inches short of his ankles and wrists. He held out a twelve-inch plastic toy diver, identical to the one in Kiri's package, which was identical to the one he had found on my beach.

Wheeler's smooth tawny face was unnaturally pale and lined. Water streaming down his cheeks was part quarry and part tears. He crouched on the silver stone and looked out over the pool.

"I brought her into this world," he said, "and now I've touched the place where she was taken out of it."

I put my hands on his huge shoulders.

"Leave me be," Wheeler said, and I moved away.

St. James was at the car, peeling off his wet suit, toweling down, and dressing.

"Vale stayed down there and taped the drowning," he said. "He likes to watch them die."

"How do you know?"

"We found this." St. James passed me a black nylon strap imprinted with yellow letters spelling the word NIKONIS. "Nikonis is the premier commercial brand of underwater camera and video gear. He taped her drowning. With an underwater light, at close range, it would be easy to do. He'll watch it over and over. That's a big part of his thrill, sitting in the dark reliving her death."

"What about Ashley?"

"He taped her, too."

"How do you know?"

"I just do."

We got in the car. St. James turned the ignition.

"We can't leave Wheeler alone out here," I said.

"That's the way he wants it. Time alone where Rio died."

Wheeler was on his feet and in motion, a hurricane of sorrow, flinging stray rocks into the quarry, punching at thin air, casting his eyes to heaven as if a divine hand might reach down and put Rio back in his arms; but there were no miracles here, not now, not in this water. Rio did not walk on the water or fall from the sky. She was gone for all time, and as the final wave of grievous admission swept through Wheeler, he dropped to the silver stone. Fists unfurled, and he buried his head in his hands, rocking rocking rocking, hope abandoned. Wheeler wept, the high pitch of sorrow swiping all the baritone from his voice, the survivor's soprano, the shrill keening fugue of the one left behind.

I had to turn away, hide my own face in the warm hollow of St. James's neck.

He wrapped an arm around me, put the Honda in gear, and slowly backed out, leaving Wheeler to grieve in private.

We traveled in silence. The spill from the dashboard lit St. James in a surreal way, accentuating his tear-stained cheeks, the white scar splitting his lip, and peregrine cuts scything his hands. I was exhausted. So was he. It was after two.

"It's been a long day," he said.

We pulled into a roadside Holiday Inn and took the last available room. A double bed, stall shower, and shag carpet the color of old blood. St. James was cold and damp from the dive. I insisted he shower first. I went next. When I came out, he was wrapped in a towel, stretched out flat on the ground next to the bed. His eyes were closed. I knelt down next to him.

"You can't sleep on the floor, St. James."

"There's only one other place."

"The bed."

"Where will you sleep, then?"

"Next to you."

His eyes opened and he studied me. There was no trace of sarcasm, no feral threat. "Why?"

"I don't want you to sleep on the floor."

"That's all?"

"That's all." I pulled the sheets back. He climbed in.

"Thank you."

"You're welcome," I said, but he was already fast asleep.

I crawled in next to him, crowding the edge, staying as far away as I could, but the bed was a double, not a king, and it sagged in the center. No matter what I did, some part of my body touched his. When I finally fell asleep, it was my elbow brushing his.

Sometime in the night I woke to the feel of his warm bare skin, his chest against my back, breath on my shoulder, arms wound around my chest, leg draped over mine. The weight of him felt good, and for a moment I hated myself for liking it; then I just gave in. There was nothing carnal in the sleepy embrace. We were simply two tired creatures seeking a reprieve from the elements, and the memory of Rio's feather-light body heavy with death and wet in our arms.

CHAPTER FORTY-FOUR

McKenzie, at half past eleven in the morning, on my cell phone, waking us. "Where's St. James?"

"With me."

Sprawled across the mattress with the covers tossed back, naked and not caring, wild hair and bare tanned skin dark against white starched sheets. He filled the bed, and I wondered how I ever thought it was big enough for two.

"You still in Boston?" McKenzie asked.

"No."

"Where, then?"

"An hour out."

"Come straight here as soon as you can. Be prepared for all hell to break loose. Hinks is on her way in."

McKenzie was slouched in his chair, eyes red and tired behind the lenses of the black-rimmed glasses. A fifth of bourbon was open on the desk. There were no cups, and I guessed Wheeler had taken slugs straight from the bottle.

Wheeler was slumped on the couch, unshaved, in worn jeans and a wrinkled T-shirt stained wet under the arms. Dark violet circles bloomed under his eyes from the long sleepless night. Emotional devastation had sucked the air out of his cheeks, leaving him gaunt. He was pale—as if his tan had suddenly faded, brittle, almost fragile. His full lips were dry and parched, the loss sucking moisture from his core.

His usual body language of battle had turned to defeat. He curled his fist to his forehead, drove it hard into the cranial bone. His other hand worked his chin, fingering golden stubble, fashioning sentences with gestures, signing emotions for which he had no words.

Wheeler's destruction was complete. The gravity of his grief flattened him, for his sorrow had but one dimension: utter despair.

Snapshots from the autopsy were scattered on a low table in front of him. Wheeler's eyes were tightly shut against them. The wild furious energy of the night before was gone. Hinks gave life to that fury now. She sat next to Wheeler, sorting through the horrible shots. I had seen her jealous, coy, sarcastic, cold, annoyed, irritated, and flirtatious, but I had never seen Hinks mad. Anger had heightened her icy beauty and sharpened her strong features.

"Oh, Christ," she whispered, palming her cheeks—fanning long fingers over her brows.

Hinks tugged the neck of her tight black sweater, glanced at Wheeler, then back at the shots. "Goddamn," she cried, shoving her knuckles against trembling lips, chewing on them as she spit out the next words: "Oh, fuck—holy Christ, Tom." She raked her hair and gripped his knee as she looked over at me, her voice shaking with barely controlled rage. "Tom says you know who did this. That you have a name—Vale—and proof that he killed AFIP's soldier, too."

"We do," I said.

Hinks passed me a snapshot. "Tom says this is him."

It was Vale, taken the day Wheeler saw us on the beach.

"Had my camera that day to get shots of the storm," Wheeler said weakly. "Don't know why I took that one. I just did."

Hinks gathered up the autopsy Polaroids. "I've lost jurisdiction over Ashley Sinclair," she said. "I'm not happy about that, but nothing I say or do is going to kick that case back to me. Rio's murder's another story. This one's all mine."

"Lowell's quarry isn't in your county," I said.

She smacked the photos against her thigh and stood. "I don't give a flying fuck where it is. Nor do I give a flying fuck about state police investigative *protocol*. Wheeler says a team of my best investigators—the whole damn department—is no match to what St. James brings to the table. That's a statement of fact, not a compliment. I only care about two things this afternoon: how Vale goes down and how soon. Every minute, every hour means another girl could be dying. Time equals death. I don't like that equation. I'll give you one other fact you may be surprised to hear. I am not interested in the Bill of fucking Rights. Far as I'm concerned, Vale lost his rights when he did this to Tom Wheeler's girl. And while state law dictates that I should bust your ass along with St. James for tampering with a crime scene, I'd just as soon drop to the floor right now and kiss your feet."

"Why?" I asked.

"For setting this up so I don't have to play it state's way, bound by regulations and law. The law doesn't apply to Vale, not in my book. I am Wheeler's friend first," she said, reaching for his hand, "and a judicial vessel second. I will do everything, I will use my position to further what has now become my personal agenda."

"Which is?"

"To wipe Vale off the face of the earth. Locate, isolate, and eradicate."

"The St. James way," I said.

"I want Vale taken down hard. Permanently and hopefully painfully." Hinks slapped the snapshots facedown on the table and dropped back to the sofa.

St. James was quiet next to me, his eyes flat, the falcon before the kill.

"Our only problem here is *the press,*" Hinks said. "We do this my way, there are a lot of facts that need never come out. But I don't have the luxury of playing wait and see. And I sure as hell don't want to worry about how the story's going to play on TV."

"You're worried about me."

"Damn right." Hinks leaned forward. "How did you feel when you went after the man who grabbed your daughter, Lacie?"

I did not reply.

"Was it enough for you to leave it to the police?" she asked. "Were you content to let law and order run its natural course?"

She rose, towered over me, then rocked on her heels alongside my chair. Her eyes were intense and clear. "Did you roll with the cops, count on them to find the man, believing that when they did you'd be content to sit in court while defense lawyers danced circles around his guilt, pulling sympathy upon sympathy explaining why we ought to feel compassion, demonstrate forgiveness, understanding? Did you do it that way?"

"No."

"And what did you do when you found him, when you were one on one?"

"I killed him in self-defense."

"Did you? Was it as cut and dried as that? What if your life hadn't been in jeopardy. What would you have done face-to-face with him then?"

In the pause that followed, Wheeler opened his eyes and stared at me. I turned to him.

"I would have killed him, Wheeler."

Wheeler then took over from his surrogate, his advocate, his friend, and now his voice was firm and strong. "I want that same satisfaction, Lacie—the same justice you took for yourself."

I looked at McKenzie. "Hinks and Wheeler have spoken for me," he said. "I'm a friend first today. You brought Rio straight to me. She was never officially logged in. We can run this any way they want—so long as you tell us you are in this as Wheeler's friend, not as a journalist."

"Of course," I said. "I agree."

"Okay," Hinks said. "I've been doing groundwork since six this morning when Tom called. The forensic evidence shows Rio was held captive for eight weeks. I talked to her friends and asked a lot of questions, trying to understand why no one missed her during all that time."

"And?" St. James asked.

"She graduated from Boston University in June," Hinks said, "then moved to a studio apartment near Harvard med school. She lived alone. I went to her place, found her phone book and made some calls. Her old friends from BU haven't heard from her since late August. They haven't been worried because they all know she had just started med school. They figure she's been in overload. There are no friends to talk to at Harvard because she never showed up for class."

"What about her rent?"

"September was paid up with a check dated August twenty-fifth. October is not paid. The last outgoing phone call from her apartment was made August twenty-sixth. Vale grabbed her right around then. I have no idea how or where. Talk to me now, St. James, from the top. This is between the five of us here in this room. Your information is proprietary. It does not go past me. Nothing goes in the jacket at state police. Now tell me about Vale."

"He is a master at changing his identity, and that makes him feel invulnerable—but not careless. He's meticulous and organized, hypercareful to not do anything that will jeopardize his safety. He did not set up Ashley or Rio as a race against time. He does not get off on risk. Quite the opposite."

"If risk isn't driving him," she asked, "what is?"

"Ego and the need to watch. I believe Vale videotapes all his kills so he can relive the thrill. And, I believe Vale's been killing for a long time—years, in fact. In the beginning, he probably kept scrapbooks of news clippings, tapes of news stories on TV. He may even have gone to the scene when the press and police were there.

"Over time, the aftermath of the kill grew to be as important a part of his thrill as the kill itself. The more he killed and got away with it, the bigger his ego grew, and the more attention he craved. Now the complexity of the experience has evolved to the point where he wants to control the media coverage. To Vale, I think, the aftermath now is an integral part of the whole kill. Public recognition—media attention is now *essential* to his work—and, as he so highly controls the conditions of the kill, so does he want—*need*—to control the conditions of the coverage. Vale has chosen Lacie as his conduit."

"He planted Ashley so I would find her," I said. "And sent me out after Rio."

"What better conduit," St. James said, "than a beautiful star newscaster, one who was once a victim of violence herself. The symmetries are irresistible to him. Fire and water. Opposites attract. His stories are all the more beautiful when Lacie tells them. He's obsessed with her and the new dimension she brings to the kill."

"From what Tom said, he's running deep," Hinks said. "How are you going to get him to surface?"

"We put Rio back in the quarry."

The room went dead silent.

"Put her back?" Wheeler's voice was an agonizing cry of a whisper. "Why?"

"It's the only way to force Vale into direct contact with Lacie," St. James said. "He's scouring the news this morning. He probably has five sets going, tuned to every channel in Boston and to CNN. He'll watch the noon news, the five and the six looking for Lacie's story about Rio. When there's no coverage, he'll get enraged and call the kill in to the police himself. The Boston stations will use their own local reporters, which will make Vale mad again. When he sees someone other than his chosen one showcasing his work, he will establish direct contact with Lacie, which is exactly what I want. Right now he's talking to her through symbols, hints, signs, sounds—everything but words. We'll return Rio to the quarry, but I promise you by midnight, state police will have been directed to her by Vale himself, and they will bring her back up."

"With a Y-shaped incision stitched in her chest?" I asked. "How are you going to explain that?"

"The body hasn't been violated," McKenzie said. "Wheeler got to me before I made the cut. The body's in one piece, exactly the way you found it, except for the hood, which we will replace."

"Doesn't this bring state police right into the case when you want them out?" I asked.

"No," St. James said. "We're light-years ahead of them. While they're going through textbook investigative procedure, I believe we'll be in direct contact with Vale."

"It's your call, Tom," Hinks said quietly.

Outside McKenzie's window, black clouds were punched with perfect circles of blue, as if Wheeler had driven his fist right through them.

Wheeler rose with a deep anguished exhalation. His sneakers squeaked across the floor. He paused at the door—and not looking back at us said, "Do it."

And Wheeler was gone.

McKenzie pinched the bridge of his nose. "Okay," he said. "Let's talk forensics."

Hinks pushed a pile of snapshots across the table to St. James and me. "I found these in her apartment," she said. "Take a look."

Rio standing poolside in competition, dressed in a swimsuit the colors of the flag. Rio, trim but powerful, that heart-shaped mark clearly defined on her shoulder. Rio with her bright blue eyes and slick honey-colored hair. Rio in the water, kicking up a storm.

"Hard to believe it's the same woman," St. James said. "In these shots she looks to be a hundred and twenty-five pounds. Maybe one-thirty. The body last night weighed in at eighty-five."

"I put a rush on the lab work," McKenzie said. "Cell blocks in her heart were dead, the result of the adrenergic response—just like Ashley Sinclair. If Rio hadn't drowned first, the cell blocks would have continued to die off, forcing her into a fatal ventricular arrhythmia."

"She would have literally been scared to death," Hinks said.

"Yes," McKenzie replied. "Again, that's consistent with my findings on Sinclair. Both women were under extreme psychological duress at the time of death, and had been for some time preceding the drowning. The mind-body paradigm's been proved by medical fact. The psychological state of fright triggers a unique physiological chain of events. Voodoo ritual's rooted in that. It's not the *magic* that really works, it's the power of the believer's own mind. But I digress. That's not what happened here. These two women drowned. What puzzles me about Rio is the weight loss. The blood tests show she was in caloric deprivation but elementally sound."

"Meaning?" I asked.

"She didn't ingest enough calories to maintain body fat and tissue mass, but she had enough vitamins and nutrients to keep her from textbook starvation. The puzzle gets more complex. The physical deterioration of her skin does not square with the time of death. Her skin tells me she's been dead in the water for three long weeks. The infection in the skin tells me she was alive for the duration of the aquatic interment. But a human couldn't stay alive in any body of water long enough for the water to do that—even in a wet suit. The infection is proof she was alive when she should have been dead. I have no scientific way of explaining that. Now, take a look at this."

He dealt out three sets of documents.

"An autopsy protocol," he said, "done two months ago up in Portland, Maine. Take a look. Tell me what you think."

We read the report carefully.

"Look at the photographs," Hinks said. "The body could be Rio, it looks so much the same. How did this come to you?"

"I belong to an international association of medical examiners," McKenzie said. "It has an extensive Web site. I laid out the weird pathology, soliciting thoughts from other ME's. Portland answered almost immediately."

"What happened with the police investigation?" Hinks asked.

"The body was never identified; the killer was never found. No other victims surfaced. The police gave up. The ME left the cause of death open. He couldn't explain the conflicting pathologies any better than I can."

I read the protocol conclusion out loud. "The advanced state of skin degeneration is inconsistent with the time of death; the infection present in the flesh is undeniably inconsistent with postmortem skin degeneration. Pathological fact offers only one explanation: The skin maceration took place while Jane Doe was alive. It's as if she was dead and alive at the same time."

"Just like Rio," Hinks said. "That takes Vale's victim count to three."

"Three that we know of," St. James said.

CHAPTER FORTY-FIVE

Vale was in a large windowless subterranean room. Outside, close by, the great Atlantic beat the shore but the sound did not penetrate, only the damp of the ocean, a salted heavy chill.

Sixteen super-size home theater units lined the cement block walls. Vale sat dead center in a swivel chair, in the dark, working a master remote. The black screens came to life and a year-old news video from WQLF in Savannah, Georgia, filled the screens.

Vale watched intently even though he had seen the tape a hundred times before.

The old news footage showed shallow tidal flats

where local boys went digging for clams. A fat-faced male reporter in a rumpled shirt stood, legs spread, feet sunk in the wet sand. He held the mike in one hand and gestured to the tidal pools with the other. A bare-chested boy in rolled-up jeans fidgeted alongside, looking wide-eyed and scared into the camera. He had been digging in the sand at the shoreline with a long wooden stick, determined to dig to China or find the biggest clam.

"I just dug and dug and dug," the boy said, "hard as I could."

Dug and dug like a dog, Vale thought, until the stick scraped something harder and longer than a shell.

"Didn't feel nothing like a clam," the boy said. "Thought maybe it was treasure from a sunk pirate ship, so I just kept right on digging."

Digging harder and faster now, fueled by greed.

What finally came up was flesh and bone, not pieces of eight.

"It was the hand first," the boy said solemnly, "then the arm after that. I just went on and dug until I found the head to that girl. She looked like she was sleeping but she wasn't breathing. She were dead. I stayed with her while my little brother ran home to call the TV station and the cops."

The camera shot widened and showed two lanky attendants picking the dead girl out of the water, packing her into a body bag. The cameraman got greedy and went for the tabloid shot, zooming in as the black bag zipper was closing over her face.

Vale punched the remote, freezing the tape on that frame. He walked right up to the screen, touched it as if it was flesh, then pushed PLAY, and the zipper went up, a black curtain closing on the fabulous final act.

Vale remembered the thrill of planting her body in the sand, but mostly he remembered the rush he got watching the television coverage when she was found, and it had awakened in him a fierce primal need for more. Television coverage became an integral part of the killing high—and now Vale chose the teller of his tale as carefully as he chose the victims themselves.

He punched the remote. Lacie Wagner's face lit up the screens, surrounding Vale like a cyclorama. Beauty times sixteen. He had been monitoring the news stations through the night, looking for her new story. He wanted to see her standing by the quarry when the body came up. He had created his own brand of reality programming, his own private network, and had picked Lacie as his star.

But the wait was growing tiresome, and Vale was feeling unsettled, angry, and tense.

He picked up his athletic bag and left his safe house, bound for the one place that calmed him.

Vale serviced the public natatorium as the pool man. It was a good job, the best.

Here he was just a nameless minimum-wage hire, skimming water, cleaning filters and greasing pumps, keeping the whole beautiful intricate system humming along. There were no set hours. As the pool man Vale could come and go as he pleased. More important, no one ever noticed a pool man. That kind of anonymity suited his purposes perfectly.

It was night, and the natatorium would not open to evening swimmers for another ten minutes. Vale in his wet suit was alone in the great vaulted space. Overhead lights were off, but the pool lights were on, turning the water into a slick blue mirror. He crouched at the edge of the deep end. His reflection thrilled him.

Narcissus at the river, he thought, *Cyclops on the bank.*

The left eye was covered with a black patch.

The right eye sparkled, an intense riveting brilliant blue.

A shaggy mustache altered the symmetry of his own elegant face, and Vale adopted body language that altered his entire physical bearing. He stuck his neck forward, rounded his shoulders, let his dark hair fall unkempt around his face. Looking at him, you would see a shy, stuttering, shuffling one-eyed man. You would feel pity for the lost eye, the dumb slow gait, and assume he had limitations beyond the physical, the way he hung his head. You would never guess the truth. That was the beauty of being a pool man. He could watch the female swimmers up close. Study them. Take his time in making his choice.

Vale had learned the power of appearance as a child, using his God-given physical beauty to hide the inner seething anger, a burning rage that expressed itself in unusual ways. It began with a goldfish, the live one he pinned to his wall. Then it was a frog, a starfish, a perch, tacked up alive and wriggling with silver stick pins, octopus arms ripped from the pulsating core, and lobster claws cut from the body of the living beast. He had performed his rituals alone at night and hid the evidence, buried it deep.

To the outside world he was the charmed one, the charming one. Top of his class at military school, popular and good looking to boot. "A beautiful child," his parents agreed. "And such a good boy. Never does anything bad." And no one ever knew, let alone imagined the truth about who and what he really was.

The big clock on the natatorium wall ticked over. Vale rose.

The pool would open in five minutes, and when the swimmers strolled in, they would see a shy one-eyed man hosing down tiles, not a cold-blooded hunter walking freely in the unknowing herd.

CHAPTER FORTY-SIX

St. James and I left McKenzie and went back to Nantucket, as if proximity to Vale's last known location would help us piece the puzzle together in a logical way, understand how Vale killed and where.

We sat in my study. St. James scanned Wheeler's shot of Vale onto the hard drive of his computer; then he loaded the autopsy Polaroids of Rio and Ashley, too. He activated the infrared connection and put the pictures up on my home theater screen. He flipped through the set choosing close-ups of each dead woman's face and clicked back and forth between them as he spoke.

"Medical school and Special Ops," he said. "Boston and Cape Cod. Ashley was a licensed diver, Rio was not. Student and soldier, two different profiles, two different hometowns. Where's the point of convergence? What's the common ground?"

"They're both blondes," I said. "And the woman who washed up in Portland was, too."

"Feels too general. Vale's precise, meticulous, and detailed. He has a different criteria for how he chooses his kills."

"Ms. Wagner?"

We looked up. Kiri Hannover was in the doorway.

"I rang and knocked but you didn't hear," she said, eyes locked on the dreadful image on the big screen.

"What brings you out here?" I asked.

"I was taking measurements for our island erosion study when I got a call from the lab. Another water sample showed up today. There was no note this time. I told the lab to go ahead and run it. The results just came in. It's fresh water, Ms. Wagner. Loaded with chlorine."

"Pool water."

"Seems to be. Sorry. I wish I could narrow it down for you better than that." She looked at the shot of Ashley again.

I walked her out to the front deck. Kiri was so tiny next to me, four feet six, standing soldier straight. Her pale blond hair glistened, wet from the rain.

"How's the swimming?" I asked, as I had asked Hinks.

"Good. I'm doing relay on the master's team this year. Butterfly's my event. Being light and small has its advantages."

Kiri went down the steps, bright in her yellow rain slicker. I watched her get in her little red SUV and back out of the drive.

I went back inside. Wheeler's picture of Vale was up now on the big screen.

"What does the pool water mean?" I asked.

"If it is symbolic in the same way the quarry sample was, then he is telling you the next victim will be found in a pool. But he hasn't given any specifics. He's toying with you, Lacie. Being deliberately vague."

I looked at the aquarium house next door. Had Rio been there that night, beating against walls in the basement while Vale was upstairs taking me in his arms? Had she been held captive at Angel's Reef, wasting away as summer eased into fall? Had I been that close to her and not even known?

"Did he keep Rio next door all that time?" I asked.

"No," St. James replied. "Vale had domestic help five days a week. He wouldn't have if he were hiding something. Vale must have a second place, a safe house where he kills."

"Here on the island?"

"Nantucket's too small. It has to be somewhere isolated but easily accessible from here, somewhere close where he could come and go with relative ease."

"I saw him most afternoons surf-casting at three-thirty."

"Which only means he was on the island at three-thirty—not that he was here in the morning or even later at night. Vale was creating the *illusion* he lived here, manufacturing patterns, habits that would become ingrained in your mind, feeding your subconscious, sending the message: This man is normal. This man has a routine. This man is wealthy. This man is okay."

"Which brings up the question: Why bother to come here, to *this* island, *this* beach, *that* house?"

"Let's focus on the remaining three sets of inconsistent facts," St. James said. "First, the radiation burns and SEATEC controlled secure dive gear Ashley was wearing are a hard straight line to SEATEC—but inconsistent with Vale's guilt. Second, Vale rented that house but he kills somewhere else. The house or the island or the beach here is important to him somehow. Third, the skin. Rio and the Portland, Maine, Jane Doe. Dead skin infected as if it were alive."

He studied the picture of Vale on the big screen and drummed his fingers on my desk.

We had been working on the assumption that Vale and SEATEC were two distinctly unconnected entities. We had never tried to connect him to the military in any way, but now I told St. James about the facial biometric database at Defense.

"We should put Vale's picture through it and see what comes up," I said.

"That database is out of my reach," St. James said. "Does Max have access?"

"Yes."

"Will he do it for you?"

"I don't know. All I can do is ask."

I sent an e-mail out to Max containing the digital file of Vale's face.

St. James and I were down to the remaining two sets of conflicting facts. We agreed that I would work on the location issue and he would work on the forensically impossible condition of the skin.

I looked out across the moor at the new house with the old pool, thinking of the unknown pool man who cleaned the old pool at night—the old pool with the beautiful scrimshaw frieze.

New house. Old pool. Conflict sitting right there in Vale's own backyard. I tried Wheeler on his mobile. He answered on the first ring. "Vale call?" he asked.

"Not yet."

I described the frieze and asked him what he thought.

"Scrimshaw in a pool?" he said. "Never heard of that."

A half hour later, Wheeler's Jeep pulled up to the pool next door.

I slipped a hooded slicker on and crossed the moor.

Wheeler was in his wet suit, wading in the shallow end, chest deep in sludge. A day had passed since St. James and I had cleared the tiles, but brown-green fungus had already reclaimed them. Wheeler was clearing windows in the algae with one hand and working his Nikonis with the other, taking close-up shots of each panel in the frieze.

"What do you think?" I asked.

"Beautiful work. Late nineteenth century, no question there. The tiles are all hand-laid and hand-colored, and then of course there's this frieze. It's a fine piece of art. The scrimshaw is done on whale teeth. One sperm whale had as many as forty teeth. The big size and flat surface were ideal for etching."

Wheeler drifted into deep water, and I helped him there, wiping down panels while he held on to the pool edge with one hand and took shots with the other.

"Whale teeth are hard, too," he said. "They hold up better than bone. But like I said on the phone, I've never seen it laid into a pool. Island architecture's carefully catalogued, as are artifacts and all types of local art. This frieze should be on record somewhere in the art or architecture archives downtown, or maybe even on file with the original property plans in town hall."

We worked quietly, wiping and shooting until Wheeler had traveled the full perimeter of the pool.

"Okay," I said. "That's the last one."

He levered himself out of the sludge, onto the edge, and heaved a great sigh. Brown water rolled off his black suit. Bits of algae clung to his knees. In the long steady rains the level of the pool had risen too high, and now the pool was bleeding, overflow seeping over the sides, spreading across the dirt and our feet in a shallow tide.

"The water's warm," Wheeler said. "Almost hot, which is why the algae's flourishing so. Another day like this, and you'll smell the pool all the way across the moor. I'm going to have a look in the pump hut and turn the damn heater down. Hot dirty water's a goddamn health hazard. Worse yet, wide open like this, kids could fall in. Little kids could come here playing, fall right in and drown."

"You holding up, Tom?" I asked.

"I've just got to stay in motion," Wheeler said. "Feel like if I stop moving I'll stop breathing, too. Crazy thing, feeling like that. I'll hose off and dress, drive into town. Dig around, see what I find. It'll help divert my mind."

*   *   *

"McKenzie called," St. James said when I walked back in. "Another match on the forensic pathology. An ME up in New Hampshire has an open case on the books from late July. Same infected maceration. The victim was female, Caucasian. Early twenties, judging from the pelvis and teeth. She was never ID'd."

"Hair color?"

"Blond."

"Cause of death?"

"Homicidal drowning. She had saltwater diatoms blooming in her bones, but her nude body was found floating in a local lake. New Hampshire's way out of range for a local grab. We still don't know the common ground. Any luck with Ashley's friend Chris Preata?"

"Not yet. I'll try her again."

I dialed both numbers, got voice mail, and left messages at each.

My desk clock ticked over to four o'clock straight up. Boston's early newscast started at five. One hour away. I wondered if Vale was worried. If he cared at all, if he would ever crack.

"You use the Net a lot for your work?" St. James asked out of the blue.

"I do."

"Ever type in your own name out of curiosity? Ever just try it to see what comes up?"

"No." I was not interested in reading tabloid gossip or news accounts of my life.

"Take a look at this."

He pointed to the big screen, at a site called The Altar.

A video was playing—a compilation of my anchor and reporting work on WRC, quick cuts strung together, a hundred split seconds of me closing the newscast and stating my name: "Lacie Wagner, WRC. Lacie

Wagner, WRC. Lacie Wagner, WRC. Wagner, Wagner, Wagner. WRC. Lacie Wagner, WRC News."

The video jumped to my first story about Ashley. I was standing on the cold shore, in the wind and the rain.

"A young woman is dead tonight . . ."

Some unknown editor had altered my original tape, adding a computerized camera zoom right past my close-up until my face filled the screen, and immediately a cut to my hands, my cheek showing the shadow of a burn, then close on my ear, so tight I could see the delicate inner bones whirling like a conch shell. Interspersed throughout were close-ups of the rain misting my cheeks, sparkling drops caught in the net of my long hair, my eyelashes, touching my lips.

The edits celebrated Lacie touched by water, and I had no doubt who the editor was.

CHAPTER FORTY-SEVEN

"There's more to The Altar Web site," St. James said. "Your WRC clip is just the first layer. See this ship icon at the bottom of the screen? That's the entry gate for authorized users. I've tried every way I know to get inside, but it's been set up too well and locked down tight with security firewalls."

"Who are the authorized users?" I asked. "And why would Vale want to prevent people from entering?"

"I can't say for sure."

"Then speculate."

"In religious terms, an altar is a place of consecrations and offerings. I think Vale is posting visual evidence—

videotapes—of his kills. It's a basic tenet of the human condition to want to share experience, and deviants—sadists—have an overwhelming need to share. The Net offers them perfect conditions to do so in blessed anonymity with others who have the same dark desires.

"Think of the Internet as an ocean with depths most people never venture into, and like the ocean it has its own bottom life. The Altar is Vale's *alter*-ego, which embodies his egotistical satisfaction. We know little about him—only that he's charismatic, persuasive, and magnetic. He presents the fantasy image of a wealthy, successful, sensitive male—and that's irresistible to women. You're living proof. He targets, kills, then shares his thrill kill with others of similar tastes."

"Why didn't he kill me?" I asked.

"You are a conduit, not a target."

"Why did he leave Nantucket in the dead of night?"

"You scared him off. Consider the chain of events. He planted Ashley because he wanted you to find her and file the first story, simply as a reporter. But then you went further, searching for the victim's identity and killer—and Vale did not want that. He never expected you to go after the truth. He never expected you to do more than report. He could not—would not—risk staying here close to you when you were so aggressively moving forward with an investigation of the death."

"Why did he sleep with me, St. James?"

"Oldest reason in the book. Because he could. Because you said yes."

McKenzie called again, at quarter to five.

"Vale?" I asked.

"Not yet. But we got three more forensic matches. Small town ME in Connecticut sent in the protocol for a nude body that washed up onshore in August. The ME in Rhode Island forwarded two, one for a female in a wet suit found floating down the river in June, the other for a nude female found in a lake in July. All three bodies had the same forensic conflicts as Rio. The victims were Caucasian females in their early twenties."

"Blond hair?"

"One was. The other two were brunettes. None was ever ID'd."

"That takes the count to six."

"Six that we know of."

I went back to thinking about conflicts.

Vale had hired his own pool man even though the Realtor had a contract with a company to service all her rental properties.

Vale chose his pool man. A one-eyed pool man who worked at night. A pool man who was not known locally at all. A pool man who took great pains to lift bramble wood and insects and dead birds out of the water, who wanted the water clean and good—but who cranked the heat up to high when he closed the pool, turning the water into a primal stew.

Vale pretended to love his fish, but he had viciously killed them.

His pool man appeared to care lovingly for the water, but then he polluted it.

These conflicts troubled me. I could not let them go. I pulled up the yellow pages for Cape Cod and called every pool-supply company listed.

One man who owned a service in Hyannis thought the description was familiar. He promised he would talk to his counter help and get back to me if he came up with something.

* * *

"Fish and Wildlife permits," St. James said. "Twenty pages downloading now. Commercial aquariums and Sea World parks organized by state. Vale must have had a black market trader or inside worker who sold to private collectors."

"You told me the species are hard to transport," I said. "His source had to be local, somewhere around here."

"There are only three possibilities," he said, scanning the list. "Boston Aquarium, Hyannis Port Public Aquarium, and a small private aquatic theme park over on the Cape. It closed down late last year, and Fish and Wildlife don't know what happened to all the fish."

"That must be where Vale bought his rare specimens. The other two aquariums would never have dealt with him."

"I agree." St. James put his working map of Massachusetts up on the big screen, flagged the location of the aquatic park, and clicked the mouse.

At seven-ten, Hinks leaned on the buzzer, wet hair shining under the porch light. She blew in electrified, energized, and went straight to my study.

"I was coming over for a meeting in town later with District Attorney Taggert, and something hit me out of the blue," she said. "There was a scandal on Nantucket a long time ago. I was a kid—and don't remember much, just enough to make me want to fill in the blanks. Have you got Internet access to press archives?"

"Yes."

"Run a search for 'Angel's Reef, Nantucket.' Let's see what comes up."

She paced and watched the big screen as I logged into the archives and typed the three words in: 480 story summaries scrolled in.

Hinks slapped the desk. "That's it," she said.

National tabloids, *Boston Herald,* and the local Nantucket daily—reporting a tragic, scandalous drowning at Angel's Reef a quarter of a century before.

"We need the crime-scene reports," St. James said. "Depositions, CSI photos, autopsy protocol—the whole jacket."

"It was state's case," Hinks said, "closed now and old. The jacket will be sitting in a warehouse up in Boston. Nantucket PD should have a full duplicate in their archives on account of the fact the crime took place here. I'm going downtown now to find it. Get a hold of Tom. Have him meet me out there."

Hinks marched out.

St. James swiveled around to his computer and went back to thinking about the skin.

I tried Wheeler but got voice mail. I left an urgent message and picked a half dozen of the headline summaries on the big screen and clicked through to the full coverage. The articles were all pure text. The story was so old, even a still photograph would not be of much help. I needed moving pictures with sound and voice—full-motion audiovisual elements.

Judging from the field day the printed press had clearly had with the story, the TV stations must have had one, too. A news clip, even one more than twenty-five years old, would give me a face and a voice, movement, a hundred telltale ways to make a solid ID.

I called WBZ in Boston, ran down the relevant facts.

"Twenty-five years is a long time," Ben said. "I'm not sure the digital archives go back that far. Anything that hasn't been digitized is in a warehouse in storage. I won't be able to get to them until tomorrow, but I'll check the archives, anyway. If it was a big enough story, it will be there. I'll call you back either way."

*　　　*　　　*

At seven-thirty, Wheeler checked in.

"Vale?" he asked.

"Not yet, but we hit mother lode. Hinks is downtown at Nantucket PD. She wants you to meet her there."

Chris Preata called at seven-fifty-five.

"I'll do anything to help," she said. "I loved Ashley like she was my own sister. Tina and I are all the family she had. The last time I saw her was Labor Day weekend. She was on leave. I went down to the Cape and stayed with her at the cottage."

"Did you come to Nantucket?"

"No."

"Do you have a fax?"

"Dedicated line right here."

She gave me the number, and I sent through the shot of Vale Wheeler had taken.

"I would remember if we had met him," Preata said when she got it. "No way I would forget a man like that."

"You and Ashley were together all the time that weekend?"

"Breakfast, lunch, and dinner every day. We even shared her room. Tina was working double shifts, so we didn't see her much. About the only thing we didn't do together was swim. I wasn't in the mood."

"Ashley swam?"

"Every day."

"At the compound?"

"No. She didn't go near the place when she was on leave. She must have gone to a park, or a club or maybe the local Y—someplace with Olympic-length lanes. Ashley swore that size counts. Took her swimming seriously. She was a real princess about that."

*   *   *

"Ashley lived in Hyannis," I said to St. James. "Rio spent two weeks in Hyannis Port in early summer. Vale must have met them there."

"He's not just grabbing girls off the street and shoving them in his car," St. James said.

"They're coming to him of their own volition, just as I did."

"He's meeting them in some socially acceptable venue, following up out of town if he must. He's working a nightclub or a bar scene, someplace where girls from all over pass through. That explains the geographic diversity of his hits. The question is, where is he working now and how?"

I logged into WRC's digital news archives, pulled one of my stories about Ashley, and watched it on the big screen.

Hinks, larger than life, standing on the shore. She looked great on tape, a striking Swedish beauty with her brilliant eyes and luminous skin moist from the rain. Her white-blond hair was a prize, the aggressive cut streaked from the salt and sun, and faintly emerald in places stained from chlorine. She was articulate, verbally adroit, and surprisingly charismatic. She spoke with confidence and pride.

"Hyannis Port may be the common town," St. James was saying, "but what's the common ground?"

"Wrong element," I said, pointing at the big screen. "We should be asking, what's the common water? See the green tinge in Hinks's hair? Swimmers get that. It's a discoloration that comes from spending a lot of time in chlorine."

I clicked over to the close-ups of Ashley and Rio, zoomed in on the faint green streaks in their hair.

"Ashley and Rio were swimmers," I said. "A pool must be where Vale harvests his kills."

CHAPTER FORTY-EIGHT

Vale loved the natatorium, every inch of the old place.

Built in the thirties, the walls, ceiling and floors were tiled with hand-colored mosaics.

The pool itself was a hundred meters long and ten lanes wide, tiled with the same classic mosaics.

Stands of spectator bleachers lined the north wall. Looking down from the last row, the natatorium looked like an aquatic mirage—a vast vault of blue, a thousand subtly different shades merged into one. During the day sunlight spilled in from huge skylights, and the sparkling water appeared to be a sea. It was a spectacular sight, but Vale preferred the view from the basement where old spectator galleries wrapped around the belly of the pool. They had been originally designed for underwater viewing of aquatic events.

Four-foot round portals were carved right into the belly of the pool. There were twelve in all, five each on the right and left sides, and one each at the center of the shallow and deep ends. The subterranean galleries had been closed to the public long ago. At the end of one was a pump room that doubled as the pool man's office, a humid, dank place that stank of machine oil and acidic chlorine. Water dripped from pipes, filters whooshed, a big gas furnace burned continuously, heating the pool.

Vale had three small Sony Watchman TVs lined up on his desk, tuned to the local Boston stations. He had been standing in his wet suit, watching Boston's local newscasts intently from beginning to end, but there was nothing about the drowning. No story, no promos, nothing at all.

Vale turned each of the small sets off, cocked his head, listened to the sounds of swimming from the pool above. Stroking arms, fluttering feet, rhythmic splashes. The swimmers were in.

Vale rose.

He left the pump room and moved down the empty spectator gallery, along the length of the portholes, tracking a young woman swimming in the lane closest to him. His breath caught in his throat. She was small—tiny, even—and pale, with a perfect face and bright blue eyes. She possessed a rare aquatic gift, seeming to fly rather than swim—hundred-meter sprints in a powerful butterfly that lifted her body right out of water and into the air.

Vale stayed alongside her throughout the five-hundred-meter heat, and when she slapped the wall in victory, his own pulse raced, sharing her thrill. She was jumping in the shallow end, celebrating her victory. Vale pressed his face tight to the circle of thick glass that separated them—his one eye devouring her, taking in the swell of hip rising under Lycra, the way the suit rode up high on her ass, the arch of her back and tiny strong thighs. She was standing on tiptoes, flexing her small feet, hands on her hips, tugging the suit down.

He touched his own crotch as need electrified him—something stronger and more pure and more powerful than lust. That something seemed to suck all the air out of his lungs, and Vale felt as if he were drowning on dry land—drowning in abject desire.

Vale moved topside into the shadows, crept under the bleachers as he watched her climb out. Team members passed by giving her slaps on her tiny back, light punches on her pale arm.

"Way to go, Kiri!"

"Now *that's* swimming, girl!"

"Hey, Kiri! You're a flying fish?"

"Hell of a race, Hannover."

Kiri Hannover. KiriKiriKiri. The tiny flying fish.

Vale stripped off his eye patch and mustache and rubbed his face vigorously with a towel. He peeled off the wet suit and swept back his hair. In a band of black Lycra that showed the swell of his manhood, his perfectly pitched erotic physique, Vale walked calmly out from under the bleachers, across the cool damp tiles, scanning the natatorium, the swimmers in the pool. His arms were relaxed, hands open at his side, long fingers curled slightly so the nails lightly scratched the flesh of his palms.

There were so many to choose from, so many who would delight. This was how he had approached Ashley. He smiled, remembering how she stood so close, looking straight into his green eyes, how she flirted and posed, attracted by Justin Vale and never imagining she knew and feared him as Andreas Villard.

There had been a special irony to that night, an irresistible symbolism in targeting a recruit who knew him as Villard. It was the ultimate test of his ability to convince. One he had passed with ease.

They were all so easy, so trusting, open, and warm. All he had to do was display charm and personality, the trappings of success. Money and chivalry melted them. He was a prize they yearned to win. Vale reveled in the ritual of landing a catch. He liked to play with them first, take each one to a long elegant meal, suck oysters from the shell, pry sweet lobster meat from claws with a fine silver fork.

Vale brushed his hands together as he watched the small swimmer towel down.

She was different from Ashley in every way. He imagined how her small bones would take the weight of his fury, the pressure of his lust. Yes, Vale thought, she was the one who would give him pleasure tonight.

He approached and smiled. "Butterfly's a demanding event," he said.

"I have a knack," the pale girl replied.

"You have talent," Vale corrected. "And, I assume, a name."

"Kiri." She smiled. "Kiri Hannover. And you are?"

"Jason," he said to the tiny blond fish. "Jason Duval."

She was smiling up at him, touching his arm, laughing and posing, wetting her lips and slicking back hair. The body language was screaming, it was so loud. And who could blame her with Vale standing so close, lithe and virile in his spare racing suit, gold diamond watch glittering on his wrist?

"I've never seen you swimming here before," Kiri said, tilting her head.

"I come from time to time when my work brings me to Hyannis. I know it seems bold, since we've only just met, but I want to take you to dinner. Do you like seafood?"

"Love it," his naïve target replied.

Vale opened the passenger side door of his car, a 700-series BMW, brand-new and paid for in cash. He held the umbrella over Kiri politely while she settled in. Her small hand reflexively stroked the rich leather upholstery.

"I have a business call to get out of the way," he said. "Five minutes tops. There's a good selection of CDs stacked in the deck, or the radio if you prefer. Once I finish, we'll be on our way."

"Take your time," she said, smiling.

He touched her cheek lightly and feathered his long fingers down her neck, measured her pulse. Her body couldn't wait.

"Young and beautiful and talented," Vale said, "and smart. Takes brains to get a Ph.D. and work at Woods Hole. Water's your subject, isn't it? You've even got a collection there, samples of water from the Seven Seas."

The tempo of her pulse picked up. Alarm. "How do you know about my work?" she asked. "We've never met before."

"I have a confession to make," Vale said as her small pale hand pressed against the door.

Kiri was on high alert, regretting having gone so quickly and willingly with a total stranger.

"I'm a consultant," Vale said smoothly, "specializing in corporate environmental affairs."

Kiri's eyes searched his, looking for truth.

"Most of my work deals with water," he went on. "Rivers, ponds, oceans, lakes. I was at Woods Hole recently and happened to see you there. I didn't have the courage to approach you at work. When I saw you here tonight—well, it felt like fate and I couldn't resist."

He smiled easily, elegantly, and tucked a stray blond curl behind her ear.

Kiri relaxed. The tiny swimmer was clearly relieved. She smiled at him almost gratefully, and her hand dropped away from the door.

"We have many areas of shared interests," he explained, utterly convincing. "I'll tell you more about my work at dinner—and we'll set off just as soon as I make that call."

Vale closed the door softly, stepped away, dialed the number, and watched her while he spoke. Kiri was comfortable, confident now, seduced by his money, thinking she was safe.

CHAPTER FORTY-NINE

"Eighteen pools in Hyannis," St. James said, "counting hotels and schools, the city park, and private sports clubs. Seven let swimmers in on inexpensive day passes; one for free. Vale could be working one or all of them."

The map of Massachusetts was up on the big screen and dotted with flags.

St. James inserted a circle, a hundred-mile radius around Hyannis, in a bright purple arc.

"His safe house," he said, "should be somewhere here."

McKenzie called in again at ten past eight. "We got five more matches on the pathology," he said. "Connecticut, New Hampshire, and Rhode Island. All young female Caucasians, all drowned. Victims were found in the following bodies of water: a reservoir, waterfall, creek, pond, and bay. That takes the count to eleven."

"Eleven that we know of," I said.

Just then, the owner of the pool service company in Hyannis called back.

"I talked to one of my counter clerks," he said. "She knows your guy. He signed up for our Loyal Customer Program. Gets you a discount and puts you on the mailing list."

"What kind of information do you have to supply to sign up?"

"Nothing much really. We take a digital photo and stick it in the computer. When you come in and ask for the discount, the cashier checks your face against the computer ID. Your pool guy gave us a first initial and last name. *L. Wagner.* The address is Nantucket. I can e-mail you the ID if you want to see it."

"I do."

It came through in color, a full frontal face shot. The pool man was wearing his parka, but the hood was down. His hair was black and parted on the left side. He had a black shaggy mustache and liver spots on his cheeks. His lips were tightly pursed, and his chin tucked in as if the camera scared him—as if everything scared him. The signature on the card was a childish scrawl. Illegible and patently false.

His face held me. Something about his face.

At eight-thirty-five, WBZ called back.

"Got it," Ben said. "Two hours' worth of clips from the late and early casts, plus a bonus: a half-hour documentary. I'm sending the digital file to you now. It's a fat one. Don't save the download on your hard drive. Burn it directly to DVD."

While the footage was downloading, Max called in on the See-Phone. His face filled the home theater screen on the wall. He did not look happy.

"I ran the photo you sent," he growled. "The biometric came up with a hit—matched to a man working at the Special Ops satellite compound on the Cape. He's an independent contractor named Andreas Villard.

"Professionally speaking, he's a top-of-the-line aquatic mercenary. He hires himself out to governments all over the world, and has done everything from booby-trapping Russian aircraft carriers to blowing up an oil company's underwater rig so they could collect the insurance.

"Villard's Canadian and has immense wealth. Money is not his motivation. He does what he does because he craves the rush. The psychological profile is harsh. He is characterized as egotistical, amoral, and intensely cruel.

"SEATEC apparently brought him in earlier this year to consult in the development and execution of training techniques for operatives in underwater tactical work. A few days ago, he disappeared. Villard has made a lot of enemies along the way. Talk is a Saudi prince put out a contract on him, chasing him into deep cover. The biometric made the match, but you'd never identify Vale and Villard as the same man."

"Can I see the docket photo?" I asked.

"I'm sending it to you now."

It came in fast, wiping Max off the screen, replacing his image with Villard's hard chiseled face: brown eyes, thick brows, and long blond hair. He was a stranger to me, a complete absolute total unknown.

Max carried on. "Villard is beyond dangerous, more than merely deadly. He is altogether something else. I'm giving you full disclosure here in an attempt to convince you to stay as far away from him as possible. I have already advised you about the limitations vis-à-vis reporting on SEATEC. Villard is part and parcel of that. There is no mandate for you to report on what is clearly a confidential governmental situation."

"It's not, Max. He's got a sideline, a whole new kind of nongovernmental thrill. That's what I'm going after now."

"I'm pleading with you, Lacie. Stay away. As far as you can."

Static graveled his voice. The connection cut, but the photo of Villard stayed bright and big, larger than life on the screen. The only feature I recognized was his mouth. Those lips. I knew their appetite, their texture and taste.

St. James networked into the infrared connection.

Face-Pro popped up. St. James put the photo of Vale that Wheeler had taken on the left of the screen; the photo Max had sent of Villard on the right. Vale/Villard.

With a few quick keystrokes he altered the right image. Villard's brown eyes flushed green. The crew cut grew out, glossy and black, receding then into a widow's peak sharp as a prow. Now the two pictures were identical.

I found Preston Porter at the number he had originally left in Washington, D.C. He gave me his fax number, and I sent Max's docket photo through while he waited on his phone line.

"Villard," Preston confirmed the instant the picture came out on his end. "Consulting advisor for underwater tactical training. He was commanding topside the night I went AWOL—he's the fuck who was going to let me die. Villard's one mean son of a bitch. Had his eye on Ashley. She said he scared the living daylights out of her."

"How many recruits has SEATEC lost so far?"

"Twelve, counting Ashley."

"How did they die?"

"In the water."

"All twelve?"

"Yes. Come to think of it, Ms. Wagner, every one of them drowned under Villard's watch."

When I disconnected, St. James asked me to put the digital shot of the pool man up on the screen. He ran it through Face-Pro. The shaggy mustache disappeared along with the liver spots on the skin, the eye patch vanished, a second intense blue eye appeared, the side parted hair swept back into a sharp widow's peak, and now we had three pictures of Justin Vale.

CHAPTER FIFTY

McKenzie called in at quarter to nine just as Wheeler's Jeep was coming up my drive. "Vale did it," McKenzie said. "He called state police and reported a dead body in the quarry."

I met Wheeler at the door. He carried his black medical bag in one hand and a cardboard box in the other.

"Vale called state police?" he said, reading the expression on my face.

"Just now."

We settled in the study. Wheeler dropped his black bag on the floor and leaned against the sill, holding on to the cardboard box like it was full of gold.

"What do you think the Boston stations will do?" he asked.

"It's too compelling for a news crew to pass up. All three affiliates will probably follow state police out to the site. You may even see some live coverage, but it's prime time on a weeknight, and I think the stations will hold the story for the late cast."

"State police have divers," St. James said, "but they want one from the ME's office on site, too."

"Who's McKenzie sending from his team?"

"That's the thing," St. James said. "McKenzie's certified. He said he's going on out, do the dive himself."

Wheeler nodded, and briefly closed his eyes.

"Where's Hinks?" I asked.

"She got hung up at the station on state business with

Taggert," Wheeler said. "Everything she found in the archives is in this box."

He took a map out of the box and spread it out in my desk.

"History's important in understanding the background to the crime. This is a copy of the original topographical survey map for the parcel next door. The property was developed back in 1908 by the owner, Charles Bennett Raleigh, a local rich whaling magnate who had a captain's house downtown.

"Angel's Reef was a showpiece of a house. He hired Angus Cooper, a local artist with a national reputation, to design the pool. He wanted something wholly original that reflected the majesty and mystery of the sea. Cooper came up with the idea of a scrimshaw frieze. He etched each panel himself, then tiled the pool and laid the frieze by hand.

"Raleigh died in 1970 and left Angel's Reef to his son Stephen, who spent summers there with his wife and his son," Wheeler said. "In 1974 the Nantucket real estate market was lousy, hit hard by the recession. Prices were rock bottom. Still, even though he was extremely rich, Stephen Raleigh sold Angel's Reef for a fraction of the property's true worth."

"Because of the scandal," I said, thinking of the news reports I had pulled off the Web. "A beautiful young woman drowned in his swimming pool."

"Right," Wheeler said. "In '74, Stephen Raleigh was fifty-seven, his wife was forty-five, his son eighteen. Raleigh's niece Callista lived in the house year-round. She was thirty-three, and a competitive swimmer, had a gold medal from the '59 Olympics. She's the one who died."

"How did an Olympic swimmer drown in a pool?" St. James asked.

"To this day there's no explaining how and why she

did," Wheeler said. "I read the autopsy protocol. There was no stroke, no heart attack, no embolism or aneurism. The autopsy showed that Callista just plain drowned."

"Tell me more about Raleigh's son," St. James said.

Wheeler dealt out three black-and-white photos, standard police shots. Left profile, right, and full frontal of the face.

"William Raleigh," he said. "Star student and athlete, a great-looking charismatic kid. Captain of the swim team and class president, straight-A honor student with a high I.Q."

St. James was watching me closely, waiting for a flicker of recognition.

I picked up the prints. Flat station house lighting made for flat shots. There was no dimension to the features, no depth of field or color. Skin did not look like flesh. The boy was stiff and unsmiling, a stranger to me.

"I don't know," I said, laying them down. "I just don't know."

He laid two more photos faceup on the desk. Callista. A close-up alive and a close-up at the morgue. A perfect oval face with full lips, a free-flowing mane of sun-streaked blond hair.

"Stunning," St. James said, "even in death."

"Yes," Wheeler said. "In his statement, Raleigh claims he was fishing with his son the day she died. No one else was with them, no one saw them go out or come in. His wife was in the village—a half hour away. Twenty-five witnesses attested to that. By the time she got home, the police and medics were already there. At first the cops suspected Stephen Raleigh."

"Why?" I asked.

"His statement about his day fishing did not match up with his son's. They claimed they were together, but Stephen said they caught no fish, his son said they caught one. Stephen said his son was wearing jeans and a T-shirt, the son said he went out in swim trunks. They couldn't even agree on what they ate for lunch.

"Then a cartographer came forward and said he was in a helicopter—flying low over Angel's Reef—taking aerial shots of Siasconset Beach that day. He came forth with photographs taken around the time Callista died. They showed that there were two people in the pool. In a blowup the police clearly identified both Callista and William. Twenty-four hours later, the mapmaker recanted. Said he had gotten the date wrong. He had taken the shots a day earlier."

"The father paid him off?" I said.

"Obviously," Wheeler said. "Stephen Raleigh built a legal wall around himself and his son, but William was of age, and he couldn't stop the investigation. The story got huge amounts of media attention. It had all the elements. Wealth, beauty, probable murder, and illicit sex. The mapmaker stuck to his story, and the police couldn't come up with anything else strong enough to make an arrest. The case was closed six weeks later. The climate here was obviously unbearable for Raleigh. He took the family across the border into Canada. No one ever saw or heard from them again—until now."

"The son, William Raleigh," I said, "has come back to the scene of the crime. He would be about forty-four or forty-five years old."

"Vale's age," St. James said.

"One more thing," Wheeler said, digging into the box. "The police found this in the pool with Callista."

He held out a plastic toy diver, wearing a wet suit, twin dive tanks, and flippers.

The mask was blacked out.

Wheeler flicked a tiny switch. The little diver began to kick.

*   *   *

"According to U.S. and Canadian records," St. James said, scrolling through pages of information on his laptop, "William's mother and father died in a car wreck ten years ago. William inherited immense wealth.

"The estate is a complex trust, a series of offshore companies, shells within shells. Ever see those wooden Chinese dolls? You open the big one up and find another smaller doll inside. You open that up and find another smaller doll inside and so on until there's one very tiny doll at the center that you can only hold with tweezers. Think of those dolls as layers in an offshore corporation. Keep digging and eventually you get to the tiny doll in the middle, but it's always a lawyer, the offshore equivalent of a solid brick wall."

"Wealth liberates," I said.

"Death does, too," St. James said. "According to Canadian records, William died late last year. I believe he has become his own creation, Vale: a living ghost, a specter, a man who changes face and name at will. His wealth and so-called 'death' bought him total anonymity—access to funds that cannot be traced, total freedom with no tracks. And no one can arrest or hunt down a dead man. If Vale is really William Raleigh."

"The WNTK download's complete," I said, cuing up the first story on the home theater screen.

Archival footage melted years away, rolled back time, taking us right into the bright summer day, walking us up to the sprawling house and manicured lawn of Angel's Reef. Fat bushes of hortensia bloomed pink against shingles weathered gray. A fountain sat at the center of an expensive stone drive, two intertwined dolphins spouting water in a fine twin spray.

The Atlantic sparkled beyond the dunes. The camera moved in a long slow pan picking up details of the

Raleigh property: land dropping down in even terraced levels, wrought-iron banisters flanking sweeping scalloped stairs, the glittering square of blue pool off the right, and beyond it, the cottage I would eventually buy, spare and pretty on the Siasconset shore.

The camera panned over a crowd of local and state police at the pool, and locked in on two medics rolling a white-sheeted gurney away from the pool. As the camera followed the procession, it picked a lone figure up on the widow's walk up on top of the house; William Raleigh, elbows resting on the railing, easy and relaxed, unaware of the camera and smiling as he looked down on the scene.

"Is that Vale when he was eighteen, Lacie?" St. James asked.

"Can't tell," I said.

The camera panned up to the drive, where a horde of reporters and cameramen gathered in a pack. The gurney was loaded into a waiting ambulance. White double doors slammed, and the camera spun around to the front door of the house.

William's father walked out wearing a somber dark jacket with gray flannel slacks. He had gray hair and a mature sun-weathered face.

"On behalf of my family," he said, approaching the reporters, "I ask the media to work in an orderly manner through proper channels. Individual members of my family are not available for public comment or interrogation by the press. Massachusetts state police is conducting a full investigation with the cooperation of the Nantucket PD. The Raleigh name is an old and good one here on this island. We will give investigators open and free access to our home. There will be no need for warrants, as we have nothing to hide.

"A tragic accident occurred here today, one none of us understands given the superior athletic condition of

Miss Callista Stephens, a former Olympic contender. But she drowned. Who can say why? No one was with her. She is in our prayers. May she find grace now in the face of God and everlasting peace."

Polished perfection.

A buzz rose from the crowd and cameras swung around, catching Eleanor Raleigh coming out with her son, William.

His skin was a smooth pale gold and his hair neatly cropped, establishment length. It was honey-colored and glossy, streaked from the summer sun and lightly tinged in places from chlorine.

He was dressed in a blue blazer and a crisp white shirt with a dark blue tie. Good twill slacks snapped smartly as he walked. His shoes were polished to a high shine. Gold flashed at his cuffs. He wore his clothes with an easy assurance and moved with slow, measured strides, hands swinging lightly, loosely at his sides.

A furrow knotted his brow, expressing concern, and concern was far from guilt. He slowed briefly for a moment and pulled up his socks. The innocence, the eternity of that one sweet, small conceit.

"Lacie?" St. James asked softly. "What about now, in this close-up?"

"He looks so different. The hair, the eye color, the age. I just can't say."

On screen, reporters shouted questions.

"William!" a reporter yelled. "We heard you were in the pool with Callista when she died."

"Hey, Billy," another shouted, "someone said it was your dad in the pool. Which story's true, Billy?"

Eleanor turned on the pack, eyes blazing, on fire with hate. "Leave us be!" she said, with none of her husband's composure. "There was an accident here, nothing more."

The cameraman went in tight on her face and got the money shot: the mother could not hide her fear.

William turned to the cameras. "Tragedy's come to Angel's Reef," he said. "Callista was family. Leave us alone now in our grief."

He was elegant, charming, utterly convincing, and more than that, he sounded so much like Vale I thought he was right there in the room. Then as if the audio cue were not enough, William's next move locked it down. He reached up and tucked a stray strand of hair behind his right ear.

"That's him," I said, my heart twisting in knots. "Vale at eighteen."

If I had been eighteen, then I would have given myself gladly to him. Even back then I would have begged him to stay.

William Raleigh ducked into the limo. Doors slammed and the glossy black car pulled away, leaving hungry cameras with only the moors, the ocean, the vast Nantucket sky, and the glittering pool, brilliant agate blue in the hot August sun.

"Were you here in '74?" I asked Wheeler.

"No," he replied. "I was in Boston, year three of med school, then five more years of residency after that. By the time I came back to Nantucket the scandal was forgotten, and Angel's Reef was just another property turned over for profit, another case of beachfront gold changing hands. Play that segment again. I want to see Vale one more time."

I hit REWIND.

Wheeler sat forward in his chair, hands clawed at his knees, wanting to dig his fist right into the screen and rip William out of time and place, alter history, twist fate so that Rio would be alive and well, a daughter he could live for.

"Take a look at that," St. James said, pointing to one of the monitors tuned to Boston's WBZ. "They're cutting into prime-time, broadcasting live from the quarry."

WBZ surprised me, using slick promos and graphics, a tabloid sensationalism that made me sick. The camera panned the quarry rim, showing troopers in high boots standing guard as a trio of divers swam Rio in—McKenzie in the lead. He climbed out first and took the body from the two state divers.

Camera crews crowded McKenzie, trying for the money shot, hungry for a close-up of the blacked-out mask and her devastated face. But McKenzie was too fast for them, shielding her with his big body, tucking her face into his chest and wrapping his arms around her. He shouted orders. An assistant opened a white sheet. It floated down, fluttering in the breeze, covering what was left of Rio, then the sheeted body was loaded on a gurney and carried away.

The WBZ cameraman had no dignity in documenting the funereal procession to the ambulance. Using a high-power optical zoom he moved right in, picking up details, a hand dangling outside of the sheet, her pale bare feet, and wet head. Wind gusted, blew the sheet off and for a dreadful split second the cameraman got his shot: a close-up of the raw red scar on Rio's face.

Wheeler—shock still in his chair, hands gouging the leather seat, then he was up—bolting from the room, slamming out the door and across my deck. I heard his Jeep door open and slam shut. Through the big bay windows we saw him cross the moor.

St. James made a move.

"Stay," I said. "I'll go. I know the weight of his grief."

CHAPTER FIFTY-ONE

Vale stood motionless, breathless, in a rage-induced freeze. The sixteen-screen cyclorama in his safe house was filled with WBZ's live broadcast from the quarry.

But Lacie was not there, just a flat-faced reporter with a bad toupee and sagging cheeks. His wrinkled tan trench coat had a rip in the collar and a stain on the cuff. He spoke in a harsh staccato. There was no elegance, no poetry, no grace—none of the fundamental beauty of Lacie Wagner's face.

She was essential to the kill. Vale had given her clear instructions to go to the site. And she was not there. He had given Lacie Wagner orders, and she had failed to execute.

A more chilling thought crossed his mind. Lacie Wagner had figured out who he was. The passing thought turned to conviction. And if she was good enough to do that, she was good enough to find him.

He would find her first.

Vale popped in a set of amber contacts, peeled off the black hair, stepped out of his leather shoes, and removed his sweater and slacks. He slipped the orange wet suit on, donned combat boots, laced them up, and checked the mirror.

Justin Vale liked what he saw.

CHAPTER FIFTY-TWO

The open pool at Angel's Reef was lit and steaming, glowing a murky greenish brown.

Vapor rose from the surface in a swirl, creating a layer of low-lying silver fog. Wheeler was in his wet suit, in the water. He had a hammer in one hand and a chisel in the other.

"The images are violent," he said. "I didn't notice at first. Look here: a harpooned whale spouting blood, Neptune raping Venus."

"There's a psychic symbolism to them we'll never understand," I said, "another language we'll never speak."

"Not true. Look here at the triple-headed hydra. The mermaid held captive in the net. Look at Neptune spearing a Siren, the grin on the face, the rapture, the glee. And the face on the medusa. It looks like Callista. These images give him power, feed his fantasy, his obsession."

He raised his tools and attacked, savagely hacking and chiseling chunks of whalebone and prying them loose with his bare fingers, tossing them into the wind. "This violence, and the evil—the seed started here, on my island, in my time."

I knelt at the pool edge and touched his shoulder, but he stayed fixed on the frieze, ripping scrimshaw out of the wall.

"Wheeler, stop. What's the point?"

He turned to me, eyes wild. "The point is that evil is here, right here in these pictures, feeding his power— power he used to get my daughter."

The hammer slammed into the pool wall. Scrimshaw splintered and white flakes sprayed out in a wild shower. Wheeler's face was contorted into a mask of rage. "It's my fault he found her, my fault she's dead."

"Don't do this to yourself. You know it's not true."

"It *is* my fault, and that's God's own ugly truth. You want me to tell you what's true, Lacie?"

"Yes."

"I taught Rio to swim—taught her to love the water. It's the one big part of me that stayed with her all those years we were apart. Her love of water put her right in Vale's reach, didn't it?"

The hammer came down and scrimshaw shattered into confetti.

St. James emerged out of the mist. "I got it," he said. "Something that could explain the skin."

Wheeler laid the hammer down.

"What do you know about the effects of water on the human body?" St. James asked.

"Medical studies have been confined to the standard exposure tests," Wheeler said.

"Beyond that?"

"Naval research, reams of it exploring the viability and vulnerability of the body in water."

"End result?"

Wheeler knew the answer by rote and spit it out in a dull monotone. "There are definite limits to how long a human can survive. Viability's determined by water temperature. Even in tropical seas, a human couldn't last more than seventy-two hours—and certainly not long enough to see the kind of maceration we saw on Rio's body."

St. James pressed. "What if the water temperature was ninety-eight-point-six degrees, the exact temperature as our core body temperature. Could a human then survive fully immersed for an indefinite period of time?"

"No," Wheeler said. "Ninety-eight-point-six degrees would be too hot."

"Why?"

"Our basic metabolic functions are a furnace, generating heat in excess of the core body temperature. That excess heat gets passed off through the skin. If the body—therefore the skin—was immersed in water the same temperature of our core, there wouldn't be any way for the body to rid itself of excess metabolically generated heat."

"The body would overheat like a car engine?"

"Worse," Wheeler said. "It would literally boil to death. Theoretically speaking, the water would not only have to be much cooler than the core body. It would have to be *exactly* eighty-six-point-five degrees. The navy used computer models and simulations to figure it out: one degree warmer, and the body would overheat. One degree cooler and the body would succumb to hypothermia."

"A human could survive indefinitely immersed in eighty-six-point-five degree water?"

"Only in theory. Water temperature's wildly erratic affected by sunlight, shade, wind, and rain. Anyway, there is no naturally occurring body of water that would stay at a consistent eighty-six-point-five degrees."

"*Naturally* occurring."

"What's your point, St. James?"

"What about artificial environments?"

"Such as?"

"Zoo exhibits, for example."

"Go on."

"Tanks, Wheeler. Aquariums. One hundred percent climate-controlled self-contained bodies of water with no tide. Assuming food and water are not an issue and you have a big enough tank maintained at a constant eighty-six-point-five degrees, how long could a human survive fully immersed: Three weeks? Four? More? Long enough for the skin to macerate and those open wounds to infect? Long enough for that?"

"Again, theoretically speaking, yes—if you don't take into account the need for food and hydration."

"You found scars on Rio's hands consistent with IV lines. What if she had been on a saline nutrient drip while fully immersed over a long period of time? Wouldn't that have been enough to sustain her life while the water worked away at her skin?"

Wheeler's eyes screwed shut, as if the physical act could shut out the truth.

St. James gunned ahead, wanting only the truth, as horrible as it might be.

"If Rio had been held captive in water maintained at eighty-six-point-five degrees," he doggedly said, "wouldn't it explain the caul on her eyes, the conflicting pathology of accelerated tissue disintegration and simultaneous infection, the death crawling over her own live skin? What if she was an *aquatic hostage* held captive in water diligently maintained at eighty-six-point-five degrees? Wouldn't it explain all of that?"

"Dear God," Wheeler said. "Yes it would."

"The Aquatic Park on the coast might have been more than just the source for Vale's rare fish," I said. "It's closed down now, and could be Vale's safe house, where he holds his captives."

"Run a search on the Web," St. James said. "Pull news stories, features, legal notices, anything at all that has to do with the park. We need a layout of the grounds and architectural plans. Find the architects if you have to, call them at home. Be thorough. I don't care how long it takes, get everything you can."

The urgency in his voice sent me running across the moor and into my study.

It took an hour and forty-five minutes of patient

work trolling through hundreds of small news stories, press releases, and general stories to find the names of the architects who designed the park, and another half hour to track down home phone numbers. And finally, as architectural plans came in over my fax, I found a feature story in an obscure magazine targeted at zookeepers.

The plans showed the park as dramatically positioned on high bluffs overlooking the Atlantic and built as a compound: one main building squared off around an outdoor amphitheater and pool for dolphin shows. A small marina was planned down at the base of the bluffs. Phase-one construction included a snack bar and pier with speedboat rentals and a whale-watching tour. The main building had two levels of exhibition halls—small exhibits upstairs and the big fish downstairs in a subterranean viewing gallery lined with twelve massive tanks.

It looked good on paper.

I read the feature article and learned the developers had made two big mistakes. They had picked the land site because it was cheap, building on rugged coastline too far north for the tourist trade. And, they had grossly underestimated construction costs. In a last-ditch effort to trim capital expenditures, they cut corners on equipment for the subterranean exhibit hall, installing aquariums that were technically too small for the kind of ocean fish on display. Animal rights activists were at the park on opening day, picketing and protesting.

Two months later the park closed down, and the property was sold to a private Montreal investor who planned to demolish the compound and build a private home. An unnamed spokesman for the investor said the fish would be donated to commercial aquariums in the Northeast where they would be guaranteed appropriate habitats. I had no doubt who that private Montreal investor was. Just then an e-mail popped up, pulling me right into the eye of Vale's dark storm.

Subject: THE EIGHTH SEA.
                  Come to The Altar, Lacie.
   Ashley and Rio are already there—Kiri is coming soon.
Click here to hyperlink in.

Kiri Hannover from Woods Hole. Kiri the swimmer. "Butterfly's my stroke. I'm fast in the water, Ms. Wagner. I promise you that."
   He had Kiri.
   I clicked the link. My browser auto-launched, and the site came up. Black letters on a red screen and atonal music, an eerie unsettling score.

Welcome to The Altar

The page changed. Black type on a blue liquid background.

There is a sea:
It is not on any map of the world
or in the collective memory of man;
a sea sailed by only one mariner
and he did not use oar, nor motor nor canvas to harness the wind
but traveled solely by the powerful pull of his own imagination;
the rising tide of a blood lust shared in the dark dreams of many men.
Come.
Come sail with me on The Eighth Sea.

The screen flashed to video of a classic five-masted sailing schooner tossing on a raging sea. A classical figurehead was cleaved to the prow: a wild-eyed siren, chest thrust out, chin up, back arched, eyes to heaven that morphed into Ashley's nude pale body stretched out on a bed. Hands sheathed in protective mitts pressed quarter-size cesium chips on her skin. Church organ music played mass for the dead.

"Ashley was chosen because she looked like you," Vale said in narration, "and the burns were for you, too. They were tattoos, brands from a flameless fire to demonstrate the power of elements you cannot see."

The screen went black.

I heard the sound of boots beating cliff scrub, dogs clawing and panting; a vicious pack in hungry pursuit. The white high beam of a flashlight slashed in, cutting through the night, locking in on Ashley.

She looked like a strange water warrior stranded on land with twin dive tanks harnessed to her back, a weight belt loaded at her waist, and a mask wound high up around her right arm. She touched the metal dive knife sheathed at her shin, then changed her mind and spun around instead, scrambling up a steep incline on all fours.

"Come on, Sinclair, let's see you run!"

The voice was military hard and totally new to me. *Villard.*

"Whoa, baby! That what you call speed? That the best you can do? What kind of soldier are you, Sinclair? What have you been thinking about in class—*fashion shows, perfume, hair curlers, getting laid? You should'a been thinking about exit strategy, Sinclair!*"

The high beam picked her up again, crouched and ready at the edge of a bluff.

"End of the line, girl! It's a long hard fall. You didn't have a good exit strategy, and now you are officially royally totally fucked!"

A Doberman lunged into the frame.

Ashley jumped.

Hard cut to black.

A broader, brighter beam of light on a rough sea.

The urgent ping of sonar locked in on its target.

A winch squeaking, squealing, shrieking, cables working, swinging the big net up out of the water, and around
slowly down to the deck.

Vale in a phosphorescent orange wet suit, taking the
netted catch in his arms, holding her like a bride.

Hard cut to white.

"Lacie Wagner!" Vale barked. "Why weren't you at
the quarry when they brought the body up? You were
specifically instructed to go to Lowell's quarry and tell
the story. What do you think this is, a goddamn nursery
school where if you feel tired or bored that you can opt
out? Quit?

"Where the fuck do you get off thinking like that?
You are a professional given an assignment. You do not
opt out—take a fucking *leave of absence*—when the
story is breaking! We know how to locate you, Wagner.
And we will. *Discipline* is the operative word today!

"You think you know about television? You think
you got the whole broadcast business locked down as
your own? Well, step on up to the Altar, pretty baby.
Step on up, and we'll show you what reality programming is all about! Are you listening to me now? Put
your bikini on, get your sweet ass in the pool, and show
me you know how to swim."

A new image flashed on.

Familiar details.

A scrimshaw panel.

Glittering blue water of a pool.

Ashley submerged in the shallows held down by
hands and arms sheathed in orange.

Water blurred time from her features, darkened the
blond of her hair. We were suddenly no longer strangers

ten years apart, but one and the same. Her face was mine—Ashley was me—and watching her die was as if I were witnessing my own death. Fear was a steel vise, an icy pressure squeezing speed out of my rocketing pulse as the sound of Vale filled my head.

"Sinclair's drowning—or is it really you down there? What's the matter, Lacie? Can't you come up for air?"

Ashley was shaking her head back and forth, eyes wide open underwater and panicked. Her lips parted, tiny bubbles escaped, the last of the air in her body, the final wet exhale.

Vale. Going on and on, talking me deep into the dying.

"I own you, I am in you, and I feel your fright. You know fire, Lacie, but what do you know about water? Two minutes is all it takes to drown, Lacie Wagner, and you now have one minute left."

Adrenaline surged through my veins.

Fight or flight, and I could not run.

On screen, my underwater eyes squeezed shut in a desperate denial. Lips parted, I inhaled, and the bright blue water flooded in. The body in the pool arched and bucked, twisted and turned, at the frenzied climax of agony. My own lungs were burning, my head bursting, panic driving hot knives straight through the center of my sternum-slamming heart.

"Feel the drowning," Vale ordered. "Feel it, girl!"

And I did. Fear was a flameless inferno burning me from the inside out, driven by Vale's nightmare voice and the contorted spasms of Ashley in the shallow end. New images strobed on the inner screen, one after the other, tropical fish I had seen in his tanks. Vale's voice shifted, turned soft and silky, a lover's caress.

"Remember *Amphiprion?*" he asked. "Or *Thalassoma lunare,* the emerald ribbon, the color of my own eyes? *Fellinas solaris* glowing orange like the sun? Remember the violet seahorses? The ruby-finned tiger? The translucent beauty of *Naso volitans* with her pale fins and fast fluttering heart? Do you recall how beautiful they were in my seven perfect seas?"

The fish disappeared, and swirling up from the water came a black, cavernous void.

"The Eighth Sea is more beautiful yet," Vale promised. "Come with me there now."

His words melted into the rushing sound of a tidal wave gathering force. Gigantic air filter systems whooshing. Tons of water circulating. Huge ventilation fans blowing hollow wind. A far-off keening cry of a dolphin calling.

"Come," Vale said, "and see my secrets revealed."

A glowing fiery red digital read-out burned itself into the upper left quadrant of the screen to the sound of fire searing into flesh: 52.4° F.

A long wide staircase leading down into a corridor lined with huge floor-to-ceiling aquatic display aquariums. The shot was wide-angle, as if taken from a camera in the ceiling at the top of the stairs.

Vale, disembodied, went on. "Digital gauges monitor water temperature, the most critical element of the habitat. If the water is not the right temperature, the aquatic specimen will not survive captivity."

The shot changed and turned unsteady as if Vale himself were walking a camera down the corridor. Tank water filled the screen. It was swirling with filth, a rancid brown green.

"*Livias vernatas,*" Vale stated, seductive and soft. "My giant ray comes from the North Atlantic and prefers his water cool."

The giant oozed into view. His wing tips scalloped with wounds, white yellow fungus crawling over his back, his belly, his face. He settled on the bottom, lethargic, sick.

The camera swish-panned to a second murky tank.

The digital readout flashed: 59.0° F.

"The giant octopus, *Halothyus julipus.* From the northeast Atlantic."

The sickening sound of ten long tentacles suctioning glass. One ominous dark eye peering out.

A third tank lit up.

The digital readout flickered: 68.6° F.

"*Homeo rathos,* the hammerhead shark. Habitat, South Pacific and the Hawaiian Islands. He measures one meter ten."

The ugly double-hammered jaw emerged from the silt. A mud colored body and powerful tail. Chunks of flesh were missing from his belly and back, the open wounds infected, oozing yellow-green pus.

The fourth tank read, 67.8° F.

"*Deadlus greganus*, the species of tiger shark found in the South Pacific."

A slash for a mouth and stones for eyes. Fungus on his fins, his jaw, his neck.

A terrible understanding filled me. I knew why he was showing the aquariums, knew exactly where he was going next. I wanted to cut the feed—but Vale's voice was a hypnotic, disabling choice.

The screen went black, but his satanic litany went on. "I've learned how to keep my prize specimens alive— it's all a matter of the correct temperature. These fish have taught me that."

The music gave way to a Bach fugue as the digital readout slowly changed over: 86.5° F.

I knew that number. Wheeler had said that a human could survive indefinitely immersed in water that is kept a constant 86.5 degrees.

"Eighty-six-point-five degrees Fahrenheit—the precise temperature necessary to sustain life indigenous to the Eighth Sea."

Water. Crystalline clear.

The fugue melted into Beethoven's Moonlight Sonata, dreamy notes scoring an aquatic ballet choreographed in Hell.

Nothing had prepared me.

Nothing I had imagined or dreamed had readied me for the pale slow spiraling form.

"Look how lovely she is," he whispered. "How graceful the death dance is."

Fungus on the back, the belly, the head.

Decomposed white curdled flesh on her legs, her breasts, her arms.

Black hair fanning out in the water, diaphanous and light, eyes open and cauled. Translucent medical tubing drifted in the water like long tentacles of a Medusa, piercing her hand and secured down with tape.

IV scars, McKenzie had said. A saline and nutrient drip.

Two long hoses snaked through the tank. They fit into a scuba regulator set in a silicone oval that sealed the bottom half of her face from nose to chin. Silicone straps circled her skull, holding the mask tightly in place.

I thought of Rio's face, the strange red raw oval, chafed all the way through to bone.

"Ingenious!" Vale exhaled.

His voice changed to the fast staccato clip of a professor instructing his class. "Commercial dive-grade air hoses fit into custom-made regulators which are set in silicone demi-masks with a watertight seal. Industrial air compressors up top on the maintenance level provide an uninterrupted air supply twenty-four hours a day.

"Feeding *Homo sapiens* in an aquatic environment presents more of a challenge. A saline nutrient drip is an imperfect solution. Some specimens rip the drip out.

Others are more compliant, understanding that the drip—like the air—is a lifeline.

"The most interesting behavior exhibited by the captives is the survival instinct. They have all ripped their masks off thinking they prefer dying to living in my gallery. Each specimen attempted suicide but put the mask back on when the drowning began. Makes you rethink the old adage 'I'd rather die first.' My specimens would rather live. Why? Because they hope their captivity will end. And indeed it does, as you've seen—my way."

One by one, Vale lit the remaining tanks.

There were seven more, eight in all, four on the left wall, four on the right, with a swiveling recliner chair placed dead center, perfectly positioned so Vale could watch.

As his camera moved down the line, the digital readout remained fixed at 86.5° F.

Bars of halogen cast a blue tinge to the water, false daylight in a never-ending night. Death would be a blessed release from this interminable liquid purgatory, a full-bodied baptismal submersion in water from the River Styx.

The supersize aquariums were ideal for Vale's diabolical intent; the glass made to withstand body blows from four-hundred-pound *rathos* and other massive ocean creatures who did not like captivity, who would fight hard to break free.

The sonata played on, scoring Vale's slow-motion dance.

These were oceanic chrysalis but there was nothing embryonic in sight, not in the long lithe forms, women in their prime, the first six dead, hanging vertically suspended or floating outstretched: pale skin flaking, hands crabbed, heads bowed, hair billowing in soft waving fans.

The eighth was alive, long legs kicking. Her head was bowed, and her arms were wrapped around her chest in a protective clench against the enemy outside. White-blond hair fanned out in a halo. Pale skin was lightly wrinkled as if she had spent too much time in the bath but it had not yet started to decay. She was a fresh catch and had not been there long. She lifted her head. The small diamond piercing her nose caught light and sparkled.

Kiri. I saw detail of the air hose feeding into the mask, how the oval was a silicone seal around her mouth protecting the air supply. Awake or unconscious, the captive could breathe, and I heard the sound of her regulator *shoo-shoosh*ing as she inhaled, *shoosh-shoo*-ing as she exhaled. Air bubbles rose iridescent in the tank twilight: silver confetti floating up instead of falling, the inverse gravity of the underwater world.

Her sightless eyes were swollen from water exposure. She raised swollen, bruised hands to the glass. With the lilting notes of the sonata came the sound of dull thudding, broken hands beating glass, her high-pitched keening cry and whispering regulator.

"Two minutes," Vale whispered, "is what it takes to drown."

The music stopped, and the whispering regulator suddenly sounded loud. *Whoo-whoosh. Whoosh-whoo.*

A digital timer flashed on screen, pulsating green and glowing: 2:00.

The whispering regulator went silent, the bubbles stopped rising and the timer ticked down slower than real time: 1:59 1:58 1:57.

"I've just cut her air supply. Watch Kiri now. Live the dying, Lacie. Travel with me now to the very pinnacle of fear."

Vale's will was a steel band, locked down tight around my own.

1:20

Grief was a hammer in my heart as I helplessly watched Kiri drown. Through my tears I saw Kiri's will to live was still strong, twisting her into a frenzy against the dying. Vale's slow-motion camera turned the movements—the bucking, arching, twisting—into agony's lyrical ballet.

:43

She tore off the mask and used the last of the air in her lungs to scream. It was a hideous hollow sound, a liquid warble fading to a muffled cry.

:20

The countdown on the clock stopped.

Kiri grabbed her mask with both hands, and I saw her gulping air, breathing deep.

"Life is mine to give and take as I please," Vale said. "Kiri has a brief reprieve. For the moment, that is, until I change my mind."

The feed cut and the screen flashed back to Max's docket picture of Villard.

CHAPTER FIFTY-THREE

I looked up and saw Wheeler in his dripping wet suit standing in the doorway. The expression on his face told me he had watched Kiri's entire ordeal.

"Where's St. James?" I asked.

"He went to the Aquatic Park."

"Without me?"

"He went alone."

I rose from my chair, stunned. "When?"

"Almost two hours ago, by speedboat."

I suddenly understood that St. James had sent me inside to get me out of the way. The betrayal stung.

"Why didn't you go along, Wheeler?"

"St. James wanted me to stay here and look after you."

"We have to call state police, send backup to the park."

"No," Wheeler said. His blue eyes were flat and hard, reminding me of the falcon before the kill. "St. James works alone. Locate, isolate, eradicate. That's his way. That was the deal."

"Not now," I said. "He hasn't seen this. He can't go up against Vale alone."

"Yes, he can. I'd bet my girl's life on him."

"Bad bet, buddy boy!"

Vale—as Villard.

Glowing orange in the doorway behind Wheeler. He wore combat boots, a phosphorescent wet suit, and had a combat utility bag at his feet. His face was blacked out with grease and framed by the orange glowing hood. His Uzi was shoved hard into the base of Wheeler's skull.

"Your fucking saint is dead. On the ground now, nose first, hands behind your back."

Wheeler went down. Vale pulled quick-action plastic snap-on restraints from the utility bag and locked them tight around Wheeler's ankles and wrists. Then he pulled a heavy commercial fisherman's net out of the bag and approached me slowly, stroking jute as if it were flesh. His eyes locked with mine, and much as I tried to see Vale the lover I had taken, I saw only the glittering hard eyes of a total stranger. But his hands were familiar, as I felt his long graceful fingers once again on my cheek, under my chin, caressing my forehead.

"We had a special time," he said. "A wild, wonderful time. You let yourself go, didn't you, Lacie? Two magical nights. Are you thinking about that now?"

I jerked my head, looked away, and still the smell of him was as intimate as his touch. The net came down over me, wet and heavy and oddly gentle. Vale fashioned it into a jute straightjacket, immobilizing me. He slung the combat bag across his back, picked me up, and jabbed Wheeler with his boot.

"Can't walk?" he said. "Well, then—roll!"

He jabbed again, and Wheeler rolled.

"Come on, boy, you can move faster than that!"

Wheeler rolled, side over side, through my foyer and out the open front door. Vale stopped at the threshold, tipped his face down close to mine, and pressed his lips against the net.

"May I kiss the bride?" he whispered.

Then he stepped over and was moving again, kicking Wheeler hard in the back, shouting him down the steps and across the drive to the shortcut in the moor, taunting and teasing, kicking him all the way to the pool next door.

It was lit and glowing. Vapor rose in a fine smoky mist.

Vale dropped me at the edge next to Wheeler. He was facedown, and I could not see his eyes. Vale nudged my shoulder with his boot, teasing, testing, ready to kick me over the edge and in. He stepped back abruptly, pulled thick boating rope out of the utility bag and bound Wheeler tightly.

"The water's warm," he said. "It's a fine night for a swim."

He pulled a loaded weight belt from the bag and cinched it around Wheeler's waist, placing the buckle release well away from Wheeler's shackled hands.

"A hundred pounds will keep you under," Vale said,

"unless you're some kind of Houdini. You were at the wrong place at the wrong time, and now you are officially fucked."

With one powerful push he rolled Wheeler into the deep end of the pool. Rancid water spilled over the edge, soaking me.

"Do you feel like swimming?" Vale said. "Would you like to go with Wheeler, or would you prefer to stay with me?"

His combat boot toed my cheek, teased my shoulder, tapped my back.

"Water or wine?" he asked. "A swim with Wheeler or a shower with me?"

"Wheeler."

I tensed against the kick, but Vale swooped down and picked me up instead. He sprinted up to a white van parked in the drive, dumped me in the back, and slammed the doors, leaving me locked in a black unlit hold.

Darker still was the final terrible understanding that a death roll with Wheeler would have been merciful compared to the death Vale had planned for me now.

CHAPTER FIFTY-FOUR

Time was measured in my own breaths. Inhale, exhale. Sixty of each equals one minute. A new equation for life. I was on my side in the back of the van, cheek pounding metal as Vale raced us through the night. Rear windows were blacked out. A sliding partition closed off the rear section from the front cabin. I smelled the stink of old fish, acidic chlorine—tasted the salt of wet netting and my own tears.

The pitch and roll of the ferry crossing were unmistakable. I lost track of counting minutes, and no longer cared, knowing we were heading for the mainland, for the Aquatic Park. Instead of counting time, I wished it would stand still, but all too soon I heard the engine kick over and felt tires speeding us over pavement. When the smooth ride turned rough, I knew we were off the main highway and on small winding country roads that were little used and poorly kept.

Somewhere along the way Vale stopped and hauled me out. Steep rocky cliffs rose to either side. I could not see breaking surf, but the sound was close. The legendary fog had settled in along with the rain—wet, heavy, almost impenetrable. He loaded me in the front passenger seat, and then we were off again, racing through the dark.

A portable DVD player sat open on the center console.

"We've had quite a night," Vale said, flashing me a big white smile. "I recorded it for you, Lacie."

He punched PLAY, and the monitor lit up.

A corridor of giant glass aquarium tanks again—identical to the one I had seen on his Internet site. The camera was positioned high, at the top of a staircase, giving a sweeping view of the whole room. It picked up the back of St. James going down the stairs, Sig Sauer semiautomatic drawn and ready at his side. He walked into the exhibition hall, dwarfed by the huge tanks. Suddenly, Vale appeared in the frame, glowing orange at the top of the stairs, Uzi raised and ready.

"Drop the gun," he said.

St. James spun around, eyed the Uzi, and reluctantly dropped the Sig Sauer at his feet.

"Hands up and locked behind your head."

St. James complied.

"Kick the weapon. Hard. Now!"

St. James kicked. The Sig Sauer spun far out of reach.

Vale shifted his aim and fired, shooting an even line across the aquarium glass. Jets of water sprayed out in high fine arcs.

"You should have brought dive tanks instead of a gun," Vale said. He aimed at the aquarium next to St. James and fired a dozen shots dead center, carving a portal in the glass. "A properly trained operative understands his opponent. Do you understand yours? What's the weight of water? Don't know? I'll tell you: one gallon weighs eight pounds."

Vale fired off four more rounds.

Water gushed out in a thundering roar, swirled around St. James's knees, and inched up his thighs in a swift rising tide.

"Each tank here holds ten thousand gallons," Vale said.

He fired at a tank next to St. James, carving a weak spot in the most vulnerable part, right at centerline.

Glass exploded. A giant wave came down, and St. James disappeared.

Vale fired again. Eleven more tanks burst in a fast and furious thirty-thousand-gallon surge. Water engulfed the stairs.

Vale backed off. Off camera, a door slammed.

Water crashed into the lens, images sputtered and fizzed, electricals popped, and then there was nothing at all but a huge silence and black empty void.

St. James. Wheeler. And now me.

Vale looked at me. His eyes were calm, cold, calculating, and totally sane. Despite Villard's amber eyes and razored hair, I saw and heard only Vale.

"They will hunt you down and kill you," I said.

"A man without a name?"

"William Raleigh."

"He's dead. The estate is run by a blind trust. The Altar has disappeared. There's no cybertrail to pick up, no way to trace my site. But the videos are out there. Somewhere, someone will always be watching Rio dying in the quarry, Ashley drowning in the pool, Kiri struggling in the tank. Technology enables."

"And wealth liberates."

"Mine liberates my fantasies and protects my identity—my anonymity."

"Why are you doing this?" I asked. I could not help it. The words just came out. "Why?"

"You'll never understand me," Vale said, "no matter what name I have. For all your intelligence, you're simply not capable. I am beyond the depths of your limited imagination. You never dreamed someone like me could even exist, yet I do. I have unthinkable desires and the ability to realize them, yet you will never understand why I do what I do."

"Why me now?"

"Because I made a mistake. I should have remained a stranger, the polite man next door whom you saw fishing from time to time. You would have gone after your story, filed the news, but your search would never have brought you within arm's length of me. There is safety in anonymity, Lacie. More than you could possibly know."

He popped the tape and dropped a new one in.

Grainy black-and-white newsreel footage played: silent film of Houdini hanging upside down, suspended in a glassed-in chest full of water.

"That is Houdini's famous water tank," Vale said. "He nearly died in it once. The piece was recently sold at auction for a record price. The sale made the front page of the Boston papers. Did you read about it?"

"Why do you care?"

He smiled. "It's a gift, Lacie. I bought the tank for you."

CHAPTER FIFTY-FIVE

Hinks, at eleven-ten, pacing the lobby of Nantucket PD downtown.

District Attorney Taggert had a long list of state business to run through with Hinks and Nantucket's chief of police. It had taken Hinks more than two hours to extricate herself. Now she paced, trying in vain to raise Wheeler and Lacie on their mobiles.

There was no answer, and that troubled her—greatly.

Wheeler, at eleven-fifteen.

Water flooded his ears, nose, and throat as the hundred-pound weight pulled him under again. He tasted the metallic sting of rancid water, and each time he surfaced he smelled the stink. Blue water turned green, sludged with fungus and algae and silt. Water he could not swim through or float on, water he would die in before the night was out.

No!

That one word was a roar.

No!

He let his body settle to the bottom. Soles flat down on the tiles, he bent his knees and put all his power into the push. He broke surface, gulped water and air, and then the lead weight was dragging him under again, into the murk, closer to death.

The weight of water was nothing compared to the hundred pounds belted at his waist. With his hands and feet bound he was destined to run out of energy. He could not go on like this forever—springing up from the deep end, surfacing long enough to get a gulp of air, then the weight dragging him under to the bottom again, where he crouched, gathered power, and sprang.

How long had he been springing now? An hour? Two? His knees ached, his thigh muscles burned. How much longer could he go? Another hour? What if he lasted three?

Then what?

It was not a question of if Wheeler drowned, but when—for this was the perfectly planned diabolical death.

At eleven-twenty Hinks helped herself to a state cruiser, and roof lights blazing, raced across the island to Lacie's house at Siasconset. Lights burned brightly in the windows, but the front door was wide open.

Hinks cut the motor, rolled silently down the drive, set the brake softly, and slipped out.

She moved silently up the steps. Pressing her body tight to the shingled wall, she edged close to the big bay window and looked in. The study was empty and lit only by one brass lamp on the desk. In that dim light, the big screen on the wall was super bright, and the man's face on it larger than life. He had short razored hair, amber eyes, and a grin that shook Hinks for reasons she could not explain.

She moved quietly inside and through the downstairs area.

Rooms were orderly but empty.

Upstairs she flicked on lights and found herself in the master bedroom. She moved to the window and looked out across the moor at Angel's Reef. The pool was lit and glowing, a dark and foreboding brown brackish green.

Something or someone was splashing.

This was not a night for swimming.

She heard the faint almost inhuman sound of a deep baritone voice shouting.

Wheeler? she thought. *What the hell's going on over there?*

Wheeler bent his knees and sprang. Cold air hit his skull. He breathed deeply; then the weight was pulling him under again as he heard someone shouting his name.

"Wheeler? Wheeler!"

He was plunging back through the sludge and hitting bottom, wondering if he had one more leap left in him. His thigh muscles were spent, his knees ached, but he had only to think of Rio, and the memory of her death gave life to his rage. He would walk on water if he had to—somehow he would survive and kill the son of a bitch. Wheeler pressed his feet down on the tile, bent his knees, and sprang one more time.

"Tom! For Christ's sake! Oh, God!"

He went under, and then she was in, on him, next to him, sinking in the sludge, fumbling at his body, feeling the rope and knots that bound him, groping at his waist, finding and understanding the weight he carried there. She groped the weight belt, found the latch, and the weight fell away. Wheeler sprang.

This time he shot straight up and broke surface, coughing and choking, sucking in the good cold air.

"*Wheeler!*"

She was crying, God bless her, and locking her arm

around his neck in a lifesaving hold. Hinks dragged him to the shallow end and propped him up against the wall, where he could stand.

"Goddamn it," she spat, fumbling at the ropes.

Water had tightened the knots.

"Fuck." She wept. "Trussed up like a goddamn turkey, tied up like a farmyard pig."

Hinks slapped at the water in anger, wiped algae off her cheek, slicked wet hair back off her face. "Who did this to you, Tom? Who? You were going to die here tonight, isn't that right? You were going to fucking drown in there, isn't that so?"

She finally worked the knots open and the rope dropped.

His knees were rubber, too weak to hold him. He fell forward. She caught him and let him lean, and the feel of Hinks against him was good. She turned his face to hers, cupped his head in her hands. By the light of the green glowing water he saw something stronger than fear in her eyes. The force of it filled him, and as she searched his face he knew she found in his eyes the same thing: adoration.

"You've got *Ruby* at the dock?" Wheeler asked.

"Yes. Why?"

"You good with her in rough seas?"

"How rough?"

"Tonight, crossing to the mainland—to the Cape Cod Aquatic Park."

"That shore's nothing but cliff. The storm has kicked up in the last hour. There's no way to make a safe landing or even navigate into a marina—not in seas this high. We'll get slammed into rock on the approach."

"Then we'll go in as close as we can, and you'll let me off. I'll swim the rest of the way."

"You're going to swim?" Hinks asked, incredulous.

"That's right," Wheeler said, grabbing the hammer and chisel that lay at the side of the pool where he had left them. "That's what I said."

CHAPTER FIFTY-SIX

We hurtled up a steep road posted with glow-in-the-dark NO TRESPASSING signs. Heavy rains had washed out sections of the bluffs, sending down heavy slides of mud and shale. Vale drove faster than he should have, but he knew the way and was confident at the wheel. A square building appeared at the top of a circular drive. Double entry doors were flung wide open to the night.

Vale eyed them. He stopped the van, cracked his door, and listened. The sound of the ocean came from far below, ferocious breakers pounding the shore. Riding under that huge sound was a shrill, high-pitched alarm.

"The compound has been breached," Vale said. "Someone has gone in."

He reached into his combat utility bag and came up with night vision gear. He donned the goggles, shouldered his gun, slipped out of his seat, gently closed the door, and went inside.

Keys were in the ignition, I noted, headlights still on high. The driver's side door was unlocked. And Vale had left me alone.

CHAPTER FIFTY-SEVEN

Whoever had come in had already left again.

Vale felt the weight of the emptiness around him, knew deep in his bones the smell and feel of a space where nothing human breathed. Dead or simply gone, he decided, eyeing a trail of blood. He flicked the master power switch, but the generator had been knocked out in the storm.

Or by the intruder.

Vale did not need electricity. He wore featherweight Army Navy PVS-7, head-mounted night vision goggles—military spec equipment designed for combat and used in Desert Storm. The unit housing was shock resistant and watertight. And, the image resolution was superb, auto-adjusting to different light sources. It even had a built-in infrared illuminator for close-up work in zero light situations.

The blacked out windowless rooms of the exhibition halls qualified as zero light. Vale fully appreciated the PVS-7 as it turned that formless pitch bright as an apple-colored day, revealing detail all around him, right down to fresh blood on the floor. He followed the trail from the entry hall into the belly of the building and up a flight of steel stairs to an access door.

Vale was certain he had left it closed. He kicked the door fully open and marched on in to the maintenance loft—a cavernous space the size of an airplane hangar positioned piggyback over the exhibition hall of big tanks. One entire wall opened to the exterior allowing for delivery and removal of big fish. The ceiling was vaulted and fitted with winches that had payloads of up to one ton. The massive aquariums from the exhibit hall below extended two feet up into this level. Tank tops were covered with heavy steel grids inset with trap-door hatches providing access for feeding and cleaning. If a new specimen was added to the tank or a sick one taken out, the entire steel grid was raised with hydraulic lifts.

Buckets of rotting fish sat next to eight tanks. Food for *rathos* the Hammerhead, and *Livias* the ray. Next to the other eight tanks were medical IV racks and cartons of saline nutrient packs—food for Vale's captives. Industrial-size air compressors the size of mini subs sat alongside providing an uninterrupted air supply—uninterrupted that is, until the compressors were turned off or air hoses cut.

Vale leapt up to the grillework now and carefully walked each row of tanks, peering down into the cavernous, water-filled gallery below. Air hoses in the first four captive's tanks were neatly sliced in two. Short stubs hung down from the grilles too far from the water surface below for any human to reach.

Vale hopped nimbly across to the facing row of captives' tanks and walked the grille. The first three air hoses were neatly and cleanly sliced from when he had cut off the air supply to the captives below. The fourth hose, however, was not. It did not dangle short and stublike as the others did, but appeared to snake all the way down from the grille and into the water. Vale opened the trap door and pulled on the hose. He brought enough up to see the slash where his knife had cut, but had not gone all the way through.

The air hose was strong industrial-strength rubber, and it looked very much like a vine. A rubber ladder for the able-bodied and fit. Jack's own beanstalk, if Jack himself had not drowned. Fresh blood dripped from the grillework. Vale swiped a fingerful and smelled, just to be sure.

Vale ran down a mental checklist.

The big bald man was at the bottom of the pool, drowned.

The longhaired intruder called St. James and little Kiri had drowned.

He studied the slit hose, the blood on the grid.

Vale cursed himself. He had assumed the latest breach had come from the outside in, not from the inside out—and knew now bone-deep that his assumption was wrong.

He dropped the hose and hurried to the far end of the loft, where seventeen massive steel valves sprouted from a wall. They were the emergency drainage systems for the tanks and corridor below. Vale quickly opened them all.

The great sucking sound of water was as loud as an explosion, hundreds of thousands of liquid gallons rushing out. The park architects had cut corners, and instead of an expensive drainage route emptying directly into the sea, the system sucked water and spit it back out onto the surrounding land. One tank would have simply wet the parkland like a heavy rain, but seventeen open and draining overloaded the pipes.

Unbeknownst to Vale, water was backwashing into the building guts, overflowing out of sink drains and toilets, and still the pressure was too intense. The main water line burst. He had inadvertently created his own man-made flood.

Foot by foot, the exhibition hall emptied, the water whirling and hissing and spiraling out. Vale waited, poised and ready, at the one semi-intact air hose. Finally, when the water in the hall below was ankle deep, Vale slithered down the air hose into the black. His goggles gave green glowing form to the wreckage. Vale kicked through the lime-colored debris, methodically searching.

Glass crunched under the thick soles of his combat boots and sliced his wet suit, nicking his shins, but Vale did not feel the cuts. The stink of rotten fish was overwhelming, but he did not cough or gag or cover his nose. No sensory information registered at all. Vale was wholly focused on counting the dead.

He walked over the giant carcass of *Livias,* the great winged ray, slipped on tentacles, and skirted the huge body of *rathos* and his hammerhead snout. He turned over five-foot-long chunks of coral reef and fake prows of old ships. Bodies were wedged under sea rock, wrapped up in kelp, buried in two-foot drifts of tank sand and shattered glass.

Vale located seven dead women, then went through again, kicking, sifting, prying, lifting, and finally sweeping shattered glass with his bare incredulous hands. The count remained at seven.

The eighth captive was gone, and so was the intruder named St. James—a longhaired Houdini with tricks of his own.

Overconfidence could be as deadly as fear. Both lead to sloppy work and errors. Vale had come to feel invulnerable—and in doing so had made a series of irreparable mistakes.

CHAPTER FIFTY-EIGHT

The earth was bleeding.

All around the van, dark soil hemorrhaged water in a fast rising tide that swirled around the tires and shook the chassis from side to side.

I could not reach the pedals, and I certainly could not steer bound and netted as I was. Using my head, I managed to turn on the overhead light and saw that the gearshift was right next to me. My hands were behind my back. I twisted around, felt the lever, and jerked it into neutral. The van rolled a few yards backwards downhill, gathering speed until the tires lost traction and instead of rolling the van was sliding, carried in a wash of fast-flowing mud. The slide turned into a spinning free fall that tossed me against the door, the windshield, the steering wheel, and dash.

High beams flashed crazily over wild scrub brush and brambles. Then the van hit a chunk of shale and stopped dead in front of St. James. He was caught in the headlights, frozen motionless like a startled deer, shirtless, barefoot, and bloody—but alive. He carried a nude woman draped in his arms. A red welt circled her mouth, and a small diamond sparkled in her nose.

Vale had been wrong. No one had gone into the compound. St. James had somehow gotten out—with Kiri.

The interior light was still on. I was as visible to St. James as he was to me.

He moved to the rear of the van. I heard the double doors open and then close. Moments later St. James had the interior partition open and was crawling into the driver's seat. Kiri was stretched out in back.

"Are you hurt?" he asked.

"No. Kiri?"

"Yes. Badly." He searched Vale's utility bag and came up with a phone. "Where's Wheeler?"

I told him, and the words were a black shroud over my heart.

"Vale?"

"In the compound," I said, "somewhere back there."

St. James punched numbers on the mobile and cursed. "Static from the storm."

He pulled a sickle-shaped glass shard from his waist. The end was fashioned into a handle with thickly wrapped tape. He cut me free from the net, sheathed the shard, and gave me the phone.

"Keep trying," he said, starting the van. "Kiri nicked an artery on her thigh. I tied it down with my shirt, but she needs a hospital."

I climbed in back and sat next to her, dialed 911, got static, disconnected, and dialed again. Vale had left a parka in the rear. I wrapped Kiri in it and dialed again. We were rolling now, St. James driving as fast as he could. His bare torso was ripped and bleeding, and shattered glass sparkled in the tangle of his long wet hair.

Kiri was semiconscious and moaning at my side.

"We're getting you help," I said, "we're on our way in."

I dialed 911, listened to static, and disconnected.

Ten seconds later, I dialed again.

The narrow road out was a steep switchback. We skidded and fishtailed at every curve. Visibility was poor. High winds chased rain in gusting sheets. The bluffs were coming down in wide wet slides, foot-high mud drifts littered with chunks of rock. We rounded a bend and hit a fresh slide, rolled into mud too deep to drive through. Tires were spinning, digging us deeper. St. James gave up, turned off the motor, and got out.

"Lock the doors," he said, "and keep trying 911."

"Where are you going?"

"After Vale. He's got a boat in the marina. When he finds the van missing, he'll probably head there."

Dripping wet, feet bare, body half nude in the cold, pale wolf eyes that could see in the dark, St. James pulled the sickle-shaped glass shard from his waist and melted into the night.

Can he do this? I thought, dialing up static.

I remembered how he moved on Rams Island, silent and light, blending into the natural world around him. He had taken a hawk from the skies and made it his own.

Bare feet and no backup.

Night was a cloak, and the fog was our friend. What hid Vale hid St. James, too.

He's a hunter, I thought, dialing again. *St. James is used to tracking. He knows the enemy; he will find a way to win.*

Wind came down hard off the bluffs, rocking the van. Kiri was crying next to me, tossing her head, clawing at air. I dialed up static and disconnected, then dialed again.

I thought of the stormy night in the quarry—how the cell phone didn't work in one spot, but a hundred yards down the road connected just fine. I dropped out and moved up over the bluff, across the broad plateau overlooking the sea, hoping open land and water would give me a good clear signal.

Standing clear in the wind and rain, my call to 911 went through.

I spoke carefully and slowly, giving all the relevant information including my name for credibility and told the operator that hostages had been killed, one was seriously injured, and a federal agent was in danger. I gave the park name, said the road was washed out, and asked for medevac air rescue and state police. When I ran out of things to say, I whispered one word—*"Hurry"*—thinking of Kiri bleeding in the van and St. James out there alone, up against Vale—glass against an Uzi and a man who lived to kill.

The call disconnected, and the powerful hand came down—a steel grip on my neck squeezing, forcing me to the ground. I tasted mud and felt the black nose of that

Uzi kissing my cheek. We were right up tight to the edge of the cliff, so close I felt the reverberations of waves pounding rock and tasted the salty ocean spray. Vale was on me, his bedroom voice warm in my ear.

"Your drowning will never be avenged," he said. "You'll be a story in the news one week, and the next you'll simply be gone. Isn't that how it goes, Lacie? The old news stories are forgotten as a wave of new ones washes in."

Behind him, I saw St. James slipping silently across the bluff, moving without disturbing the air, stepping so lightly he barely touched earth. His glass shard was drawn and ready.

Vale touched his lips to mine, gave my mouth his warm moist breath. "Do you want one more taste of me before the water takes you?" he said. "Be honest. Do you want that now?"

St. James. Pale gray eyes bright with a predatory shine. Mine must have flickered as he approached. Vale, so close, did not miss that small reflex. He spun off, the Uzi tucked tight and ready just as St. James jumped, the curved glass shard a sharp killing claw aimed at his prey.

Vale fired, and even as bullets shredded St. James's chest, the power of his lupine leap propelled him right into Vale. The two men went down. St. James's curved claw sank deep into Vale's left shoulder. Blood spouted from the orange neoprene. Vale threw St. James's slack body off and rose. Enraged like a wild wounded beast, he reached for me, and over the sound of the crashing surf and wind came a deep guttural sound I had heard once before.

Wheeler in blue scrubs. Wheeler at Rio's autopsy. Hallucinations, Lacie. Wheeler is dead.

But he was not.

Wheeler in a black wet suit was sprinting across the plateau, hammer raised and ready to strike.

Vale turned, faltered, undone by the arrival of a man he was certain was dead—and that split-second hesitation was all the time Wheeler needed. Before Vale could raise the Uzi, Wheeler swung the hammer and slammed him hard in the forehead.

Vale staggered back. The bluff gave way beneath his feet and slid, taking Vale down. He dropped the Uzi, clawed at cliff scrub, and grabbed a thick root. It held. He was hanging on with one hand, body dangling over the edge. I crawled forward and saw Vale dangling, a hundred feet above white foaming surf and huge breakers slamming rock.

Wheeler unzipped his wet suit and pulled out the chisel he had used to destroy the scrimshaw frieze. He lay flat out on the ground, leaned over the edge and stared down at Vale.

"Fucking Houdini," Vale said.

Wheeler calmly placed the point of the sharp chisel between the thumb and first finger of Vale's root-gripping hand.

"How did you get out of the pool?" Vale asked.

Wheeler tapped the chisel lightly with the hammer, enough to split Vale's skin and draw blood, but not enough to release Vale's hand from the root.

Vale looked down at the water again, up at Wheeler, then me.

He could have gone on for years—decades perhaps—with his quiet perfectly planned kills. But his ego had driven him to search out a very public documentation of his private executions. Ego had seduced him into taking unacceptable risk.

Now he saw death as his SEATEC recruits had, and like his female captives, Vale now knew the agony of waiting. He now knew how *inevitable* felt. Wheeler planted the chisel and drove it in deep into the nerves and muscles of Vale's hand.

Vale shrieked—but held on tight.

Surf crashed against rock below, sending up gales of white water spray that wet us.

Vale glanced down again, then up at Wheeler, and closed his eyes.

"Look at me!" Wheeler ordered.

Vale did.

Wheeler planted the chisel over the knob of his center knuckle, then turned his face to the sky in divine apology or seeking divine approval—I wasn't sure which. He drew a deep breath of air and when his lungs were filled, he lifted the hammer, hesitated, and looked at me.

I was the sole witness to this execution, and while it felt morally right, it was criminally wrong—if the facts were told.

I was a friend that night, not a journalist.

I nodded once sharply, closed my eyes, and turned away.

Wheeler roared with deep primal satisfaction. He brought the hammer down.

Chisel shattered bone. And Vale let go.

CHAPTER FIFTY-NINE

St. James was on his back, next to me.

His bare chest was a shredded mass of tissue and blood and white shards of bone. Sweat beaded his face, blood seeped from a dozen different gunshot wounds, his breath was ragged and wet.

Wheeler knelt alongside and fashioned bits of my clothing into makeshift bandages.

"I got through to 911," I said. "Help is coming."

"There's nothing more I can do," Wheeler said. "We have to wait and pray."

"Kiri's alive. St. James got her out. She's in a van down on the road. Go to her. See what you can do."

Wheeler hesitated.

"Go," St. James managed.

Wheeler nodded and rose.

St. James looked up at me, wolf gray eyes glazed, shining a world of hurt.

I peeled my gloves off and touched his chilly forehead.

"Help is coming," I promised. "Help is on the way."

I put my ear to his chest and listened to wet sounds inside, blood in the lungs, a heart skipping beats.

"Talk to me, St. James."

"Vale. Tell me about it."

"You took him down. He went over the edge. He's gone."

"I won," St. James said. "Vale died first."

I tried to cover St. James, block out the cold, but it was everywhere at once, wind and rain and my own body like ice. I could not make him warm. We waited an eternity, me running my ruined fingers through his wet hair, picking out glass, trying to talk away his pain, and when the sound of sirens came in on the wind, I took his frozen hands in mine.

"Help is here," I said. "You're going to make it, St. James."

"Sweet lies falling off your factual lips."

"You're going to make it, St. James."

"Darling Lacie, never ever telling me the truth."

"They're sending a helicopter to fly you out."

"Tell me another lie."

"You're going to make it."

"Pretty Lacie raining down tears on a man called St.

James. The only color you wear is elemental, in your
eyes and hair: blue sky for eyes and fire for hair. Indigo
eyes and tears running blue. Careful now, girl. Cry long
and hard enough, rivers of pain will wash the color right
out. You'll look in the mirror and find your blue eyes
turned black."

"St. James . . . "

"Don't let tears wash the color from your life."

"St. James . . . "

"Browning. Elizabeth Barrett Browning as written to
Robert. *Sonnets from the Portuguese.* The Indian's an
aesthete and poet even in death."

"You're not dying, St. James."

"Lies from an angel, tropical rain falling from her
lips. Don't cry for me now."

The sound of helicopters came on the wind. I looked
up and saw three aerial searchlights swinging, washing
us in pools of light. St. James's eyes were open, fixed on
the sky as if the chopper was his falcon winging down
from her place of pride.

Wind from the rotors ripped through my hair, tan-
gling it in front of my eyes, and for a moment I could not
see St. James. I touched his lips, felt the reassuring puff
of his warm breath. I laid my cheek next to his.

"Tell me another lie," he said softly. "Tell me you
would've made love with me once, that you know it
would've been good."

St. James's slack body was heavy in my arms, and I
embraced him hard, as if that was my answer—as if my
own powerful will could keep him anchored in this life.

One of the three choppers came down a safe distance
away.

I heard men shouting. A team of medevac paramedics
emerged from the mist, lugging gurneys and heavy
cases. They shouldered me out of the way. Suddenly I
could not see St. James's face or his body, only the cloud

of white jackets dropping down and a short time later a billowing starched white sheet. I didn't know if I should think of it as a blanket or a shroud.

I grabbed one of the team and told him about Kiri. He took two of his men and ran off toward the van.

A second chopper landed, and moments later state troopers came running in with high-power searchlights, radios, and raised guns. Black ponchos and heavy boots.

"Where's the shooter?" a trooper asked me.

"There." I pointed to the edge. "He went down."

He shouted orders to his men and radioed the search and rescue helicopter hovering overhead.

As he shot more questions at me, getting details of the dead at the park, a pack of news choppers flew in overhead. Every newsroom has a young reporter who does nothing but listen to the 911 police scanner. The Boston newsrooms had obviously all heard mine. The choppers settled down, and field teams poured out with minicams and cordless mikes, lights and cameras all aimed at me.

I squinted into the glare trying to identify faces, station call letters, looking for a friend. Questions came at me like bullets. Someone tapped me on the shoulder.

"Ms. Wagner?"

I turned and saw Benjamin O'Brian's eager young face.

"We're set up to do a live feed," he said. "WRC's hot-linked in."

He held out a mike. Behind me, EMS workers loaded St. James onto a gurney.

"Do you feel up to it, Ms. Wagner?"

"It's what I do, Ben." I took the mike.

"On five, then." He counted down and I spoke.

"Seven women are dead tonight, and so is the sadist who killed them." The words came slowly at first, tears on my cheeks mixing with rain. "There is one survivor, and the man who saved her may not make it through the night. In the process of investigating the death of Private Ashley Sinclair, this reporter uncovered a story rooted in evil—a legacy of murder begun a quarter of a century ago."

Somehow, despite the trauma and shock of all that had happened, the thousand-pound ache in my heart, I found solace in my work, a strange catharsis. As the rain came down, the words rolled together and the story—my version—poured out.

In the weeks that followed, the feds went through the motions, but investigative incentive ran low. Nothing of value was recovered from the park. On the Net, The Altar had disappeared, but I believe Vale simply moved it just as he had claimed. Somewhere someone is sitting in the dark, watching the drownings, Ashley in the pool, Rio in the quarry, and God knows how many more.

Kiri was his last captive, the only one to escape Vale's tanks alive. She told the investigators all she knew—which was not much. Vale had been charismatic, charming, and elegant. They met at a pool. He invited her to dinner. It seemed so innocent, simple, and good. So easy and right to say yes.

Her flesh healed, but the scars on her soul will take much longer. She had been touched by evil, she had invited it in, and that one dreadful truth will mark Kiri—as it has me—for the rest of our God-given days. And even as we move forward into the future, away from the past, we will silently wonder what made Vale who he was and why when we looked at him, we did not—could not—see beyond the beauty to the monster underneath.

Eyes are not windows to the soul. I looked straight into the eyes of evil and saw only green quiet waters, gold corneal tingeing sparkling with cultural elegance, the promise of passion, the stirrings of desire. I gazed into luminous emerald eyes of evil incarnate and felt nothing but warm, wanted, and safe.

We must fear those who walk among us unnoticed with dark desires and deep running tides, men whose souls harbor oceans of evil teeming with plots and plans for new ways of enacting the oldest crime in the book, men who delight in hunting their own species in endlessly innovative diabolical ways.

"Technology and money," St. James had said, "are the great enablers. We are in a new century and yet the great *faiblesse*—the inherent weakness—in the human soul remains. The conduits have changed, but fundamental evil has not. I don't believe it ever will. Men are born killers, not made."

I learned later that it wasn't the fall that killed Vale. It was not even St. James's perfectly pitched glass or Wheeler's hammer blow. With a pair of knees shredded from the rocks, bleeding and helpless in the raging sea, Vale drowned. Saltwater diatoms found blooming in his bones were forensic proof. And cell blocks killed off in his chest proved he had been conscious when he drowned, very aware and terrified at the time of his death.

McKenzie performed the autopsy. Wheeler assisted. There was no mention made in the protocol of the shattered bone and severed tendons in Vale's right hand.

The killer, Vale, had simply stumbled in the fight with St. James and gone over the edge of the cliff—just as I had reported on the news and said in my statement to the police. It is the only version Hinks knows, and thus far Wheeler has left it at that between them. He told me he wanted to move forward with her, together, away from the past. Theirs is a loving, fiercely intimate relationship; nonetheless, Wheeler has elected to quarantine that dark part of his heart, hold it back from Hinks, as is his right. What happened that night on the cliff is between Wheeler and God and Rio.

As for the rest of us, the detailed facts of how Vale went down do not matter—only that he was gone for good, and if you believe in karmic justice, it feels right that in the end the water took him—that he was conscious when he drowned.

Vale had many names, and changed personae as effortlessly as he changed shirts, adopting identities as they fit his purpose. He had many names, but I think of him first and always as Vale—the mariner who claimed for his own and sailed the Eighth Sea.

I often watch the tape of the story I filed from the cliffs, mesmerized by how that last dead night comes alive on my big screen: the EMS team in the background loading the gurney with St. James, the hovering chopper and hot lights, troopers in black rain ponchos pouring in, Vale's orange glowing body in the rescue harness. But one detail transfixes me: the sight of my own bare hands holding the mike.

I had taken off my gloves when I touched St. James and forgotten to put them back on. When I first saw them I felt shame—that I had put those ravaged appendages on public display; then I remembered St. James's words: "They are symbolic of the source of the currents of your life," he had said, gliding through the coves at Rams Island in his birchwood canoe. "Your hands are living proof of the dark waters you've swum through, proof that your life will never be calm like a lake. It's your destiny, Lacie, your fate. There's no shame in that."

He told me I have an old soul, that I've seen too much evil for someone still young.

"You must not let tragedy associated with elements wipe the beauty and power of those natural forces from your life," he had said. "You must find strength in the elements, not fear."

St. James said that life is all balance, like his canoe. He counseled me to counter darkness and evil with happiness and light—to live and laugh and ride each day like a wave, as if it is the last.

At night I try to direct my dreams as if they are films, carefully scripting dialogue, placing props, cueing sounds so my sleep is filled with good things—I try, but in the long hours between midnight and morning I relive that night and the ache in my heart is so heavy, I wake up in tears, weeping for all the drowned girls, the ones we found and all the others we never knew.

"Think of the one you saved that night," Hinks says. She tells me to think of the countless women we spared the same ungodly fate. "If it hadn't been for you, Vale would have gone on killing for years to come. Think of the ones you saved, Lacie, only of that."

I try to see it her way, but every night the tears wake me, and when I fall back asleep the worst of my dream inevitably unfolds.

The imagery is water, the cold Atlantic on a bright winter day. I am swimming, and although my feet are kicking, I am struggling against the tide, my body is leaden, and I do not move. The girls are all around me, long lithe forms in water so clear I can see their ruined faces, the white-cauled eyes and cottage cheese skin. The girls reach out, and although I am close, I do not have hands enough to hold them, to pull them up to the surface, and the sound scoring my dream is something worse than the fury of fire or my own father's final infernal shrieks.

It is an aquatic fugue. The echo of wet voices. Wailing girls who cannot breathe. Keening cries and thumping fists. It is the sound of ten girls drowning, inhaling water when they are dying for air.

I live their deaths every night in my sleep.

"Don't," St. James once cautioned. "Don't walk down those dark roads."

I try, but somehow the dark stories find me, as if all I have been through has marked me, and when they come my way, I am compelled to follow.

The stories pull me forward, always forward, out of daylight and into night.

EPILOGUE

It is late spring; yesterday I high-stepped into the sea at Nantucket, consciously banishing images of Rio and Ashley. I closed my eyes, fell back faceup to the sun, and *I swam.* My hands were tiny lateral fins, sea horse small and fluttering, trilling through water, offering some guidance like a rudder, but mostly they floated useless at my sides. The principal propulsion came from my size-nine feet and powerful legs kicking, left-right-left, propelling me free-bodied and able through the deep salt sea.

"Kick!" St. James ordered from the waterline. *"Kick!"* Glacial water pooled in my solar plexus, warm sun heated the tip of my nose.

"Kick, kick, kick!"

I heard his voice and saw him wading in the shallows with his cane alongside me, chest still battered and bandaged, shoulder in a sling, pale eyes shining a world of pride, loving hands waving me in.

"Kick, Lacie, kick! Swim to me now."

I fight the fear still, the darkness and night. I think I always will. But there is a deep fierce comfort in having St. James by my side—his proud high cheeks, the power of his smile, teeth flashing white like the lip-splitting scar, the dozen other new battle marks streaking his beautiful face—and his fire-colored hair tumbling down in a tangle, begging me to run my ruined hands through it. Lourdes for the fingers, come touch it and be whole.

St. James.

The sound of wind rushing through peregrine bells, strong wings flapping.

Water stroking the shore.

St. James.

"Kick, Lacie, kick! Swim to me now."